I0600335

Copyright © 2025 K. Arbegast

All Rights Reserved

No part of this publication may be reproduced, distributed, or transmitted in any form or by any means, including photocopying, recording, or other electronic or mechanical methods, without the prior written permission of the publisher, except in the case of brief quotations embodied in critical reviews and other certain noncommercial uses permitted by copyright law.

ISBN: 979-8-9991326-0-4 (Paperback)

Any references to historical events, real people, or real places are used fictitiously. Names, characters, and places are products of the author's imagination.

Front cover image and book design by K. Arbegast.

First printing edition 2025.

1

GRAVE VISIT

Noah clenched a daisy in his fist as he stared down at the gravestone. Its polished surface caught the low rays of sunlight trickling through the trees, a reminder that the day was rapidly approaching its end. He threw a glance over his shoulder at his friends picnicking a ways back at a wooden table as his fingers unconsciously tugged at the few leaves studding the flower's stem.

With a sigh, he knelt and laid the flower before the stone. He paused there with his head bowed, breaths quickening as horrible overwhelming loss swept over him. He squeezed his eyes shut and stood in quiet remembrance as the sun slowly lowered towards the horizon.

He eventually rose and meandered back to his friends, winding between rows of nearly identical gravestones to the table where three figures were unpacking sandwiches. All of them, himself included, were students of Oakridge Community College. The school was situated down the road from the cemetery in the suburbs of the city of Glenmore.

"This better not be bologna," the girl named Leah said threateningly as she took a wrapped bundle from the backpack her brother Brian had set out. Both siblings had fair hair cut to slightly above shoulder length, though Brian's was more curly, and reddish-brown eyes.

"It's *all* bologna. The whole container went onto that sandwich," Brian said with an evil smile.

Leah narrowed her eyes at him in mock suspicion and

opened her sandwich to reveal sliced turkey and cheese. She grinned and immediately smacked Brian before chomping into the food.

Noah smiled as he sat down beside Brian. Noah had decided on a whim to be an orientation leader back during the beginning of the fall semester, as he was currently in his second year of college and felt confident enough in his own knowledge about campus life to do a decent job introducing new students to the lay of the land. Brian had been one of a dozen kids assigned to his group, and Noah had rapidly grown attached to the good-natured and surprisingly capable young man. They had made arrangements to room together (along with another first year whom Noah still barely knew, two months later) and had grown to consider each other like brothers in that short time. He'd met Brian's sister in the first week of classes and found her to be equally good company.

The small form of May sat across from him, laughing with a hand over her mouth at the siblings' antics. Noah hadn't technically invited her on their outing, as he barely knew her. She was good friends with Leah, however, and Leah had asked if she could tag along. She spoke very little, though Noah had noticed she did seem to sneeze a lot. She had a very pretty face with East Asian features.

Noah glanced at her warily as she began to lean back for the umpteenth time, inhaling like she was coming up for air from the depths of an ocean. She explosively sneezed once more, then quickly stifled herself, rubbing the tip of her bright red nose.

"Sorry," she squeaked. "I promise it's just allergies."

Leah nudged her playfully. "We'll see about that in three days, huh?"

"I'm not sick. It's not the *Wager*. It's not even a cold," May grumbled.

Noah's expression went blank. His smile returned half a second later, but the momentary slip didn't escape anyone's notice. The two girls shared an uncomfortable look.

"Sorry," Leah said unhappily. "I wasn't... I wasn't

thinking."

Noah just sighed and shook his head, squashing down the flash of grief. The *Wager* was far too popular a subject of discussion for him to have not long since grown inured to its mention.

Brian looked between them before grabbing an armful of sandwiches from his backpack and distributing them around the table. Each one was wrapped very neatly in a delicate white cloth, in typical Brian style.

"You doing okay?" Brian asked hesitantly after Noah had gratefully received his sandwich.

Noah nodded as he lifted the fold of cloth, carefully unwrapping it. Something about it being so nicely packaged made him want to handle it with the same care Brian put into its assembly. Once the sandwich was framed by the unfurled petals of the cloth, Noah smiled and looked at his friend. "Well, I miss her. Of course. Thanks for coming out here with me."

Brian took a large bite of his own sandwich and nodded seriously, then opened his mouth and started talking. Unlike May, he didn't cover his mouth, so the action sprayed Noah with food detritus. "I don't know what I would do if I lost someone like that. You seem to handle it pretty well, but... uh, we're here for you, you know? What kind of lousy friends would we have to be to leave you alone today?"

Leah nodded vigorously along with his words, and May smiled supportively despite only having met him a scant few hours earlier.

Noah grinned at Brian and bit into his sandwich. "Hmm, I only invited you for your expert cheffery. I would definitely be despairing all by my lonesome right now if you didn't do such excellent work with these sandwiches."

Brian scoffed and cheerfully punched him while May and Leah laughed.

Comfortable silence overtook the table as the four of them finished their food. By the time each of them were shaking the crumbs out of their napkins, the shadows had lengthened enough to make Noah glance around at their darkening surroundings and roll his cloth napkin up pointedly.

"I don't want to be stuck out here when it really starts getting dark. Way too many small hard tripping hazards lying around this particular environment."

"Yes, that seems like a highly ironic way to go out," Leah agreed, rising from her seat.

The other two followed suit without complaint, with Brian carefully re-folding everyone's napkins before placing them one at a time back in his backpack.

They collectively made their way onto the cemetery's gravel path. It wound around the edge of the clearing before veering into the woods, cutting through a small section of it to eventually end up at a paved road.

Noah tried to take one last look at the gravestone marked by a freshly cut daisy, but it was already too dark to make it out among the rows of identical grave markers.

Walking into the trees was like passing into a dark veil. Noah followed his friends down the path nearly blindly, gazing around at their surroundings ineffectually and lamenting their decision to visit the cemetery so late in the afternoon. His vision was like a bad camera in the dark, full of shifting grainy artifacts.

Nearly a full minute passed before Brian suddenly blurted, "Hey, I've got flashlights!" His tone implied he had only just remembered this fact.

They all stopped as he sheepishly fished them out of his backpack, pulling out two. Each had a slim handle that widened into a square socket. Noah knew they were both dull black metal despite it being too dark at the moment to properly see their color. Brian carried them around everywhere, although Noah had never seen him actually use them until now. Brian gave one to Noah and kept the other for himself.

Noah flicked his on and shone it around. The gravestones cast long, square shadows in gridded patterns as he swung the weighty light back and forth.

They walked quickly, all of them eager to get back to
the main road. The gravestones were soon left behind and
replaced by thickly growing trees curving over the path.

After about thirty seconds Brian began to slow down for
no immediately apparent reason.

"Why are we stopping?" Leah demanded.

Brian silently thrust his flashlight forward. Noah peered
ahead, realizing with an unpleasant jolt of surprise that the
path diverged into two, the gaps in the forest staring back at
them like hollow eyes.

"I don't remember a fork in the path," Brian said.

2

PATH LESS TRAVELED

Noah peered down each trail, a strange feeling passing over him.

"Yeah, there wasn't one," he said quietly. "Although I've only been down this way a few times. It's been months since I last visited; I'm not exactly familiar with the trail. We must've missed it on the way here."

"I guess so," Brian muttered. He took a few steps down the left path, his flashlight swiveling around, looking for a familiar landmark. He quickly came back and did the same the other way.

Noah watched him with resignation growing in the pit of his stomach. The trails were framed by identical drooping branches. They were indistinguishable.

"We'll just have to pick one of them," he said. "It's only a short walk if we go the wrong way. It probably comes out a bit further down the road."

Leah groaned and started walking after Brian, who was still looking in vain between the two paths. "No way we managed to get lost on this tiny freaking trail."

"Not lost, necessarily..." May said hopefully. "I mean, it's a fifty/fifty chance, right?"

All thoughts immediately went to the *Wager*. The phrase 'fifty/fifty' was used so often describing it that the words themselves seemed to carry the weight of the sickness.

"Er, you know..." May said quietly, sighing.

The four of them looked at each other, flashlights

reflecting strangely off their eyes, the point-blank lighting making faces appear like masks. The night seemed to grow colder as they stood there.

"Well, let's go," Noah said finally. "We're wasting daylight."

"Ha, I wish," Leah mumbled.

They moved forward, slowly at first, hesitant to leave the junction behind. But as it fell behind them they started walking faster and faster, sticking tightly together as they shuffled along. Their breaths seemed loud and quick in the stillness of the woods.

"This is fun," Leah said suddenly, causing the other three to jump slightly. She continued blithely, "I've always liked going on walks in nature. Brian, remind me to get out in the great outdoors more often."

Brian sighed. "Sure thing." He looked around, considering. "We can probably turn around now. The path out isn't this long."

"No, we're almost there, look," Leah said.

A few steps further proved her words true. The gravel path petered off into nothing, leaving the group standing in a small dark clearing. Colossal trees plunged up from the earth in a circle around them. There was no road in sight, although they could distantly hear the sounds of vehicles through the trees.

"Well, we reached the end of the path, but it's the end of the wrong path," Noah said, voicing the obvious. "I guess we picked the wrong way." He pointed his flashlight into the mesh of trees across the clearing, towards the sounds of traffic. "Sounds like we're close, though I don't really feel like bushwhacking my way to the road."

Leah shrugged. "Me neither. Let's take the path back then."

"Wait a moment," May said. "What's that?"

Noah turned to see her pointing into the darkness to the right of his flashlight's beam. He shone his light out where she was gesturing, and a moment later Brian's beam joined his own. The light struck a stout shape recognizable as a small building.

"Does somebody live out here?" Leah wondered, squinting ahead.

"I feel like we would have noticed some kind of private property signs along the way if that were the case," Noah said. "Although it would have been extremely easy to miss them."

Brian was walking forward, prompting everyone else to drift along reluctantly behind him. His flashlight was still trained on the structure.

"I think it's a mausoleum," May piped up suddenly. The four of them stopped in front of the building and stared up at it like hapless tourists. It had the shape of a small ancient monument, with two sets of columns supporting a pediment and a couple steps leading up to the door.

"Why's it so far from the cemetery, then?" Leah asked.

Nobody had an answer to that.

Noah left the others behind to circle the structure, but there wasn't much to see. The side and back walls were plain. When he had looped back to the front he paused, and on a whim mounted the steps, grasped the handle, and tugged. He jumped back like a startled cat when the door unexpectedly opened an inch.

All three people standing behind him immediately yelled, and May sneezed panickedly.

"WOAH! What do you think you're doing?" Brian demanded.

Noah quickly shut the door and backed away. "I didn't expect it to be open! Who leaves these things unlocked anyway? That's just careless!"

"Oh, so it's *their* fault. You're totally free of accountability here."

"What's the accountability for? No harm done," Noah scoffed, his heart racing despite himself.

Brian shook his head. "Forget it. Let's just get back to campus."

"Good idea," Leah said, skipping forward to snatch the flashlight from Brian. "It's my turn with the flashlight, by the way," she added as she pranced away.

"You don't get a turn!"

"I think she just did," May said dryly as they watched her disappear down the path, the light bouncing away between the trees.

Brian sighed despondently as they hurried back into the woods after his sister. "I swear, she acts like a child sometimes," he complained.

"You are children, you puny little first years," Noah said.

"Oh, come off it, you're only a year up!" Brian snapped.

Noah shrugged, supremely aloof. "Seems like a big difference to me."

Leah was close enough now to have heard enough of their conversation to know she should feel affronted. She was walking slowly so as to let them catch up, and seemed about to respond when she stopped moving altogether and tilted her head.

"What is it?" Brian asked quickly.

"Shh, I heard something," Leah whispered.

Immediately the four of them went dead silent. Nobody wants to run into anything in a dark woods, and the thought of someone or something being nearby sent a frigid chill trickling down Noah's spine.

Leah was shining the flashlight directly down the path, so they all saw exactly when a doglike shape crossed into the beam, barely in range of the illumination. Its eyes turned towards them suddenly, two white unblinking dots. Noah felt his entire body freeze up, from his heart to his fingers, as he stared back and felt for the first time in his life that he was prey, that he was being hunted, and that his life was in imminent danger. His friends' presence faded away until he felt he was standing utterly alone in the sights of a predator.

The creature tilted its head back and an eerie howl spread across the woods. The sound multiplied as more distant voices joined in, growing into a haunting siren.

Wolves, Noah thought numbly.

3

WE CAN HIDE

"Oh, it's a wolf," Leah said.

It took Noah a few seconds to register her nonplussed tone, and he wondered somewhat sheepishly if he were the only one to have panicked.

Brian clapped his hands. "Ay, buddy! Get off the trail!"

Noah grabbed Brian's arm before he could clap again. "Are you mad?"

Leah looked at Noah's pale face and laughed lightly. "It's okay, it knows we're here. The best thing to do is make ourselves big and loud. We see a lot of wolves back home and we've never been attacked. Just don't push your luck and do something stupid like panic."

Noah looked wildly between them and was slightly gratified to see that May looked just as wide-eyed as he felt.

"Okay. Well, I've never seen a wolf before in my life, so this is a very new and exciting experience for me. Is it normal for it to be getting closer like this?"

Leah didn't take her eyes off the beast. It was better illuminated now, creeping forward with its eyes locked on them. It was smaller than Noah had always imagined a wolf to be, though that didn't make it seem any less threatening.

"We can back up," she said. "Not too quickly."

"The clearing is just behind us," Noah said. He took steady steps backward alongside his friends, resisting the urge to simply bolt away as fast as his legs could take him. "We can hide..."

"Don't you dare finish that sentence with anything close to 'in the mausoleum'," Brian warned.

"Hey, you're the one who said it," Noah said. "It would be a good place to hide."

"Suit yourself," Brian retorted. "I've had plenty of encounters with wolves and I've survived all of them without having to hide in a random shady-ass mausoleum."

"What's so shady about it? Just because it's ominously separated from the local cemetery and is unlocked for unknown reasons doesn't make it of any more dubious character than your average mausoleum. It sounds like you're making excuses to yourself, if you ask me," Leah said.

They reached the edge of the clearing and drew closer to the building. The wolf prowled calmly after them, not closing the distance, but not letting them draw away.

The group came to a stop in front of the door, and the wolf paused a few meters away in turn, unblinking. After several seconds two more identical creatures slipped out of the woods and padded to the first one's side.

"Alright, no need to dawdle, everybody in," Noah said, putting the flashlight between his teeth and grasping the handle once more. He pulled it open, heart stuttering as the door opened just a couple inches before sticking stubbornly on some invisible obstruction. He wrenched on the handle with all of his strength, and the door grudgingly rewarded him with three more inches before the handle suddenly snapped off in his hand and its two bolts clattered to the ground. He swore under his breath and shifted his grip to the edge of the door, but was unable to open it further. May was already slipping inside, displaying not the slightest hint of hesitation.

"Is that wide enough for you two? Hope so," Noah said to the siblings, and squeezed inside after May. The flashlight's handle bumped the edge of the door frame as he entered, knocking the flashlight out of his mouth and making his teeth hurt.

It was at least fifteen degrees cooler in the mausoleum than it was outside, and it was not a warm night to begin with.

His teeth chattered as he stooped to retrieve the flashlight, which had rolled a few times and come to a stop against a wall. Its beam illuminated May's lower legs as she stood against the opposite wall.

A moment later Leah popped in. "My idiot brother is so scared to be in the vicinity of a couple of corpses that he's about to become one himself," she hissed. She sounded angry, but her expression was near tears.

"Brian!" Noah snapped, stepping up to the entrance. "Get your ass in here!"

Brian was leaning against the wall next to the door, peering inside the opening, sweat shining on his temples. "It's okay," he said shakily. "I think I'll just-"

Noah couldn't see the wolves from inside the mausoleum, but Brian suddenly flinched violently and without a second thought Noah grabbed his friend's shoulders and yanked him inside. Half a second later a wolf bounced off the wall and turned to growl at them. The beast lunged forward, its gnashing jaws slotting narrowly into the opening before its shoulders caught on the door and it was unable to push further inside. Its maw snapped furiously, panting hot air, its eyes and teeth glinting.

Noah gripped his flashlight tightly, holding it over his shoulder like a baseball bat, then brought it down fiercely on the beast's snout.

It let out a pained whimper and withdrew just long enough for Noah to pull the door shut. He gripped the handle as tightly as he could even after the door had shut all the way, holding it closed as if the wolf would somehow figure out a way to open it without a handle from the outside.

But ten seconds passed, and there were no audible sounds from outside besides the ongoing howls of the other wolves circling the mausoleum. Noah gradually relaxed and stepped away from the door.

He looked at his friends' pale faces and exhaled. "Okay. What now?"

4

THERE WAS INDEED A CORPSE

The interior of the mausoleum was quite small, being just a single room lined on one side with a wall of labeled crypts. The far end of the room housed a raised dais with a stone coffin in the place of honor. A bust of a snarling creature was carved into the wall above the coffin. All four of them twitched backwards when the beam of Noah's flashlight landed on its fearsome countenance. It might have looked like a normal human if the face weren't so grotesquely twisted by its wild expression. It stared down at them with an animal hunger in its eyes.

"Well, that's only completely horrifying," Leah said after a moment, exhaling. She walked closer, mounting the steps and circling the coffin to peer closer at it. "It's crazy lifelike. If it was carved by hand, whoever made this must have been a master."

Noah got the feeling she would currently be stroking its stone face if it weren't out of reach. He kept the flashlight trained on the statue for her benefit as he stepped closer to Brian, who was sitting quietly on the ground, his back against the wall. His backpack was in his lap.

"Sorry for pulling you in," Noah said.

Brian looked up at him and chuckled unhappily. "Thanks. I mean, you saved my life, man. So I forgive you." He looked around. "Even if this place is creepy as hell."

Noah smiled. "Well, yeah. Not my first choice for escaping a couple of crazy wolves. Definitely would've picked somewhere with some heating, to start with."

Brian raised an eyebrow. "I have some hand warmers, you know. There's a couple in my bag." He unzipped his backpack and fished around for a moment.

Noah laughed. "Of course you do. Is there anything you didn't bring?"

Brian handed his friend a small plastic packet and frowned. "Snacks. I have some water, though."

"It's fine," Noah said. "Ideally we won't be here long enough for that to matter. The wolves should definitely be long gone by morning, right?"

Brian shuddered. "I hope so. They aren't acting like the wolves I'm used to, though, so who knows."

"Hey, can I have this for a second?" May asked.

"What?" Brian looked over to see her pointing at his flashlight, which Leah had balanced on the floor to point straight up. "Yeah, that's fine."

Noah started kneading the hand warmer to activate it as he watched May take the light and walk across the room to investigate the crypts. She crouched to peer at the names engraved into each marked square.

"This isn't the Latin alphabet," she said after a moment. "I don't recognize the characters at all."

"Maybe the family spoke a foreign language," Leah said from where she stood over by the carving on the wall. "They probably wanted their graves to be in their mother tongue or something."

"Must be some rare language," May said, straightening after looking at the names for another minute.

"Holy crap," Leah suddenly breathed.

They all turned to see what had caught her attention. She had for some questionable reason climbed onto the lid of the coffin and was face-to-face with the bust, staring intently at its mouth.

"What? What are you doing, Leah?" Brian asked, alarmed.

"There's a lever," she said excitedly. "It's tongue is a lever, I think. I'm going to pull it."

"Woah, hold on a moment!" Noah said quickly. "It could do anything. We're in a random family's mausoleum. Who knows if they were crazy enough to rig traps like some kind of ancient tomb?"

Leah stopped. "You really think it's that dangerous? Why would they make the trap so hard to find?"

Noah hesitated. "I mean, it's a long shot, but I've seen so many movies of people more or less in this exact situation that I would feel like an idiot if I made the exact same mistake as everyone else." He paused, watching Leah practically bounce with excitement. "I can't deny I'm curious now, though. I'm starting to see why everyone always pulls the lever."

"Let's put it to a vote," Leah said, suddenly glaring menacingly at her brother and May. "All in favor of pulling the lever and probably finding an awesome stash of gold and riches left behind by this family to the one worthy enough to find their secret lever."

She raised her hand hopefully, then grinned as Brian and May both raised their hands as well with sheepish looks towards Noah.

Noah threw up his hands. "Fine! But if I die because of this moronic decision after escaping from freaking *wolves*, I'll never forgive you all, I swear."

Leah grinned. "Aw, we'll be fine." She wrapped her fingers around the protruding tongue and pulled down.

It didn't budge.

Leah sputtered and glanced around awkwardly. "I thought I saw a hinge mechanism," she muttered sheepishly.

Then she adjusted her grip and pushed the tongue upwards.

It slid up with a crunch. Leah almost fell off the coffin as a series of clicks ran down the wall. Then the lid started to slide open, and she did fall off, toppling to the floor as she lost her balance.

Her head poked back up after a second, and she glanced at her friends before slowly leaning forward to peer inside the coffin.

She immediately grimaced and recoiled. "I suppose I shouldn't be surprised that there's a corpse inside," she said. She looked up with an odd expression. "Although, guys, you should take a look at this."

"I'll pass," Brian said, looking sickened. "Does putting the lever down close it back up? Let's try that right now."

"No, there's something else in here," Leah said. She started to reach in, but stopped with an uncomfortable expression and withdrew her hand.

Noah sighed deeply and walked over, looking down into the coffin.

There was indeed a corpse, but it had an ancient look about it and wasn't as gross or smelly as he feared. The skin was like aged yellow paper drawn tight around its bones. Its hands and feet were, disturbingly, locked down by strips of metal to the base of the coffin. It had black wispy hair and no nose to speak of.

Around its neck was a necklace of thin silver links, with a large square locket of the same color resting on its chest.

As Noah looked down at the corpse, May drew up beside him to get her own look at it. She glanced sideways at Leah. "Is this necklace what you were trying to get at?"

Leah shrugged. "Yeah, I wanted to see if I could open it. I'm not sure I want to touch it, though."

May raised an eyebrow and impassively grabbed the pendant. She lifted it closer to herself, leaning forward when the chain went taut to get a better look at the unlocking mechanism. Seeing two small knobs on each side of the square, she nodded slightly and compressed them both simultaneously. They clicked into place easily and the two halves of the pendant slowly cracked open like a book, ticking gently.

The three of them leaned forward to see what lay within, only to recoil as a vast amount of black smoke-like dust blew out from the pendant. At the same time, the corpse began to shudder like it was being electrocuted.

5

IT'S ALIVE

May sucked in a gasp and dropped the pendant back into the coffin, stumbling back. Leah and Noah fell backwards in surprise.

The cloud expanded quickly, billowing out of the wide-open box and filling the small enclosed space with a smoky haze. Noah pulled his shirt up to cover his nose and mouth, creeping forward to stare in horror as the body started twitching and jerking against its metal bonds.

"What the hell?" Brian yelped from the far wall, seeing smoke fill the space. "What did you do?"

"May did something dumb," Noah tried to say, but started coughing instead.

He broke off with a choking noise as the corpse's flimsy, sunken eyelids pulled open to reveal gaping skeletal sockets. The lack of eyeballs did nothing to lessen the feeling that it was somehow staring straight at him. It pressed itself forward, lifting its torso a few inches off the base of the coffin before falling back. It leaned back and forth, suddenly managing to pull one of its shriveled hands free of its metal shackle, and the undead creature clawed itself into an upward position, grasping Noah's shirt before he could escape its range.

Noah shuddered at its touch and wrenched himself violently away. He couldn't get free of its grasp, though, and began to panic as the corpse tugged him closer to the coffin. He wrapped both his hands around the thing's wrist and heaved away mightily, but simply could not overcome the dead creature's unnatural strength.

Brian had started screaming at some point, and now he ran up beside Noah and started punching the corpse wildly, punctuating each blow with a yell. It didn't seem to mind overly much. When Brian realized his gallant attacks were altogether ineffective, he switched tactics and began attempting to pull Noah away from the cadaver's grasp instead. It craned its neck towards him, opening its maw hungrily.

By now the smoke pouring from the pendant had begun to peter off, and after a moment Noah realized the corpse seemed to be weakening in equal measure. He felt a surge of hope, feeling the thing's grip loosen, before the battle came to an abrupt end as the body went slack. It unceremoniously slid limply back into the coffin, its head rolling to the side. The pendant clattered and belched a few last clouds of dust into the air.

Brian and Noah fell to the floor, gasping for breath.

"I don't think I can take any more," Noah said, flopping onto his back. "Two near-death experiences in one night are... way too many."

Brian was shuddering all over. "That was terrible." He looked around, finding Leah and May cowering wide-eyed against the far wall, and pointed at them. "One of you get this coffin closed. Maybe burn the body in there before you close it, actually."

For a few moments, neither of them moved, but then Leah slowly stepped forward and approached the coffin. She skirted around it nervously, looking sideways at the motionless body within. She screwed up her face unhappily, then seemed to summon her courage and stepped gingerly up onto the coffin's stone rim. From there she reached up to the statue on the wall and clicked its tongue back down into its original position, then quickly hopped back to the floor as the coffin's lid began to slide shut.

They all watched the gap slowly close, only relaxing once the corpse inside was sealed away once more.

"So, what just actually happened?" Noah said after a minute. "Because last I checked, dead things are supposed to stay dead."

"And the pendant. What was that?" Leah demanded.

"I think we found something we shouldn't have," May said quietly. "You saw those shackles on the corpse, right? Whoever laid it to rest here knew something was wrong with it. This might look like a mausoleum, but it's really a prison."

"A prison for the dead," Brian said heavily, and shivered again.

Noah exhaled and watched the dust in the air swirl around in response. "We probably shouldn't be breathing this stuff in."

"You think?" Brian said flatly, shooting him a look.

Leah glanced towards the door. "The wolves are still howling out there. If we leave this room, we're right back where we started."

Noah turned toward Brian. "I don't suppose you've got any gas masks in that backpack of yours."

His friend sighed. "You suppose right. If we get out of this I'm definitely getting a couple, though."

"For the next time we find ourselves in the burial places of the cursed dead, huh?" Leah said, elbowing him.

He coughed and pushed her away. "Obviously."

Leah sighed and leaned against the wall, sliding down it until she was sitting on the floor. "How about water?"

"That, I do have," Brian said, procuring a bottle and tossing it over. "Drink whatever you want, I've got a bunch."

Noah picked up his hand warmer from the floor. He had dropped it when the zombie had lunged at him. It was still quite hot, so he held it to his chest with both hands with a sigh. He hadn't felt the cold while he was fighting for his life, but now that he was calming down the chill was quickly becoming perceptible to him once more. Laying on the floor as he was, his body head was quickly leaching away into the stone, but he didn't bother to get up.

"I guess we're going to be sleeping in here tonight," he

said. "If we can get to sleep in the first place."

"Not sure how likely that is," Brian said with a glance at the coffin standing ominously across the room.

Even with the lid sealed shut, none of them could forget the thing inside, separated from them by just a few inches of stone. It had seemed to be dormant in the last moments before the lid slid over it, hiding its desiccated form, but who knew if that dormancy was permanent. It had displayed such great strength that Noah had no trouble at all imagining it suddenly pressing the lid off the coffin and crawling out to consume them all.

Despite these anxious thoughts, he eventually closed his eyes and was overcome by sleep.

6

EVERYTHING'S TOTALLY FINE

Noah awoke some time later feeling terribly lightheaded. He groaned and rolled over, causing the hand warmer which had long gone cold to tumble to his side. He looked around, rubbing the back of his head and remembering where he was. One of the flashlights was still on, which let him see his friends passed out in a row on the floor to either side of him. A couple of Brian's hand warmers were scattered around their prone forms.

Noah stood up slowly, grimacing as he felt all of his limbs alight with pins and needles. He stretched gingerly and wiggled his fingers, but couldn't seem to work the blood back into his limbs.

Wondering what time it was, he gave up stretching and walked over to the door, pausing to listen for any wolfish sounds outside. He couldn't hear anything, but then again, Leah and Brian were both snoring like a couple of buzz saws. He tried to wait for a moment of silence, but they seemed to be synchronizing their breathing to produce a constant racket. Frustrated, he considered just waking them both up, but figured it couldn't hurt to just crack the door slightly to gauge how bright it was outside. In the unlikely event that a wolf had sat patiently right outside for hours on end, he wouldn't be opening the door wide enough for it to get in.

He took a deep breath and pushed the door open just an inch. Sunlight poured into the mausoleum, probably for the first time in a great number of years. The thought brought a grin to Noah's face. Feeling confident, he peeked out to scan the clearing outside and then pushed the door open as much as he could.

As the door opened, he saw for the first time just how much smoky dust had been trapped in the mausoleum. It had been difficult to gauge how much was swirling around them with the single-point light sources of the two flashlights. Noah gulped nervously as dark clouds streamed out of the crack in the door and dissipated into the bright day outside. It was an awfully high concentration, especially considering how long they had been sitting around in it. And this was what was left of it after a large part had escaped through the mausoleum's hopefully highly effective ventilation system.

Noah patted his chest nervously but couldn't sense any obvious pain in his lungs. *Maybe we accidentally stayed out of the worst of it by sleeping on the ground*, he mused. It was possible the smoke from the pendant acted like normal smoke that rose from a fire, and naturally drifted upwards. *Or maybe it's the heat that causes it to rise*, Noah reflected. He couldn't remember the exact mechanics of why smoke behaved the way it did.

There was no use worrying about it at this point. Now that he knew it was morning, Noah had no qualms about waking his friends up. May was already stirring a little, as the ray of sunlight happened to strike her across the face. She protested the sun's brightness with a hand thrown tiredly across her eyes and unhappy grumbling under her breath.

Leaving her be, Noah walked over to stand between the pair of snorers and nudged them both with his foot until the grating noise mercifully trailed off into blissful silence. They awoke quickly, although their quick transition to awareness may have been expedited by Noah kicking them with a little more force than was strictly necessary.

Once the four of them were all fully awake, they were all more than eager to get out of the cramped room of the mausoleum.

"Do any of you feel kind of lightheaded?" Leah asked after

they were all outside. They filed onto the gravel path, finding it a lot more pleasant in the light of day than they had last night.

"You're feeling it too?" Brian asked with a surprised look at his sister.

"I'm definitely feeling it," Noah confirmed.

"I am as well," May said.

"Oh no, there was definitely something in that smoke," Leah said worriedly.

"You think it was the smoke?" Brian asked, kicking a pinecone along the path.

"Well, what else could it have been? I suppose there could have been fumes or something in the mausoleum, if it didn't have proper ventilation." She frowned. "Corpse fumes, that doesn't sound any better."

"I'm also having a little trouble waking up my arms and legs," Noah said. He almost kept that to himself, but now that he knew they were sharing at least one affliction he was curious if there was more to the uncomfortable pricking in his limbs than a simple bad night's rest.

Leah's head snapped over to him. "Same here."

Brian and May just nodded with grim expressions.

Noah rubbed his forehead. "Now I'm scared to wonder what we were breathing in. I thought it was just dust or something."

"That much dust in a little pendant?" Leah said incredulously. "No way that was normal dust. I'd bet you anything that whatever was going on to make the corpse act like a zombie is very closely related to whatever produced all that smoke." She paused and tilted her head. "Was it dust? It kinda seemed like dust to me at first, but it filled the space and stayed in the air like smoke."

Brian shrugged tiredly. "Does it matter?"

Leah scowled at him. "Hey, I'm just trying to reach a consensus here."

Brian rolled his eyes. "It looked like smoke to me."

Noah raised an eyebrow. "I was thinking it was dust," he

insisted, mostly to be contrary.

Leah looked pointedly at May, who looked between the three of them with a startled expression.

"I don't know, it kind of seemed like dust," she said uncertainly.

"There we have it. We've been infected with a terrible disease, probably on par with the *Wager*, by mystery corpse dust," she said with finality.

They reached the fork in the path and chose the correct trail to take them back to the road, looking awkwardly at each other as they proceeded onto the right path.

"To think we would have had a perfectly nice, normal night in our own beds if we had just picked the right way home," Brian said wistfully.

"I don't know, it kind of makes for an epic story," Noah said. "Provided we survive the terrible dust disease, of course."

"I hope Paul didn't worry too much last night," Brian said, then chuckled and continued sarcastically, "I'm sure he immediately took note when we weren't back at the dorm at our usual time, and filed a missing persons report, along with notifying our housing advisor and campus security."

Paul was the roommate of Brian and Noah. He was a nice enough person, but Noah doubted he had put much thought into their absence, if he even noticed it at all. The kid went to bed at an entirely too reasonable hour and usually woke up after Brian and Noah had left for their morning classes.

"I want to stop at the corner shop before we go back to campus," Leah said.

"Yeah? What for?" Noah asked.

Brian shook his head with a sigh. "She's gonna get canned soup and claim it'll cure death itself."

Leah glowered at her brother. "Canned soup is the ultimate treatment for any ailment. It'll take care of our deadly dust disease before we even get into the first stage of debilitating weakness. Minestrone, to be exact. You doubt now, but just you wait. You'll see how right I was when you're miraculously cured."

Brian shot a sideways look at Noah. "She's somehow maintained this opinion for eleven years despite never seeing the slightest evidence in favor of it. Her belief in soup is inspiring in its inanity."

Leah stuck her nose in the air. "I'm going to pretend I didn't hear that."

Brian nodded, continuing to talk to Noah as if his sister wasn't right beside him. "Yeah, that must be how she manages it. She ignores the multitudes of signs that she's an absolute lunatic."

Leah pointedly turned away and struck up a conversation with a baffled May.

Brian chuckled, and after a moment Noah cracked a smile as well, letting the joy of a beautiful morning fill his thoughts. He never thought he'd hold such an appreciation for a regular old breeze, but he found himself enjoying the fresh air as it stirred gently through the trees. The sound of the leaves rustling seemed like the most pure and calming noise in the world. He was disappointed when the rumbling noises of traffic gradually overcame the quiet of the woods.

7

THE CORNER MARKET

Soon enough they cleared the trees and turned off the trail onto a paved sidewalk. They passed the trailhead sign, which read *Oakridge Cemetery Nature Trail - Hours: Dawn to Dusk*.

The street they were now walking along was lined on both sides with a stone brick retaining wall topped by cast iron fencing. Large oak trees towered from each side, spreading their branches overhead and creating a pleasant canopy. The occasional vehicle drove slowly down the two-lane road.

Noah listened to Leah trying to convince May that soup was a perfectly acceptable breakfast food, preferable, really, to any other possible option, for a few minutes before taking pity on her and interrupting.

"So, soup is great and all, but are we really not going to see a doctor or something? I feel like we should tell somebody what happened last night. Maybe someone has an explanation."

Brian scratched his head. "I don't know how legal our actions were. Maybe if we didn't break into somebody's tomb, I'd feel more comfortable about getting professional help. I agree we should at least pay a visit to the health center once we're back on campus to see what they have to say, though."

"Hey, I didn't 'break' anything," Noah said. "They left the door open. They probably wanted visitors to pay their respects to the dead there."

Brian gave his friend a doubtful look. "That's not how it

works."

"Well, then we just don't tell anyone! Problem solved. We went to the cemetery, left at a normal hour, slept the night in our own dorms, and woke up feeling a little ill. There's no reason they can't figure out what we've come down with and treat it if we give them our symptoms, right?"

"That sounds fine to me," Leah said. "Brian?"

He shrugged. "Sure, we'll just lie to the people who only have our best interests at heart."

"Oh, come off it. They'll probably talk to campus security, who will talk to the police, who will talk to us about how we suddenly have to pay whoever's mausoleum we stayed in a big fat fine for disrespecting their dead or trespassing on their land or whatever," Leah said.

Brian looked down. "We wouldn't have to tell them *everything*." He sighed. "It's fine, though. We can lie."

"Great, it's decided," Noah said.

"I don't want to lie," May muttered.

Leah looked over, annoyed. "What?"

She seemed to shrink. "What if we have something truly dangerous? They'll be able to help us better if we tell them what really happened. And I know one of the nurses there. She wouldn't share anything that would get us in trouble."

Leah sighed. "She might not have any control over what information gets shared. I don't know about you, but I can't afford to deal with whatever consequences arise from someone making a fuss. You think I wanted to sleep in a mausoleum? The situation was outside my control. Outside the control of any of us, and I harbor no guilt in keeping the exact events of last night something that I keep quiet. It might be a little uncomfortable, May, but I'm asking you to do the same."

May considered her words for a minute. They reached a somewhat busy intersection and stopped to wait for a break in traffic.

After they had crossed, May finally shook her head. "I don't know. You're talking about this like we've committed a mortal sin. We were just dealing with some unlucky circumstances and made do with the resources we had available. Even if we went right to the authorities and told them every detail, I believe they would understand we were only trying to survive. I need you to let me think about it."

Leah was clearly unhappy at her friend's response, but she nodded. "Okay. But we have to reach a decision before we go to the doctor. I don't want you to start recounting everything all of a sudden."

By now they had reached the beginning of the commercial section of town. This area was so close to Oakridge college that it was practically part of its campus, so the landscaping was tidy and a lot of the two-story shops lining the road displayed college merch in their front displays.

Noah and his friends strolled past the various storefronts, aiming towards the Corner Market at the far end of the street. It was like the poor forgotten cousin of the other buildings, and indeed outdated not only every store on the street but the campus itself. The floor tiles were approximately the same shade as a ripe banana and the brash blue-tinted lighting fixtures buzzed like they were hiding hornets' nests. The building was small, cramped, and the quality of maintenance both within and without had led many a customer to believe it was in danger of running out of business any day.

In reality, it saw more sales than all of the other shops on the road combined, simply due to the fact that every student on campus relied on it- and it alone- for groceries and casual shopping. The current store owner, a startlingly large man named David, knew the names of nearly all of them.

They reached the front entrance of the Corner Market, a single black door with the hours of operation listed on a handwritten note taped to the inside of the window. Leah breezed inside and beelined for a particular aisle.

"I guess that's where the soups are," Noah said, watching her vanish around the corner.

"Yeah. She comes here every week just for soup. It's completely absurd." Brian shook his head. "I think she started getting it all the time as a joke, but at some point it kind of got absorbed into her psyche and became a genuine obsession for her."

"I can see that," Noah said, as she reappeared from the aisle with an armful of cans and a huge grin on her face.

"I've got enough for all of us," she said brightly when she had drawn up beside them. "Do any of you need anything else before we go?"

"I'm going to use the bathroom," Brian said.

"You sure you want to do that here? You know what the restroom is like," Leah warned.

Brian smiled tightly. "Oh, I'm well aware. I'm quite desperate."

"I think I'll use the bathroom as well, actually," May said.

The two of them walked speedily off towards the back of the store.

"I've been out of milk for a few days, might as well grab some while we're here," Noah said. "You can go check out if you like, I'll be quick."

He wandered off towards the refrigerated section. As he stood in front of the rows of dairy products, trying to find the brand he liked, he suddenly coughed. A small cloud of black dust bloomed from his mouth.

8

EVERYTHING MIGHT NOT
BE TOTALLY FINE

Noah's heart dropped at the sight and he looked around to see if anyone had noticed. There were a couple of people standing further down the aisle, but none of them were looking in his direction. Waving his hand quickly through the cloud to dispel it, Noah gave up trying to find his particular brand, grabbing a random carton of milk and hurrying away towards the front of the store where the cash registers were located. He noticed Leah was already paying for her absurdly large amount of canned soups and decided to get in line at another register.

Are our lungs all full of dust? He wondered, growing more anxious with every passing second. *This could be even worse than we thought.*

It came his turn to pay and he pulled out his wallet. His fingers were so numb that it took him a lot longer than it probably should have to pull out the appropriate number of bills. He had been unpleasantly aware of the pins-and-needles sensation pricking at his hands all morning, but only now realized how much it interfered with his fine motor control. Luckily for him, he only had to extract a few dollars. Most of the items sold at the Corner Market were just as cheap as one would hope from such a tired looking store.

He held the money out to the guy manning the cash register, none other than David himself, and realized with horror that he was about to cough again. Recognizing that he wouldn't be able to stifle it before it came out, he tucked his head down into his elbow and prayed that David wouldn't be able to see the dust he feared would appear.

There was to be no hiding it. The sinister cloud bloomed around his arm and polluted the air around the checkout station, prompting the several customers in line behind him to swiftly back away. David wasn't so quick to move, and tiny particles coated the lenses of his glasses and clung to his clothing.

Cringing, Noah squeezed his eyes shut momentarily and took a deep breath. "I'm sorry about that," he said as David stared at him in surprise. "I'm a little sick at the moment, I sincerely apologize."

David waved his large hands through the cloud and coughed loudly to clear his lungs, drawing the attention of everyone nearby who had failed to notice the initial burst of dust. May and Brian had gotten back from the bathroom at some point and looked over curiously from where they were waiting by the exit. Their eyes bugged out of their heads as they recognized the odd dust from the mausoleum drifting through the air around Noah.

"That's not a healthy habit, son," David said as the air finally began to clear.

Noah's attention shot back to him in surprise. "Oh, that's not- I mean, I don't smoke," he was quick to assure the man.

David smiled at him and took his glasses off, beginning to clean them on the hem of his shirt. "You don't need to bother with any of that, son. I'd just like you to know that your lungs won't thank you for the habit. Take it from me. I was hooked for twenty years before I managed to quit." He held his lenses up to the ceiling lights, peering closely at them. He frowned and brought them back to his shirt, rubbing the lenses more fiercely.

Noah held his hands up, feeling his cheeks turning red. "I appreciate the advice, sir, but I don't need it. I've never smoked in my life."

David continued as if he hadn't said anything, "The best way to do it is to replace the habit with something else. Start substituting one for the other and before you know it you're chewing gum instead of giving yourself a dozen chronic diseases. It'll be hard, son, but I believe in you."

Noah buried his face in his hands. "Thank you, sir."

He grabbed the milk and hurried out of the store. His friends stared worriedly at him as he rushed by, but he just shook his head and gestured for them to follow him outside.

"What happened?" Brian asked as soon as they were back out under the sun. They set off along the street, continuing in the direction of Oakridge Community College.

"Well, David thinks I'm a smoking addict now. Because of this," he said with a sigh, and forced a cough. Dust spewed out in a foreboding mass.

"Oh, no," Leah whispered. She glanced around and let out a small cough of her own. Dust flew into the air, swirling into the cloud Noah had produced and further darkening the air around them.

They all stared at the haze, dread settling like a lead blanket over their shoulders.

"Are we dying?" Brian asked.

Leah punched him. "Of course not. It's just a little dust. We have soup, we'll be fine."

Brian didn't look very reassured, so Noah added, "Plus we're also going to the doctor. We can see if the office is open as soon as we get back on campus. I'm sure they'll give us something to clear everything right up."

May smiled. "Especially if they know where the dust came from."

Leah rolled her eyes. "Did anything about that zombie's pendant look like established science to you? They're not gonna have a clue what has happened to us."

Noah looked anxiously back at the store and said, "I hope it's not contagious. If so, I might have just gotten David sick."

They all looked back in the direction of the Corner Market, though by now they were in the middle of the Oakridge campus and the store was out of view. Eventually Leah rubbed her neck and shrugged. "It's too late to do anything about it now. Either the dust is harmless or we're walking safety hazards. The best thing for us to do is just get back to our dorms and lay low until we can see a doctor."

Noah nodded. "Yeah, I need to put my milk in the fridge regardless. And I'm taking a shower before we do anything else."

Brian exhaled. "Oh boy, a shower sounds so nice right now."

A few quick minutes later they arrived at Leah and May's dormitory and the two girls stepped away to the main entrance. May disappeared inside while Leah paused on the threshold, holding the door open with her foot. Noah doubted she'd be able to open it again if it closed, what with her hands full of soup.

"Oh, do try not to cough on people! You don't want to be responsible for infecting half your dorm!" she said.

"I'll be careful," Noah said seriously.

Leah smiled. "See you guys at the health center in half an hour?"

Brian looked at Noah before nodding. "See you then."

9

SHOWERS

Noah and Brian made their way to their own dorm, sticking to the side of the thoroughfare and doing their best not to spew black dust everywhere. Several half-stifled coughs broke out despite their efforts, and though Noah hoped they did a sufficient job of smothering the resulting clouds, he couldn't help but feel that they were putting everyone they passed at risk. He imagined a black streak forming in the air behind them wherever they stepped, creating a hazardous line through the center of campus like a tripwire awaiting unsuspecting victims.

They finally arrived at their dorm, only a few buildings down from May and Leah's. Far from feeling relieved to be off the sidewalk, Noah's worry only deepened as he opened the door and stepped inside. Now that they were in an enclosed space, any dust stirred into the air would linger indefinitely. Any person who walked where they had passed would be in danger.

"Should we even be in here?" Noah asked quietly after a kid walked by them obliviously.

Brian shrugged helplessly. "Probably not, but I need a shower. Let's just make it quick and get back outside as soon as possible."

They passed another couple of students on the stairs, recognizing all three of them. Noah felt more and more guilty as he climbed to the fourth floor and walked quickly to his room. They had no idea how contagious the dust was, but Noah didn't want to find out by waking up to the entire campus being infected. They could be carrying a deadly sickness, and here they were walking around their dorm like nothing was wrong. Were they being selfish?

Probably, Noah thought glumly as he unlocked his door. He held it open for Brian and followed his friend inside.

"Oh, hey, Paul," Brian said.

Paul was working studiously on his laptop with headphones on at his desk. He didn't seem to hear Brian, so Noah walked over and put a hand on the desk, being very careful not to exhale whatsoever as he stood over the small blond-haired kid.

Paul startled and paused his music, pulling his headphones down to rest around his neck. He stared at Noah and Brian in surprise. "Don't you guys have class right now? What's up?"

"We've got something of a... of a cold. We're not going to class today," Noah said. "Don't mind us." He turned and put his milk in the mini fridge at the base of his bed.

Paul glanced uncertainly between them before shrugging and dropping his headphones back on.

Noah and Brian quickly changed out of their clothes and grabbed a towel and bottle of soap each before leaving Paul once more alone and stepping out of the room.

Noah was thankful to see that the hallway was clear of students, and let out a few raspy coughs while he felt comfortable that no one was around. He was just starting to relax a little when they arrived at the dormitory showers and walked in to find the room chock full of students busily washing themselves.

"Is it always this busy at this hour?" Noah asked Brian, dumbfounded. He usually showered before bed and had never seen so many of the showers being used at the same time. They were lucky to find two empty adjacent stalls.

Brian shrugged nervously and cleared his throat. "I don't know. Steam supposedly makes you have to cough less, so we might be fine." He waved a hand through the misty air. "And if not, hopefully the air is so foggy anyways that nobody will even notice."

Noah scowled at his friend and responded in a low voice, "The goal isn't to hide that we're sick from everyone, it's to keep them safe."

"I guess so." Brian glanced sideways at him. "It's hard to care about that right now though, when we don't really know if it's harmful or not."

Noah felt differently, but he didn't press the matter. "Hey, is it just me, or is there absolutely no hot water right now?" He'd never had to put the shower knob to the highest setting, but right now he had it cranked all the way and the water was barely luke-warm.

"It's probably 'cause half the building decided to shower at once," Brian grumbled. "I'm not getting any hot water either."

The kid in the stall next to them overheard their conversation and looked over in surprise. He seemed to hesitate before saying, "Are you guys trying to prove something, or what? You look like you're standing in a blasted steamer! I can feel the heat from here!"

Noah blinked in surprise as he realized the guy was right. Him and Brian were single-handedly steaming up the showers to the point he could barely see his friend despite standing just a few feet in front of him.

"Oh, no," Noah said to himself. "This has got to be another symptom. We've gone numb."

Out of curiosity, he turned the shower knob all the way to the other side and waited a few seconds. He couldn't discern any change whatsoever in the water temperature, so he turned to the random guy showering next to him.

"Hey, is this cold?" He stepped back and gestured to his shower.

The guy gave him a very strange look, but he narrowed his eyes and stepped over to stick his whole arm under the showerhead. He backed away with a shiver and a scowl. "Yeah, it's cold, dumbass. What are you playing at?"

Noah frowned. "Nothing at all. I guess I'm having some

issues sensing temperature at the moment."

The guy snorted. "Sure. Whatever, man."

Noah usually found showering to be a relaxing activity, but without being able to feel the heat of the water he found himself disappointed. He finished his shower with the temperature at the coldest setting and dried himself off unhappily.

"I hope all these symptoms don't hang around for long," he said to Brian as they wrapped their towels around themselves and stepped out of the showers.

"Tell me about it. I was looking forward to a nice warm shower, but it felt like nothing. Like standing in the rain. Not even that. I could barely feel the water at all."

They passed two students in the hallway but Noah barely noticed them. He glanced down and suddenly pinched his arm as hard as he could. There was no sensation of pain whatsoever.

"This is dangerous," he said after a moment. "Anything that has this strong of an effect on us has got to be directly impacting our nervous system. We could end up paralyzed."

Brian shot him a startled look.

Noah continued, "And even if that doesn't happen, if we can't feel anything, then we have to be really careful that we're not damaging ourselves. All sorts of normal activities are balanced by our awareness of when something is starting to hurt. Without that we can get injured way too easily."

He coughed and waved aside the dust.

Brian looked contemplative. "So far our lungs, circulation, and now our nervous system has been impacted. What the heck was in that mausoleum?"

10

A MATTER OF LIFE AND DEATH

They got back to their room and dressed themselves. Noah was unable to stifle a small cough before he finished changing, and he and Brian shared a worried look and glanced over at Paul. The kid was still doing work at his desk, bopping his head slightly to his music.

"I hope he'll be okay," Brian said, grabbing his backpack and stepping out of the room.

Noah looked down guiltily. "Yeah."

They entered the stairwell and descended the stairs, emerging by the building entrance at the ground floor and at long last stepping out into the sunlight.

Finally feeling comfortable enough to take a deep breath, Noah sighed deeply and watched a few small dark wisps drift away from his face.

"It's getting worse," he commented.

"Let's go find out what's wrong with us," Brian said, setting off. "C'mon, I want to beat the girls there."

Noah forced himself to smile good-naturedly. "Oh, that'll be easy. They're probably still in the shower."

Brian grinned. "They don't stand a chance."

"You know, maybe not, if they figured out that they can't feel heat and the problem isn't that their showers are cold. Showers aren't so nice without hot water."

Brian narrowed his eyes. "That's right. Dammit! We've lost our main advantage." He glanced around, his eyes alighting on the nearby bus stop, where a shuttle was just pulling in. "Aha! This will be our path to victory. They won't think to use public transportation to skip a five minute walk."

Noah pulled his friend back before he could get out of reach. "Don't tell me you're thinking of sitting in an enclosed vehicle with several dozen other people just so you can beat the girls in an imaginary race."

Brian rubbed his neck sheepishly. "Oh, you're right. We'll have to settle for beating them on foot."

Noah rolled his eyes. "The bus would take longer than walking anyway. It won't leave the bus stop for another few minutes at least, and then it will visit every spot of interest on campus and half the spots of no interest for no reason, and probably drive off campus too for good measure. We'd have been everywhere but the health center by the time Leah and May got there."

"It sounds like you're speaking from experience."

"That is correct," Noah grumbled. "I genuinely have no idea why anyone uses the shuttles."

"It sounds like you just haven't figured out the campus shuttle schedule."

"No, I'm sure that's not it."

After a few minutes the squat building of the campus Health Center came into view, squashed between the much larger Public Facilities and Campus Safety buildings.

"I've actually never been here before," Noah said, approaching the front entrance.

Brian raised his eyebrows. "I've been once. Remember when I thought I'd fractured my arm back in the first week of classes? Well, when I came to see a doctor they said it was just a 'bone bruise'- still not sure how bones can be bruised, honestly- and they basically told me to get over it. I haven't felt the need to return since. If we had anything less than whatever we picked up last night, I'd just try to sleep it off."

They walked into a small lobby with couches and cushioned chairs arranged around a low central table stacked with brochures and magazines related to campus life. The walls were painted lime green and yellow, the campus colors.

May and Leah were already seated in the corner in a small cloud of black dust. Both of them were reading a pamphlet they must have picked up from the display on the table.

"No way!" Brian exclaimed. "How'd you get here before us?"

"I don't know what you mean," Leah said. "We took our time to clean up and get ready. You can thank yourself for taking your sweet time getting over here."

Brian looked at Noah, dumbfounded. "They're joking, right?"

Noah shrugged. "Guess we should've been faster." He sat down on the couch next to them. "Have you talked to the receptionist yet?"

"No, we were waiting for you guys to arrive."

"Oh, then no point sitting around any longer." Noah stood right back up and walked over to the front desk. There was no line, so he and his friends were able to crowd up around the counter. A sliding glass partition separated them from the guy sitting inside.

"Good morning," the receptionist said with a smile. He looked about the same age as Noah, and he wore a name tag that said *Robert J.* "What brings you here today?"

"We need to see a doctor," Noah said. "Right away. We're all sick."

Robert's expression smoothed over and he calmly pointed to a paper taped to the glass partition between them. "Scan that QR code to set up an appointment. I don't know how busy the doctor is today, but most students are able to get a meeting with her within forty-eight hours."

"We can't afford to wait that long," Leah said quickly. "Can you just check if they can't meet with us now?"

Robert glanced between them, fiddling with the top button of his shirt. He finally shrugged and gestured to the QR code again. "That link will bring you to a page that will tell you when the doctor's earliest open time slot is."

"Let's just check," May said quietly, holding up her phone to the paper. While she fiddled with the link, Noah turned back to the receptionist.

"Is there no one else qualified to talk to us? You can't tell me there's just one doctor taking care of a few thousand college students."

Robert adjusted his glasses. "There are indeed several other doctors. We have three psychiatrists in the office at the moment, and we usually have a second physician, but he is currently out of town at a conference. He will be returning in four days."

"Well, that's just great," Noah grumbled, turning to May. "How about that link? Does the doctor have any open appointments today?"

May squinted at the screen. "The next available appointment is... Wednesday."

Leah threw up her hands. "That's two days away! We can't wait that long!"

Noah turned back to Robert. "I understand that the doctor is very busy right now, but I believe it would be in everyone's best interest if we could get an appointment sometime today. We don't know what we're sick with, but we have reason to believe it's serious, and we have no idea how contagious it is. We're just trying to keep everyone safe."

Robert sighed. "Look, I'm obviously no physician, but it sounds like you should just isolate yourselves for a few days until it blows over. I can't give you a note or anything to excuse you from classes, but," he smirked, "lack of a doctor's note doesn't stop most students from skipping class whenever they feel like it."

Noah clenched the edge of the counter and resisted the urge to roll his eyes. "We're not just trying to get out of classes. This could be a matter of life and death!"

Robert just sat there calmly. "Is there anything else you need?"

Noah turned away, disgusted. He started to walk towards the exit, but then stopped and looked around the room. It was completely empty aside from the four of them. Feeling angry and reckless, Noah cleared his throat and started coughing.

11

THAT GOT THEIR ATTENTION

He ignored his friends' alarmed looks and merely focused on coughing over and over with as much force as he could muster. A dark cloud formed around him, faint and wispy at first, though the entire room soon came to be cast in a dark gloom. It felt strangely satisfying to expel so much dust out of his body, although the amount that was filling the air around him was beginning to get a bit worrying.

Brian looked like he was about to say something, but Leah elbowed him with a dark look in her eyes, and so they just stood silently and watched Noah cough and hack like he was trying to throw up last week's lunch.

After nearly a minute Noah finally snapped his mouth closed with a final wheeze and smiled.

"Sorry about that. That's just one of our symptoms, I'm sure you understand." He exhaled through his nose and dark smoke trickled out his nostrils.

He could barely make out Robert's shocked expression through the glass. Dust had drifted through the cracks around the edge of the partition and begun to fill his side of the office.

"If you're wondering if inhaling the smoke has gotten you infected with whatever we have, don't worry! We're wondering the same thing, since we have no idea what it is."

Without another word Robert stumbled to his feet and fled the room, leaving his chair slowly swiveling in a circle.

Noah's expression went flat as the receptionist disappeared from view, and he stepped back to slump into one of the lobby's comfortable plush chairs.

None of them said anything for a minute. At some point some poor student tried to enter the room through the main entrance, but they took one look at the ominous wall of smoke inside and backpedaled, retreating quickly out of view.

"That was an interesting tactic," Leah said eventually.

"Let's see if it works," Noah said shortly. It would be unfortunate if the receptionist ended up getting sick, but it was better than them wandering around cluelessly and infecting everyone they came across for two days. Even if they restricted themselves to their dorms, they would still have to leave occasionally, and it would be difficult to convince Paul to exercise the same level of caution.

Brian dropped into a chair next to Noah and dust visibly puffed into the air as the cushion compressed.

"They're gonna have to deep clean this whole room," his friend said.

Noah sighed. "Yeah, probably."

May looked around. "I can't be alone in thinking it's a little scary how much dust is floating around. All of this was *inside* of Noah. We're probably all carrying around this much dust inside of us. You'd think we'd be able to feel it somehow, but somehow I don't feel sick at all."

Noah smirked. "Oh, and I could have kept going, too. I just thought this was enough to make my point."

"That we have some kind of horrifying disease?" Brian asked.

"Well, yeah."

"How much longer do you think we should wait around in here?" he asked. "It would be kind of rude to just leave the room like this, don't you think?"

"Let's give them ten minutes. They were kind enough to give us entertainment, after all," Noah said, picking up one of the brochures off the table. He scanned the title, 'Rhinopathica Pendula: What You Need to Know', and laughed shortly. "Hey, take a look at this ancient thing. It must have come out in the first few weeks after the *Wager* appeared; it uses the old name."

Brian grabbed another identical brochure off the table and raised his eyebrows. "Well, would you look at that."

"I'm not surprised the name changed. 'Rhinopathica Pendula' hardly rolls off the tongue. Everyone probably forgot about the original name as soon as the catchy nicknames started popping up," Leah said.

Noah opened the pamphlet out of curiosity and, steeling himself, read a few lines aloud.

"'*Rhinopathica Pendula (RP) is a newly identified disease that has prompted the medical community to reassess established paradigms of human pathology. The etiology and mode of transmission of RP remain unclear, with no evidence of predisposition across specific demographics. During the prodromal phase, the disease primarily affects the upper respiratory tract, with symptoms emerging shortly after exposure. Rhinorrhea is the sole confirmed symptom at this stage.*

"*Within 72 hours of onset, all affected individuals advance to the critical phase. Approximately 50% of cases resolve spontaneously, with full restoration of respiratory function and no lasting complications. In the remaining 50%, the disease progresses rapidly, impacting vital organs such as the lungs, heart, or brain. This progression, referred to as the Fatal Outcome, is variable in presentation but universally results in death within one minute of onset. To date, no cases of survival following the Fatal Outcome phase have been documented.*'"

Noah looked up with a blank expression. "Well, they've got it all correct. Seems like no one's made much progress since this was published."

"You would know better than us," Brian said delicately.

The door to the back office suddenly opened, prompting everyone to look over at it hopefully.

A relatively young brunette woman stood framed by the doorway, waving her arm to clear the air as dust rushed around her to fill the sudden vacuum. She wore a white jacket that was a mix of a lab coat and dress shirt, and had a surgical mask strapped to her face.

She let the dust settle in the air around her, still standing in the doorway, her eyes roaming around the dark haze the room had been draped in. At long last she made eye contact with the four friends sitting in the corner.

"So, you're the ones who've been causing Robert so much trouble."

"We need your help," Noah said quickly, cutting her off before she could say anything else.

"...I can see that," she said dryly. She turned and started walking away from them. "Follow me to my office."

12

DOCTOR'S OFFICE

The four friends stood up in a rush and hurried after her. *Finally, we'll get some answers*, Noah thought.

She led them down a brightly lit hallway and past a couple offices before turning into one with a placard marked *Dr. Iris Jansen, M.D., Physician.*

"Sit down," she said brusquely, gesturing to the four plastic chairs that had been set up against the wall. A fan was running in the corner by the door, blowing towards the open window. Generic photographs of rolling outdoor landscapes were framed on the walls.

"First of all," she began, "I'd like all of you to know I have sent another student who had properly scheduled a meeting with me back to their dorm so that I could speak to you four. I'm not saying this for the purpose of making you feel guilty, only so that you understand I am taking your plea for help seriously."

They all nodded.

"Thank you for taking the time to help us, Dr. Jansen," May said.

The doctor nodded. "You're welcome. Now, Robert told me you don't know what's wrong, but that you're convinced it poses a significant risk to yourselves and to your fellow students. When did you first start experiencing symptoms?"

They all glanced at each other before Leah spoke up. "Just earlier this morning, Doctor. We came here as soon as we realized something was wrong."

She nodded. "Have you done anything unusual in the past forty-eight hours that you can immediately think of?"

Noah kept his face neutral and fought the urge to look at his friends.

"Not really. I guess we went off campus yesterday evening, but we only went to the cemetery."

"Oh? Were you paying your respects to someone in particular?"

Noah swallowed. "My mom."

The doctor focused in on that like a detective sniffing out evidence. "I'm sorry for your loss. Do you mind sharing how she passed?"

Noah shook his head. "She got the *Wager*. She didn't get the good outcome."

He could see her lose interest in the subject as soon as he mentioned the *Wager*, clearly realizing there was no connection to their current ailment.

"I see. That is truly unfortunate." She wrote something down on a tablet on her desk. "So, I see you are all experiencing some unusual respiratory conditions."

All four of them were exhaling small amounts of dust with every breath, only for the dark clouds to get whisked away by the air blowing from the fan and shunted out the window.

"Yeah, but that was like the third symptom," Leah said.

"Let's just focus on the smoke for now," Dr. Jansen said. "Do any of you spend significant amounts of time in smoky environments?"

"Actually, it's dust," Brian and Noah said simultaneously. Leah and May nodded.

Dr. Jansen raised an eyebrow. "Is it, now? What makes you so sure? It resembles smoke to my eyes."

They didn't have a good answer to that, so eventually Noah just shrugged. "Nothing, really. It just feels correct."

"Alright, then." She wrote something else down. "My question still stands, however. "Have you been doing any cleaning? Been in a dusty area?"

Brian looked at Noah. Noah thought for a moment and

concluded the mausoleum was not dusty, nope, and answered "no" without elaborating.

The doctor nodded shortly. "Have any of you ever smoked or are currently smoking?"

They all shook their heads. She made a note. "I will measure each of your oxygen levels before you leave today," she said. "For now, let's move on to your other symptoms. What was the first sign that something was wrong this morning?"

"I felt really light headed," Noah said. "And my whole body had that pins-and-needles feeling, like it was asleep. Not so much anymore, though. I've been totally numb for about an hour now."

The doctor looked at each of them in turn. "Is this true for the rest of you as well?"

"Yeah," Leah said. "I can't feel anything. I touch something, and I can see my hand touching it, but it doesn't feel like anything is there. It's really weird. And probably a sign that something is awfully wrong." She looked anxiously at the doctor.

"We'll see," Dr. Jansen said evenly. "It sounds like you are experiencing poor blood flow. Are there any other symptoms you have taken note of since this morning?"

Noah thought about it and shook his head. "That's everything. That I've noticed, at least."

None of the others had anything else to add.

"In that case, I will take this moment to retrieve the pulse oximeters to measure your blood oxygen levels. I will be back shortly. Please stay seated with your hands below your heart to prepare for the test."

The doctor stood and strode out of the room.

"She has no idea what's wrong with us," Leah said after a few seconds.

"I'm getting that feeling as well,"Brian said. "Hopefully this blood oximeter thing gives her enough information to at least let her treat us, even if she doesn't know the name of whatever we have."

"I really hope that there's nothing to worry about," May said. "That would be nice."

A few minutes later Dr. Jansen reappeared, pushing a small plastic cart ahead of her. There were a few plastic blue-and-white clips on a small tray on the cart, along with a stethoscope and a small mallet.

"I have decided it would be prudent to take the basic measurements that you would be tested for at a regular physical check-up. We will start with your heart rate. The pulse oximeter will also record your pulse, but I am interested in listening to it myself."

The doctor knelt by Noah first, equipping the stethoscope. She placed the chest piece below his heart and held still for a few seconds. Eventually she leaned back and asked, "Are you holding your breath?"

"No," Noah said. "Should I be?"

"Please don't. I can hardly pick up your pulse in the first place. Kindly take a deep breath."

Noah did so, exhaling a stream of dust.

Dr. Jansen ignored it, concentrating fully on picking up the sound of his heart. She finally nodded, wrote briefly on her tablet, and moved on to Brian next. She listened to the pulse of each of them before returning to her desk and reclining in the seat.

"I'm going to be straight with you; the heart rates you are all displaying are low enough to be adequate reason to send you immediately to a facility better equipped to keep you alive than we."

They all sat bolt upright. "Is that what you're going to do?" Brian asked. "Are we going to be okay?"

"The reason that I haven't already called an ambulance is that you four should already be unconscious, yet you are all alert and conversing normally with me. That is sufficient reason for me to conclude there are abnormal factors at play that I'm unaware of. I plan to determine what those are."

13

YOU WON'T FEEL A THING

She picked up the two blue-and-white clips from the cart and stood up. "You have been in a resting position for long enough that you should all be ready to measure your blood oxygen saturation. Your symptoms lead me to believe that it will be atypically low. Please clip this to your index finger."

The doctor handed Noah and Brian each their own oximeter, and they clumsily secured it to their fingers. They sat quietly for a minute. Noah swung his finger back and forth, feeling odd that he couldn't feel the device itself yet was able to sense the slight weight resistance, the tiny amount of extra force required to move the digit.

"That should be sufficient," Dr. Jansen said, glancing at the readings and bringing up her pen to write them down, then pausing and looking back at the oximeters. Her eyes narrowed.

"If the data these are displaying is accurate, I am unsure how you are still conscious, let alone alive," she said bluntly. "Quite frankly, it's impossible. A human is not able to survive off such a low saturation of oxygen in their blood. Your heart rate is reasonable, if surprisingly low, but the oxygen levels are just absurd. Are you even breathing?"

She paused, and looking like she could hardly believe what she was writing, made a note of each of their readings.

It was the same story with May and Leah.

Looking dazed, Dr. Jansen put the two oximeters back on

the cart and grabbed the mallet.

"I'm sure you've done this before. It will just be a light tap on your knee."

She knocked the mallet against Noah's knee. He felt nothing, of course.

"Relax your leg," the doctor said. "You're too stiff for this test to produce accurate results." She knocked once more in the same spot, then to Noah's surprise started tapping around his knee and adjusted herself so that she could tap several points along his arm. After a minute she stood up and ran a hand through her hair. "Alright, for one reason or another, you've got zero deep tendon reflexes. None that I tested, at least. What on earth is going on with you?"

Noah felt like he was watching her carefully composed persona gradually fall apart at the seams as she struggled to understand the information being presented before her.

She rounded on Brian and administered the same array of taps against his legs and arms. As she moved between muscle tendons, growing ever more flustered, Brian looked sideways at Noah with a bewildered expression, making him laugh.

"There's nothing funny about this," Dr. Jansen said testily without looking up. "The four of you should be on the verge of death. You should need to be hospitalized. You should not be sitting around laughing at each other as if nothing is wrong."

The doctor moved to Leah and began rapping on her with the mallet.

"It doesn't feel like anything is wrong," Noah said. "Except when I'm supposed to be feeling something. And then that just feels weird."

"You should be-"

"Look, I get that we should be freaking out. But this obviously isn't your average sickness. There's as much happening here that shouldn't be as things not happening that should be. So let's all agree to forget whatever assumptions we might have about how a sick person is supposed to behave and work together on getting us back to normal."

Dr. Jansen stopped midway through knocking on May's

ankle like she was trying to hammer a nail into it and looked at Noah with a stricken expression. "You're absolutely right. I apologize for my unprofessional behavior. May I ask what your names are?"

"It's Noah."

"Brian."

"Leah."

"May."

The doctor smiled. "Nice to meet you all. I'm Dr. Iris Jansen."

"I know," Leah said, and Brian elbowed her.

"We're making a fresh start," he muttered.

Ignoring them, Dr. Jansen sat down in her chair and gently set down the mallet. "I wonder if this is how the first doctors to discover the *Wager* felt. Completely out of their depth, like none of their training was enough to prepare them for something so different. A whole new paradigm of medicine that nobody has even begun to understand."

Brian nodded hesitantly. "After the patient died, maybe. They wouldn't have known anything was wrong until the person had passed away without warning."

Dr. Jansen nodded. "Yes, of course. We're lucky in that regard; there's still time to figure out what's happening. Right now I'm thinking the best course of action is to contact the medical center downtown to get you moved there for further testing. They have equipment leagues above anything we could hope to get our hands on here. I'm sure they would be just as interested as myself in discovering how you're still alive."

She picked at her surgical mask and added, "To be honest, I'm starting to wish I had put on a full-face gas respirator mask, if only we had any. This escalated quite a bit further than I was expecting."

"I think we can all say the same," Leah said.

"Speaking of which, have you interacted with many people since you began displaying symptoms? Depending on how contagious this sickness is, we could find ourselves with a serious problem on our hands."

Suppressing a sigh as he thought back to how many people they had run into in the past several hours despite their dubious efforts to stay out of the way of the general public, Noah could only give the doctor a worried grimace. "Too many people to count. Pretty much the only thing we can do at this point is hope that it doesn't spread easily. If the sickness is transferred to another person as easily as them inhaling some of the dust we're producing, then things are going to get bad really quickly."

The doctor nodded. "Best case scenario, you have all somehow picked up a noninfectious disease. You are, however, wrong that the only thing we can do now is hope."

Noah glanced up. "How so?"

"Preventative measures. I plan to have the four of you stay at a housing complex at the edge of campus. Have you heard of the spot we used to send students who came down with the *Wager*, before it was known if the sickness was contagious?"

They all nodded.

"We get to stay there?" Leah asked excitedly.

Dr. Jansen inclined her head. "It is the best way to ensure you do not come into contact with any more people until we have additional information."

She stood and stepped closer to the cart next to the door, opening a small drawer under its top counter. "One last thing. I would like to take a blood sample from each of you." As she spoke she extracted four vials and four needles from the drawer.

Noah couldn't help a shudder from passing through him at the sight. He had always hated needles. It's fine, he told himself. This is the best possible time to get poked by one. I won't even feel it.

Even so, he grew nervous as she pulled on a fresh pair of gloves and approached him with a needle in one hand and an elastic band in the other. She swiftly wrapped the band around his arm and poised the needle over his flesh.

"You won't feel a thing," she said with a smirk, and

inserted the needle.

He winced in spite of himself as he watched the small vial fill with red liquid. *The problem isn't that it hurts, it's that there's a needle sucking blood out of my body. That's a perfectly reasonable thing to object to.*

Soon enough it was finished, and Dr. Jansen calmly released the pressure on the elastic band and withdrew the needle. She stoppered the vial, labeled it quickly with a permanent marker she procured from seemingly nowhere, and laid it on the cart. "Put this on," she said, passing Noah a band-aid.

He nodded faintly and began picking at the wrapper as she grabbed another needle and vial and started wrapping Brian's arm.

Noah quickly realized that he wouldn't be able to get the band-aid open on his own. His fingers felt like they sometimes got when he stayed outside in the bitter cold for too long, and returned indoors only to find he was so numb he couldn't untie his own shoelaces. Embarrassed, he was about to lean over to ask Leah for help when he remembered she wouldn't fare any better. He placed the bandage back on the cart instead, feeling silly.

He glanced down at the puncture spot on his arm, mollified to see it wasn't bleeding at all. He settled back in his seat to watch Dr. Jansen finish drawing blood from each of his friends.

14

EVEN THEIR HAZMAT SUITS
ARE ON BRAND

"We should have some form of results within forty-eight hours," Dr. Jansen said. "I will have someone bring you back to the health center when it is time for us to discuss the test results. I want to keep you as involved in this process as possible. If at any point before then you wish to speak with me about anything regarding your sickness, please feel free to call me." She handed each of them a card with her name and number.

"I will also be in contact with your roommate," she said with a stern look at Noah and Brian. "Since you felt it would be fine to pay him a visit."

Noah glanced down guiltily, but the doctor was already moving on.

"And finally, I would like each of you to wear one of these for the foreseeable future," she said, opening the drawer on the cart once more and pulling out what looked like four regular digital watches. "These will monitor your heart rate and blood oxygen levels. They will automatically alert me if either value drops too low. They are waterproof, so feel free to keep them on at all hours of the day. They do not need to be charged."

"Sweet," Brian said, attempting to wrap it around his wrist, only to give up with a stumped expression. "Um, do you think you can fasten it for me?"

Dr. Jansen looked amused. "Ah, yes. Of course, my apologies."

She affixed his watch, then the rest of theirs when it became apparent none of them currently had sufficient dexterity to secure the small clasp.

"Good thing I won't feel it if it starts chafing," Noah said. "I don't think I'd be able to get it off on my own."

Dr. Jansen led them out of her office. Instead of taking them out the main entrance, she had them follow her out a back door that opened into the small parking lot behind the building.

"We're going to have to close off the main lobby," she said. "It will be quite the hassle to clean it up safely."

Noah ducked his head. "Sorry about that. Not my brightest decision."

Dr. Jansen gave him a sideways look. "So you did it on purpose."

"Er, I mean it wasn't my proudest moment. I would never do something so stupid intentionally, obviously."

"Of course."

A lime-green van with the campus logo emblazoned across its doors turned into the parking lot and pulled up to the curb in front of them.

"That will be your ride to your new housing," the doctor said. "The driver is aware of your unique situation and is wearing appropriate safety attire."

The window slowly rolled down, revealing a person in a full-body lime green hazmat suit. Their face was partially concealed behind a gas mask that they were wearing underneath the large plastic shield of the suit. The person nodded at them.

"Wow, even their hazmat suits are on-brand," Leah said. "How come you didn't get one of those?"

"There was not one easily accessible in the Health Center, and I did not believe it would be necessary to take the time to retrieve one from the Campus Safety building," Dr. Jansen said. "Believe me, it's a decision I'm actively regretting. I will be monitoring my health in the coming days."

She opened the van's door for them and stepped back. "I recommend each of you give your parents a phone call to inform them of what is happening. I'm sure they will be quite interested in this morning's events."

They all nodded obediently and filed into the van. The driver rolled the windows down as soon as they entered the vehicle. They all waved at Dr. Jansen as the van pulled away, and she cracked a small smile and waved back.

Noah half expected their driver to remain silent for the duration of the ride, but as they turned out of the parking lot he spoke up. "So, you guys have some sort of crazy virus or something? Never thought I'd have to wear a full-on hazmat suit for this job."

Noah was surprised at how bluntly their driver was speaking about the whole situation, but Leah easily picked up the conversation.

"Yeah, I guess. What's the suit like? Does it make you feel super safe?" she laughed.

The driver shrugged. "I suppose so. Though the thing cuts off most of my peripheral vision, and it's way too hot. I put on one too many layers this morning. How was I supposed to know I'd be told to put on a freaking hazmat suit?"

Leah glanced at her friends and said, "Feel free to blast the AC if you want. We won't be bothered."

"You sure? Don't mind if I do, then." He pushed a few buttons on the dashboard and a moment later the sound of rushing air filled the van.

The air blew for a minute before the guy waved his gloved hand in front of the vent and sighed. "Fat lot of good it'll do me if this suit doesn't let any cool air in. I swear, it's almost as if Oakridge cheaped out on their hazmat suits. There's got to be versions of these things with cooling systems built in, right?"

"They probably hoped nobody would ever actually have to use them," Leah said.

"You'd think so, but apparently the whole medical staff

had to wear these to work every day for a few months while they were still figuring out what was up with the *Wager*. Took 'em a while to decide that it wasn't contagious. Sure am glad I wasn't working here back then. In those days I was still delivering pizzas for that restaurant up the road. Now that was a fine job... ah, here we are."

He pulled to the side of the road and hit a button that opened both the van's doors. They all clambered out and peered at their new living quarters. It was a row of contemporary townhouse-style homes painted in shades of red and orange. Each housing unit had a small balcony on the second floor.

"These look really nice!" Brian enthused. "Do they really just sit empty all the time now that you're not isolating students who come down with the *Wager*?"

The driver waved his hand back and forth, leaning out the window to talk to them. "Well, they've always spent most of their time unoccupied. The incident rate for the *Wager* is something like one in ten thousand, so even in the early days I doubt all four units were ever filled. Anyways, Oakridge still gives students the option of moving in here if they happen to get the *Wager*. Most of them choose to spend the time with their family, but there are exceptions. There's actually a kid staying there right now, poor thing. Not sure what their name is, but I'm sure you'll see them on the lawn out back at some point."

He withdrew back into the van and grabbed something from the console. "In any case, here are your keys. One unit for the guys and one for the ladies."

He handed May and Leah the keys tagged with a 2, while Brian and Noah received the keys for unit 3.

"Alright then! Everything should be fully stocked, but call the number on the kitchen table if you need anything. There's a whole staff whose only job is basically to help you guys, so don't hesitate to actually make use of their service. Any questions?"

"Will we get our backpacks? My laptop is in there." Brian

looked anxiously at their driver.

He tilted his bright green head. "I'll make sure they know you want it. They should have it to you by this afternoon."

"Awesome, thanks."

"Excellent. The name's Dan, it's been a pleasure. I'll see you around." He waved a gloved arm and pulled away.

15

NEW LODGINGS

"Is this place sweet or what?" Brian asked, all but tugging his friend to the front door.

"It's definitely an upgrade from our dorm room," Noah agreed, thinking about Paul and worrying for a moment that he'd get lonely, but then realizing there was a good chance that the kid once again failed to realize that Brian and Noah had temporarily moved out.

Noah glanced over at the girls unlocking their own door and they all waved at each other before entering their respective units.

Inside, they were met with a surprisingly spacious sitting area immediately to the left of the entrance, and a staircase disappearing up to the second floor on their right. At the rear of the sitting area, against the far wall, was a kitchenette with a window overlooking a pleasant view of a meadow ringed by dense woods. The color palette was mostly shades of gray with a few red and orange accents. Noah observed there was a complete lack of carpeting, and that even the cushioned seats in the sitting room had a plasticky appearance.

Noticing a horizontal coat rack attached to the wall behind the door, they hung both their keys on one of the hooks. Noah found himself irrationally wishing he had a jacket or something to hang up.

"I want to see our rooms," Brian said, immediately setting up the stairs.

"Alright, me too." Noah followed him to the second floor,

which had a short hallway with three doors. Brian was already going down the line, opening each one and peering inside eagerly.

"Bedroom, closet, and... bedroom. Nice, both bedrooms have a balcony. The bathroom must be downstairs."

Noah looked inside the second bedroom and saw it was furnished with a twin captain's bed and a small desk with a piece of beige paper folded to stand upon it like a tent. His name was printed on it so as to be clearly visible from the door. The closet was open to reveal shelves stocked with a couple sets of clothes. The back wall was almost entirely made of glass, with a door leading out to a view over the meadow behind the housing unit.

"Hey, I think this room is supposed to be mine," Noah called to Brian, glancing at the namecard. There was no response, so he took that as agreement and walked over to the closet to investigate its contents. *No way these are actually my own clothes that they took from my dorm.*

To his vague relief, it turned out to just be a few brand-new outfits from the local clothing store. All the tags were still attached. They weren't his exact size, but they were close enough that Noah suspected whoever had picked them out had been informed of his approximate weight and height.

"Wow, free clothes. Looks like my college tuition is finally starting to pay for itself," Noah said to himself. He closed the closet and wandered out to the balcony.

Brilliant midday sunlight streamed down, putting a smile on his face. He looked out over the meadow and saw it was divided into four sections by a couple rows of bushes extending a short ways from the building. Out in the open meadow beyond the bushes, a picnic table was positioned near the center of the lawn. Surrounding most of the meadow was a wire fence, presumably installed as a safety barrier to prevent students from entering the wide river that curved gracefully behind the meadow. Its dark, slow-moving water reflected the trees of the woods just beyond its banks.

Noah tilted his face towards the sun and closed his eyes

peacefully, only to slowly frown He silently rebuked himself for expecting to feel any warmth, and with an unhappy sigh, he returned inside. As nice as the view was, he didn't feel like standing around to appreciate it at the moment.

He walked back out into the hallway and poked his head into the other bedroom to see Brian lying spread-eagled atop his bed. His eyes were open, and he turned to look at Noah when he noticed him hovering by the door.

"So, what do you think of this place?" Noah asked his friend.

Brian shrugged. "It's awesome. Did you see the clothes in the closet?"

Noah nodded with a faint smile. "Yeah. It's kinda weird, somehow."

"Oh, so it's not just me, then. It feels awfully strange for some rando to have picked out the clothes I'll be wearing. I mean, don't get me wrong, I appreciate that I won't have to wear this same outfit for who knows how many days straight, but they could have at least let us get some stuff from our dorms."

Noah walked over to sit down at the desk. It had Brian's name on a card upon it, printed just the same way as the one in his own room. "I don't think you realize the harm that even one quick trip could do."

Brian shrugged again, looking tired. "Sorry if I'm not showing a high enough level of concern for your taste." He turned his head to look up at the ceiling. "I know you're not going to want to hear this, but it seems like everyone's sort of overreacting. I mean, yeah, nothing about what's happening makes sense, but it's not *bad*, per se. It's not as if we're in pain or anything. So when I see everyone rushing around to make stuff like this happen- stuff like getting us our own private townhouse- I can't help but feel like we're taking advantage of our position, somehow." He looked back at Noah. "You know?"

Noah blinked. "The reason all this is happening isn't because of the symptoms we've shown so far, necessarily. I think it's more because it's something new. Its potential is totally uncharted in every way. If anything, I believe people are underreacting. They should be trying their best to gather up everyone we've come into contact with this morning and treat them all as carefully as they're treating us.

"I understand where you're coming from, but I don't think you should be worrying for that reason. I'm sure everyone will be quite pleased if all this blows over, not upset we exploited them somehow."

Brian sat up with a pensive look. "That makes sense, I guess. You're probably right."

"Oh, I know I am," Noah grinned. "C'mon, let's see what they have for us downstairs."

16

THE ONE WITH THE *WAGER*

They ended up walking around opening all the drawers and cupboards and going through them like they were raiding the place. To their disappointment, most of the storage spaces were empty. The shelves in the living room were bare of any books or other items, and the kitchen cupboards had only a few sets of utensils and dinnerware.

The one exception was the refrigerator, which was stocked with some pre-made meals.

Peering inside the fridge, Noah was suddenly reminded of the milk he had bought earlier that was now abandoned in his dorm. He sadly realized he might not get back to his own room in time to drink it before it spoiled and made a mental note to text Paul that he could have the milk if he wanted it.

"What do you want for breakfast?" Noah asked.

"Breakfast? It'd be lunch by now, wouldn't it?"

"I guess so." Noah glanced at the band on his wrist, forgetting for a moment that it wasn't a regular watch. Instead of the time, it displayed two values. His heart rate per minute was currently vacillating between 12 and 13 and his SpO2 was 52, although that number was blinking and had the message *Please remain in a resting position for accurate results* scrolling by underneath the number. He had no reference for how abnormal those values were or what they were supposed to be. He looked over at Brian and wondered what his stats were at, but decided against mentioning it. His friend seemed to be in a better mood, in large part due to something he had just found in the fridge.

"No way! They got us mac-and-cheese!" Brian crowed, pulling out a cardboard bowl with a plastic sheet sealing the contents. He brought it over to the microwave and looked serenely out the large window as he waited for it to cook, perking up as he noticed something.

"Hey, there's someone out in the meadow," Brian said. "It's not either of the girls."

Noah stepped up beside him and squinted outside. A figure was walking away from the townhouses towards the lone picnic table out in the middle of the field. They had cropped blonde hair and were wearing a loose long-sleeved blue shirt with white pants.

"I bet that's the student with the *Wager*," Noah said, staring at them and wishing they would turn around so he could see their face. After a moment he realized he could just go outside and say hi instead of staring out the window like a creep.

"Take your food outside, I want to go meet them," Noah told Brian. He went to the back door and slid it open.

"Okay, just let me grab a fork," Brian said agreeably. He joined Noah a moment later and they walked out into the field together.

They stopped a safe distance from the figure sitting at the table. Noah could tell it was a girl now that they were closer. She seemed to be looking out into the woods.

"Hi," Noah said.

She turned quickly to stare at them in surprise. "Oh, hi there. Both of you have the *Wager* too?"

"Uh, not exactly," Brian said after a second.

The girl had light gray eyes, making her curious glance at them seem intense. "Well, what are you doing here, then?"

"We're sick with something else," Noah said. "The school is having us stay here until they know how dangerous it is."

She tilted her head. "They don't know?"

"They only know enough to be worried."

The girl seemed intrigued, and she gestured at the bench

across from her with a small smile. "Want to take a seat? Or are you too scared of the *Wager* to come any closer?"

Her tone was provocative enough to make Noah want to step forward, but he just shook his head. "I don't want to get you sick. The whole point of us staying out here is to stay isolated."

She just laughed. "Oh, I'm not worried about whatever you have. I know I'm not going to survive my *Wager*."

Noah didn't budge. "You don't know that. There's no way to tell ahead of time."

She shrugged. "Well, I can. I can feel my end coming like a beast hunting me down, and it's been patiently waiting for its time to strike. I will die tonight."

Her proclamation was grim, but the tone was one of acceptance.

Eventually Brian looked at Noah, who sighed and walked over to the table. "If you insist. Just don't say we didn't warn you. I'm Noah, by the way."

"Brian," his friend said with a nod.

"My name's Sophie," the girl said, sniffing and quickly rubbing her nose. "So, what's up with you two?"

"We're dying," Brian said dramatically as he plopped his lunch onto the table, and Noah elbowed him.

"Medically, we might be in dire straits," he allowed. "But for one reason or another, we feel fine."

"Dire straits?"

"Er, low heart rate and blood oxygen, numbness."

"That doesn't sound that bad."

"That's what I'm saying!" Brian said, pointing at her and looking at Noah. "See, I'm not just a careless idiot trying to get everyone sick!"

Noah glanced down at his wristband. "Right now, my bpm is... ten. I'm no expert, but that seems low, right?"

Her jaw fell open. "Ten? You should be in a hospital! How are you alive right now?" She turned to Brian. "You absolutely are a careless idiot. Ten bpm is insane."

"Oh, is it?" Brian said, looking contemplatively at his own

watch.

Noah noticed movement up by the townhouses and looked up to see Leah and May exiting their unit and beginning to walk towards them across the grass.

"Here come the girls," he said.

Sophie raised her eyebrows and turned to glance at the pair heading over. "You're not the only ones with these weird symptoms?"

Noah shook his head. "There's four of us. We all got sick just earlier this morning."

"Hey, you two," Leah called as she got closer. "What happened to staying away from people? Have you forgotten why they moved us out here?"

"She said she doesn't mind," Brian said defensively. "She'll die tonight anyways."

"Brian!" His sister snapped, appalled.

"No, it's true," Sophie said.

"Sophie?" May asked suddenly. She walked up to the table and looked at the other girl with wide eyes. "You got the *Wager*?"

"Oh, hey, May. Yeah, I guess I did."

"I didn't even know! Why aren't you with your parents? Don't they live just down the road?"

Sophie ducked her head. "I'm sorry, I should've told you. If it makes you feel any better, I hardly told anyone. I didn't want to have that conversation over and over, and I didn't want everyone to worry about me. And as for my parents..." she trailed off with a hard look in her eyes. "They didn't want me to come home once they found out I had the *Wager*. They only live a few miles from campus, but the morons are convinced it'll spread to them."

May looked shocked. "That's terrible."

She shrugged. "It is what it is. I just wish I were doing more with my final days than sitting around feeling sorry for myself."

She shook her head and forced a smile. "Anyways. That mac-and-cheese smells good."

Brian startled and glanced down at his bowl like he'd forgotten it was there. "Does it?"

Sophie looked at him curiously. "Is your sense of smell affected?"

"Apparently," Brian grumbled, picking up his fork with a troubled look in his eye. "I won't complain so long as I can still taste the food. If I can't appreciate the glory of mac-and-cheese, then I take back everything I said about this stupid sickness being no big deal."

They all looked at him as he tasted the food, Sophie with amusement, the other three with suspense.

Brian chewed and swallowed with effort, a thunderous expression growing across his face. "This is a CATASTROPHE. Where are the doctors? We need to get this fixed right now."

He pushed away his food with a disgusted look and stood up. "I'm going to call Dr. Jansen."

They watched him storm across the field and disappear inside.

"Well, at least he's motivated to help the doctors now," Leah said.

"I'm sure they'll be interested to hear about the new symptoms," Noah added. "Even if it might not get them any closer to a solution. Or even an explanation."

"This is probably the most inconvenient symptom yet," Leah said thoughtfully. "I haven't really been bothered by the other ones, but this will be annoying. I like being able to taste food."

"Well, I can still taste," Sophie said cheerfully. "Are any of you going to claim that mac-and-cheese?"

"Go right ahead," Leah said. "No need to rub it in our faces or anything."

Sophie grinned and tucked in.

17

REASON FOR CONCERN

As Noah watched her mow through the bowl of cheesy pasta, he realized the last thing he had eaten was the sandwich Brian made for their cemetery visit last night. The unusual morning had made him forget all about breakfast, and it was only now that he realized he wasn't even hungry. *Add it to the list of symptoms*, he thought.

He gazed at what was left of the mac-and-cheese and wondered if he should force himself to eat something anyways. Just because he didn't feel hungry didn't mean his body didn't need food. If anything, it would be a waste not to make use of the meals someone had prepared for them. It wasn't every day he got food free of charge.

Before he could make up his mind to go inside and get something to eat, Brian reemerged from the house and trudged over to their table.

"What'd the doctor say?" Leah asked.

"She thanked me for the info, but said that we'll just have to wait for the test results before we can really start hoping for any updates. I asked when they'll finish making an antidote and she got really evasive." Brian slumped into the seat. "I'm stuck like this forever," he moaned disconsolately.

"Hey, we'll get to the other side. Things have a way of working out," Noah said optimistically.

"The only thing I see coming on the other side of this mess is a miserable existence. A life without joy. Without meaning." He looked on the verge of tears.

Noah shook his head. "Leah with her soup and you with your pasta. You're both way too attached to random food for your own good."

Noah heard a dull thump and looked up in concern to see Leah with her forehead against the table.

Sophie stopped eating for a second to glance sideways curiously. "Did she just die?"

Leah pulled herself upright and shot Sophie a dirty look. "No, you jerk, but I might as well have. What will I do without soup? It's the only thing that keeps me going some days."

Noah put his head in his hands. *I swear, the people I call my friends. This is ridiculous.* "You could still eat it if you wanted to."

"It's not the same," Leah said mournfully. She stood up. "I'm going inside. I need time to recover from this."

"It was nice to meet you," Sophie said. She turned to May. "And I'm glad I got to see you again before it was too late. I'd say we should catch up sometime, but..."

May shook her head. "Don't say that. I'm right here, let's talk."

"We can go in," Noah said quickly, nudging Brian. His friend nodded.

"Yeah, I have homework I need to get done."

Everyone turned to look at him. Leah stopped walking away like the weight of the world lay upon her shoulders and straightened to stare back at her brother. He glanced around uncomfortably. "What?"

Leah shook her head. "We have every excuse to take a break from schoolwork right now. Nobody expects you to be all studious while you're valiantly fighting for your life against a terrible, unexplained illness."

Brian scratched his neck. "I don't want to fall behind. What else am I going to do here, anyway?"

"Oh, I don't know. There's a television in the sitting room, go watch a movie or something. Or call our dear parents to tell them that we've gotten an illness previously unknown to man..."

That reminded Noah that he should call his own dad before he forgot. He left the siblings to their bickering and headed inside. As he passed through the kitchen he glanced in the direction of the fridge, but he just couldn't summon the energy to bother eating anything and he ended up going straight upstairs to his room.

He flopped onto his bed and buried his face in the pillow. It had a slightly plastic feel that made him wonder if he might accidentally suffocate himself if he fell asleep, but he allowed himself to relax. *I probably don't even need to breathe by this point anyway. My whole body is shutting down.*

After a minute he began to consider how stupid it would be to die from making that kind of assumption, and he grudgingly rolled over.

Might as well get this out of the way, he thought, pulling out his phone. He dialed his dad and tried to think of the best way to phrase his situation as he waited for him to pick up.

"Hey, Noah. What's up?"

Noah closed his eyes. "Hi dad. There's something I need to tell you."

"Oh no. Who is it?"

Noah looked down at his phone. "What?"

His dad laughed. "Nothing. What's going on?"

"So, I went to the campus health center earlier today."

There was silence on the phone.

"I talked to a doctor- my friends were there too, we were all feeling a bit off- and the doctor thinks we all have some odd kind of rare illness. She ended up putting us in this nice little housing unit on the edge of campus where we'll stay until she knows if it's safe for us to be around people."

Noah ran his words over in his head and nodded to himself. That didn't sound too terrible.

His dad didn't say anything for a few seconds. Then he asked, "Are you doing okay? Are you in pain?"

"We're doing great; we're not in any pain, and they've given us everything we need to be comfortable here."

An exhale came through the phone. "What exactly made

you decide to go to the doctor this morning?"

"We, ah, noticed we were breathing out something like dust, which is the main thing that tipped us off. We were also feeling a little numbness."

"Dust? Numbness? What's the dust from? Where are you feeling numb?"

"We... aren't sure," he lied. "And the numbness is everywhere, I guess. I've had no sensory input besides sight and hearing for the past couple hours."

"Hmm. Well, don't go jinxing yourself by phrasing it that way."

Noah gazed out the balcony window and debated whether to share the rest of the symptoms. They were all a step up in terms of reason for concern and they sounded scarier than they felt. Eventually he decided to just spit it out, if only for the sake of honesty.

"There's something else. Just... a couple other symptoms."

His tone must've made his dad nervous, because he heard a short inhale. "Yeah?"

"Again, we all feel fine, but our heart rate has dropped a bit. Well, a lot. And apparently there's not enough oxygen in our blood or something."

"How low?"

Noah looked down at his wristband. "It's at 8 right now."

As he spoke he realized it had decreased just over the past couple minutes, and he felt a spike of worry. Pushing it aside, he added, "And my pulse ox level is 49, if that means anything to you."

"You need to be at a medical facility. Right now." The voice on the phone was suddenly stone cold. "Stop talking to me and call your doctor immediately. I'm getting in the car now. I'll see you in a few hours."

"Dad, wait, it's a ten-hour drive! Honestly, I'm okay, you don't need to-"

The phone beeped.

Noah put it down with a sigh.

18

SMALL EMERGENCIES

Noah looked back at the display on his watch and regarded the numbers. He still felt normal, but the heart rate was starting to get awfully low, and he was a little nervous at what would happen if it hit zero. He put two fingers on his wrist for a few long moments and held himself motionless as time stretched on without a pulse. Just as he was about to panic, he smacked himself as he remembered he wouldn't be able to feel anything regardless of whether his pulse was there or not. He flipped his wrist over and saw the bpm value was still at 8.

Feeling quite silly, Noah decided to go downstairs to eat something. He typically never missed a meal, so it was strange that he still wasn't especially hungry. He would have already called Dr. Jansen about it if Brian hadn't beaten him to the punch.

He found Brian slumped in what would probably have been an uncomfortable position in one of the chairs in the sitting room, eyes closed. As Noah walked past him into the kitchen, it occurred to him that he should probably check if his friend was okay.

"You doing good?" he called. He opened the fridge and panned his gaze over the neatly packaged bowls and plates. In normal circumstances, this would have been a dream come true. Free food, pre-made for his convenience. Maybe someone like Brian who liked to cook would wish for more options to make something himself, but Noah himself had never seen the allure of the culinary arts.

Instead of feeling pleased, though, he felt only reluctance as he grabbed a dish with some kind of ground meat and vegetables and carried it over to the microwave. He set his food to cook for a minute, noticing that May and Sophie were still outside at the table. He suddenly became aware that Brian had never responded to him.

"Brian?" Stepping quickly into the sitting room, he grabbed his friend's shoulder and shook it roughly. Brian's head rolled to the side lifelessly.

"Oh, no." Noah looked around as if he would see someone or something to help laying around nearby. He picked up Brian's limp arm and turned it so he could read his heart rate. The number didn't read 0, but it was uncomfortably close, at 5. Noah couldn't see Brian's chest moving. He tried to feel if he was breathing, putting his hand in front of his slightly agape mouth for a second. He let his hand fall down in frustration as he immediately recognized he wouldn't be able to feel any breath.

Panicking and feeling useless, he ran into the kitchen and picked up the card on the table with Dr. Jansen's phone number which she had given them earlier. He pulled his phone from his pocket and began to dial.

As he was entering the numbers, his food finished cooking and the microwave beeped loudly.

Noah ignored the sound and moved his finger over the dial button, only to pause as he heard a sigh from the other room. He turned to see Brian shifting in the chair, pushing himself upright and yawning.

"Brian!" he yelled, dropping the phone in surprise. "Are you alright?"

"Shh," his friend said, peering over at him. "I'm just resting."

"At this hour? It's the middle of the day," Noah said, feeling relieved. He left his phone on the table and crossed the room to retrieve his food.

"We've had a busy day," Brian grumbled. "Can't I have a

minute of sleep without you freaking out about something?"

"It can't hurt to be cautious," Noah said. "It looked like you had, well, died."

"Don't be dramatic," Brian sighed. "We're still around as of yet."

Noah set his bowl on the table beside his phone and took a seat. He looked at the mound of food, feeling not a trace of an appetite, and told himself it was for his own good.

He picked up his fork and took a bite. He chewed without feeling or tasting anything at all, and then forced himself to swallow.

"I'm beginning to see why you were so upset when you tasted that mac-and-cheese," Noah said.

"Don't remind me," Brian sniffed.

Noah glared down at the bowl like it had personally wronged him and tried another bite. Before he could swallow, a wave of revulsion passed through him and he spat it out involuntarily, gagging.

Noah pushed the bowl away. "Dr. Jansen would be happy; I think I finally feel as sick as I'm supposed to be. That was awful."

"That's what I said, but you only mocked me," Brian said, placing a hand in mock grief over his heart. He walked into the room and dropped into a seat at the table.

"If the sickness doesn't kill me directly, I might starve to death," Noah muttered. "I won't bring myself to eat anything else like this. I don't think I could even if I wanted to." He looked outside at the two girls sitting together at the table. "I wonder if Sophie feels like eating another unwanted meal."

"Just throw it out, don't be weird," Brian said. "It's ground beef and green beans; who would want to eat that, anyway?"

Noah looked at him. "Just because it's not mac-and-cheese doesn't make the food worthless."

"Hey, I like other foods. I have quite the open mind when it comes to culinary options."

"Says the guy who literally only eats pasta and one specific kind of sandwich."

Brian drew himself up indignantly and opened his mouth to respond, only to stumble and grab the edge of the table with a dazed look. "Woah. What was that?"

"What was what?" Noah asked worriedly.

Suddenly, for a split second, he felt all of his limbs go slack. He regained control of himself before he toppled completely off the chair, but he was left with an odd feeling. He sat there with a distracted look in his eyes, trying to figure out what exactly was different.

"Something's wrong," Brian said. He looked at Noah, brows furrowed, then shifted his gaze outside. Sophie was helping May sit up out at the table. She must've been leaning a little too far back, because she had fallen backwards to the ground.

A few seconds later Leah ran out from her own housing unit. She raced across the field towards May and Sophie, and they shared a few words between them before looking anxiously over their shoulders at Brian and Noah's unit.

"Come on," Noah said, leaving his nearly untouched food on the table to hurry outside towards the girls with Brian in tow. They drew up beside the others and slid breathlessly onto the bench opposite them.

"Did you all just-"

"Yeah," Noah nodded at Leah. "What do you think that was? And why did it happen to us all at the same time?"

"I don't know why it was so synchronized, but I think I know what it was," Leah said darkly. "Look at your watch."

Noah glanced down.

The screen displayed two flashing zeros.

19

THEY WERE JUST TRYING TO HELP

"**B**ut I feel fine," Brian said, glancing up from his watch.

"Yeah, that's kind of the motto of the day," Leah snapped. "Obviously, how you feel is not an accurate indicator of your current state of health."

"So what, are we all seconds from death?"

"I didn't say that. We've survived thus far, right? What's one more unexplainable condition?"

Noah looked around. "Somehow, missing a pulse all of a sudden seems a lot more strange than everything else combined. There's a big difference between having a low heart rate, even a weirdly low one, and suddenly lacking one altogether."

"I would have thought it would feel different," Brian said. "I mean, in a bad way. Seeing how a person kind of needs a functioning heart to survive. What's it doing in there anyways, just sitting like a useless lump? I don't tolerate lazy vital organs." He knocked his chest sternly like he could start his heart back up through sheer discipline.

"I do feel a little different, though," May said.

Noah glanced at her and nodded in agreement. "It's obvious something's missing. You expect a pulse, and when it's not there, you kind of sense the inverse of it, like a ghost of a pulse."

They all sat quietly, trying to feel what he described. Sophie looked around at them awkwardly and scratched her neck.

"So, if your hearts have all really stopped, how are you all still alive? Or am I missing something?"

Leah shrugged. "Wish I knew."

All of a sudden there was a commotion from the direction of the housing units. They looked over to see a small army of campus health workers stream around the side of the building and run at their various top speeds towards them. They all wore lab coats and respiratory masks, both of which were lime green. A couple of them carried emergency rescue stretchers.

"Lay on the ground!" one of them barked as they approached.

"Are we being arrested?" Brian asked playfully.

"I thought there were only four of them," Noah heard one of the health workers mutter.

"Which of you has the *Wager*? Please step aside," the initial guy said impatiently. Sophie backed away with her hands in the air and a bemused glance at the four friends.

"Please lay on the ground," he repeated, stepping closer. "You don't have much time."

"Much time for what? I think you're more worried than you need to be, here," Leah said, waving her hands placatingly, even as she lowered herself onto the grass beside the picnic table. Noah and Brian shrugged at each other and did the same. May was already lying on the ground, her head tilted to the side to stare at the health workers with an entertained smile.

"Your heart rate has just hit zero," the first guy said gravely as a couple of the other green-suited workers knelt beside them and started dutifully performing chest compressions. Two others went between them, confirming they had no pulse. "We need you to be in a prone position, or else you'll end up injuring yourselves when you lose consciousness."

The four of them stared at him from the ground for a couple seconds.

"Is that going to happen soon, or..." Brian said eventually.

"Er, yes," he said, looking unsure. "Very soon."

"Did nobody actually tell these people what our situation is?" Noah asked his friends, his voice jumping each time the guy pressed his chest. "He seems genuinely worried for our lives. We're not actually in any danger, right?"

The man currently performing CPR on Noah was unbothered by his words, his eyes fixed intently straight ahead as he pressed in a steady beat. Noah didn't feel anything, of course, and he lay there wondering when someone would realize that something was amiss. This guy clearly didn't mind that he was doing chest compressions on a perfectly conscious and apparently unconcerned student.

"Look, how about we just all make a field trip to Dr. Jansen's office? Maybe you'll be more willing to listen to her when she says that all this is unnecessary," Leah said, pushing away the worker trying their best to restart her heart. She stood up, ignoring their protests, and glared at her friends. "Get up, guys. This is a waste of time and you all know it." She rounded on the health workers. "Take us to the health center. Use the stretchers if you want, I don't care."

"Miss, please lay down-"

"Put the stretcher down and I'll get on that. Then you can take us to the doctor."

The worker hesitated, unsure how to respond. He seemed baffled as to how Leah was still upright and conversing with him and was perhaps wondering if he had somehow found the wrong group of students. Eventually he gestured for the workers to cease their resuscitation efforts and for the rescue stretchers to be laid out beside each of the prone students.

Noah's vision lurched as two workers lifted his body onto the metal frame and strapped him down. He turned his head to watch Leah brush aside the people trying to help her, laying on the stretcher herself and folding her arms calmly behind her head with a smirk.

In short order they were being carried across the field.

"Bye, guys!" Sophie called cheerfully, settling back into her seat at the table to watch them leave.

Noah lifted his head off the stretcher and waved. "See you."

She shook her head slightly, and then they were around the corner and she was out of view.

Noah frowned at her response. She still ostensibly had a fifty percent chance of survival, yet she had already given up all hope of living past the day. Sighing unhappily, he allowed himself to relax back onto the stretcher and close his eyes. With his only sensory input being the muffled shuffling of feet all around them, he suddenly felt as though he were floating weightlessly in an empty void. It was jarring to know with certainty that he was being moved and jostled through space, yet be informed otherwise by all sense of touch. The impression of being adrift in space grew stronger as his mental image of the environment around him faded. Eventually he decided he didn't care much for the sensation and he opened his eyes. His surroundings fell reassuringly back into place.

By now they had been taken to the front of the building. A few campus vans were parked along the curb with emergency lights strobing, painting the entire area in flashes of red. As they approached, two of the workers stepped forward to open the rear doors so that the stretchers could be carried within. Noah was lifted into the vehicle and set on a long bench along the wall of the van. May was brought in right after him and set on the opposite bench. She seemed fascinated by the entire situation. When they made eye contact she gave him a grin.

There were four workers in the back of the van with them, sitting on each side of their stretchers.

"I don't suppose I can sit up now that we're in here," Noah said.

The workers exchanged glances. "It's best you don't," the one sitting by his feet answered gruffly. "It's starting to look like this was all a false alarm, but I'd rather be safe than sorry under these circumstances."

"So what, did you all get alerted by our wristbands, or did you get a call from Dr. Jansen?"

The worker gave him an amused look and tapped a small radio clipped to her shirt pocket. "I don't know about any wristbands. We were alerted by campus safety of the emergency."

So Dr. Jansen must have called the safety people, who called these guys. I guess it's no wonder some information got lost in transit.

"I wouldn't say that it was a false alarm," Noah said. "It's just not much of an emergency. From my perspective, anyway."

"You had no pulse," one of the workers by May's stretcher said coldly. "I tested your heart rate myself. Nothing else makes sense, but the one thing I'm sure of is that you're absolutely right that it was no false alarm. I'm just praying we get you to the health center before your body starts reacting like it's supposed to without a pulse. You're living on borrowed time right now."

"Well, I must have gotten quite the fat loan."

The worker chuckled shortly. "So it seems you have."

20

YOU COULD PROBABLY HAVE
PICKED A BETTER TIME

Now that they weren't being carried around by hand, Noah felt comfortable enough shutting his eyes, and he allowed himself a few minutes of rest.

He usually wasn't able to fall asleep so quickly, but he must've drifted off almost immediately because the next thing he knew he was being jolted awake by someone shouting seemingly straight into his ear.

"Hey, stop that," he said, opening his eyes.

The worker that had been shouting went silent with a yelp and stepped back quickly.

They had arrived at the health center; he could see the building through the open doors of the vehicle, which they were still inside. For some reason there were two square pads on his chest. All four health workers were crowded around his stretcher, staring down at him in alarm.

"What? What is it?"

"You were completely unresponsive," one of them said. "No breath, no pulse, no reaction to shaking or touch."

"Oh," Noah said. "You said you already knew my heart rate was nonexistent. I was just resting."

"It didn't look like resting. It looked like death." The health worker shook his head. "We were waiting for you to lose consciousness, and then you did just that. What did you expect us to think?"

Noah looked at May. To his surprise, she looked shaken as well. "They're right, Noah," she said. "They used a defibrillator on you and everything."

"Oh, is that what these are?" He picked at the two square white pads on his chest. "I didn't feel it."

"Of course not," she grumbled.

"Everyone can't just freak out every time one of us wants to take a nap," Noah said.

The worker narrowed her eyes. "What if one of the times, it isn't just a nap? Nobody would be able to tell."

Noah scratched his neck. "Sure they would, after enough time had passed."

She looked at him like he was crazy. "You're going to have to accept that people will get nervous." She glanced outside and exhaled. "Regardless, we've arrived. I've got half a mind to tell you to walk after your little stunt, but since you're still technically on the verge of death- past the verge, really- I suppose we can bear to carry your stretcher inside."

Noah sat up. "It's okay, I don't mind walking."

"Lay down," she barked.

Noah complied.

They lifted the stretcher and carried it outside. The others were waiting for them by the back entrance.

"You weren't sitting around for long, were you?" Noah asked as he was brought closer to Brian and Leah. Leah was sitting upright with her legs dangling off the edge of the stretcher, and neither of the workers carrying it seemed brave enough to tell her to lay down properly.

"Nah, we just got here," Brian said.

"Oh, good. I kind of fell asleep on the way over," Noah said.

"Seriously? It's like a five minute drive," Leah said. "That's kind of impressive, to be honest."

"I'm glad you think so. My attendants were not so pleased with me. I'm starting to realize that the only way to wake one of us up if we fall asleep is with sound. I mean, they electrocuted me, for crying out loud, and I slept right through it."

"Well, that makes sense," Leah said with a shrug. "I don't think it'll be much of an issue anyway. I typically don't need to have somebody shake me awake in the morning. I just use an alarm, like a normal person. That will still work."

Brian nodded. "And if it doesn't work, I'll just scream at the top of my lungs until you get up, no worries, man."

Noah shot him a look. "Glad to know I can count on you."

"Of course," Brian said, looking pleased.

As they talked the workers carried them into the building. They must have been informed that the front entrance was closed, because they didn't even try to use it and had them brought straight in the back door.

A couple of wheeled gurneys were lined up against the wall immediately inside, and the workers quickly transferred them onto the much more easily transportable beds. Leah simply stepped off her stretcher and hopped onto the gurney, while the others were carefully lifted from one frame to the other. From there it was a short trip down the hall to Dr. Jansen's office.

They stopped outside her office, as there was just no feasible way to fit all of their gurneys inside, and one of the workers stepped inside to let her know they had arrived.

"Well, why don't they come in here themselves?" Her voice carried easily from the office, and a moment later she stepped out into the hall. She took one look at them all on the gurneys and her eyebrows shot up.

"Why are they being transported like this?" She asked the closest worker.

He looked confused at the question. "It's standard procedure, Doctor. We responded to a call that their hearts had stopped."

"And how long has it been since that call?"

He rubbed the side of his head. "Uh, maybe twenty minutes."

"Have any of them fallen unconscious at all in that time?"

The workers beside Noah pointed at him immediately.

"Yes, he did."

Noah threw his arms up in exasperation. "Oh, come on! It was just a nap!"

Brian glanced at him. "You could probably have picked a better time."

Noah rolled his eyes. "I didn't expect to fall asleep in a single minute. I only meant to rest my eyes."

"Put the gurneys away," Dr. Jansen said, pinching the bridge of her nose. "You all have satisfied your job; feel free to go on your way. Well done for getting them here, I suppose." She turned her gaze on the four students. "Get off those things. We need to talk."

She spun on her heel and stepped back into her office.

Noah shrugged apologetically at his attendants and hopped off the gurney. "Thank you for trying to help us," he said.

The guy looked bewildered. "Of course."

Noah followed his friends into the doctor's office.

21

WE'RE NOT CORPSES

"Somehow I am unsurprised to see you all in seemingly perfect health despite having had no heart rate for the past twenty minutes," Dr. Jansen said.

"Then why'd you make an emergency call?" Leah asked pointedly. "You could have just called us yourself to ask how we were doing."

"I could have," the doctor acknowledged. "But that would only have been fine if you were indeed stable. I made the call on the off chance that you were in as much danger as your pulses indicated. If that had been the case, the time it took to call you personally would have likely doomed you."

"Oh. Thanks, I guess."

"You are welcome. Now that you are here, I would like to discuss today's developments."

"Developments? You mean test results from the blood samples?" Noah said hopefully.

"No. I am referring to the situation here on campus concerning the spread of your sickness."

Noah felt a sinking sensation

"It's been spreading?" May asked.

"Indeed. There have been about a dozen reports of symptoms in the past three hours. All but two of which were from students currently residing in your dorm halls. We must assume this is only a fraction of infected students, because despite our best efforts, many of them do not feel that it is necessary to contact the health center when they suddenly begin breathing dust and losing all sense of touch." She turned to Brian and Noah. "I took it upon myself to call your roommate Paul when I became aware that the illness was spreading."

Noah leaned forward. "Is he okay?"

"He has been infected."

Noah put his head in his hands. "Oh, man." A thought occurred to him and he looked up. "How about Robert?"

"Who the heck is Robert?" Leah asked.

"Robert is one of the receptionists who work in this building," Dr. Jansen said. "He is the one who helped you this morning. To answer your question, Noah, he is one of the two known individuals not residing in your dorms who has fallen ill."

Noah nodded. He hadn't expected any other answer.

"What are you doing with all these sick students?" Leah asked.

"A school-wide announcement has been released informing everyone to isolate themselves if they are aware they have been exposed to the dust, or if they are displaying the known symptoms of the illness. I am currently in the process of convincing the college board that they need to lock down the campus until we have more information about what is happening."

"Woah," Brian said. "That's going to affect a lot of people."

Dr. Jansen gave him a hard look. "You might have done well to consider that before you waltzed through your dorm this morning."

He winced.

Noah just sat there in shock. It felt like everything was slipping out of control way too quickly. If they had only been a little more careful, they could have single-handedly prevented the entire mess that was beginning to unfold.

"How big is this going to get?" he asked quietly.

They all looked at Dr. Jansen.

"It depends on how soon the campus is shut down and how effectively people obey the announcement. Based on the rate of infection so far, and my previous experience with college students... this will get worse before it gets better."

She suddenly clasped her hands and straightened. "Anyways. I would like to administer another round of physical testing."

"That's fine," Leah said. "Same stuff as before?"

"More or less."

"Uh, alright."

"I'll make it quick," she assured them, grabbing a pen light off her desk and flipping off the lights. She left the open window uncovered, which allowed plenty of light into the office.

They were sitting in the same places as they had that morning, with Noah closest to her desk, so the doctor started with him. She did exactly as Noah expected and shone the light into his eyes one at a time.

"Interesting," she said, leaning back. "Your pupils were reactive. The response was minimal and delayed, but there was noticeable miosis."

That's kind of weird, Noah thought as she moved to the others and found the same result. *Why would that be working when hardly anything else is?*

Dr. Jansen seemed to be wondering the same thing. "I can't say I expected these results, but perhaps I should have. After all, your sight has been one of your few bodily functions to remain functional throughout this ordeal. The illness does not seem to affect vision thus far."

She set the light down, turning it off and switching the office's overhead light back on. She then picked up something else from inside her desk, but kept it hidden in her closed fist. She turned to them and for the first time seemed to hesitate.

"Now, you are under no obligation to submit yourselves to this test," she said in a tone that did not fill Noah with eagerness for whatever she had in mind. "This would not be considered part of a standard examination."

Leah narrowed her eyes. "What is it?"

Dr. Jansen held up a single-bladed razor. The blade was

sealed in a slip of airtight plastic. "If you so choose, I will make a small incision on your arm and lower leg."

Noah's eyes bugged out. "Why would you want to do that?"

"I am curious how your body has been regulating its blood pressure. In a normal scenario, the blood in a corpse will settle due to the lack of circulation. Yet you are displaying no signs of swelling in your lower limbs."

"Aren't there other ways to take someone's blood pressure?" Brian asked. "You don't typically see doctors pulling knives on their patients. Also, we're not corpses."

"I will gain more information with this method. Your unique symptoms would mean you feel no pain, though I understand if you wish to skip this test. And I apologize for the comparison; you are correct. I was merely pointing out the established effect that a lack of circulation has on a body."

"I'll do it," May said, surprising everyone. She pulled up her sleeve and pointed to her upper arm. "Here?"

"Er, that works," Dr. Jansen said after a moment. "Alright."

"May, you don't have to," Leah said quickly.

"It's okay. If this is helpful to the doctor, then I can put up with a little cut," she said with a smile. "It would hardly be the worst of our worries, right?"

Noah remained silent, feeling uncomfortable. This seemed like a massive departure from standard operating practice. Also, he couldn't exactly pin down the difference, but Dr. Jansen seemed to be acting a little differently than when they had met with her earlier. He was trying to figure out if the two were related when something suddenly occurred to him.

"Hey," he said.

Everyone looked at him.

"Who's that other person who got sick? The second one who's not from our dorms."

Dr. Jansen looked at him for a few seconds before taking off her respiration mask, letting a dark cloud spill out.

"That would be me."

22

INCISIONS

Noah maintained a neutral expression as she looked at him, perhaps seeking a reaction. He thought he saw accusation in her eyes, though that might have just been him feeling guilty.

"Aw, that sucks," Brian said.

Dr. Jansen glanced at him with brows raised. "I would say so, yes."

This is personal for her now, Noah thought. It's not just our lives on the line anymore.

The doctor briskly replaced the mask on her face and pulled on a pair of blue elastic gloves. She then smiled at May and knelt next to her chair, unwrapping a square alcohol wipe and scrubbing it over the girl's arm and lower leg.

May sat with an impassive expression, watching the doctor do her work.

"Are you ready?" The doctor asked. Her tone was kind, yet Noah couldn't help but narrow his eyes. Before she revealed her own infection, it would have been reassuring that she cared deeply enough about helping them to make such an unorthodox move. Now, he couldn't help but wonder if it was desperation for her own health that drove her bold decision. Was she acting in their interests, or her own? What else would she be willing to do?

He wished he could tell if May was sharing similar thoughts, but she displayed no outward signs of doubt in the doctor.

"Yes. I'm ready."

Dr. Jansen nodded, roughly tearing away the wrapping on the razor in a single motion and making a swift slice. The blade dipped smoothly in and out of her shoulder. May flinched slightly, perhaps having expected a shallower cut, but she didn't say anything.

"And now your leg," Dr. Jansen said calmly. May was wearing shorts, so the doctor simply wiped the razor with another antibiotic swipe before making a second incision on the outside of her calf. May didn't blink this time.

The doctor sat back to observe the results with an intent gleam in her eyes.

Despite his misgivings, Noah was interested to see what she was able to glean from this test. He leaned forward out of his seat to get a look at May around Brian and Leah.

Each wound was marked by a bright red line, but there was no other sign of spreading blood.

"You still do not feel any pain, correct?" Dr. Jansen asked.

May cleared her throat. "That's right."

Dr. Jansen leaned over to grab a plastic container from her desk. She unscrewed the lid and dropped the used blade inside, then replaced the container on her desk.

"Interesting," she said. "Neither incision is bleeding. There are no signs of settling blood in the lower limbs, implying a notable blood pressure and circulation, yet here the blood acts as expected without a pulse and does not seep excessively from the wounds. There is no visible difference between the two incisions."

As she spoke she pulled out her tablet and made a few quick scribbled notes.

She glanced at the other students. "Further testing would be beneficial...?"

They all looked at each other unwillingly. Noah shook his head.

"Perhaps not today," the doctor said easily. "Regardless, this has been informative. I appreciate your cooperation with my unusual request, May."

The girl nodded.

Dr. Jansen grabbed a band-aid and fingered at the wrapper. They watched her struggle for nearly half a minute.

Finally May spoke up. "It's fine, I don't need a band-aid."

The doctor frowned. "You should cover the incisions."

"Unless you want to bring another person in here, I don't see any of us being able to open those things," Leah said. "You might as well be wearing oven mitts."

Looking like it physically pained her, Dr. Jansen put down the unopened band-aid. "Unfortunately, I must agree with that assessment."

"You don't have any other tests, do you?" Noah asked nervously.

"No. Those are the only two I had planned for you this afternoon. I would have prepared more, but I believe it would be redundant, as I have been in contact with a downtown medical complex by the name of Insight Labs. They are very interested in meeting you four. I have arranged a trip tomorrow for you to visit their testing center."

"Wait, you did what?" Leah said, standing up angrily. "We never agreed to that. Why are you only mentioning this now?"

"It is my duty to ensure the health and safety of all students attending Oakridge Community College, and this is necessary for me to effectively perform the job with which I have been entrusted."

"No, it's not. Plenty of students have the illness now, whether we like it or not. Find a volunteer, and if there are no willing students, volunteer yourself. You'd be just as good a test subject as any of us. We're not going to go to this medical center. Right, guys?"

Noah and Brian nodded their assent. Leah rounded on May. The quiet girl bobbed her head quickly.

"Yeah! So, sorry, but you're going to have to find someone else," Leah said. She crossed her arms.

"You don't get a say in this," Dr. Jansen said coldly. "As the campus physician, I know better than you what is in the best interest of this community. You have the most developed case of infection and thus are the best choice. You will be picked up tomorrow morning at nine. Ensure you are ready to leave at that time."

The doctor sat down in her chair and reclined back. "There is currently a van waiting for you in the back parking lot. It will return you to your isolated housing units, where you will continue to reside for the foreseeable future. I suggest you don't make them wait."

Leah audibly ground her teeth, glaring hatefully at Dr. Jansen before stomping out of the office. They could hear her footsteps all the way down the hallway until she opened the exit door and slammed it shut behind her.

"Let's go," Brian said quietly, looking upset. He walked out with May close behind, leaving Noah alone with the doctor.

"What are they going to do to us?" he asked.

"Whatever they deem necessary," Dr. Jansen said. "They are known for getting results."

Noah swallowed. "Okay," he said, and left her office.

23

I'LL PASS ON THIS GROUP ACTIVITY

Their driver turned out to be none other than Dan, garbed in his neon green hazmat suit.

"Have you been wearing that all day?" Leah asked, sliding into a seat next to May.

"Nah, I just threw it on again when they sent me to pick you up," he said. "Man, I can't imagine if they made me wear this all day. That would be the worst."

"Not as bad as you driving us around without it," Noah said lightly.

"You haven't worn one of these things. I wouldn't be so sure," Dan laughed. "Though to be honest, it doesn't feel as hot as it was earlier, thank goodness."

Noah's head shot up. "Would you say you're feeling numb?"

Dan shrugged carelessly. "Uh, no. Why?"

"It's one of our symptoms."

Noah could see the moment their driver realized what that meant.

"Wait one second," Dan said slowly, swiveling in his seat to peer at them through the plastic screen of the hazmat suit. "That campus announcement earlier, with the warning about symptoms and whatnot..."

"Yeah, that's kind of our bad," Brian said.

"Woah," Dan said. "Makes me glad I have this thing on after all." He wiggled his gloved fingers.

"Hey," May said suddenly. "I feel kind of weird." She

looked around, seeming unsure of what exactly was wrong. She rubbed her arm unconsciously, then looked down in surprise. "Uh, guys, look at this," she said quietly, turning slightly in her seat with her sleeve pulled up to give them a view of her shoulder.

They all craned their heads to look.

"Well, holy crap," Brian said. "That was fast."

May prodded at the spot where Dr. Jansen had cut her arm, but the mark had nearly disappeared. A faint pale line was all that remained of the wound. She lifted her leg and they saw the same had occurred on her calf.

"The spots feel warm," she said in surprise. "That's the first thing I've felt all day."

"No way," Brian said. "Is this the first sign of our return to normal?"

"It's already starting to cool down," May said glumly. "So probably not."

"How would that even work, anyways?" Leah asked. "Is it even possible for us to go back to normal now that so much of our regular vital functions have been dead for so long?"

Noah glanced at her with knitted brows. "This would pretty much be worst case, but what if the illness is the only thing keeping us alive, somehow? And when we don't have it anymore, we just die like we normally would have without a pulse?"

"You're saying that we need the sickness now," Brian said, not seeming fond of the idea at all. "That our only two options are to die or to be stuck like this forever. I'm not liking the lack of a 'continue life as normal' alternative."

"Yeah, but who knows. That's just my theory," Noah said.

Brian shuddered. "You better be wrong."

"I'm hungry," May said.

"Good luck with that," Brian said. "Food tastes terrible right now."

"Oh, that's right," May said, frowning.

"You just healed two wounds within the span of a few minutes," Leah pointed out. "That's kind of incredible. Maybe that's why you're hungry."

"Hey, that's right," Brian said. "Damn. Now I wish another one of us took the crazy doctor up on her offer. We could compare how we felt."

"We could do it ourselves," Leah said.

They all looked at her, and she shrugged. "It was just a suggestion. We don't have to, obviously."

"No, it's not a bad idea," Brian said. "Especially if there's decent evidence that we'll immediately heal from it anyways. Which is rather awesome, by the way. I know it could randomly kill us at any moment, but now that I'm thinking about it, I'm starting to come around on this whole sickness thing."

Noah glanced between them. "You do realize how insane it sounds when you say you don't mind the sickness that's getting you to purposefully wound yourself."

"Hey, does it really count as a 'wound' when it's totally painless and heals within minutes?"

"Yes, it does. I'll pass on this group activity."

"Eh, suit yourself," Leah shrugged. "We only really need one of us to do it to see what happens."

Brian glanced at her. "Hey, how do you suppose we should go about the DIY method?"

"There's probably a knife in the kitchen that would do the job," Leah said, tapping her chin thoughtfully. "Hey, Dan, I don't suppose you have a pocket knife on you?"

"I think I'll keep myself out of this project of yours," Dan said.

"Aw, don't worry, it's doctor-approved," Brian said.

"Psycho-doctor approved," Leah said under her breath.

"She's scared," May said. "She doesn't know what's happening to her. Or to us."

"That doesn't make it okay for her to throw us into the wringer," Leah said heatedly. "Those scientists at Insight Labs have been cracked down on a dozen times for breaking all sorts of safety laws. They keep saying they've fixed themselves up to standard, and then they're in the news next week for lobotomizing somebody."

Dan nodded from the front seat. "You'd do well to stay far-WOAH!"

He slammed on the brakes, making the van screech in protest of the sudden deceleration. There was a dull thump on the windshield. Everyone in the vehicle was jerked forward.

Noah peeled himself off the chair in front of him and looked out the windows, trying to see why they had stopped.

"I couldn't even see them until they stepped right out in front of the van," Dan said dazedly.

"What? A person? Dan! Did you just run over a student?" Leah demanded.

"I- I think I did," he stammered, throwing the door open and rushing out onto the road.

Noah exchanged wide-eyed looks with his friends.

"We weren't moving too quickly," Brian said hopefully. "Right?"

They exited the van, curious yet apprehensive of what they would find.

Noah's heart sank as he rounded the vehicle. Dan was standing over a twisted form draped over the curb. There were pavement burns across the victim's forearms, face, and chest, visible through his torn Oakridge T-shirt. His left leg looked terribly misaligned. The only positive sign was the lack of spilled blood.

There were a couple other people nearby on the sidewalk, looking at the scene with transfixed horror.

"One of you needs to call an ambulance," Dan yelled at the bystanders, then turned to Noah and his friends peeking around the corner of the van. "Get over here and test his pulse. I have too many layers on to do it properly."

"We won't be able to, we've got no sense of touch," Noah said quickly.

Dan blinked. "Oh, right." He looked around, noticing that nobody was on the phone, and pointed at the closest person. "You. Call campus safety right now."

The girl looked startled and glanced around her,

presumably hoping he was pointing at someone else, but she finally nodded and got her phone out.

Leaving her to it, Dan knelt beside the injured student and flicked a lever on each of his cuffs that let him pull off his outer gloves. He then peeled off a second pair of gloves and gently raised the guy's wrist, pressing his fingers firmly against it. Noah leaned forward as he waited for Dan's verdict.

"I don't feel a pulse," Dan said eventually, letting the wrist drop. He rubbed his eyes and stood up miserably.

The driver began to walk back over to them. Before he could take more than two steps, the body laying behind him suddenly lurched, its hand shooting out to grasp his ankle.

"Woah!" Dan yelped, toppling to the ground. He looked behind him to see the student's head lifted to stare right back at him.

"What? He's not dead!" Brian said, stepping closer, only to recoil as the student hauled himself forward and clamped his jaw onto Dan's leg.

24

I DON'T KNOW WHAT'S
WRONG WITH ME

"The guy's crazy!" Noah yelled, running forward to help their driver.

Dan was shouting incoherently, shaking his leg and causing the student's head to wag back and forth. As soon as Noah was within reach, Dan grabbed hold of his hand and managed to tear himself free of the kid's grip. They stumbled towards the van, while the student fell backwards onto the grass.

Dan and Noah stared down at the guy chewing fixedly on a small piece of Dan's leg. Even as they watched, the scratches across his upper body started knitting themselves rapidly closed, leaving behind unblemished skin. His leg popped a few times but remained in a visibly broken position.

Noah looked on in disgust as the student swallowed and pushed himself upright. He took a step toward them, wobbling slightly on his yet unhealed leg. Everyone backed up quickly, but the guy didn't move further.

"What the hell were you thinking?" Leah bellowed at the student. "He was trying to help you!"

The student blinked, and to Noah's surprise, spoke coherently. "I know. I'm sorry." He wiped his mouth and stared at Dan in a way that made Noah uneasy.

"Then why would you try to eat him, you maniac?"

"I don't know," he said, sounding confused.

At that moment the growing sounds of sirens reached a crescendo and an ambulance pulled around the corner. It pulled to the side of the road right in front of their parked van and a couple workers leapt out. They seemed thrown off when they saw the injured guy standing on his own two feet right in front of them.

"Are you the one who got hit?" a worker asked.

"I guess so," he said, looking around. "It doesn't even hurt, though."

"We were told you had not survived the crash," a second worker said. "Someone took your pulse and found none."

"Wait a moment," the first worker interrupted. "Are you another one of those people with that infection?"

"What infection?"

"The one that everyone on or nearby campus got five emergency emails about," the worker said slowly. She rubbed her temples when the guy just shrugged cluelessly.

"Well, it's easy enough to check," she sighed. "Do us a favor and force a few coughs."

"Uh, okay." He did as instructed, and to no one's surprise, dust came out.

"That's been happening since lunch," he said, unconcerned.

"And you didn't think to call the health center?" the worker yelled, exasperated. She blew out an irritated breath. "Oh, forget it. You might not be in any pain right now, but that clearly doesn't mean you're not injured. Get in the ambulance, we'll take you to urgent care."

"Be careful," Dan warned them as they approached the student. "He attacked me right after I checked his pulse."

The workers stopped in their tracks and turned to him with raised brows. "How so?"

"He bit me," Dan said, sounding like he could hardly believe his own words. "He seems reasonable enough now, I guess, but he did this to my leg." He pointed down.

A small red gash marred the skin above his right ankle. Blood flowed freely from the wound, running down and staining his socks dark red.

They all looked back at the student, who seemed to shrink. "I don't know why I did that," he protested weakly. "I won't attack anyone else. I'm not some lunatic."

"We might want to call in campus safety for this," one of the health workers said. He turned to Noah and his friends. "And you'll need another driver. Just sit tight for a minute, please."

Dan let the workers help him into the ambulance and lay him down on a bench. Noah watched through the back door as they cleaned the wound and poured antiseptic fluid over the whole leg before wrapping it up.

Meanwhile, a few other health workers cautiously stepped closer to the injured student.

"What's your name?" one asked.

"It's Jack," he answered. He suddenly threw his hands up and shut his eyes tightly. "Stop! I'm sorry, don't come any closer. I don't know what's wrong with me."

Everyone backed off cautiously.

"I'm so hungry," he said. His eyes started to glaze over, and he stepped towards the closest person.

One of the workers standing by the ambulance noticed what was happening and shouted in alarm. "Everyone back up! You four students, get into the ambulance."

Noah gladly retreated after his friends towards the emergency vehicle. He kept a careful eye on Jack, but the unstable student barely seemed to notice them hurrying to safety. They scampered around the back of Dan's van and stepped up into the back of the ambulance. It looked exactly the same as the one they had been in earlier, except it was staffed by a different crew. A worker shut the door as soon as they were all inside, and they gathered around the window together to peer out anxiously at the scene unfolding outside.

"So, May," Leah said under her breath. "When you said you were hungry a few minutes ago, this isn't what you meant, is it?"

May looked at her nervously. "I- I don't think so. I mean,

it's not that bad."

Leah held her gaze for a few moments before nodding and looking back outside. "You better tell me if that changes at any point."

Jack seemed to have regained a measure of control over himself. He wasn't chasing after anyone at the moment, at least. The few workers unfortunate enough to be left standing outside were surrounding him in a very loose circle, trying to keep him contained until campus safety arrived.

Before long the sound of sirens heralded the approach of security. Two SUVs pulled up behind the van and the ambulance, forming quite the line of green campus vehicles, and safety workers spread out to replace the cordon around the injured student. Jack seemed willing enough to let them guide him into the back of a vehicle, although he snapped like a wild dog at anyone who got too close. Each time that happened he would immediately draw back and look miserably at the ground. Noah almost felt bad for the guy, watching him cringe back and forth.

"If we can't find another driver for you, we can bring you to your dorms," a health worker said.

"We were actually headed to those housing units for students with the *Wager*," Leah said. "And no, we don't have the *Wager* ourselves. It's a different sickness."

"That's fine, we can drop you off there," the worker said without batting an eye.

The last few people who needed to board the ambulance did so quickly, eager to get away from the scene, and they were soon back on the road.

Noah and the others kept glancing at each other, full of questions, but there was an unspoken agreement to wait until they were alone to discuss anything.

"It's been a busy day," the worker beside Dan sighed. "Lots of calls. Everyone's getting sick and there's been half a dozen minor car accidents on the roads around campus because the driver supposedly couldn't feel the pedal."

Noah swallowed. "That's terrible."

"Well, nobody's been seriously injured, thank goodness. I just wish people would take all the warnings going around more seriously. We're lucky nothing worse has yet to pass." He looked outside as the vehicle slowed to a halt. "Is this your place?"

"Yup," Noah said, standing up. "Give the driver my thanks for the ride. And Dan," he added, "I'm sorry all of this happened while you were just trying to get us home."

"Don't be," he said firmly. "It wasn't your fault. I'm not sure what's going on with you guys, and to be honest, I don't want to know. I wish you the best, though."

They clambered out onto the sidewalk.

"I hope you heal up quickly," Brian said.

"Thanks. You seem like a nice bunch of kids. Try to stay out of trouble, yeah?" He held his hand up in a wave as the door shut and the ambulance pulled away.

25

MIRACLE SICKNESS

They walked up to their respective doors, only to discover they didn't have their keys.

"Oh man, we left the keys inside," Brian said, watching Noah tug ineffectually on the handle. "How do they expect us to get in?"

Noah looked around. "Do you know how to pick a lock?"

Brian rubbed his hands together. "How hard can it be?"

Noah glanced over to see what the girls were doing, just in time to see them disappear around the side of the building.

"Uh, I think May and Leah are walking around back," Noah said. "I guess the back door should be open, right?"

"Oh. Good idea," Brian said, pulling his eye back from the keyhole. They followed the girls around the building to the back entrance, which was indeed unlocked.

"That's not very secure," Noah said as they walked inside.

"It's convenient for us," Brian said with a shrug.

Noah noticed his cold bowl of ground beef and green beans was still sitting on the table. He grimaced at it and quickly threw it in the trash.

"Hey, I was going to eat that!" Brian complained, then laughed at Noah's incredulous look.

"Yeah right," Noah said. "I bet you wouldn't eat that for a hundred bucks."

"That sounds like a great deal. A minute of pain and misery for that much cash? Easiest decision of my life."

A tapping at their back window caught the boys' attention,

and they both looked towards the sound. Sophie was standing right outside the glass with a big smile. She saw them looking and gestured for them to come out.

"Want to go see what she wants?" Brian asked.

"Well, it would just be awkward to ignore her now."

They joined her outside.

"For all the fuss those health workers put up, I sure didn't expect to see you all back here so soon," she said. "What happened?"

There was a gleam in her eyes that Noah hadn't noticed earlier, and she was all but jumping up and down.

"A lot," Noah said. "What's got you so worked up?"

"Look at this," she said brightly, clearing her throat and letting out a cough. Dust was expelled from her mouth.

"You seem awfully happy to have come down with our weird illness," Noah said.

"Oh, can you tell?" she grinned. "Why on earth would I be happy about getting a sickness that mysteriously lets you survive impossible conditions? Or have you both forgotten that I'm scheduled to kick the bucket in a couple hours?"

Noah and Brian stared at her.

"You think this is your free pass to surviving the *Wager*?" Brian gaped. "I don't want to put your hopes down, but... that seems unlikely."

"That's okay. I'm fine with unlikely," Sophie said. She skipped ahead of them towards the picnic table. "Come on, I already got Leah and May out here."

Noah watched her hop into a seat at the table and turn to the girls excitedly, blowing dust all over the table.

"Imagine how crazy it would be if she's right," Brian said.

"Well, completely ignoring the side effects that may or may not include eating people, nobody would be able to prove whether it was just her getting lucky with the *Wager* or if our sickness actually saved her life," Noah said. "I bet it would spark a lot of studies, though. If she's lucky enough to survive past tonight, the poor girl is going to be a huge target for that Insight testing place. She'll be in there right after us."

"What testing place?" Sophie asked curiously, overhearing the last few words and turning to face them.

"Oh, the big shady place down in the city," Noah said. "Didn't you say your parents live nearby? If you grew up in the area you've probably heard of it."

"The Insight Labs medical campus?" She asked, recognition sparking in her eyes. "Hold up, you guys are going there? You think I'll be sent there?"

"Well, I can't say for sure about you, but we've all been scheduled for testing there tomorrow."

Genuine fear spread across her features, and she looked wordlessly between the four of them.

"He's right," Leah said with an angry shrug. "Doctor's orders."

Sophie scowled. "What sort of lousy doctor sends their patients to that kind of place?"

"One who is too scared for her own life to give a shit about anyone else," Leah spat out.

"Scared for her own life? Oh, did she get the sickness?" Sophie wondered.

They all nodded.

"What's she so scared about? Honestly, it's misleading to call it a sickness. It's a miracle."

"Tell Dr. Jansen that," Brian muttered. "She didn't even know that the sickness might make you go crazy- I don't think she did, anyway- and she still didn't hesitate to throw us at Insight Labs at the first sign of danger."

Sophie narrowed her eyes. "What do you mean, 'crazy'?"

"Well, there's this one infected kid that tried to eat our driver," Brian said. "It might not be related. Maybe."

"It's related," May said.

Leah shot her a look. "How do you know?"

"I nearly took a bite out of Dr. Jansen when she cut my arm," she said.

Brian scooted away from her with a panicked look.

May scowled at him and added, "But it was only for a second. It caught me by surprise, you know? I figured out pretty quickly that I didn't want to do that. Like she wouldn't taste good. Obviously, I mean, people wouldn't taste good..." she trailed off.

Leah elbowed her. "What did I say about telling me when you want to eat people!"

May looked away. "I hoped it was just a momentary weird thing," she admitted.

"Well, do you still feel hungry?"

"Not around you guys," May said. "Honestly, I was fine until we got into the ambulance after we hit that kid. The drive here was terrible."

"You think it's because we're all infected too?" Noah asked. "I mean, the goal of any disease is to spread itself. Maybe it has a built-in function to keep you from going after anyone who also has it."

"But that would mean Dan's infected," May said uncertainly. "And he said he wasn't feeling numb."

"We didn't get numb until a few hours after we got the sickness," Noah reminded her. "If he's been wearing the suit for a while, he won't have even noticed that he's breathing out dust 'cause there's a gas mask built into the thing. He could have gotten sick from someone else when he took the suit off, and then before he could notice the symptoms, he had to put the thing back on to pick us up again."

"Okay, so Dan's basically confirmed to be infected," Brian said.

Noah shrugged. "Maybe not. The other option is that the hazmat suit protected him and made him look less tasty to May."

May grimaced at him, but he only shrugged at her. "I'm just trying to figure out what's happening here. The sickness spreads so quickly. If people aren't careful, it won't just be an issue on our campus. It'll be everywhere. The current situation is going to look like a little puddle of water next to the nuclear blast site that we'll be dealing with."

Silence settled over the table.

"Oh, boy," Brian said finally. "This is going to get so bad."

26

SHOULD BE COMMON SENSE

Sophie leaned back and stretched. "Well, it won't matter to you guys if you're locked up at Insight Labs while everything goes down. If I were in your position, I would do everything in my power to stay far, far away from that place. You go into their labs, you won't walk out the same."

"I appreciate the advice and all, but how would you suggest we actually go about it?" Leah asked. "There's a reason they still haven't been closed down, and it hasn't been because of a lack of effort on behalf of the entire local community. There's a lot of money behind that place. They get what they want, and right now, Dr. Jansen has us dangling in front of them like a juicy cut of meat. They won't just let us go if we ask nicely."

Sophie shrugged. "I'm not saying I have a solution."

"We could just leave," Brian said. "We're not exactly locked up right now."

"My man, we attend this college," Noah said. "I've invested too much time and money towards my degree to just walk out. They don't have to lock us up; we're trapped by everything we've given up to be here."

"I'm not saying we disappear forever," Brian said. "Just until this infection gets through its worst stages. We'd only have to hide long enough for Insight to decide we're not worth the effort of finding and picks another poor sap to be their lab rat. Hopefully Dr. Jansen."

Noah thought that was actually a good point, but May

shook her head.

"They wouldn't experiment on a fellow doctor," she said. "They'd pick a student."

"Well, as long as it's not one of us, I'm fine with that."

"You shouldn't be," May said.

Brian rolled his eyes, causing May's expression to darken.

"If you run away, you're just as selfish as the doctor," she said quietly.

Brian's eyes widened. "Don't compare me to that scum," he growled. "She's the one who went and got the attention of the beast; I'm just trying not to get eaten. If it starts looking at other prey, that's not my fault, it's Dr. Jansen's."

"Maybe that's true," May shrugged, "but would you be able to live in peace with yourself if you knew a fellow student had faced the tests meant for you?"

"Yeah, I think I would, actually."

"What if you found out that the student had perished?"

Brian threw his hands up. "Sure, I'd feel terrible! But I'd still rather it be them than me. You can't tell me to sacrifice myself. That's a decision you only get to make for yourself."

Noah watched them argue with a small frown. In this case, he had to agree with Brian. It would be stupidity itself to present themselves on a silver platter to Insight Labs. There was no guarantee they would even seek a replacement if they disappeared, although he had to admit it was likely.

With this in mind, he spoke up. "Brian, if you decide to run away tonight, I'll join you. I'd want to have more of a plan than just getting off the campus, and I don't want to be on the run forever, but I think hiding is probably our best option at this point. Dr. Jansen said she's trying to close the school anyways while the infection still poses a threat."

"I'll run away too," Leah said, making May turn to her in disappointment.

"Hey, don't give me that look! I'm not going to let the person who wants to eat people guilt me into doing anything."

Looking like she was quite caught up in the unfolding drama, Sophie raised her hand. "Me too. I want to run away."

They all looked at her.

"Okay," Brian said finally. "But why? Nobody's asked you to be their lab rat."

"Yet," Sophie said. "Besides, if this dust infection thing doesn't save me, then I don't want to have spent my last few hours cooped up in this place." She hesitated, then added, "I think I'd like to see my parents before I run out of time with the *Wager*."

Brian shrugged. "Well, I'm not going to stop you. Although I'd hate for you to traumatize them by showing up on their doorstep only to drop dead."

Sophie smirked. "But that would be funny."

Noah rubbed his eyes. "Alright. If this is actually happening, we need to figure out exactly what we're doing."

"Easy," Brian said. "Wait 'til it gets dark and walk off campus. We can cut straight through the woods behind the meadow here, come out on a back road, and from there we can walk wherever we want to go. As for food... well, I don't know about May, but the rest of us haven't gotten injured yet, so let's just hope it won't be an issue."

"I never said I was going," May said.

"Well, would you rather be with us, or locked up in a lab somewhere?" Brian asked.

She closed her eyes. "I don't know. I don't want to go on my own."

"You should come with us," Sophie said, and Leah nodded. "C'mon May, don't throw yourself at the shady lab."

"What if we get caught running away?" she asked.

Sophie seemed to realize the girl was on the fence about it, and she quickly responded, "Again, it's not as if we're criminals doing time. It's just a school. Any kind of repercussions we end up facing if we're somehow caught in the middle of our great escape can't possibly be as bad as whatever medical terrors you'll be subjected to if you stick around. Besides, we won't get caught."

"Okay, what if we're overreacting to the whole 'testing' thing?" May said, shamelessly abandoning her previous two arguments. "We don't even know what they're going to do."

"Do you want to bet that whatever they have planned is going to be stuff you're comfortable with?" Leah asked. "This isn't your friendly family physician, May. They've killed people before and gotten away with a light slap on the cheek."

"As far as I'm aware, the people who lost their lives at Insight knew that what they were doing was dangerous," May said. "They were desperate and basically sold themselves to risky science for cash. We're in a completely different situation."

"This is ridiculous," Noah said, standing up. "We're trying to convince you to not throw your own life away. Nobody in their right mind- or not in incredibly desperate straights- would ever allow themselves to be a patient of Insight Labs. You hold no responsibility for whatever they choose to do if we run away. I know I barely met you twenty-four hours ago, but I really don't want to see you left behind tonight. I'm not going to sit here any longer to argue about something that should be common sense."

Noah got up and started walking inside. He had turned the handle halfway when a shout came from behind him.

"Wait," May said. "I'll go."

Noah smiled. "Glad to hear it. I'll meet you all out here at ten PM. 'Ensure you are ready to leave at that time', yeah?"

"Ok, Dr. Jansen," Brian yelled.

Noah chuckled and stepped inside to pack.

27

TENDENCY TOWARDS
VIOLENCE

Noah stood in his assigned bedroom upstairs and looked around, wondering what he should bring for their grand getaway. *Spare clothes*, he thought. He went to his closet and pulled out a couple outfits, wrapping everything up in another shirt and tying it to act like a bag.

Now if I just hoist it over my shoulder on a nice big stick, I can look like every depiction of a homeless kid ever made.

"A bindle, that's what it's called," Noah muttered.

He glanced over at the bed. He wouldn't even get to sleep in it for a single night. "Ah, such is the cost of freedom," he laughed quietly to himself. He wondered for a moment if he should bring along one of the blankets from the bed, then remembered he wouldn't need to worry about getting cold. The best it could be used for was maybe an impromptu draped shelter, and Noah didn't feel like carrying it around for that.

He tried to think of anything else to bring. Usually when he went on overnight trips he brought a huge bag filled with everything he might possibly need. But even if he wanted or needed all that stuff now, most of it was either still laying around in his dorm or about six hundred miles away in his dad's house.

He straightened, suddenly remembering that his dad was driving that distance right now. He had forgotten all about their phone call. *Oh, man. He's gonna get here right after we've disappeared.*

Noah rubbed his face, trying to tamp down the sudden spike of stress. He pulled out his phone and stared at it, wondering if it would be a mistake to tell his dad that they wouldn't be around.

I'll ask Brian, he decided, picking up his hobo bundle and stepping out of the room. He checked the other bedroom as he passed the door, but it was empty, so he walked downstairs to find Brian in the kitchen peering into the fridge.

"Feeling hungry?" he asked, half joking and half nervous that his friend was indeed looking for something to eat.

Brian quickly shut the fridge. "No, I'm just trying to think if there's a way around the injury-induced tendency towards violence that seems to be becoming a trend for infected people. There must be something that could work as a substitute for fellow humans."

"Anything in there look like a potential alternative?"

"No," Brian answered, snorting. "I can't believe any of this stuff ever tasted good."

"I'm sure there's a solution," Noah said. "There better be one. I know I don't want to have to worry about trying to eat people if I happen to pick up a scratch."

"I'm surprised it hasn't become more of an issue already," Brian said. "I mean, someone with the sickness has got to have gotten injured by now. Is there an announcement about it yet?"

"Not that I've seen," Noah said. "And I've gotten all the other public safety warnings without any issue. The communications people might just not know yet."

"Well, they will. They've got that Jack kid in custody. They'll figure it out real quick. Maybe people will start to take this whole thing seriously then."

"Don't count on it," Noah muttered. "Well, I actually came down to ask you about something."

"Yeah?"

"I called my dad earlier and told him about what's going

on, or at least what we knew at that time."

"Did you tell him everything?" Brian asked nervously.

"All of our symptoms, yeah."

Brian ran a hand through his hair. "Oh, no. What did he say?"

"He said he's gonna drive down to see me in person, for whatever good he thinks that'll do. He'll be arriving in a few hours."

Brian shot him a startled look. "He's gonna freak out if you're missing."

Noah sighed. "That's why I'm debating whether to tell him that we're going to be off campus for a while. Nothing specific, just enough to make sure he doesn't go ballistic."

Brian nodded slowly. "I think you should do that. Maybe wait until we're actually gone, just in case he tries to call Oakridge right after you hang up to warn them about our imminent unplanned departure."

"Yeah. That sounds reasonable. My only worry is that he'll get caught up in this mess if he's in the area. I'd hate for him to get infected by someone. Or eaten, God forbid."

Brian scratched his head. "Maybe you should call him now after all. Try to convince him to turn around."

"Well, I know how he thinks, unfortunately. I tell him it's too dangerous for him to visit, he'll just become all the more determined to get here. It's as if he thinks his mere presence will drive away all maladies. The guy's just gonna get himself killed." Noah buried his face in his hands. "I don't know what to do."

"Hey, man," Brian said, awkwardly patting his shoulder in a gesture neither of them could physically feel. "Do you want to ask the girls if they have any ideas?"

Noah shrugged. "I dunno. They don't know my dad. I know I'd be better able to come up with the right combination of words to get him to just turn around, though I don't have a clue what those would be."

"You could tell him the truth," Brian suggested. "That you're hiding so you don't get dissected in a lab."

Noah glanced up. "You think that would work?"

"It's worth a try. Tell him that the doctor is sending you to Insight tomorrow, and get a sense of his reaction before you decide whether to confess that we're gonna run away."

Noah nodded. "Okay." He smiled at his friend. "Thanks."

"Of course. Do you want me to leave the room while you make the call?"

"You can stay. Provide me with some moral support."

Brian took a seat at the table and watched Noah dial.

"He better pick up," Noah said.

28

I WOULDN'T LIE

His dad picked up on the first ring. "Hello, Noah. Is everything okay?"

"I'm doing fine at the moment, yeah. I just wanted to share some updates on what's planned for tomorrow. Keep you in the loop."

"What's happening?"

"Have you heard about Insight Labs? The big medical lab in the city here?"

"Can't say that I have. Why?"

Noah looked at Brian. *This is going to be more difficult if he doesn't already have the background knowledge of what Insight is like.*

"They're a very experimental place," Noah said carefully. "We're going to be sent there tomorrow morning."

"How long is your appointment? I was hoping to stop by to see you."

"It's less of an appointment and more of an... uh, abduction," Noah said. "We said we didn't want to go, but the doctor is basically forcing us. We weren't given a choice."

"Why wouldn't you want to see their doctors?"

Just spit it out, Brian mouthed.

"They've killed people, dad."

There was no response, so Noah blazed forward. "We aren't being sent there for our own good; it's so that some scientists over there can satisfy their curiosity about this odd little sickness. And because our campus doctor hopes they'll find a cure, or something."

"Have you talked to anyone about this?" Noah's dad snapped. "Because this is not how a school should be treating its students. If what you're saying is true, it's unlawful."

Noah scratched his neck. "Uh, we haven't really talked to anyone. But that's besides the point! Insight Labs isn't part of the college. They operate independently, above the law in every way that counts. They've decided they want us, and nothing anyone does will stop them."

"Why the hell does this Insight place need to see you so bad? What's so interesting about this sickness of yours?"

Noah sighed. "It's new. That's really all the reason they need. They're probably excited that it will open new branches of scientific discovery or some crap."

"I'd like to have a word with whoever gave them your name."

"No, you wouldn't. She's a pathetic excuse for a doctor. And it wouldn't help anything, anyway. It's too late now." Noah looked at Brian and crossed his fingers. "There's nothing I can do at this point short of running away."

"Hmph. If this mess is half as bad as you're making it sound, maybe that's not such a bad idea."

"But what about our studies?" Noah flashed a mischievous grin at his friend.

"Your life is more important than your grades." He let out a sigh. "In fact, I'd prefer if you got out of there. I know it's a lot to ask, but-"

"Don't worry about it, dad. I trust you. If you say I should run, I'll run."

There was silence for a moment. A short exhale carried through the speaker. "I'm proud of you, Noah. I don't know if I could be so brave."

Brian waggled his eyebrows at his friend. Noah ignored him.

"Well, I should probably start packing, if I'm really going to do this," Noah said.

"Oh, yeah. Of course. I'll text you the address of the hotel

I'm staying at in case you want to stop by- I still want to see you, Noah. Call me whenever you can. Don't do anything too reckless, okay?"

"I won't," Noah promised. "See you later."

"Later, kid."

Noah hung up.

He turned to face Brian with a smug grin. "That went pretty well."

"See, I knew it would work," Brian said, pleased. "All it took was a teeny tiny bit of family manipulation."

"At least I didn't lie," Noah said defensively. He paused in consideration. "At least, I don't think I did. Yeah, I wouldn't lie to my father."

"Of course not," Brian said. "Speaking of promising not to do anything reckless, want to see how quickly we can heal a stab wound? We never got around to testing the limits of our regeneration."

Noah stared at him. "What about the side effects?"

"There's nobody who's not infected nearby," Brian said. "You won't hurt anyone."

"Let's just classify that as a terrible idea and agree to never try it," Noah said. "I think I'll go upstairs to try to get a few hours of sleep before we leave. You should do the same. Who knows when we'll next have proper bedrooms."

"I guess so. Not that it matters. We could sleep on a pile of rocks and it would feel no different from a warm, soft bed. I don't know if I'd be so willing to run away otherwise."

"Hey, it's more than just the physical comfort of a mattress," Noah said. "There's something to be said for knowing you're in a private and secure place as you fall asleep."

Brian thought about that. "Yeah, you're right. I don't know how much rest I'll be able to get, but I suppose it would be silly not to try. I don't really need to do anything else to prepare."

"It's weird, isn't it? Not having to bring all the usual stuff? All sorts of clothes for different weather, food, drink. I'm not even going to bring a toothbrush."

"Well, you either won't need one, or you really, really will," Brian said.

Noah frowned. "Hmm. Maybe I should bring a toothbrush. Not to assume the worst or anything."

Brian shrugged. "I think I'll just take a change of clothes and a comb. Just because we're gonna be homeless for a little while doesn't mean we gotta look it."

Noah stood up from the table. "Set an alarm before you try to get some sleep. It would be really lame if we slept right through the night and woke up to the people from Insight knocking on the front door."

"The girls would wake us up."

Noah shot him a look.

"Oh, stop worrying. I'll set an alarm for myself."

Noah gave him a nod and headed upstairs. Resolving the issue with his dad had taken a huge load off his shoulders. He was glad he had thought to get Brian's opinion on what to do instead of blundering his way through a conversation that would probably have only made things worse.

Feeling optimistic about their prospects, Noah kicked off his sneakers and sat on the edge of his bed, taking his own advice and setting a quick alarm for himself. He got up to set his phone on the desk and flip off the light switch. There was still quite a bit of evening light streaming in through the large window. He frowned and went over to it, pulling the stiff shade across and casting the room into pitch-darkness before he could realize how thoroughly the screen blocked out all light.

The feeling of weightlessness returned in full force near-instantly. Noah quickly reached out to uncover the window, but his hand must have missed the shade, because no light returned to the room. He cast about in front of him blindly and senselessly, rapidly losing awareness of his surroundings. Without visual confirmation he began to doubt if he were moving his limbs at all, or if he were just standing there motionlessly. He tried to strike out with his hands but heard no sound. A moment later a thump reverberated through his head as if someone had struck the back of his skull. Noah gasped and tried to duck forward, but there was no further noise to indicate what was happening.

"Brian! Come here!" He shouted for his friend.

He felt himself slipping into panic as he waited in vain for some sort of sense of place to return to him. There must have been some illumination bouncing into the room around the edges of the window or from under the door, but neither of those sources of light were very bright to begin with and his eyes were not strong enough to pick out anything from the void that surrounded him.

Finally, what seemed to be an eternity later, he caught the sound of footsteps approaching.

"Noah?" Brian asked from outside his room. "What is it?"

"Can you- can you just open the door?"

Knowing his friend was right outside, Noah's panic receded, leaving a prickle of embarrassment in its place.

"Uh, sure," Brian said. A moment later blessed light cascaded into the room, dispelling the abyss. Noah found himself looking up from a surprisingly low vantage point.

"What are you doing?" Brian looked down at Noah laying on the floor. "Are you okay?"

He had fallen at some point without noticing. Now he was laying there with his feet by the window and his head by the center of the room, staring straight up. Noah quickly picked himself up.

"Sorry, I'm such an idiot," he said. "I was just trying to turn off the lights. I didn't realize it would get so dark."

Brian seemed puzzled, but he only nodded. "Is that all you wanted?"

"Yeah. Thanks. You know, I just figured out something else we should be packing."

"What's that?"

"Flashlights."

Brian shrugged. "We might have to rely on our phones for that. I haven't seen any honest-to-goodness flashlights lying around."

With that he left the room, careful to leave the door cracked. Noah quickly slid the window shade open a few inches as well, just to be safe.

Feeling shaken, Noah climbed into bed and hesitated before pulling the sheets up over himself. He didn't want to imagine how long he would have been incapacitated in his own room if Brian hadn't been nearby.

He closed his eyes. Absolute darkness settled over him once more, but rather than growing anxious, he relaxed with the knowledge that he was tucked safely into bed. A deep sense of peace filled him and he was asleep within seconds.

29

GREAT ESCAPE

The alarm woke him up as planned. Noah smiled as he got up to turn it off, feeling tentatively hopeful about what the night would bring. His brief mishap in the dark was a good warning to be careful about operating in poorly-lit conditions. It would be annoying to deal with such an obtrusive weakness, but there was nothing to be done about it. Even perfectly healthy people had trouble in the dark.

He was still feeling quite pleased about how smoothly he had handled the situation with his dad. Everything was in place for him to make a straightforward getaway with his friends. It would be a small break in routine for a few days before he had to return to his regular studies. Maybe- possibly- it could even be *fun*.

He looked at the bed and, feeling somewhat silly, thought about stuffing some pillows under the blankets in the shape of a sleeping person. Eventually he decided to just leave it be. Maybe whoever came to pick them up would think they had simply missed the appointment by accident. Leaving behind such ineffectual and obvious signs of deception could only hurt them and arouse suspicion.

All of his things were downstairs, so he left the bedroom without a second glance. *I hope I never see the inside of that room again,* he thought spitefully. *It would have been nice enough if the school just left us alone during our time here, but Dr. Jansen kind of ruined the whole experience by dragging Insight into our business.*

His smile slipped at that thought, but he brightened again once he walked into the kitchen and saw Brian trying to fit a couple folded towels into his swollen backpack. They looked to be from the bathroom upstairs.

"What happened to just bringing some clothes and a comb?" Noah asked. He put his face up to the window and squinted outside, trying to see if the girls were already out there, but he didn't see them. He turned back to the table.

Brian somehow finished pressing the towels into his bag and managed to shut the zipper over them. "No point leaving these behind. It could be useful to have towels in a number of situations, and it's not as if I'll feel the strain of the extra weight. If Oakridge didn't want us to take our towels with us when we ran away, they shouldn't have left any in our house."

"You're lucky they got your bag back to you in the first place. Otherwise you'd be stuck with a knotted wad of clothes like me."

Brian grinned. "You should have asked for your stuff when you had the chance. A guy swung by to drop it off while you were napping. It still has everything in it that I packed for our cemetery visit yesterday evening, which means we have our flashlights back."

Noah's face lit up. "Hey, that's fantastic!"

Brian looked smug. "I know. Things work out when you pack properly." He gave Noah's clump of clothing a doubtful look that Noah pretended not to notice.

"It's kind of insane how much has happened in the past twenty-four hours," Noah said. "I mean, everything was normal yesterday. Who could've guessed that we'd end up getting the whole campus shut down?"

"The first sign that things were beginning to go wrong was that horrible mausoleum," Brian reflected. "I knew we should have just stood our ground and fought the wolves like men."

"Very, very dead men," Noah said. "Don't be silly. Those things would have totally eaten us if we hadn't found a place to hide."

"Speak for yourself." Brian crossed his arms. "I carry bear spray."

"Yeah, and it's definitely buried under twenty pounds of miscellaneous items at the bottom of that bag. You were about half a second from getting slammed by a wolf before I pulled you inside the mausoleum."

"If May were here she'd probably say something about how we should have bravely laid down our lives for the greater purpose of keeping the disease locked up away from society."

"Well, May's a little crazy," Noah said. He checked the time on his phone. "We should go outside. It's nearly ten."

Brian shouldered his massive backpack and Noah slung his sack over his shoulder.

"Bye-bye, housing unit number three," Brian said cheerfully as they exited the back door.

There was a small porch light next to the door, but all it really managed to do was emphasize how dark the far side of the meadow was.

"Uh, maybe you should get those flashlights out now," Noah said.

"...I think I will."

As Brian began the unenviable task of fishing them out from his overstuffed bag, Sophie and then Leah and May stepped out from their respective units.

"Here," Brian said finally, handing Noah a light and tucking the second one under his elbow so he could close his bag back up and heave it onto his back.

The girls crossed between the pools of light cast from each door to meet Noah and Brian.

"Is everyone all set?" Sophie asked.

She had a backpack like Brian's, though not nearly as tightly packed. May and Leah each had hobo bundles nearly identical to Noah's.

Noah expected to see some sign of displeasure from May, but she seemed just as excited as the rest of them to get off campus.

"All right, there's a wire fence that runs around the edge of the field," Sophie said, then pointed out into the dark. "If we cross it over there and head north, we shouldn't have to ford the river back behind the meadow. The fence isn't anything too crazy; we shouldn't have any issue climbing it. Except you, Brian. You might want to toss your backpack over ahead of yourself. That thing looks like it weighs fifty pounds."

"Don't worry, I can't even feel it."

"Sure, but that doesn't mean your body has physical limits you shouldn't exceed. You might want to reconsider bringing all that before we leave."

Brian looked like he was actually thinking about it, but he ended up just shaking his head. "Everything I packed is essential."

"Somehow I doubt that," Leah said.

"Let's wait until we're off school grounds to have this conversation," Noah quickly interceded.

They moved away from the building, out into the meadow. Noah was quite glad to have the flashlights. Maybe there was a danger of being seen, but in his mind the risk was completely outweighed by how badly they needed the light to see. The twin beams of light cut through the dark like knives through warm butter, paving their path forward.

They passed the picnic table, looking somehow ominous in the way it loomed out of the dark at them, and soon enough the fence Sophie had mentioned came into view.

It was a simple metal-wire fence, probably intended more to demarcate the edge of the property than to keep people in or animals out.

"Careful of the wires along the top," Sophie said. "It's not barbed, but some of them are a little sharp."

She hopped over it with impressive dexterity considering the double impediments of the darkness and the clumsiness that came with being fully numb.

Brian did as she had advised and quickly passed her the flashlight before slinging his backpack onto the other side of the fence. He picked his way up and over with considerably less skill, but he got himself over.

May and Leah joined them without any issues, leaving just Noah to climb the fence.

"Take this," he said quietly, passing Brian and Leah his bundle and the flashlight.

He braced a foot in one of the small gaps in the wire, hoping that he had enough of his weight braced on his toes to get him over, and stepped his other foot onto the top of the fence. The wires sticking up under his foot bent slightly as he shifted forward, his disconnected sense of touch making him feel oddly like he was piloting a suit. From there he crawled the rest of his body over the top and let himself drop down on the other side to join his friends. There was a strange resistance on the right half of his body before his feet touched the ground.

As he accepted his things back from the siblings, he was quite surprised to suddenly feel a peculiar warmth bloom along the bottom of his right forearm. He held his arm up and shone the light at it curiously.

He stifled a gasp, making the others all look in his direction.

"Oh, no," May said.

The flesh was split open, dividing his arm nearly in two from the base of his wrist to the inside of his elbow.

30

AND THIS IS WHERE THINGS
START TO GO DOWNHILL

Noah tried to flex his fingers. His first reaction was concern that the injury would render his hand unusable, and to his alarm, his fingers only twitched slightly when he commanded them to close.

Then the edges of the gash began to subtly pull themselves together like a stubborn zipper, and Noah lost his train of thought. He staggered from the sudden hunger that rose up from within him.

"Get back," someone murmured.

Noah looked at the one who had spoken, swallowing, barely comprehending their words. He instinctively stepped after the closest person as they retreated to prevent the distance between them from widening. The grip of his left hand loosened and his bundle of clothes dropped to the ground without his notice.

A part of Noah was half-heartedly struggling to drag himself out of the haze that had enveloped him. It was a hopeless prospect, however; the warmth in his arm continually dragged his attention back within himself and to the terrible gaping emptiness that demanded to be filled. Nothing else mattered.

He locked eyes with the young man standing perfectly still just a few feet away.

That's Brian, he thought distantly, but he found he didn't care.

Noah closed the distance between them without warning and reached towards him, planning to drag him closer. He forgot his fingers weren't functioning and only managed to slap weakly against his arm. Brian pushed him firmly away, sending him stumbling backwards into the fence.

Noah furrowed his brows, frustrated, feeling a lot less keen to go after his friend all of a sudden. Even that brief touch was enough for him to know instinctively that it would not be worth the effort. It would not gratify his hunger.

He looked around, disregarding the four people around him, knowing they were worthless. He needed to find someone else. He turned his gaze to the buildings of the main campus, barely visible behind rows of trees and the townhouse-style building they had been staying in. There would be plenty of people there. Full of eager thoughts, Noah started walking along the fence. He didn't bother attempting to climb directly over it. He had barely managed with two functional arms; attempting it now would be a waste of time.

"Where is he going?" a worried voice asked behind him.

Now that he had a plan, he found his mind had cleared enough for him to recognize the question and respond appropriately. "I need to visit the campus to grab something to eat," he said, smiling happily to himself. He didn't bother to look back at them.

"Oh, man. Guys, he's definitely gonna eat someone," the same voice said.

Several pairs of footsteps rapidly approached him from behind. He ignored the sound until he was suddenly lurched backward and he glanced down to see a hand tugging on his left arm.

Without a second thought he snapped at the hand, causing it to swiftly recoil. He smiled and continued forward at a faster pace, nearly to the end of the fence, only for someone to tackle him bodily from behind. He collapsed promptly to the ground.

He tried to get up, but a weight on his elbows and heels

rendered his struggles ineffective. As he realized he was trapped he grew angry, turning to see who was holding him down.

"Brian," he growled. He should have expected that they wouldn't understand. He urgently needed to eat; with every passing second he was acutely aware of his energy draining away to fuel the healing wound on his arm. Here he was withering away, and his own friend was trapping him, forcing it to happen.

"You need to stop," Brian hissed. He looked over at May. "How long will it take him to calm down?"

She threw her hands up. "I don't know! Compared to him, I barely had a scratch. I was never in danger of running off after people like this. I suppose the hunger reduced somewhat once the cuts finished healing, although it never completely went away." She looked down at Noah with an unreadable expression.

Brian flipped over Noah's arm, ignoring his friend's pathetic efforts to escape. "Well, the wound definitely is still open. Who knows how long it'll take for it to fully heal."

Sophie sighed. "We should have just gone out the front door and walked around the fence into the woods. We couldn't even get off the freaking property without everything going wrong."

"Hey, we'll get past this. Right, Noah?"

Noah moaned pitifully, feeling as though his entire body were shriveling away into nothing.

"See? He's doing great. We just need to wait a minute or two and we can get moving again."

"He doesn't look great," Leah said, crouching down to shine the flashlight at his face. "Are you sure he'll be okay if we just keep him here?"

"Are you seriously suggesting we let him go?"

Leah shrugged. "No. I don't want to be responsible for some random kid getting eaten. And I don't think Noah would feel great about that after the fact, either."

"Yes, I would," Noah said. "Let me go."

"Shut up, Mr. Zombie," Brian said.

"Hey, I think I heard that everyone on campus was staying out in the middle of the woods tonight," Sophie said.

For a moment Noah sent a glance out into the woods, but almost immediately he turned back to glower at Sophie. "Liar."

She sighed. "There might be someone out there."

"No, there isn't."

Sophie put her hands on her hips. "Can't you just get a hold of yourself? Think how terrible it would taste to bite someone. You'd regret it immediately."

"Yeah, you're right. I've changed my mind. Let me go."

"Don't let him go," May said.

"Wasn't planning on it," Brian grumbled.

"Can't we move a little further away from the road?" Leah asked. "Anyone driving by can see us crouching out here like a couple of guilty gremlins. Someone is bound to call campus safety. Or campus safety will see us themselves."

"I have an idea," Brian said suddenly. "Can one of you open my backpack? There are a few towels at the top right inside. I just need one."

"Sure," Leah said, quickly retrieving a medium-sized bath towel. "What are you going to do?"

"Watch," he said. "And then tell me I'm a genius."

Brian swiftly wrapped one of the towels around Noah's face like a blindfold and tied it behind his head, then quickly stepped back

Noah gasped. "No," he whispered, going motionless for a moment before bucking and thrashing with all of his remaining strength. His left hand scrambled at the towel without managing to dislodge it from his head. Brian watched calmly as his friend's movements became weaker and weaker until he lay completely still.

"I feel like we just killed him," Leah said, staring down at him.

"He'll be fine. He's just completely immobilized."

Noah whimpered.

"Oh, be quiet. This is for your own good. Leah, give May the flashlight and help me pick him up."

They scooped him up in a two-man carry and retreated as quickly as they were able back away from the road. They reached the spot where they had initially crossed the fence and stopped there, staring into the dark woods. The trees were relatively dense, although there wasn't much undergrowth, which would make traversing the land much easier. They would face no worse obstacle than the occasional fallen tree.

"Are we seriously going to have to carry him all the way through?" Leah groused. "C'mon Noah, aren't you better yet?"

"Yes! Take off the blindfold."

She didn't bother to respond, but after a moment she sighed and doubtfully checked his arm. Though it was noticeably smaller, the wound was still brightly visible against the pale flesh of his forearm.

"You realize we can see the injury right in front of us. We can tell you're not healed." She cast a second glance at his arm before looking up across him at Brian. "Has he always been so thin?"

"I'm wasting away," Noah lamented.

Brian shrugged helplessly. "He just has to hold on until the cut closes up."

Sophie noticed Noah's clothes nearby in a pile on the ground and scooped them up, and then they took their first steps into the woods. It was quite strange to be back under the trees in the dark for the second night in a row. May and Sophie held the flashlights. May was a lot better about keeping the ground directly under their feet illuminated, while Sophie kept pointing the light off into the trees at every little sound.

Eventually May looked over at Noah's limply hanging form with a frown. "What if he gets injured again at some point? I mean, it's bound to happen. It'll probably happen to all of us. We can't just infinitely walk around like this without eating anything; we'll run out of energy eventually."

"That's an excellent point, thank you, May," Noah said. "I completely agree that the only reasonable decision is to let me free. You can just wait for me here, I'll be quick."

"There's got to be something else we can eat besides people," May continued as if Noah hadn't spoken. "It just doesn't make any sense. It's all calories, when it comes down to it."

"Nothing about this blasted sickness makes sense," Brian said. "I've given up trying to make sense of it."

"Even if it's outside our understanding, it has to be working on some sort of logic," May said. "Everything that has occurred so far must have happened for a reason."

"It'd be nice if Insight grabs someone else to experiment on and figures it out," Brian said.

May gave him a disappointed look.

"Through gentle and humane research, of course," he added hastily.

31

SORRY I TRIED TO EAT YOU

They picked their way between trees, heading roughly north. There was a back road that they would eventually run into, and from there they would have to decide exactly where they wanted to go next.

"I did some tests before we left to see if there's any form of regular food that still tastes good," May said.

Brian winced. "I kind of thought about doing that, but I just couldn't make myself try anything."

She dipped her head. "Yeah, it was a distinctly unpleasant experience. But based on what we've seen so far, I wondered if raw meat would be more palatable. Trust me, it's just as nasty as it sounds. I really don't know what else would be a possible food option at this point."

"There are no other options," Noah said weakly. "It has to be alive."

They looked at him. By now his arm was nearly fully healed, although the rest of his body was in a poor state. His limbs were like sticks and what little they could see of his face beneath the table was gaunt. He looked like he hadn't eaten in weeks.

With the blindfold blocking out all sense of sight, Noah's entire world was the constant pangs of hunger wracking his body. If he were not so tired he would have been shaking uncontrollably. He dipped in and out of consciousness every few seconds.

"You're almost there, buddy," Brian said. All that was left

of the formerly gaping gash was a dull red line. Though it was nearly gone, Brian couldn't help but notice that the rate of healing seemed to be slowing down as it neared completion.

"I don't think he's going to suddenly regain all the body mass he's lost from this," May said. "Honestly, I wouldn't be surprised if his condition doesn't improve at all until he eats something."

Nobody knew what to say to that.

In the next minute the last remnants of the wound disappeared. They drew to a halt, looking expectantly at Noah.

"Let's put him down," Brian said.

They lowered him gently onto the earth, which was covered in a thick blanket of dead leaves and twigs. Brian tore away the towel blindfold to find his eyes closed and his expression peaceful.

"Wake up, Noah," he said.

He was as motionless as a corpse.

"Uh, maybe we should have let him run off and do his thing," Leah said.

May shot her a dark look.

"What? Remember that kid we ran over? He only needed a tiny little bite out of Dan to heal most of his injuries."

"Well, we're in the middle of the woods now," Brian said. "Not many people around here."

"He just needs a minute," May said hopefully. She nudged him with a foot, and his head flopped to the side.

"This whole regeneration thing kind of sucks," Sophie muttered. "The effects from the healing are worse than the actual wound."

"He would probably have been fine if we hadn't incapacitated him and carried him off into the woods," Leah said.

"Stop acting like we should have let him eat someone," May said, exasperated.

"Look at him!" Leah yelled. "He's a freaking skeleton! It's no wonder he's unconscious!"

"Well, should we pick him back up and keep moving,

or are we going to wait around for him to wake up?" May wondered.

"We can try to wake him up," Brian said. "We're far enough away from campus that it should be safe to yell, right?"

They all shrugged, so he bent down by Noah's ear. "Noah! Now is not the time for a nap! Wakey wakey!"

They waited a few seconds, but there was no reaction.

"I don't think you were loud enough. You should scream at him," Sophie recommended.

"I don't want people to think there's a murder happening out here," Brian said.

Noah suddenly twitched, and everyone's attention shot back to him. He slowly curled himself into a ball and let out a quiet moan.

"Noah! How do you feel?" Brian asked quickly.

"Awful," he mumbled in a barely audible voice.

"Can you stand?"

Noah cracked his eyes open and reached up, letting Brian pull him upright. It was easy; he was terribly light.

Brian tried not to wince at his friend's appearance. In the harsh light of the two flashlights he seemed just as pale as a ghost. His arms and legs were like trembling toothpicks and his eyes had a hollow cast. Overall, he was nearly unrecognizable.

"I'm hungry," he said. He clasped his arms around himself and looked around miserably. "I'm really hungry."

"You're not going to run away, though, right?" Leah asked. "Or try to come after us?"

Brian glanced at her. Noah hardly looked capable of supporting his own weight, let alone running off or attacking anyone.

"I don't think so," Noah croaked.

"Great, let's keep moving," Sophie said. She pointed the flashlight ahead and stepped away impatiently.

"How much time do you have?" May asked her.

She scratched her head. "About an hour, give or take

fifteen minutes. I want to see my parents before it starts getting close."

"Okay. How far away are they from here?"

"Only a couple miles. I'll be able to say for sure once we're out of the woods and I can see where we are exactly."

Brian helped Noah take a few shaky steps after them. Leah noticed that they were having trouble and came around to help support Noah from his other side.

"I'm sorry about this," Noah said. He looked at Brian. "Sorry I tried to eat you."

His friend waved a hand. "Aw, don't worry about it. You weren't very good at it anyway."

"Hey," Noah protested. "I was handicapped."

Brian patted him gently on the back. "I don't mean anything by it, buddy. I'm sure you would've made a very capable zombie."

His words seemed to hearten Noah somewhat.

It went unsaid that Noah was absolutely in a worse state now than when he had initially injured himself. Brian was sure that without support, his friend would immediately collapse to the ground like a poorly stacked Jenga tower.

Nevertheless, they made steady progress through the woods. The sheer density of darkness within a night-shrouded forest is a considerable thing, and whether it was because of their newfound vulnerability in the dark or just regular human instinct, they all found themselves feeling quite wary of their indistinct surroundings.

Before long they emerged out onto a short clearing. A dark road devoid of vehicles stretched to either direction. The woods continued on the other side.

"So, which way?" Leah asked.

Sophie looked down the road both ways, rubbing her chin. "Hmm. Right, I think. Yeah."

"Great, glad to know you're one hundred percent certain that's where we should be heading. Let's go."

Brian and Leah helped Noah hobble onto the asphalt and they began making their way down the road.

"What are we going to do if a car comes along?" Brian asked. "There's a chance someone might stop to try to talk with us to see if we need help or something."

"I dunno, switch off the lights and hide in the woods?" Sophie suggested. "We probably won't see anyone. This road is pretty much only used during big campus events."

A small dark-furred creature suddenly scampered onto the pavement just ahead of them. None of them noticed it until it crossed directly into the path of their flashlights. It recognized their presence in the same moment and froze. A bushy striped tail and mask-like features marked it as a raccoon.

"Aww," Leah began to say, but a second later it turned tail and leapt from the beams of light back the way it had appeared.

Without warning Noah lunged forward after it, pushing Brian and Leah away in a surprising display of strength and diving off the road after the creature.

32

LIKE NORMAL PEOPLE

"Woah!" Brian yelled in surprise. "What are you doing?"

"What do you think he's doing?" May asked dryly.

"Oh. I guess raccoons are on the menu, then," Brian said, squinting into the dark in an effort to see if Noah had successfully caught the thing.

A short, high-pitched squeal told him all he needed to know, and he grimaced.

Sophie finally turned the light onto Noah. He was hunched over, his back to them and the raccoon clutched in his hands. The creature was not struggling, probably because it was missing a large part of its neck.

"Noah?" Brian asked.

His friend didn't even glance at him. He took another bite and continued chewing.

"Well, if this works out, it looks like we've found something edible besides people," Sophie said hopefully.

Brian stepped towards Noah, but Leah put a hand on his shoulder. "Maybe let him finish first," she said.

They watched as Noah slowly devoured the animal and did their best to tune out the sounds that the process produced. Brian found himself glad that his friend was turned away from them, hiding the worst of the details.

"This is insane," Leah muttered. "What kind of sickness makes people act like this?"

"I'm just glad it was a raccoon and not a random guy taking a walk," Brian said.

At long last Noah polished off the last of the raccoon, or at least what of it he seemed interested in consuming. Bits and pieces of bones and fur lay discarded at his feet. He stood there for a moment longer, licking his fingers.

"You, uh, feeling better now?" Brian asked.

Noah turned back to them with a face covered in blood. A trace of black dust seeped from the corner of his mouth. They all quickly took a step back, but he just smiled slightly and nodded. "A bit better, yeah. It's not the ideal meal, but it works."

"If you say so," Brian said.

"You've got some of it on your shirt there," Leah pointed out. "Well, it's everywhere, actually."

"Hmm?" Noah looked down and scowled. The entire front of his shirt was painted red and clung damply to his chest. He held his hands up a little, seeming unsure what to do.

"Here," Sophie grumbled, teasing out a clean shirt from the bundle of clothes Noah had packed and holding it out to him at arm's length. "I definitely do not want to show up to my parent's house with you wearing that."

Noah pulled the bloodstained shirt off and used the relatively clean backside of the garment to wipe off his legs, arms, and face. He then balled it up and threw it into the darkness of the woods.

"Thanks," he said gratefully, taking the fresh shirt from Sophie and pulling it on. It hung loosely on his gaunt frame.

"Fantastic, now you only look like a sick and starving guy on the brink of death, and not one who's also a murder victim," Leah said.

Noah frowned at her. "What?"

"I would've thought you'd have filled out a little after eating an entire raccoon."

"A person would have been better," Noah said casually. "An animal isn't as compatible."

"Compatible?" May asked, glancing over with a strange

expression.

Noah paused and scratched his neck. "I don't know why I phrased it that way. The raccoon was like... a junky snack. It might have been satisfying at that moment, but it's not exactly a good meal."

"Great, we're back to eating people," Sophie sighed.

"It's not all bad," Noah said. "I can walk on my own now. That's an improvement."

"If you can walk, you can carry your own stuff," Sophie said. She threw his bundle at him and he somehow reacted in time to catch it. "Also, should I be worried about letting you near my family? Are you going to be able to control yourself?"

Noah briefly closed his eyes. "Yeah. It might be a little uncomfortable, but I won't- I won't do anything."

She looked intently at him, trying to gauge if he was just trying to convince himself he would be fine. "Well, if they start to look too tasty, get out of there, okay?"

Noah nodded. He kicked a pebble along the side of the road. "I can't believe this is even something I have to worry about now," he muttered. "This is ridiculous."

"Tell me about it," Brian agreed. "People are going to freak out when they start hearing about this. It's completely scary."

They walked in silence for a few minutes until May eventually looked up with a frown. "If the school tries to track us down, is it really such a good idea for us to be somewhere so obvious? They're bound to check if we have any family in the area."

"They're not the freaking FBI," Sophie said. "But I guess I see your point. I only wanted to pay them a short visit anyway. It would be irresponsible for us to stick around long, especially with Noah here who's one stubbed toe away from losing his mind." She ran a hand through her short hair and sighed. "It's probably a mistake to go there at all. I don't care, though. I want to see them one more time before the *Wager* hits. Partly in case it really does take me out, but also because I'm pretty sure the dust sickness will keep me alive. I need them to see that they worried their little heads off for nothing."

"We don't have to come in," May offered. "I don't mind staying outside while you visit them."

Sophie considered that. "That could work."

Leah quickly shook her head. "If you're worried about your parents' safety, I don't think you should be alone with them. It would be safer if we're all there so we can help control the situation if anyone somehow gets injured. I don't know how much you plan on telling them, but even if you're completely open about everything, they won't be prepared to defend themselves against you suddenly trying to eat them if worse comes to worst."

"If there are more of us in the house, there's a higher chance of something going wrong," Sophie said slowly.

"Yeah, but if you're on your own, the consequences of an accident would be worse," Leah said. "Do whatever you want, though. There's going to be some danger involved no matter what."

Sophie shook her head. "I don't know now. I'll see what the best option feels like once we get there. They might not even be home."

"Call them," Noah suggested.

"I would, but they haven't been answering my calls for the past twenty-four hours." Sophie clenched her fists. "They think if they stick their heads in the sand that everything will be fine."

"Uh, are you sure they'll want to see you tonight?" Brian interjected.

Sophie growled. "Oh, I'm sure they won't, but I don't care. I want to see them, so they're gonna have to face me whether they like it or not."

"Alright then," he said, clasping his hands behind his back. "I'm not one to intervene in family matters."

Despite her words, a nervous air came over Sophie as they continued walking. They reached an intersection and turned right. The first few houses began appearing along the road, along with the occasional welcome streetlight.

May wrapped an arm around her friend. "It'll be okay. Once they see you they'll be glad you visited them," she said softly. "They're just scared that they'll lose you, and they don't know how to deal with their fear."

Sophie bobbed her head quickly. "Yeah, I know. Thanks."

"How far did you say we have to walk?" Noah grumbled with mock fatigue. "We've gone at least fifteen miles already. I've never walked so far in my life."

"We've walked around two miles," Sophie said with a cross look. "The house is a few streets away yet."

"We should have taken a car," Noah opined.

Sophie rolled her eyes.

Despite Noah's complaints, it wasn't long before Sophie stopped in front of a small two-story Tudor house. There were two cars parked on the steeply slanted driveway.

They hung back as Sophie began trudging up to the house, but she beckoned them after her. "I think I'd like you to stick with me, if you don't mind. I know this is a really weird situation. You don't have to if you don't want to."

"We don't mind," May was quick to assure her.

"We don't?" Brian said under his breath, causing Leah to elbow him. They followed Sophie to the doorstep.

"They might be asleep," Sophie said anxiously.

"We can tap their bedroom window," Noah suggested.

Sophie gave him a weird look. "Or we could knock on the front door first like normal people."

She took a deep breath and did exactly that, rapping quickly against the wood.

"Louder," Leah said.

Sophie hammered on the door and then kicked it with a boot for good measure.

"Woah, they're going to think someone's trying to break in," Leah said quickly. She glanced sideways. "Your parents don't own firearms, do they?"

Sophie let out a nervous laugh. "Not last I checked."

She lifted her hand to knock again, but May grabbed her arm. "Listen, they're coming."

They all went silent. Footsteps slowly approached the door and a moment later the face of a middle-aged man appeared in the small glass window. He blinked owlishly at the five of them standing on his doorstep. Then his gaze focused on his daughter and his jaw fell open.

33

PHYSIOLOGICALLY CHANGED

"What," he mouthed, shocked. He glanced behind him. "Cassy!" he yelled. "Sophie's here!"

He withdrew from the window and they heard the bolt unlatch. The door opened to reveal him standing in checkered pajamas. A woman in exactly the same outfit appeared around the corner a second later, and she hesitated at the sight of them all before rushing forward and embracing her daughter.

"Hey, mom," Sophie mumbled.

The woman pulled back. "What are you doing here? Who are these people?"

Sophie smiled. "These are my friends. They were kind enough to come out here with me."

Her parents looked doubtfully at the four students standing behind her. "What's wrong with him?" her dad asked, pointing at Noah.

Noah blinked and froze in place, licking his lips. He had somehow halved the distance between them without realizing it. He swallowed as he stepped slowly back into line with his friends.

"Get it together," Brian whispered harshly into his ear. "These are Sophie's parents. Not your dinner."

Noah shook him off and cleared his throat. "Nothing's wrong with me," he said indignantly to the dad. "Mind your own business."

"You're the one who showed up in my home," he retorted.

"He's sick," Sophie said quickly. They weren't breathing and she didn't see any sign of dust from him at the moment, so she felt comfortable enough adding, "It's not contagious. And it's not the *Wager*, either."

"What the heck is it, then?"

"...We're not sure," Sophie admitted.

"How'd you even get here?" her mom asked, looking out the window and failing to see a car they might have taken.

"Oh, we walked. The school said some fresh air would do me good, and who am I to argue with such an esteemed establishment?"

"They told you to go for a walk at 11 PM?"

"Yeah, can you believe it? I think they're trying to skip out on dealing with my body when I get whacked."

Her parents gaped and seemed to come to the realization that their daughter might very well keel over at any moment. She was at the final hour of the *Wager*.

"You shouldn't have come here," her mom said.

"Well, I did. I'm not gonna walk all the way back to campus now."

They looked at each other. Sophie's face was set stubbornly, while her parents seemed close to panic.

"I suppose you might as well sit down," her dad said finally. He led them into the sitting room, where it quickly became apparent that there would not be enough seats for everyone. Sophie's mom brought in two more chairs from the kitchen. Noah tried to take a seat beside the dad, but Brian quickly took him by the shoulder and guided him to an empty chair on the opposite side of the room. Sophie shot him a thankful look as they passed her.

"I don't think so, buddy," Brian muttered.

Noah sat down obediently and did his best to look like he wasn't actively thinking about eating anyone. He wasn't sure if he succeeded, based on Brian's worried glances.

He knew on a basic level that his thoughts and desires were being influenced by the infection he carried, but that didn't stop it from being effective. Whether it was a function of the sickness or not, he couldn't find within himself any shame for his quite drastic shift in appetite. He knew if he attacked Sophie's parents at this very moment, he would feel no remorse for having consumed a human being. He knew he should, and that he would have been thoroughly repulsed by the idea even a day prior. But he had been physiologically changed by the sickness, and it left him sorely lacking any form of guilt concerning his hunger. He retained at least enough self-awareness to recognize that fact.

"I'm Travis," Sophie's dad introduced himself, breaking Noah out of his self-reflection. "And this is Cassandra."

His wife offered a strained smile.

"Does anyone want a drink of water or anything?" Travis asked.

"No," all five students said simultaneously.

"Oh, excuse me," he muttered.

"Sorry," May squeaked. "I can take some water if you want me to."

He smirked at her reply and just shook his head with a long-suffering sigh.

"Should we change?" Cassandra wondered aloud, her words directed towards her husband. "It just doesn't seem right to host guests in our pajamas."

"I think wearing pajamas is a good sign that it's too late for anyone reasonable to be showing up without warning," Travis said.

"The only reason it was without warning was because you haven't bothered picking up the phone all day," Sophie said accusingly.

"We just wanted you to be getting rest," her mom protested. "You should be saving your energy."

"For what?" Sophie snapped, her voice rising. "Either the *Wager* hits or it doesn't. There's no in-between. The least you could have done was be available to your daughter on what may be her last day alive."

"We had faith in you," Travis said.

"Really? I don't think that's true. Because if you did, you

wouldn't be acting like I've already died." She glanced at the time and smiled savagely. "We'll see soon enough if your faith was justified."

Noah noticed that she failed to mention anything about her hopes regarding the interaction of the second sickness she carried on the outcome of the *Wager*. He shrugged to himself. If she wanted to keep her parents in the dark, that was her decision. Even if it made him somewhat uncomfortable that she was making them worry more than they perhaps had to.

Travis and Cassandra were growing more anxious by the minute, and everyone except Sophie shifted uneasily in their seats. Noah began to regret agreeing to accompany her inside. He looked over at the parents sitting obliviously just a few feet away and had to swallow again. It would be so easy...

I should leave, he thought, but he couldn't make himself stand up.

"So, how's your day been?" Cassandra asked her daughter in a hesitant voice.

Sophie stared at her in disbelief. "You're asking me now?"

"Of course, Soph. We care about you."

Sophie snapped to her feet. "Well, then you should have acted like it. All I wanted..." she drifted off, her expression going blank. A slightly confused look crossed her face.

"What?" Travis asked. "What did you-?"

She stumbled to the side before collapsing across the carpeted floor.

34

DO YOU HAVE ANY PETS

Everyone stared down in shock. It was one thing to know someone had the *Wager*, and another to watch it knock someone to the ground before their very eyes. Perhaps they hadn't truly expected anything to happen. It was difficult to imagine that such a seemingly healthy person could be so suddenly and completely taken out.

Cassandra was the first to react. "Sophie," she breathed, sliding to the floor in a single motion to kneel over her daughter. "Oh, my girl."

She pressed the back of her hand to Sophie's cheek and picked up her limp hand. "She's not breathing," she choked. Tears sprung from her eyes.

Noah shared a glance with his remaining friends. *Should we tell her that's normal? I would feel kind of bad if we got her hopes up for nothing.*

None of them said anything, so he kept his mouth shut.

Travis joined his wife on the floor. He gently took Sophie's hand and gave it a squeeze. "Get up, Soph," he murmured. "Come on. You're strong."

At that moment Sophie's eyes flicked back open.

It took everyone a second to notice, as she made no other bodily movement. Her eyes were unfocused and absolutely still. Cassandra let out a shout of excitement, only to immediately fall back into concern when there was no other sign of life.

"What's happening now?" Travis asked suddenly, peering

close at his daughter's face. He gasped. "Oh, it's awful. I can't look."

"Let me see," Cassandra commanded fearfully. She pulled him away and gave a cry of her own at what she saw.

Blood was beginning to trickle from every orifice on Sophie's expressionless face, pooling in her eye sockets and streaming down her cheeks. Cassandra leaned away in horror, nearly falling over as her daughter's body twitched and began shaking in small violent jerks.

"What's happening to her?" Brian demanded.

"She failed her *Wager*," May murmured.

"It's like it's melting her brain," Leah said with quiet dismay. "How horrible."

The shaking grew weaker and weaker until Sophie lay still once more. The carpet around her head was stained in a dark splotchy halo.

"No," Travis said, trembling. "Why did this happen?"

His wife leaned into him with disbelief across her face. They clutched each other like a stranded man at sea would clutch his only buoy.

Noah looked on with a frown. He had just met Sophie a few hours ago, but so much had happened in that time that he felt like he had just lost a childhood friend. He glanced at May, who really had known Sophie. She had a fixed look in her eyes, an almost angry twist to her brows. She seemed to be mumbling something under her breath.

Noah tilted his head toward her, trying to pick up her words.

"You're not gone," she muttered. "You can heal."

Noah's eyes widened and shot back to Sophie, then to her parents mourning beside her.

So subtly he almost thought it was his imagination, her bloodied face grew gradually gaunt, her eyes and cheeks sinking marginally into the holes in her skull. Blood no longer ran freely and was beginning to dry and crust along her skin like a dark red webbed mask.

Her eyes twitched nearly imperceptibly as her eyelids

started working in small increments to clear the red gunk obstructing her vision.

Noah's attention shifted to her splayed-out limbs and he saw her skin was tightening like shrink-wrap around her bones. She slowly took on a starved appearance, though nobody else appeared to notice the change.

Sophie finally managed to clear her eyes sufficiently to view her surroundings and she stared wildly about the room with horribly bloodshot eyes. There was no recognition in her gaze, only a terrible urgent need.

"Get away," Leah yelled in surprise, rising hastily to her feet. Before anyone could react or figure out what, exactly, they were supposed to get away from, Sophie reared up with such force as though someone had shoved her to her feet.

"Sophie!" Cassandra cried gleefully at her daughter's miraculous revival, but the word morphed into a scream as Sophie lunged teeth-bared towards her. She sank her teeth into her mother's shoulder and her momentum carried them both right back down to the floor.

Travis gaped in absolute bewilderment at the sudden turn of events.

"Help your wife, you idiot!" Leah yelled, diving forward to grab Sophie's narrow frame and attempting to pull her gnashing jaws away from Cassandra. Sophie was just weakened enough for Leah to be able to yank her out of biting range, though not so weak as to allow herself to be completely dragged away.

"What is she doing?" Travis spluttered. "Sophie, stop it!"

"She's a zombie," Leah said in a distracted voice. "She'll eat you too if you're not careful. Help me get her off your wife, will you?"

The man took a hesitant step forward. Sophie was straining desperately against Leah's restraining grasp, lurching forward over and over in mindless repetition and falling just short each time.

"She needs to eat something," May said. "Do you have any pets?"

Travis turned his traumatized gaze on her. "What?"

"A dog, a cat? Maybe a horse?" May said optimistically.

"Ducky," Travis said slowly.

"Unless it's an unreasonably large duck, it won't be enough," May said.

"She's our kitty," Travis said.

May blinked. "A cat is still too small."

"She's a pretty big cat."

"Well, where is she?" May glanced around. "Ducky might need to be sacrificed."

"She's outside somewhere," Travis said. "God knows where."

"I think the cat duck is a lost cause," Leah ground out. "Would anyone mind lending me a hand? Sophie is half an inch from eating her own mother right here." She swiveled suddenly towards her brother. "Brian! You're the one with the insta-win towel method! What are you waiting for?"

"Oh!" Brian yelled, jumping up. "Come on Noah, we can be useful." He set his backpack down beside his sister and knelt down to fish frantically in its pockets. He furrowed his brows, finding only empty space where he knew he had packed them.

"They're not here," he muttered.

Noah decided not to tell his friend about how he had stealthily taken the towels out of the backpack and thrown them into the woods while he wasn't looking.

Brian settled for pulling out a white tech shirt. He sidled closer to Sophie, holding the shirt tensely in front of him as he waited for an opening, and looked back when his friend didn't appear next to him. "Noah?"

"If I get any closer, I'm helping Sophie with her meal," he said honestly. "I don't think you want me to pitch in here."

"Oh," Brian said. "Maybe stay right there then. Good, uh, self-awareness."

Noah nodded shortly, sheer restraint putting a twitch in his eye. "Let me know if you want me to help, though. I'd be very willing to take part."

"Don't you worry, I have it covered." Brian tried to wrangle the shirt around Sophie's head, but she noticed what he was attempting to do before he could succeed and shrieked angrily in recognition of the tactic they had used to subdue Noah. She ducked away and grabbed the sleeve, trying to yank it away.

"Oh, no you don't," Brian growled. He smacked her hand aside and quickly dropped the hem of the shirt around her head.

They watched her expectantly, but she easily shrugged out of it and turned her attention back to Cassandra.

"What?" Leah said, sharing a glance with Brian. They both then looked at Noah.

"Hmm?" he asked. "Why are you looking at me like this is my fault?"

"You're the one who demonstrated that we can't function in the dark," Brian said.

Noah shrugged. "The room is too bright. It only works in perfect darkness; you have to turn the lights off."

Brian threw his hands up. "If we shut off the lights we'll be just as incapacitated as Sophie."

Travis looked over with an attentive look in his eye that made Noah nervous.

"That's right," Leah muttered, oblivious to Travis listening in. She sighed as Sophie continued pulling dumbly against her hold like a rabid animal. "What can we even do now?"

Travis trembled in the corner, clenching and unclenching his fists as he watched the events unfolding in his living room. He finally seemed to make up his mind about something and turned on his heel, stumbling out of the room.

"Hey!" Brian yelled. "This is your family, you coward!"

A moment later Travis returned from the kitchen with a chef's knife in hand. It was long, sturdy, and looked very capable of dealing serious damage to a human body.

"Woah!" Brian choked, completely taken aback. "Who are you planning on using that on? Your daughter?"

"My daughter's dead," he said morosely.

"I don't think you understand what's happening here," Leah said quickly. "You'll only make it worse if you hurt her more. It's better to try incapacitation."

"Yes," he said. "With a knife." He raised the blade forward. It was shaking like a maraca. "I have to be strong for Cassy."

Sophie managed to snag a small bite while the siblings were distracted. Cassandra screeched wordlessly, trying to pull away, but she couldn't break Sophie's grip.

Leah yanked Sophie's head back. The crazed girl snapped at her angrily before turning back to strain her jaws towards her mother.

"All you need to do is get yourself and your wife out of here!" Leah yelled at Travis. "Do you *want* to murder Sophie?"

Travis' knuckles were white. "Look at her. It's just like you said. She's- she's a zombie. She'll just attack someone else if I run away, and I can't let my feelings put others in danger." He pointed the knife at them. "Move aside. You think I want to do this? Don't make it any more difficult for me."

Brian turned to look at Noah. "Stop him," he said quickly.

35

HUNGRY

Noah didn't give Brian any time to change his mind. He leapt from the seat like a man shot from a cannon, flying across the room in an instant and latching onto the man.

"Woah! Watch it!" Travis yelled in surprise. Then Noah tore away a small piece of his arm, and the man shrieked, wrenching himself back and pointing the knife at him. "Ow! What the- you're another one!"

Noah barely heard him. He gnawed on his prize, a blissful expression passing over his face as he finally felt some of his energy return to him.

"I don't know what I expected," Brian groaned, watching Noah chewing happily away. "I just need you to keep him off us, Noah!"

Leah shot her brother an irritated look. "What did you think would happen, you idiot?"

"He looked like he had himself under control," Brian protested. "Noah, stop!"

Noah registered Brian's words and chose to ignore them. Travis presented a perfect opportunity; he could satiate himself while also protecting his friends. Besides, now that he'd started eating, he didn't feel like stopping so soon.

He stepped forward eagerly, but Travis waved the point of the knife threateningly at his chest, making him hesitate.

"That's right, don't come any closer," the man warned. "I'm going to walk past you now. Don't try anything."

Noah stared at him unblinkingly. If this man was willing to kill his own daughter because she was a so-called 'zombie', he would have no issue slaying him as well. Noah narrowed his eyes. The guy was trying to get him to lower his guard.

With an angry yell, Noah leapt forward.

Travis' eyes widened and he braced the knife in front of him.

Noah didn't pull back. He wrapped his hands around the man, pulling him close, and chomped at the base of his neck. He paused just long enough to observe that Travis had driven the blade of the knife deep into his chest, and mentally shrugged before planting his face back between the man's neck and shoulder. Usually that would be a concern, but with the lack of pain, it didn't seem like an issue that needed to be immediately addressed. Heat spread in pulsing waves from the wound, siphoning away his energy, yet Noah found any vitality lost was replenished as soon as it disappeared. He just had to keep eating. A strange pain seemed to scrape at the interior of his skull, but he pushed the annoying sensation aside.

Travis scrambled weakly to escape Noah's assault. He was already backed against a wall, leaving nowhere for him to run. He let go of the knife and tried to press Noah's head away, but Noah just chomped on the man's hand in an automatic motion as soon as it neared his mouth.

Travis screamed raggedly, gasping for air between his cries. He slowly dropped down the wall, losing strength, and Noah leaned down after him easily.

"Noah, stop," someone pleaded beside him. Noah looked up to see May.

"Do you want some?" he asked after he swallowed his current mouthful.

She froze for a moment before shaking her head. "Noah, this isn't right. You're going to kill him if you don't stop."

"Okay," Noah said, picking at a bit of Travis stuck between his teeth. "I'm still hungry." Why couldn't she just leave him alone? He itched at the warm spot on his chest.

May finally noticed the handle of the knife stabbing a hole through his shirt into his ribcage, and she grimaced. "Oh," she muttered. "Let me take that out for you, okay?"

Noah glanced longingly at the man cowering against the wall, but he nodded grudgingly. "If you must. But be quick."

"Come over here, I need better light," May said, guiding him gently away from Travis' shaking form.

"Come on, it's plenty bright," Noah complained.

"Let's go in the kitchen," she suggested.

"Why?"

"Stop complaining."

Noah followed her into the other room. She pulled out a chair at the table and gestured for him to sit down.

May pulled a face at the knife, but set her jaw and took hold of the handle. She heaved back on it and the blood-streaked blade came silently unsheathed from Noah's chest.

"Ugh," she mumbled. "That's horrible."

Noah stood up. "Thanks."

"Wait," she said quickly. "Sit down."

"What now?" he asked crossly.

"You've already eaten plenty," May said calmly. "You don't need any more. Just stay here until the parents leave."

"I need to eat," Noah said, aggravated. He pulled up his shirt to look at the wound, but it had already closed. He poked at it in confusion.

"See?" May asked. "You're all healed. Don't let your hunger control you. You don't need it right now."

Now that Travis wasn't sitting enticingly right in front of him, Noah found he was able to consider his current state more carefully. The urgency he had felt as his energy was being actively drained away had disappeared. "I can stay here," he said slowly, surprising himself. "But I don't know how long I can resist. He's- he's right there," he murmured, nearly standing up to wander back into the sitting room before he got ahold of himself and he forced his body to relax.

May smiled at him. "Good. I'm going to go help Travis get outside. All you need to do is stay right here. If you feel like it's getting too difficult, you can call for me and I'll come right back. Is that alright?"

"I can do that," Noah said quietly. He began to feel ashamed that she had to treat him like this. Like some kind of dumb needy child. *I won't need her help*, he promised himself.

Suddenly Travis burst into the kitchen, flinching at the sight of Noah, and skittered across the room to a door beside the stove. He flung it open and stumbled through, descending the staircase that was revealed.

"Hey, where are you going?" May called after him. "You need to get out of the house!"

Travis' only response was a distant frightened yelp.

"That idiot," May muttered, staring down after him into the basement. "What does he think he's going to do down there?"

"I can go help him," Noah offered.

"I think you're confusing 'help' with 'eat'," May said lightly. She looked towards the living room. "Let's forget about him for now. Cassandra still needs help, though I have no idea how Sophie is winning out against three people. She's not exactly a large person."

She left Noah behind to hurry into the sitting room.

Noah wished he could help too, that he could be assured that he wouldn't just make their job twice as difficult. He wanted to team up with his friends to save Sophie, and maybe even Sophie's mom too. Yet even as he thought about going over, another part of him knew he was just trying to make up an excuse to get closer to Cassandra. He couldn't even trust his own motives, he thought angrily.

As he was trying to pinpoint the exact rationale of his conflicting thoughts, a distant "A-ha!" came floating up from downstairs.

A second later, every light in the house went out all at once.

36

ENTIRELY THEIR FAULT

Had the sun not long since dipped under the horizon, there would have been some amount of light filtering through the blinds of the window in the kitchen. But the late hour meant that with the interior lights shut off, there was simply no visibility to be had.

The sharp scuffling sounds of movement in the sitting room disappeared, allowing Noah to hear the frightened sobs of Cassandra.

If I can get over to her, nobody will know if I take a few bites, he was unable to stop himself from thinking. He shook his head, struggling to shut out the useless thought. It would be impossible for him to cross the handful of feet into the other room, even with the woman's cries to guide him. Already he felt himself sinking into the familiar numbness of the void, his limbs disappearing from his awareness until all he was aware of was his own thoughts. He tried to stretch his hand out in front of him, but it was as if his brain had forgotten that he had an arm to begin with. The best he could do was hope he would still be upright in the chair when he regained his senses. The lack of any immediate noises of impact gave him hope this would be the case.

He eventually picked up the sound of Travis climbing the stairs. The man must have been unfairly exploiting his ability to feel to allow him to sense his way up.

Then the door opened, revealing that he actually was using the dim light of his phone to see.

In a moment of spectacular self-discipline, Noah refrained from immediately demonstrating why it had been a moronic decision to turn on a flashlight after going through the effort of shutting off the house's electricity. Instead he calmly said, "You should turn that off."

Travis shone the light at him uncomprehendingly, so Noah narrowed his eyes and stood in a sudden, startling motion, then took a small step towards the man.

He didn't truly intend to do more than scare him into better caution, but Travis reacted with a scream loud enough to probably wake his neighbors and his arms spasmed in surprise, sending his phone flying.

It bounced off the corner of the table and fell to the floor, skittering and spinning before coming to rest with the light shining upwards.

Noah stopped in front of Travis anticlimactically and watched him shrink against the wall across from him, arms raised against the attack he was certain was imminent.

"Well, go on," Noah said. "Take your light and get out of here."

The man slowly straightened, fright and uncertainty clear on his face. "I thought you were-" he began.

"Hurry up!" Noah snapped, ducking down to grab the light and holding it out to him. "I'm not sure why I'm even bothering to help you, so get out of here before I change my mind!"

Noah was beginning to severely doubt the man's intelligence by the time he finally took the phone back. He snatched it quickly like a small starving animal might take food from a person.

"If you don't turn it off, Sophie will fight you," Noah warned. "You can judge for yourself if that's worth your ability to see. Just know that she'll be worse off than you in the dark."

"Thanks," Travis muttered. He covered the light with his hand, judging how dark the room became, and seemed unhappy with the total lack of visibility.

"I'll turn it off if things get out of hand," he decided, and he grabbed the knife off the table before stepping quickly into the sitting room.

Noah moved a little to get a good view of the proceedings, but didn't dare get any closer. As nervous as he was about how Travis would use that knife, he knew he would only make things worse by getting involved. All it took was one momentary lapse of control and his friends would be dealing with him and Sophie simultaneously.

Noah was hopeful that the situation would resolve peacefully now that Travis had control over the light in the room. It was essentially an off-switch for everyone except him and his wife; as long as he played his cards well, he could hypothetically escape without any further bloodshed.

The weak beam of light swinging into the room acted as a clapboard for action to resume. In the brief respite afforded to her by the dark, Cassandra had managed to drag herself away from the others, but she was bleeding so heavily from her wounds that she had barely managed to clear the room before collapsing from weakness.

Noah's friends had ended up haphazardly scattered across the floor. They stirred as light fell into the room, struggling to regain their senses.

Through sheer random luck, Sophie happened to be the closest to Cassandra, and she immediately honed in on the fallen woman. She dashed across the room, reveling in the lack of pesky restraining friends, and dove upon her mother.

"NO!" Travis yelled, darting after her. He pushed past the three students, bracing the knife towards Sophie's back as he moved.

Noah's breath would have caught if it wasn't already gone. The man hadn't hesitated to stab him earlier, but he had been cornered and caught by surprise. Looking back on it, Noah had more stabbed himself onto the blade than been truly attacked by Travis. It was an entirely different thing to run after someone and stab them from behind, let alone if that person was one's own daughter.

Travis must have truly believed that he had no other option, because he didn't flinch away. He drove the weapon down into the back of Sophie's neck, pulled it out, and punctured the same spot over and over in brutal repetition.

Noah's stomach twisted, but Sophie didn't even react. She was too engrossed with her meal to notice anything was amiss. Her flesh was healing at impossible speeds, nearly closing up completely between each plunge of the knife.

Everyone else froze, watching the violence play out between the family. Nobody knew who they should be trying to save anymore. They had been protecting Cassandra, and now Travis had taken over that job, although his method was considerably more violent. So much for no bloodshed.

Travis was not deterred by the slow progress. He whittled steadily away, a terrible grimace fixed on his face.

Is he really going to be able to kill her? Noah wondered nervously.

Sophie finally looked back, becoming aware of the warmth in her neck, and tried to bite Travis' arm. Unlike Cassandra, however, who was now presumably unconscious, Travis fought back. He grabbed Sophie's head and slammed her skull to the ground beside Cassandra, receiving a terrible bite to his wrist in the process. Gritting his teeth at the pain, he planted a knee on her back and twisted her head to the side to regain access to the same spot on her neck, getting right back to his grisly work.

Without a steady intake of food and energy, Sophie's healing became a lot less effective. Her limbs shriveled further and further into sickly skeletal things even as the wound in her neck deepened.

She's lost, Noah suddenly knew.

Travis had the same thought. He raised the knife for one last blow and brought the blade clear through Sophie's neck.

Her head came clean off and dropped to the floor. The expression left on her face was inhuman, completely twisted by hunger. Some blood- oddly dark blood- dripped from each side of the decapitation wound, though not nearly as much as there would normally have been.

She was fully and completely dead.

Travis heaved deep breaths, just looking down at what he had done. The knife dropped from his hand alongside tears from his bloodshot eyes.

"Cassy," he said, leaning down to his wife. "Cassy, I did it."

There was so much blood around her that Noah was certain the woman had already died, but to his immense surprise her eyes cracked slowly open.

"What did you do?" she asked softly.

Travis looked at the beheaded body of his daughter. "I saved you from a monster," he whispered.

Cassandra turned her head weakly to gaze into Sophie's lifeless eyes. "That's my daughter," she breathed. She didn't breathe back in.

"No!" Travis growled. "I killed the zombie! You're safe!"

There was no response. He was kneeling beside two corpses.

For a very long moment, nobody moved. Travis slowly drooped to the floor as though he had no energy left to remain upright.

Then, in one sudden movement, he grabbed the knife off the floor and turned to the four remaining students.

"Why did you come here?" he demanded hoarsely. "What made you think you should come anywhere near my family?"

Noah was suddenly struck by the recognition that this tragedy was entirely their fault, starting from when they had first agreed to sit beside Sophie at the picnic table. If they had stayed inside, Sophie would never have gotten their sickness. She would have passed away in her little housing unit without anyone being the wiser, and her parents would've been informed the next day.

"This was a horrible mistake," Noah said. "All of this."

Travis' hollow eyes bored into him. "Damn right, it was. You've killed my family. I don't even know your name, and you've destroyed my life."

Noah didn't know what to say. He had to look away.

Travis waved the knife, forcing his attention back to him. "I hope you never forgive yourself for what you've done tonight. It better haunt you to the day your miserable life finally ends."

"I'm truly sorry," Noah mumbled.

Travis stared at him for a long moment. "This is your fault, too," he said, and turned the blade of the knife to face his own chest. Before anyone could do anything, he pushed it into his heart.

37

WHAT NOW

"No!" May yelled, rushing to his side. "Why would you do this?"

Travis glared hatefully at her. "You've taken everything from me. I see no reason to suffer needlessly through a life without my only sources of joy.

"Besides, I know how this looks! You think there's any future for me where I'm not locked up for killing my kid?"

May gazed at him sadly. "There isn't anymore."

We didn't take everything from him, Noah thought grimly. *He still had his life. He chose to take that from himself.* Of course, that fact didn't excuse any of their choices leading up to this point.

Leah and Brian drew up beside May, but there was nothing any of them could do. Travis clutched the knife shakily against himself as if one of them would try to pull it out, though none of them made any move to do so. There was no coming back from a pierced heart, not with the terribly slow regeneration of an uninfected person. His muscles slowly relaxed as blood loss drained his strength, and his head drooped to his chest.

He went from listless to dead within the minute. Just like that, Sophie's family was gone. All that remained were three cooling bodies laying beside one another. None of them had died with a tranquil expression, though even if they had, the sheer quantity of blood surrounding them would have tipped off any uninformed viewer that they had not gone out peacefully.

Noah gazed bleakly at the scene. He had never been exposed to anything close to this level of violence in his uninfected life, and the scene now spread out before him felt sharper, more real than anything he'd ever faced before. He was glad the sight of the bodies no longer filled him with hunger. He knew instinctively that it was because they were no longer alive, not a result of a change in his symptoms, but he took solace in the moment of self-composure regardless. He was not proud of what the sickness was turning him into, but if this were the closest he could get to normalcy, he would enjoy it while he could. *I just have to stay away from anyone who doesn't have the sickness,* he thought gloomily. *Then I can live life like normal. Well, mostly normal.*

For a moment he allowed himself to indulge in a highly implausible fantasy, imagining what it would be like if everyone at Oakridge got infected and a community formed where they could all exist without worrying about eating each other. *I probably shouldn't hope for that outcome, as nice as it sounds.* Any new students would have to be okay with willingly infecting themselves; it would need to be a requirement of enrollment. He laughed aloud at the thought. A zombie campus. The amount of signage warning away normal people would be crazy.

"What the heck do we do now?" Brian asked quietly.

"Definitely not stay here," Leah said.

"Let's talk in the kitchen until we know where we want to go," May suggested.

They did as she suggested, keen to get out of the sitting room. Leah snagged a chair so that there were enough seats for them all around the table.

"We're not thinking about going back to campus, right?" Noah wanted to confirm.

The siblings exchanged a glance and shook their heads.

"We should warn people about how the *Wager* interacts with the sickness," May said. "I'm not saying we should personally go back to campus to tell everyone, but we should make sure the information gets out there. There could be more people like Sophie who think they've found an effective cure."

"I doubt there's anyone else on campus with the *Wager*," Noah mused. "And to be honest, we should've seen it coming. It's not like we didn't know what would happen if someone got injured."

"I didn't connect the dots that the *Wager* kills people by destroying their internal organs," Leah said. "My brain kinda skipped right to the instant death result."

"Yeah, unfortunately it wasn't so instant. I wonder how close it came to actually killing Sophie before the healing kicked in."

"We're getting off track," Brian interrupted. "We can't stay here. We are not stealing Sophie's house after killing her family."

"We could go see your dad," Leah said to Noah.

He slowly turned to her with a murderous look and she held her hands up. "That was a joke. Don't eat me."

Noah rolled his eyes.

"We know how family get-togethers end up," Brian said. "Nearby relatives are off the table."

"Maybe we should've just stayed on campus," May said. Before anyone could argue, she tried to explain, "More than just preventing this whole disaster with Sophie, I think we might really have been able to help Insight find out more about what's wrong with us. I get that they have a bad track record with their patients, but would that really be an issue for us? We wouldn't feel anything they did, and they would be very highly motivated to avoid injuring us. Going to them is our best shot at ending up with a real cure."

"You make a good point," Leah reluctantly conceded. "But part of the original reason we left was because the visit to Insight wasn't presented to us as our choice. Dr. Jansen should have asked if we were interested in an appointment. If she had only made all the same arguments you just did, we probably would have agreed. Going about it in the way she did only served to scare us all away."

"We can still go back," May said. "They don't have to know we ever left."

"Except that Sophie will have mysteriously disappeared. Some concerned neighbor will eventually find her and her parents here, and who knows what sort of conclusions will be made from there," Brian said.

"Speaking of which, we should call the police once we leave the house. I would feel horrible if we just left the family rotting here indefinitely," Noah said.

Leah looked a little uncertain at the idea of involving law enforcement, but Brian and May nodded, and she didn't argue. "Fine. So I'm guessing since nobody has thrown out any ideas yet that don't involve turning ourselves over to Insight, we have no clue where to spend the night?"

May scowled. "We should just keep it in mind as an option."

"If we need to we could literally just lay down somewhere in the woods," Noah suggested. "Nobody would find us there."

"But we'd be so vulnerable," Brian protested. "If we're sleeping, we won't know that we're being eaten alive by wolves or whatever until it's too late. We would never know what happened, we'd just be gone."

"We could go back to the mausoleum," Noah said half-heartedly, the mention of wolves reminding him of the place. "We never told anyone where we got the dust. Nobody would look for us there of all places."

"Do you really want to walk all the way there?" Brian wasn't keen on this suggestion. "That ancient zombie is still in there. Unless it somehow got out and is now roaming town."

"Well, the zombie was inert for most of the time we were there," Noah said, mostly just to argue. "It was pretty much a regular dead body until we touched its pendant, and I'm like ninety-nine percent sure it returned to normal after we covered the coffin back up. Plus, we're zombies too, now. It won't eat us. Probably."

"I think going to the mausoleum is a good idea," Leah said

suddenly. When they looked doubtfully at her, she explained, "We should get that pendant. It's definitely involved with everything that's happened so far; if anything can help us find a cure, that necklace can. We'd have to be stupid not to go after such an obvious potential windfall."

Brian groaned. "Well, I don't want to be infected forever. Maybe it's worth the risk. If going back to that freaky place will help us find a way to get back to normal, then I say screw it. Let's go." He stood up and pushed in his chair.

Noah stood up as well. "I'm good with that. I don't want to hang around here any longer."

"Fine, but we still need to figure out what we're doing in the morning," May reminded them. "As safe as it might be, I don't want to be staying in a mausoleum for the next several days."

With no further reason to stick around, they got up from the table and made their way to the front door. Noah glanced briefly at the bodies and shuddered. His friends kept their gazes averted from the sight altogether as they picked up their various bags and clothes where they had been thrown aside in the sitting room.

When they had all their things, they opened the door and exited the household.

38

'ZOMBIE' FEELS DEROGATORY
SOMEHOW

Lounging cooly on the sidewalk was an enormous white cat with a yellow collar. It hadn't been there when they first walked up to the house.

Upon noticing it, everyone's heads swiveled to stare at Noah in panic, but he didn't make a move towards the animal.

"What? I'm not that desperate," he said. "It'd take a lot for me to go back to non-human food."

"I wish you meant that in the normal sense," Brian muttered. "When did you get so weird?"

"Hey, we all have the same sickness," Noah said, crouching down to pet the cat. It started purring immediately.

"Let's get moving," May said, watching Noah nervously.

He straightened. "You guys have no trust."

"And I think we're well justified in that. Let's go."

They kept walking, leaving the cat behind. It meowed pitifully at their retreating backs but thankfully didn't try to follow.

"That stupid animal might have saved Sophie's family if it weren't prancing around outside," Leah said.

"Ducky's a smart kitty," Noah defended the cat, feeling irrationally protective. "It knew it'd be dinner if it went inside, and Sophie might well have still been hungry afterwards. Not sure what'll happen to it now that its family is gone, but I'm sure it'll figure things out. Cats are resourceful, you know?"

"...Sure," Brian said. "You gonna call the police now?"

"Not until we're a couple blocks away."

They turned left off of the driveway and set off with May leading the way. Noah wouldn't have known which way to go, but she seemed confident enough that he didn't question her choice in direction. Brian and Leah already had the flashlights out; the sparsely placed street lamps left large swathes of the road in shadow.

"You realize there's a decent chance somebody will figure out our involvement," Leah warned. "It's not that I don't think you should make the call, but you need to be aware that we could find ourselves in some serious trouble."

"I'm aware," Noah assured her. "But as much as Travis obviously blamed us, we're not personally responsible for any of the deaths in that house. Although we could have prevented... well, everything, probably, I have some confidence that we won't be convicted of murder if they work out that we were there. We were just a couple of poor bystanders."

"Insight could get us in trouble if they tell the authorities about our sickness," Leah worried. "All it would take is somebody over there catching wind of the awful thing that happened nearby and sticking their noses into the situation. Their scientists could probably take one look at the scene and know exactly what went down. It wouldn't exactly take a master of forensics to figure out that Sophie was eating Cassandra. They could make the argument that we put the family in danger just by our presence; the possibility that we could also get wounded, and they'd be right."

"We could say we didn't know about the danger," Brian said uncertainly. "Though I'm not sure anyone would believe that."

"Look," Noah said. "I know that it might not be the most cautious or logical decision to call the police to a scene we were involved in, but I'm not calling them out of a commitment to our fine legal system. I'm doing it because I'd feel like absolute garbage if I left a family to rot in their own home."

"No, I feel the same way," Leah agreed. "Which is why I'm not going to try to stop you. Get out your phone and call them now. We're far enough from the house. We don't want to wait until we're at the mausoleum; they can probably track the call."

"Alright." Noah got his phone out and hesitated nervously. "I've never actually called the cops before," he admitted.

"I can do it," Leah offered easily.

"No, it's fine." He steeled himself and dialed.

Soon a man's voice answered. "What's your emergency?"

Noah was suddenly kicking himself for not planning out what to say. What should he do, just straight up say a whole family had died? "Uh, something really bad has happened. The address is..." he trailed off and looked around in alarm.

"80 Birchwood Lane," Leah sighed, rubbing her temples.

"You hear that?" Noah asked the phone.

"80 Birchwood Lane, yes. Can you share any more details about the reason for your call?"

"Three people have died." Noah decided to just spit it out. There was no reason to be furtive about it. "Two of them died to stab wounds and one was... um, eaten alive."

"Are you in a safe place currently?"

"Yeah. The guy who stabbed the first person turned the knife on himself afterwards. We're not at the house anymore."

"*That's enough,*" Leah mouthed at him.

"Um. Have a good day," Noah said, interrupting whatever the guy was trying to say next, and hung up. Worried that they would try to call him back, he immediately shut off his phone.

"You could have ended the conversation better," Brian grumbled.

Noah punched him without looking over, not noticing that the shot missed him by a foot. "I didn't say anything I shouldn't have, did I?"

Leah shrugged. "We should be fine. They'll go to the house and see what happened. I say we've done our job."

"I kind of wanted to just give the guy the address and hang

up," Noah confessed. "I guess this is better, though."

Brian chuckled. "Good thing you didn't. That would've been suspicious as heck."

They turned onto another road and Noah was glad to recognize the stone brick wall lining each side of the road.

"Hey, we're practically there already!" Brian said in surprise. "Going to the mausoleum might not have been such a bad decision after all."

"Were you ranking the options based on how far you'd have to walk to each one?" Noah asked accusingly.

"Of course."

They began to hear the sound of sirens distantly behind them, though no vehicles drove down the road they were currently walking along.

"Good. They'll find them," Leah said. "I might actually be able to sleep tonight."

Noah nodded. "This is the spot, right?"

They had arrived at the sign marking the entrance to the trail.

Brian pointed at where it said *Hours: Dawn to Dusk* and smirked. "Aw, guys, we have to pick another destination, the trail's closed."

Leah walked past him onto the trail, not slowing in the slightest. "We're zombies; we're supposed to wander around in the dead of night."

"'Zombie' feels derogatory somehow," Brian mused.

"Oh, do we need proper non-offensive terminology now? What would you prefer?"

"I'm fine if people want to think of us as zombies," Noah commented. "Otherwise we're just plain cannibals. At least this way we have an excuse for how we're acting."

"How you're acting," Leah corrected. "We haven't eaten anyone."

"Don't you have to be an actual corpse to be a zombie?" Brian wondered. "If you forget about our lungs and heart not working at the moment, we're not dead. Nobody would be able to tell anything's wrong with us until we try to eat them."

"Yeah, Sophie's parents sure made that clear," Leah muttered.

"Functioning lungs and heart are a pretty strong indicator of life," Noah said. "There's a reason Dr. Jansen got so freaked out."

"We're special," Leah said drily. "Special zombies."

"But not for much longer," Brian hoped. "We'll get this pendant and it'll reveal the secret to un-zombifying ourselves. Then we can go back to campus and cure everyone else, and everything will go back to normal."

Brian's flashlight suddenly turned off, prompting the friends to all look at him.

"Uh, I didn't turn it off," he said, just as surprised as the rest of them. "It must have died." He clicked the button several times and shook the device, but it remained dark.

"It's okay, we have another one," May said.

"I would have liked to have a backup," Brian muttered. "Nothing to be done about it now, I guess."

They continued into the darkness of the woods.

39

ILLUMINATION

"Reseat the batteries," Noah suggested. "Sometimes that works."

Brian shot him a disgruntled look. "You want to try that? Have your fingers magically regained their fine motor function?"

"Ah, right. Never mind."

"I'm just glad I thought to bring along a spare. Leah, protect that thing with your life."

"Of course," she said stoically. "We can pick up new batteries tomorrow morning at the Corner Market. We'll have to convince someone in town to install them for us."

"I wouldn't be surprised if the store is closed," Noah said. "I definitely infected David."

Brian shook his head in disappointment. "I liked David. Why'd you have to get him?"

"Oh, like any of us had any clue what was happening."

"I don't even know where else we could go to get batteries," Leah admitted, ignoring Brian's teasing. "I go to the Corner Market for everything."

"I'm sure there's another viable place somewhere around town," Noah said, although he had no idea where that might be. He was just as reliant on the Corner Market as every other Oakridge student.

"This light better not give out tonight," Leah said threateningly, shaking the remaining flashlight as if she could scare it into proper behavior. "It's pitch-black inside the mausoleum; we'll be trapped if the light happens to die overnight."

"Uh, I really don't like the idea of that happening," Brian said worriedly. "Maybe one of us should stay outside while the rest of us investigate."

"And sleep outside, too?" Noah shook his head. "We have to be careful about where we sleep. I mean, people generally are, but with the way we are now, we especially can't afford to leave ourselves out in the open like that. I'd say it would be a better idea to leave the door cracked all night, but then animals might get in and we'd be no better off than if we were outside."

May looked at Brian. "Did you bring any candles and matches?"

He grinned in surprise as she jogged his memory, pleased at his own foresight. "Hey, I did! There's our solution. We'll have to keep a careful eye on the light to make sure it doesn't go out, but it's still safer than relying on a couple of old batteries. We can take shifts or something." He furrowed his brow. "Although, I'm not sure how good the ventilation is in there. I'd hate to give us all carbon monoxide poisoning."

His three companions stared at him.

"We're not breathing," Leah said.

Brian blinked at her and then rubbed his eyes. "Sorry, yeah. It's been a long day. Although in my defense, it's super weird that we're just casually not breathing without any issues."

Noah focused on his own lack of breath for a moment and tried to inhale. He honestly couldn't tell if he was filling his lungs with air or not without the sensation of air moving past his lips. He held a hand to his mouth and attempted to exhale, but of course he didn't feel any breath on his deadened fingers.

His friends watched in concern as he struggled to produce a breath. It was such a similar action to breathing that it should have been easy, but no matter how hard Noah tried, he couldn't tell if he was expelling any air.

"I don't think I could breathe if I wanted to," Noah finally said, his tone neutral. He looked at Brian. "You're right that it's super weird. Oxygen is needed for our cells to perform cellular respiration. It's needed for life!"

"I'll take your word for that," Brian said with the obliviousness of someone who had probably failed ninth grade science.

Noah rolled his eyes. "It's basic biology. If we aren't using oxygen to produce energy, then what are we running off of? What's our power source?"

"As gross as it sounds... flesh?" Leah suggested tentatively.

Noah shook his head. "None of you have eaten anyone yet, and you're all functioning fine. Me and Sophie only got hungry when we were injured, which implies that whatever mysterious energy is fueling our usual activities doesn't contribute toward regeneration. As soon as we get hurt, our own bodies suddenly become up for grabs, and we start shriveling away unless we can get ahold of something to eat."

Noah nodded to himself, then paused with a confused expression. "Except, that doesn't make sense either! Energy from food can usually only be utilized by cells when in the presence of oxygen, so I have no idea how I've managed to gain energy from digesting a whole raccoon and a bit of a person when I haven't had breath or a heart rate since lunch."

"Maybe we're breathing through our skin," Brian said excitedly. "Like frogs!"

Everyone else gave him an incredulous look.

"Hey, frogs are cool," Brian protested.

Noah pinched the bridge of his nose. "I can agree with that, but there are so many reasons why it's unlikely that we have suddenly gained the capability to perform cutaneous respiration.

And even if we had, it wouldn't help us without proper circulation. How do you think oxygen gets to your cells?"

"Look, just because you're a bio major doesn't give you the right to shoot down my awesome ideas," Brian complained. "We don't know anything for sure. Would you have thought we could even be alive right now? This conversation in itself is a miracle of science. Don't tell me something can't happen just because it's 'unlikely'."

"You're right," Noah admitted. "Maybe we are breathing through our skin at this very moment. Maybe we'll wake up tomorrow and have completed our full transformation into frogs! It's unlikely, but anything's possible! Right?"

"Now you're just being facetious," Brian grumbled. "Forget I said anything. What were you talking about? Digesting things?"

"Maybe you haven't digested anything," May murmured to herself. She looked over hesitantly. "I have no idea what digestive insanity happens when one of us eats something- I mean, you ate a raccoon; that's not normal- but maybe the food is being used in a completely different manner than usual. Some way that optimizes it for healing somehow, though I have no idea how that would be. I'm no bio major."

"I bet Insight could figure it out," Brian said.

"Not that you would ask them," Leah said with a sharp look at her brother.

"No, I'm just saying." He squinted ahead and groaned. "Guys, we're at the cemetery. We missed the trail to our mausoleum."

"No way," Leah complained, but he was right. The light traced the contours of the gravestones ahead of them.

"Well, let's go back, then," Noah muttered. "It's how we found the trail the first time anyway; with any luck we'll stumble across it again in the same way."

The four of them turned around and headed back the way they'd come.

"Should we be worrying about running into those wolves again?" Noah asked. "They're probably long gone, right?"

"Actually, we should definitely be worrying about running into them," Leah said nonchalantly. "Wolves sometimes roam the same area for multiple nights in a row. They could be stalking us right now."

They all looked behind them, but the trail was empty.

"Or," Brian said pointedly, giving his sister a disappointed look, "they could be several dozen miles away by now. The pack probably isn't around."

"I can't hear any howling," May said hopefully.

"Wolves typically don't howl when they're tracking prey," Leah informed her.

"Okay, let's stop with the ominous wolf facts," Noah said.

She shrugged. "They're either here or they're not. Nothing I say will change that."

"Yes, it will," Brian admonished her. "The universe will punish you for pushing your luck. You'll summon a whole new pack of wolves to our location."

"I think I see our junction," Noah interrupted excitedly.

"Hey, you're right," Leah said, shining the light forward. "Sweet, we didn't waste our time coming out here."

They wordlessly filed onto the correct path. After they had been trudging along for a minute, Leah's flashlight alarmingly began to sputter a little. Their surroundings flashed in and out of darkness, making Noah feel dizzy.

Leah smacked the light and it stopped flashing, although it was about half as bright as it had been. "I think this one needs new batteries, too," she said. "Brian, can you get those candles out now? This thing could die at any moment and I don't want to find out the hard way if the moonlight is bright enough to see by."

"Yeah, give me one second," Brian said. Leah shone the light at him as he dropped his bag to the ground and dug around in one of the pockets, coming up a moment later with two tea light candles and a matchbook. All three items looked completely unused. He struck a match and lit one of the candles, then handed it carefully to Noah. "Don't let the wax spill on your hands."

Noah nodded and watched the small pool of liquid grow around the wick as the wax melted. It was strange to be leery of hurting himself for a reason other than pain.

Brian quickly lit the second candle for himself and let the match burn almost to his fingers before pinching it quickly with his other hand. He tossed the small stub of cardboard to the ground, zipped up his bag and stood up.

"Turn off the flashlight," he told his sister.

"You sure?" She seemed nervous about it, but did as he requested.

For a split second their eyes struggled to adjust to the dimmer illumination of the candles, everything going black except the two weak flickering points of light. Before they could begin to lose sense of themselves, though, their sight crept reluctantly back until they could all see each other once more. It was a warmer, more fluttery sort of light, but it would serve their purposes until they could get new batteries.

Noah had never relied on a candle as his only source of illumination, and he was pleasantly surprised by its brightness. He'd only ever seen candles burn in a room already lit with electrical lights, and it undersold how much light such a small flame could put off.

"I have a couple more candles, so we should hopefully be good until morning," Brian said. "We can keep the flashlight close at hand if there's any emergencies. But there won't be any, right, Noah? You're not going to drop your candle."

"Of course not."

"I'd light more candles for May and Leah, but I don't have enough to be careless with how we use them. I'm trying to be at least a little conservative here."

"It's okay," May reassured him. "We just need to stick close together and we'll be fine."

They walked along the trail until the clearing came into view, and they slowed as they moved towards the mausoleum. The stocky structure was nearly invisible until they were right in front of it.

"We made it," May said quietly.

"You didn't expect us to?" Leah asked with a small smile.

"I half expected it to have disappeared," she said. "Not for any real reason, I guess."

"Let's just get inside before the wolves can make a surprise return," Noah said.

The door was still missing its handle, which would have been quite a problem if it hadn't been left slightly ajar.

Without another word, the four of them slipped inside.

40

DON'T TELL ME I JUST BURNED MY OWN FINGER OFF FOR NOTHING

Everything was just as Noah remembered inside the mausoleum, including the coffin across the room in the place of honor. It was the first thing his eyes were drawn to, seeking confirmation that it was still firmly shut.

"Alright, I vote that we wait till morning to grab the pendant," Leah said, pulling the door closed behind them. "In case it wakes up that zombie again. I'd like to get a good night's sleep before we have to deal with that, and it would be great for there to be actual sunlight outside so we can escape if we need to."

"Excellent idea," Noah said, setting the candle carefully on the ground and then flopping down beside it. "I need sleep."

"You took a nap right before we left," Brian said.

"I don't care. Wake me up when it's morning. Extremely late into the morning. I'm not skipping school just to wake up at seven AM."

"We all need to take a shift to watch the candles," Brian informed him sternly. "So you're going to miss out on a few hours of sleep no matter what. I'll let you pick when you want to go, though."

"Why can't we just use the lights on our phones?" Noah complained.

"My phone lasts about fifteen minutes when I turn the flashlight on," Brian said calmly. "And I know yours isn't much better."

"Fine, I want the last shift."

"Great. And while we're all still awake, let me say this: if at any point we get down to the last candle, wake everyone up so we can move outside. It would be better to be exposed outdoors for a few hours than to be trapped in here with no light. Understand?"

They all nodded seriously.

"Great. I'm going to put all the candles right here along the wall. We have three more; keep track. Always keep at least two burning."

"Yes, sir," Leah said.

Brian gave her a look. "Don't mess this up. I don't want to be trapped in a mausoleum forever."

"I don't think any of us do," she replied. "We'll be careful."

"Can I go to bed now?" Noah asked.

"Yes," Brian sighed. "Go right ahead."

Noah relaxed onto the stone floor. When he had slept in this spot yesterday, it had been bone-chillingly cold and quite literally hard as rock. Now, to his sensibilities, at least, it was as comfortable as any mattress.

This sickness might suck in a lot of ways, but it sure makes it easy to get to sleep, was his last thought before he drifted off.

He dreamt of hunger.

The next thing he knew, a voice was speaking into his ear, pulling him unwillingly into consciousness.

"It's your turn, Noah."

He groaned and rolled over to find May crouching beside him, her eyes reflecting the dancing orange light of the candles beside them.

"The sun will rise in about an hour and a half," she whispered. "I just lit the last two candles. They should last us until morning."

"Alright," Noah mumbled. "Enjoy your sleep."

He watched jealously as she lay down beside Leah and closed her eyes, going motionless. Usually as a person fell asleep their breathing gradually slowed and deepened, but May displayed no such visible transition. If his own experiences were anything to go by, though, she was already halfway to dreamland.

He slouched against the wall. *Now I just have to stay awake for ninety minutes.* He looked over at the two candles. They were both obviously freshly lit. Stacked up beside them were three empty aluminum tealight casings.

Noah had no idea how long a single candle was supposed to last. He peered at the small blocks of wax and couldn't help but think they looked far too small to burn for more than even twenty minutes.

He shrugged and leaned back. Clearly, he had very little experience with candles. They were arguably a sort of technology all in themselves.

Noah glanced at his friends. They were laying nearly shoulder-to-shoulder along the wall. The longer he looked at them, the more uncomfortable he began to feel, and it took him a minute to realize it was because of how still they all were. Of course they weren't breathing, but there were also no small shifts or twitches as they slept. It was uncanny. He wondered if the three of them had noticed the same thing during their shifts.

He had to look away after another moment, the uncomfortable sensation strengthening into a tangible dread. It felt exactly like he was trapped in a small, dark space with three corpses.

Stop it, he admonished his brain. *It's just my friends, and they're not dead. I'm as much dead as they are. Get over it.*

Besides, we're in a mausoleum. There's an actual zombie in here. That's the one I should be worrying about.

The thoughts did nothing to ease his anxiety. *At least I'm not in danger of falling asleep now,* he thought. No matter how comfortable he might be physically, his mind was too tense for him to drift off.

Almost as soon as he convinced himself his own anxiety was a good thing, he began to calm down. A few minutes passed and he once again found himself fighting to keep his eyes propped open. He knew that if he shut them for even a moment he would be asleep before he knew what had happened.

He gazed at the candles. They had hardly burned through any wax or wick. *I could just crack the door and go to sleep. The sunlight would shine inside in the morning, and the candles would probably still be burning anyways.*

Even as the thought passed through his mind, he knew he wouldn't do it; there was a reason they had discarded that idea from the beginning. Wolves might not be able to fit through the small opening, but plenty of smaller scavenger-type critters would fare just fine. And while Noah knew they weren't dead, any animal that happened to wander inside would think differently. A bit of bad luck and they could be completely consumed by morning, whether it be by rats or any other opportunistic critter.

He stood abruptly and began pacing up and down the length of the room. Anything to stay awake. He made a dozen laps of the mausoleum before he started worrying that he was just exhausting himself further, and he sat back down.

He felt so tired that he wondered if the sickness was affecting his energy levels. He wouldn't be surprised in the slightest. *I'm going to crash,* he realized. He wouldn't make it to morning.

He glanced around the room in one last lethargic search for something, anything, to force himself awake. His eyes lingered on the lever and coffin, but he quickly disregarded them; he might be desperate, but he wasn't stupid.

His sight then fell upon the twin flames of the candles, and he stared into their hypnotizing depths for a good twenty seconds. His eyes suddenly widened and he shook himself. He knew how he could guarantee he would stay awake. He slid himself towards the candles with a dangerous plan coalescing in his mind.

The problem was that he was too comfortable. Sleep was hovering within tantalizing reach; all he had to do was relax slightly and he would be unconscious. But he knew there was a way to make himself significantly uncomfortable.

This might be even more idiotic than messing with the coffin, he thought dully. *My mind is definitely addled by sleep deprivation. That, or the sickness. It's one or the other for sure.*

He waved a hand over one of the flames. There was, of course, no sensation of heat. He had to check; it would have been quite unfortunate if he had a random weakness to fire that he only found out about once it was too late.

He withdrew his hand, picked up the candle, and leaned back against the wall with it placed carefully in the palm of his hand. He stared at it for a long moment, wondering if this was a dumb idea.

He finally shrugged to himself and extended his pointer finger, letting it sit within the flame. The fire wrapped smoothly around his skin, forming a pronged shape. He held his finger there a moment longer before lifting it out, revealing the worst burn he had ever gotten. The charred skin popped and peeled before his very eyes, making him wince, but he didn't look away. The damaged skin soon fell away and was replaced with freshly grown flesh. In less than sixty seconds the finger was indistinguishable from his other digits, if perhaps a bit cleaner.

Noah sat perfectly still, waiting for his hunger to make itself known, but all he could feel was a faint pang in protest of his regeneration.

He frowned. Apparently that wasn't enough damage. He hesitated for a moment before inserting his finger back into the flame. A slight warmth seemed to radiate from the candle, but he knew it was because his body was working to heal the burn damage rather than the actual temperature of the fire.

He let his finger sit there for well over a minute, his finger warming with every passing second, before he decided enough was enough and he lifted it from the flame to examine it in morbid interest.

The digit was charred black and glowing like an ember. He

waited patiently for it to heal, but there was no visible change.

Growing slightly worried, he poked tentatively at it and tried to curl the finger, only for the top bit of his finger to break off at the knuckle.

"Aw, man," he muttered, disgusted. He nudged the crumbling thing away, unintentionally causing it to disintegrate into a lump of unrecognizable ash, and refocused his attention on what remained of his hand.

Don't tell me I just burned my own finger off for nothing. I'll never hear the end of this.

He squinted closely at the stump. Much to his relief, it was growing back, albeit quite slowly. Slowly was a relative term, of course. Flesh visibly extended from the raw tip of the finger, gradually thickening and reforming into its normal shape.

Noah braced himself for the hunger, but even so, it came like a kick to the gut, forcing him to double over. He needed to eat.

This is all part of the plan, he reminded himself. *Keep it together.*

If he had known he would have to regenerate half his finger from scratch, though, he might have thought twice about burning himself. It might not have been as bad as the fallout of healing a split arm, but it still left him in a desperate state.

Noah looked longingly at the door.

I could just step outside for a quick minute to grab some food. I can take my phone light. That'll give me at least fifteen minutes. That's plenty.

He stood up.

Stop, Noah thought, feeling like he was arguing with another person rather than himself. *I can eat in the morning. I need to stay here for my friends. I am in control. I can do this.*

He wrenched his hand back from the door handle. If he were breathing, he would be taking quick, agitated gasps, but the pressure was contained within his mind.

He forced himself back down into a sitting position.

I should check if the sun has risen yet, he found himself thinking, but immediately recognized the thought as the trap it was. He pulled out his phone and powered it on instead, checking the time. He still had to wait over an hour for sunrise to come.

Easy, he told himself.

He imagined locking his own limbs to the floor, holding them unyieldingly in place. He would not move for anything.

Noah locked his gaze onto the candles and settled back. He would make it to daylight.

41

THE WORST FORM OF
IMMORTALITY EVER

Noah fell into a meditative state as the minutes slowly passed, his thoughts on a careful leash that brooked no deviation from his self-imposed immobilization. He came up with countless reasons to leave the mausoleum, to crack the door, to check the time, and he parried them all without moving so much as an inch. It was an endless circular track of pulling his mind back from its hungry intentions, recollecting himself, and waiting for his own thoughts to inevitably rebel once more.

The candles burned slowly lower and lower. The air in the room was so still that the flames stood perfectly straight in two motionless flecks of light. Noah used them as a focus for his thoughts, letting them pull him back into control each time he was on the verge of losing himself. They became the eyes of a serpentine beast, echoing the hunger he felt, commiserating with his plight. He honed in on them until everything else faded away. It was a state comparable to the void of complete darkness; a floating, weightless sensation, but the candles served as his anchors, and he did not feel lost.

He became so completely transfixed that he failed to immediately notice when his friends finally began to stir and awaken. The quiet rustling sounds they produced were automatically seized and set aside before they could be allowed to affect his meditation, and he was quite literally blind to everything besides the twin candles.

He was only shaken from his trance when the flames began to quiver, shaken from their perfect stillness by the movement in the room.

Noah blinked slowly, the carefully restrained feedback loop in his mind finally springing free. He allowed himself to shift a little, half expecting to feel sore, but his limbs were as insensate as he had become accustomed to.

"Morning," Leah said, sitting up. She was the first to fully awaken. Her eyes fell upon the candles, then shifted nervously to Noah. "Cutting it close, are we?"

"Hmm?" Noah suddenly realized both candles were barely hanging on by their last dregs. A thin layer of transparent liquid was all that remained in either cup.

He had completely lost track of the remaining duration of either candle. "Yeah, I figured they would last us until morning," he decided to say, not particularly wanting to admit the colossal mistake he had made.

"You should have woken us up before they got this low," Brian said disapprovingly, brought to wakefulness by their conversation. "Either one could die at any moment."

Leah stood up and walked over to the door, bracing her hands on the handle. "It is morning, right?"

Noah didn't say anything. He had spent so much effort to stay inside that it felt strange for them to be opening the door with so little fanfare now. He shook the feeling off.

"Yeah, the sun should be up by now," Brian answered for him, checking the time on his phone.

His words were proven true a second later as Leah heaved the door open and blinding sunlight cascaded inside.

A wide smile spread across Noah's face. I made it. There'd been a dozen moments over the past hour when he had lost hope that he would be able to hold out. It felt like a small miracle that he was now standing with his friends in the slanted rays of the morning light. Part of him wanted to push past Leah to rush outside right away, but he held himself back with an effort of will.

Leah left the door open and turned to wake up May, who was only halfway to consciousness. Brian leaned over to put out the candles, but before he could, both flames suddenly winked out, drowned by the melted wax they had been weakly fluttering over. Smoke twirled from the black nubs of spent wick.

Noah and Brian shared a wide-eyed look. There had been hardly five seconds to spare between the door opening and the candles dying.

There might have been time to open the door before the last of the embers went out, Noah thought weakly. He decided to believe that would've been the case, if only for his peace of mind.

Neither May nor Leah seemed to notice that Brian hadn't been the one to blow out the candles, and Noah supposed they were probably better off not knowing.

"Are we ready to grab the pendant?" Leah asked.

"Absolutely. Let's get out of here," Brian answered. "Would you like to do the honors or should I?"

"I've already had to pull the lever twice," she said. "I think it's your turn."

Brian grumbled to himself but trudged nonetheless to the coffin. He climbed slowly up onto the lid and tilted his head back to stare at the stone bust leering off the wall.

Noah gazed at its ravenous maw, wondering just how purposeful the choice of expression was. Had the artist known of the sickness that was sealed away beneath its snarling countenance? The design couldn't be a coincidence.

Brian reached into the sculpture's mouth and gave the tongue a tug.

"Push it up, not down," Leah said wearily.

"Ah, right." The tongue-shaped lever slid into place. Brian stepped quickly to the ground before the coffin began to unseal itself.

They all tensed slightly, ready for any sudden movement from within.

"We're fine," Brian said after a few anxious moments with

no sign of motion. "Come on."

His companions reluctantly stepped up beside him. Noah was suddenly afraid that they would look inside and see nothing but broken shackles.

To his relief, the sunken face gaped lifelessly from the coffin.

"See, it's dead," Brian said. He reached cautiously towards the pendant. They had failed to close it when they first visited the mausoleum, and it lay with its two halves spread like an open book.

As his fingers brushed the knobbed metal clasp, the lower jaw of the corpse fell open with a soft clack. Brian recoiled with incredible speed of reflex, but there were no other signs of life. Noah wondered skeptically if gravity was the culprit for the movement.

"Just grab the thing already," Leah said impatiently.

Brian sent her a dirty look. "I'm getting to it." His fingers hovered over the metal box nervously before he gathered his courage and seized it, snapping it shut and yanking the item back over the body's head. He tried to pull it completely off in one motion, but the chain caught in the small of its neck and refused to shift further.

With a deeply unhappy sound, Brian gingerly scooped his hand beneath the skull and lifted it so that he could pull the chain the rest of the way off.

To everyone's alarm, the body's hands suddenly lifted jerkily from its sides, reacting to the theft. Its eyes fluttered open.

Brian yelled and stumbled back with the pendant in hand. "Close it!"

May climbed onto the ledge of the coffin, carefully avoiding the uncovered side where the body was exposed.

Noah watched the zombie warily. It certainly seemed unhappy that its pendant had been taken, but it hardly had the energy to lift its own hands, let alone put up a fight. It trembled impotently as May flicked the lever and the lid drew slowly over its shriveled form.

To Noah's amusement, May dropped into a sitting position atop the coffin and let it carry her sideways as it closed.

A moment after the coffin sealed, they heard the two dull thuds of what Noah assumed to be the body's arms falling limply to its sides. There were no further sounds of movement.

"Like taking candy from a baby," Leah said cheerfully.

"A really, really ugly baby," Brian said.

"Uh. It can probably still hear us."

"You think?" Brian exclaimed, looking alarmed at the idea.

Leah shrugged. "Well, we didn't lose our hearing when we got the dust. If this zombie has the same sickness we do, and I think it's safe to assume it does, then why wouldn't it be able to hear?"

Noah furrowed his brows. "Not to be overly pessimistic, but is this going to be us one day? Is this sickness really just the worst form of immortality ever?"

Brian gave him a nervous look, but Leah shook her head. "We can die, obviously. Look at what happened to Sophie. It just takes a ton of damage."

Noah nodded, but privately he wondered what would happen if nobody were to go to the effort of chopping their heads off. If they were left uninjured, what would happen when they passed the point that they would have died of old age? It felt like such a long way away, almost too far into the future to bother worrying about, but Noah couldn't help but worry about what their fate would be if they were unable to find a cure. Clearly, death hadn't been the end for the poor guy that had been entombed here.

"I wish we could talk to whoever made this pendant," Brian said. "I bet they would know all about whatever is happening to us."

"Also, the coffin has shackles built conveniently right in," May added. "Shackles are not a normal part of a coffin. Whoever installed them had to know about the dust, or at least they knew enough to be worried about it. Although, on second thought..." she trailed off and her brows creased as she recalled the previous night. "The shackles broke almost immediately when the zombie first awoke. I would have expected them to be able to restrain a halfway decomposed corpse, even considering the age of the material. It's almost... agh, this sounds insane, but it's almost as if they were designed to give unknowing visitors a false sense of security."

Leah met her intense gaze. "Shackles on a dead body doesn't really seem like the best way to avoid alarming visitors. Unless said visitors were already somehow expecting it to be not so dead. Not sure where they'd get that idea, though."

May shrugged. "Yeah. I might be reading way too much into it. And besides, you'd think they'd have made the lever easier to access if this whole thing was supposed to be some sort of trap." She glanced sideways at the stone lid. "There's some writing carved here. It's not English, but it's possible that it's some form of warning."

"I saw the writing earlier but kind of assumed it was just the name of the person," Brian said, peering over. "I guess that would be a stupidly long name though. Maybe it is a warning."

May took her phone out to take a picture of it. "If we can figure out what language it is, we can probably translate it."

"Oh, good idea," Brian approved.

May smiled and slid off the coffin. "Alright, enough's enough. Let's get out of here."

"Time to find out if the entire town has been infected," Leah said brightly. "Hey, if everyone's sick, then there's no reason to close stores, right? Maybe the Corner Market will be open after all."

"I don't think we should be hoping that everyone has gotten sick just so that we have an easier time buying batteries," Brian scolded her.

"Eh, I didn't say I was 'hoping' for anything. But you're right that it would be convenient."

They gathered the five empty candle casings off the floor

and exited the mausoleum. Nobody noticed the small pile of ash that used to be Noah's finger.

I should tell them that I need to eat, he thought. *But then they might not want me to go into town, and I really don't want to settle for eating another random animal.*

They set off along the trail.

42

I THINK MY JUDGEMENT MAY BE
SERIOUSLY COMPROMISED

Noah was glad his stomach didn't make any grumbling sounds as they walked, because that would have been a pretty obvious giveaway that something had happened overnight. It once again raised a few questions over how much of their digestive systems had been messed with by the sickness, but at the moment Noah was just glad for the secrecy it afforded him.

After a few minutes of walking, a squirrel happened to dash across their path. Noah watched it pass in front of him without so much as a twitch. *I've graduated to better fare than that,* he thought haughtily. He glanced stealthily at his friends to see if they had such low standards so as to be tempted by the rodent, but they didn't seem to have even noticed its passing. *Eh, I guess they're not hungry at the moment. Good for them.*

"It's eight AM," Brian said as they reached the three-way junction and took a hard right. "People are gonna show up to our housing units back on campus in an hour. Technically speaking, we haven't broken any rules yet-"

"Haven't broken any rules?" Leah interrupted, laughing. "I'm not sure Dr. Jansen would agree with that."

"We've already established that we don't care what she thinks," Noah said.

Brian gave them both a flat look. "Once it hits nine, we're

going to have to worry about Insight tracking us down."

"That's fine," Noah assured him. "It won't take that long to stop by the Corner Market." *And to grab a snack along the way.*

A worrying thought suddenly occurred to him. "What do you think the chances are that everyone's actually been infected?"

"Everyone?" Brian asked. "I'd be awfully surprised if *everyone* is sick, especially if you're referring to the entire town population. If we're just talking about Oakridge students... Well, it's possible, I guess."

"Oh, no," Noah said.

"I know, it's terrible," May agreed sorrowfully. "So many people are going to be panicking and wondering what's happening to themselves."

Noah glanced at her. "...Yeah."

All he needed was one nice, healthy, uninfected person taking a walk. He looked around with a smile. The sun was shining, the temperature was probably great. There was no excuse for anyone to be staying inside on such a beautiful morning.

"Something's put a spring in your step," Leah remarked. "What's there to be so happy about? I could use some good news."

Noah looked around guiltily. "Ah, I'm just enjoying the weather. There's probably lots of people out and about right now, wouldn't you agree? It's hard to stay indoors on a day like this."

Brian squinted at him for a long moment. "Are you feeling okay? Is there anything you'd like to tell us about?"

Noah zipped his mouth shut. *Darn it, what'd I say?* He mused over his words, but failed to find anything wrong with them. He settled for giving his friend a shrug and a bright smile.

"You're never this happy," Brian muttered. "The last time you were this happy was..." He suddenly stopped walking and turned to his friend.

"Noah," he said, stony-faced. "When and where were you injured?"

Leah and May stared between the two of them.

Noah wouldn't meet Brian's eyes. "What makes you think I've been injured?"

"Point to the spot."

Noah swallowed and gestured to his finger.

"When?"

Noah cleared his throat. "Just a few hours ago. During my shift. I was feeling really tired…"

Brian put his face in his hands. "Oh, you idiot. What did you do?"

"It's not important, is it? Let's keep walking." He stepped forward, but nobody else moved.

"Noah, what did you do?" Leah asked.

He kicked at a small rock at the edge of the trail. "I stuck my finger into a candle."

They all stared at him.

"On purpose? What, pray tell, made you think that was a good idea?" Brian demanded, flabbergasted.

"I would've fallen asleep if I didn't do anything," Noah protested.

"You were barely doing your job anyways," Brian retorted. "The candles would have gone out without you saying a thing if we hadn't just so happened to wake up in time." He turned to the girls. "Do either of you realize that we were literal seconds from being trapped in the mausoleum? We'd still be in there right now, completely helpless, if Leah had waited five seconds before opening the door. We'd probably still be there in a year, or ten. Possibly a lot longer than that."

They turned their startled gazes on Noah.

"Is that true?" May asked.

Noah rubbed his eyes unhappily. "I don't know. I suppose so. I was just trying my best to stay awake and not leave to get something to eat. I guess I lost track of the state of the candles at some point."

May blinked, seeming to struggle to wrap her head around

how close they had been to catastrophe. "You should have just woken us up," she said finally. "I would have taken your shift for you."

"Huh," Noah mumbled. "I didn't think to do that. I'm sorry. I feel pretty dumb." His footsteps slowed as he realized the thought of waking them up had never even crossed his mind. It should have been an obvious solution to his predicament, but he had been so razor-focused on the idea of escaping and seeking out food that he had failed to realize there was a much more reasonable course of action. "I think my judgement may be seriously compromised," he mumbled.

"No kidding," Brian yelled, punching him. "Not only did you make that stupid decision, but you also tried to hide your hunger from us."

"I'm sorry," he muttered again. "I thought you would try to stop me from going into town."

"Yeah, and you're absolutely right," Leah replied. "You're not going anywhere near civilization until you eat. There's squirrels everywhere; grab whatever one takes your fancy."

"Oh, come on!" He complained. "Would you want to eat a squirrel?"

"No, but I wouldn't want to eat a person, either, so I don't think I'm the right person to ask."

"I couldn't even catch a squirrel if I tried," Noah grumbled. "The things have turbo engines for legs."

"Well, you'll have to come up with a solution. It doesn't have to be a squirrel. You could find something slower."

"Like that," Noah said, his eyes lighting up.

His friends all turned to look down the path at whatever had caught his attention.

"Oh, no," Brian muttered.

A guy in a green Oakridge jacket was walking obliviously towards them with his dog on a leash, coming into view around a bend in the path about fifty yards away. He saw them all looking at him and waved.

Brian grabbed Noah before he could tear off towards the man. "Wait! He could be infected," Brian said desperately.

"You don't want to eat him if he's infected."

Noah shook his head. The guy looked too old to be a student. Judging by the jacket, he was likely an alumni. He probably hadn't been on campus in years.

"He's not infected. I just need a little bite," he pleaded. "Nothing vital."

Brian glared at him. "You don't need anything. Your finger is fully healed."

"It took a lot out of me," Noah argued. "You know the whole digit fell off? It takes a lot to regenerate a whole limb from scratch."

They gave him a dumbfounded look. "From a candle?" Leah asked doubtfully. "How did you manage that?"

Noah shrugged. Brian looked like he was going to say something, but Noah continued before he could open his mouth.

"Besides, isn't this guy the ideal target? Nobody's around to panic or get in the way. We won't end up with a mess like we did at Sophie's house."

"The fact that you're coherently arguing your case shows that you're still in control of yourself," Leah pointed out.

"Of course I'm in control. I'm not being forced to do anything against my will."

Leah shared an exasperated glance with Brian and May. "Do you even hear yourself? The sickness is literally talking out of your mouth. I get that you're hungry, but can't you just hold yourself back just for a minute until this guy passes us?"

"Absolutely," Noah said, but although he wasn't struggling against Brian's hold, his eyes didn't stray from the man for a second. The person was close enough now that he could probably overhear their conversation. The dog started barking.

"Alright, blindfold time," Brian said.

"No!"

"Yup, since you apparently can't be trusted around people anymore, this is what we're going to do every time we cross paths with anyone. Get used to it." He nodded at Leah, who wordlessly circled around them out of Noah's field of vision. Before he could think about what she was doing, something descended across his eyes. It was a thin material, to the point that light could still pass through it, giving him hope that they had misjudged their choice of blindfold. Then to his terrible disappointment, a second and third layer appeared, completely blocking out all light.

"What?! Did you plan this?" He cried out in abject betrayal.

"Of course. We'd be silly not to, especially when you gave us such a great opportunity by going to sleep so early last night."

Noah's limbs gradually loosened against his will. He soon heard the sound of leaves rustling below him.

"Am I being dragged?" he tried to ask, but someone must have shoved something into his mouth, because the words were incomprehensible.

Half a minute passed, and then he heard an unfamiliar voice. "What's going on?"

Noah's hunger reared up in reaction to the voice, which sounded terribly close.

"Free me," Noah demanded, but the words came out as two indistinct syllables.

"Don't mind our friend," he heard Leah say. "He's having a seizure. We're used to it, though; this is the safest way for him to deal with it."

"Are you sure? Hey, kid, are you alright?"

"He's great," Brian answered for him. Noah tried his very best to struggle, to break free from the void. Desperation filled him at the knowledge that the man stood so close, but even when he felt that he would give himself an aneurysm from sheer effort, he couldn't move. His body simply seemed too far away, completely inaccessible.

"Well, I'm no doctor, so I'm not sure how much help I could offer you anyway. If you're sure you're all fine, I'll leave you be. Enjoy the weather, yeah?"

"Thanks, you too," May said.

His friends, the traitors, waited for well over a minute before they finally decided to remove Noah's bindings.

"I think that blindfold/gag combo worked splendidly," Brian said. "It's good to know we have such a perfect solution to Noah's problem."

"I'd like to see how you feel when it becomes your problem, too," Noah snapped. "Because it will, sooner or later.

"I would only have taken a tiny little bite, anyways. You're acting like I can't control myself."

"'Cause you can't," Leah said. "It's okay, though. That's why we're looking out for you."

"But I still need to eat," he groused. "You didn't help at all."

"We'll find something else."

They continued down the path, keeping a careful eye on Noah as they went along.

43

PEOPLE TASTE BETTER

Much to Noah's disappointment, they did not come across any more people before they reached the end of the trail.

"You're just delaying the inevitable," Noah said as they started walking along the sidewalk. "I'm going to eat someone at some point."

"After you were injured last night, you could barely walk," Brian reminded him. "But you seem to be doing just fine now. I know this isn't what you want to hear, but from our perspective, you just seem really eager to eat people despite there being nothing actually wrong with you. You can't expect sympathy from us about that."

Noah couldn't even put into words how unfair he felt his friends were being.

"Is the road closed today?" May asked. "Where are all the cars?"

The four of them peered back down the road. There was no sign of any kind of roadblock, but there wasn't a single car in view either. The section of the road they were currently on cut through the middle of the woods that encompassed the cemetery nature trail, which meant there were no houses, either. It was one long, empty stretch of space.

"Is it our fault, you think?" Leah wondered. "Is the whole community in lockdown?"

"This doesn't look good," Brian said.

"No, not at all," Noah agreed. "Who am I going to eat

now?"

"You could at least pretend that you're normal," Leah sighed. "Instead of reminding us every five seconds that you've gone completely crazy."

Noah gave her a hurt expression.

"What? May got hurt yesterday, and I don't hear her wondering where the closest human snack is."

"I only got a little cut," she spoke up quickly. "Noah has it plenty worse than I do."

"Thank you," he said, feeling pleased that someone was finally understanding his plight.

"But that doesn't excuse your actions," she suddenly continued. He glanced at her in surprise and flinched at the hard look in her eyes. "If I were you, I'd refuse to go near anyone before I was one hundred percent sure it would be safe for everyone involved. I would consume whatever animals I needed to so I could assure myself that I wouldn't pose a threat to other humans. You should be ashamed of the way you've been behaving, putting yourself above others."

"He can't help himself," Brian said hesitantly. "He obviously doesn't really want to eat people. That's not who he is. It's whatever the sickness is doing to him."

May glanced at him. "You and your sister are acting like it's no big deal for some reason, but it's not okay, Noah. You're not trying hard enough, and sooner or later, it's going to cost someone their life. You can't just treat this like a bad cough that you have to soldier through until it goes away, not when so much is at stake. I just want everyone to be safe, can you understand that?"

Noah recoiled. "Easy for you to say," he spat out. "You might have gotten a little cut or two, but you obviously have no idea what it's like. I can barely hold this conversation with you just because all of my willpower is being spent on not sprinting towards the nearest house I can find. I know you think I'm crazy, and it doesn't really feel like I am, but maybe you're right. I can't even remember what it was like to look at a person without feeling hungry. It feels normal, you know?

And I bet you'll feel exactly the same when you're in my place."

"The only reason you're having so much difficulty controlling yourself is because you're not taking the alternatives you know are available to you. We've already established that animals are a viable substitute, and you're completely ignoring it as an option."

"Yeah, because people taste better," Noah said, rolling his eyes that he had to voice the obvious. "Which again, you would understand if you were injured like I was. Want to see if you can hold yourself to your words? Let's take off a couple fingers and see what happens."

"Stop it, Noah," Brian muttered.

"Tell her to stop first," he retorted. "I'm only defending myself."

"No, you're not. You just told her to cut off her fingers. Everybody needs to calm down."

Leah nodded. "We have more important things to worry about. How bad do things have to be for the roads to be shut down? We're concerned about Noah, but there could be another dozen or more people just like him wandering around causing chaos. The town wouldn't close the streets for just anything."

Even before she finished speaking, a low rumble filled the air, heralding the approach of vehicles from around the corner. A moment later the source of the noise emerged into view, and a line of heavy armored-looking trucks came trundling down the center of the road with no regard for traffic lines. Noah's mouth fell open as he recognized one of the vehicles as an honest-to-goodness tank. The rest weren't far off, ranging from massive utility vehicles to armored cargo trucks. *Is the whole military coming to pay Oakridge a visit?*

He tensed as the convoy got closer and closer, but not a single driver slowed down or acknowledged them in the slightest. Soon the trucks were thundering right in front of them, so close Noah could almost imagine the ground trembling beneath his feet. He could see the drivers wearing bulky black gas masks through the open windows.

"Hey, that one's from Insight!" Leah shouted over the rumbling noise. She pointed at one of the trucks near the middle of the procession. It was only slightly smaller than the tank and boasted six massive wheels. If it didn't have Insight's bright blue logo plastered across its side, it would have blended right in with the rest of the envoy.

"Who let them join in?" Brian said in dismay. "I didn't think they were with the government!"

"They're not," May said.

They watched the vehicles turn one-by-one around the corner towards the Oakridge campus.

"Well, that doesn't bode well," Leah muttered.

"Imagine if all that is to pick us up," Brian said with a dark chuckle.

"No way," Noah replied. "Something's happening on campus. And if it's not related to our sickness, I'll eat my foot."

"Please don't," Leah said.

"I doubt any stores will be open around Oakridge," Brian said.

"Then why are we still walking that way?" Noah asked.

"Don't you want to see what's happening?"

"We're on the run, Brian! We all saw the Insight logo drive by. Call me crazy, but I don't want to head towards the people who are trying to lock us up in a lab!"

"Things have obviously gotten out of hand since Dr. Jansen called Insight yesterday. I don't think anyone will be overly concerned about us peeking around a little."

"You don't know that."

"All these people that just drove by probably aren't infected."

Noah stared at him for a moment. "Excellent point. Very excellent point. Guys, I think we should check out the campus."

44

I AM IN FULL CONTROL
OF MYSELF

Apart of Noah hated that he was letting himself be led around by his stomach, but he was genuinely too hungry to care. He was finding it harder and harder to be bothered by the judgement his actions would bring upon him. He would go back to 'normal' once he got cured; no point worrying about it until then.

They reached the town and started passing the first storefronts, all of them dark and empty. No people strolled the sidewalks. The only signs of life, strangely enough, were the campus shuttles rattling occasionally up and down the road. Noah soon realized that the ones heading away from campus were full of people, while the vehicles traveling back were empty.

"They're shuttling away the students," he said, nodding at the most recent bus to pass them by.

They stared warily after it. Kids sat squashed against the large square windows, some of them staring out with bored expressions. Noah made eye contact with a few of them, and in each instance the person did a double take. Nobody expected to see him or his friends casually strolling through town when it was so clearly in the middle of a lockdown.

"You wanna bet all these people are infected, or not?" Brian asked. "I can't imagine they'd throw everyone in together. They'd know better than that."

"It could be either," Leah replied.

Noah squinted after the bus, wondering if his instincts would kick in to inform him if they were good food or not, but he got nothing. They must've been too far away.

"Let's find out," he said to himself, rubbing his hands together.

They soon found themselves outside the Corner Market. It was just as closed as everything else. There was a new sheet of paper tacked beside the one with the store's hours, looking very clean and white in comparison. Brian read it aloud.

"'CLOSED for obvious reasons. Go home, idiot'."

"That's not very professional," Leah commented.

"One of his employees probably made the note," Brian said with an unbothered shrug. "And it's a justified sentiment, anyway. We are kind of idiots. Do you see any other people out taking a walk?"

"I'm surprised there aren't more military-type people around, with how many trucks went by," May said. "I thought the whole town would be swamped."

Then they went around the side of the store, just a few more steps, and stopped short.

Spread out across the shallow grassy basins of Oakridge's sports fields was what looked to be a full army camp. The vehicles that had passed them earlier were only the tip of the iceberg, latecomers to a much larger operation; on one side of the fields was a row of large brown tents, while the rest of the area was swarming with what must've been the whole student body. From their elevated viewpoint, the four friends could see the many lines that students were being painstakingly arranged into, all leading into one of the dozen or so brown tents. Students would enter on one side and soon be led out the other, directly to a row of campus shuttle buses lined up on the gravel road running down the side of the field. When a bus was full, it would pull onto the main road and turn either back towards campus or in the opposite direction, towards town.

As the next bus came their way, they wordlessly agreed to

edge around the side of the store and out of view. They hadn't had any issues with any of the previous buses, but seeing the full extent of the operation made them nervous.

"I don't want to end up on one of those," Leah said.

"You aren't curious where-"

"Nope. Not even a little," she cut off her brother.

"We should find out what's happening," he said.

She squinted at him. "You sound like Noah."

Noah, who had been nodding in agreement with his friend, gave Leah a peeved look.

"I'm curious as well," May said. "We should ask someone if they know where everyone is being driven off to."

Leah gazed at her incredulously and pointed down. "Do none of you see all the soldiers? How do you propose we get past them without ending up in the lines ourselves?"

They all peered down at the fields. Now that it had been pointed out to him, Noah noticed a very loose perimeter of soldiers casually encircling the entire area. At the moment they were merely strolling about with a threatening demeanor, but each of them held an oddly long and narrow rifle-esque weapon, more than ready to react to any trouble.

Noah swallowed. In the back of his mind he had been waiting for a good moment to dash down onto the field, but he could see now that there would have been no chance he made it past the subtle sentries. Even if the soldiers currently seemed more concerned with keeping people in than out.

"So, yeah," Leah said. "I'm quite happy with observing from our current perspective."

"We could get a little closer without too much risk," Brian said. "Close enough to overhear if someone's talking about what's going on, which I guarantee you most people are. I say we go for it. Even if we get caught, what's the worst that would happen? They can't be sending off an entire campus's worth of students to their deaths. It's probably some form of quarantine, maybe even a treatment facility. We just need more information."

Noah opened his mouth to agree, but all three of his

friends turned a thunderous gaze on him and he snapped his jaw shut.

"We know exactly where your motives lay, Noah," Brian said. "You don't need to argue for going down to the field; we're well aware that you're all for it."

He blinked. "Okay."

"Insight is sticking their filthy hands into this mess," Leah said. "They've got their trucks and their people all over the place. That's enough to tell me I want no part of whatever is going on down there."

"We're not walking into the middle of everything and turning ourselves in," her brother argued. "There are plenty of nice big vehicles conveniently parked between us and them. They're practically asking for someone to sneak over."

"You and May can go down," she allowed after a moment of thought. "I'll stay here with Noah."

"Hey!" he yelled. "I am in full control of myself."

"You can't say that when all you mean is that you won't be fighting your own instincts to eat the closest person. You'll only get yourself killed anyway. This isn't some poor helpless family; these are armed soldiers who have definitely been warned to look out for anyone behaving exactly like you."

He looked stricken and fell silent for a long moment. With an uncharacteristically serious expression, he nodded. "You're right. Let me go down. I promise, I won't do anything to endanger any of you. Or myself."

They all stared doubtfully at him.

"Let me prove I'm not just a dumb zombie," he pleaded. "You can even bring the blindfold."

Brian's mouth twisted. "Oh, we're definitely bringing that."

May scowled at the two boys. "Don't tell me you actually trust that he's not going to just run after the nearest bystander. Why risk anything when Noah can just stay here?"

"Let me do this," he insisted earnestly.

Brian looked between the girls, makeshift blindfold already in hand. "I'll be ready if he tries anything. We can treat this as a test."

"Fine." Leah threw up her hands. "But I'm going too, then."

"Okay," Brian said easily. "I'm not worried about you suddenly deciding to eat someone."

Noah just smiled at his friends. "Are we ready?"

Brian grabbed his arm. "Yeah. Come on."

They crept quickly down the hill, beelining for the nearest truck. All of them crouched down even though the vehicles were more than tall enough to conceal their forms, fearful of presenting themselves as large targets. It made them look exceedingly suspicious, but it wasn't as if anyone was supposed to be walking around outside of the military cordon anyway, standing upright or otherwise. Noah could only hope that the nearby soldier didn't suddenly decide to turn around while they were still out in the open.

The four of them made it to the first truck and dashed onward to the next without pause. This second one had a large covered cargo bed, which Noah glanced at nervously. It was big enough for people to theoretically be sitting inside. Nobody emerged, though, and they safely continued away.

"Okay, we're close enough," May said. "There's too much space before the next truck."

"We're not close enough to hear anything. There's no point stopping here," Brian said evenly.

May gave him an unhappy grimace. Her whole posture was tense, but she went with them when they stepped out towards the final vehicle. Noah kept his eyes firmly on the closest soldier, standing about twenty meters away. They didn't seem interested in looking away from the students on the field at the moment.

Leah and May were faster than him and Brian, simply by virtue of them being able to run freely. Brian wasn't about to let go of Noah, not when they were so close to so many people. Regardless, all four of them made it to safety without issue.

"Easy," Leah whispered.

They crowded around the edge of the truck, some kind of

boxy utility vehicle, and waited to see if their efforts would be rewarded.

There were plenty of people standing around close by, and the sound of chatter filled the air, but it was all indistinct, carrying from further away across the field.

"Why isn't anyone in this line talking?" Brian muttered. "What are they doing, just standing around?"

He risked a quick glance around the side of the truck, then pulled back with a displeased look on his face. "Everyone nearby is on their phone."

"Should we go to a different truck?" Leah asked.

Noah looked around. There were no other vehicles parked anywhere near the field.

"Do any of your phones still have a charge?" Leah asked. "There might be a school announcement or something."

May pulled out her phone. "Good idea. Let me check my email real quick."

They all sat down to wait.

"The connection out here sucks," May muttered.

Another minute passed before she perked up. "Hey, look at this. There was a campus-wide message last night. Everyone was told to show up at the fields at seven this morning."

"Seven? Do you think that would have included us?" Leah asked. "I wonder if this would have taken precedence over our trip to Insight."

"Does it say anything else?" Noah wanted to know.

May frowned. "No." She put her phone down and went quiet, just listening.

All of the conversations tangled into one muddy mess of words, making any individual phrases indecipherable. Noah was about to suggest they get away from the field and back to safety when the words "already found a cure" floated over to them from somewhere nearby, making all four of them go absolutely still.

"Did you-"

"Shh," Leah held a hand up, and Brian went silent.

They strained for all they were worth to catch more of the conversation, but it had disappeared back into the muddle of hundreds of voices.

"Do you think they really figured it out?" Brian asked. "Because if so, I don't care what you guys are doing, I'm walking over there right now."

Noah didn't know how to feel about the idea that there was already a cure. He searched himself, trying to make sense of his own emotions, and slowly realized... he didn't care. He didn't feel like he needed to be cured of anything. Sure, he was hungry, but that would stop being an issue as soon as he could get away from his friends for a minute. Not that he would try to do that, he quickly reminded himself. It was just bound to happen on its own sooner or later.

Then his dad popped into his mind for some reason. He found himself wondering what he would do if the man was right beside him. Would he be able to stop himself from doing to him what Sophie had done to her own mother?

I'm not as far gone as she was, he thought. *She was totally crazy. Her brain was melted. I only lost a finger.*

Even as he tried to convince himself, the only emotion he could feel was the nagging hunger, a constant needle pricking at his will. He shut his eyes. *I wouldn't hurt my dad. Right?*

He suddenly stood up and stepped out from behind the truck.

"I'm getting into line."

45

HUMAN DIAGNOSTIC TESTER

Taken by surprise, Brian was nearly pulled out into the open after Noah before he released his friend's arm and stepped quickly back into concealment.

"Don't be rash," he hissed, but Noah paid his warning no heed. He smiled reassuringly at them and began crossing the short stretch of grass towards the nearest line.

His friends watched on in frozen alarm, certain he was about to eat someone, or at the very least be caught and questioned. Instead, without anyone else the wiser, he calmly stepped into the throng of bodies and attached himself to the end of line like he was just a regular student doing as he was told.

"What should we do?" Leah asked, gripping the edge of the truck as she stared out at him.

"I wasn't planning on jumping into this mess until I knew exactly where everyone was being sent," Brian said. "But now I have no idea what to do. How about you?"

"Whatever you decide," Leah replied quickly. "I just want to stick together."

"Well, it sounds like there might actually be a cure," he said hesitantly. "Maybe Noah has the right idea. My only concern is what the cost could be."

"It looks like everyone is being treated, or at least being sent somewhere to be treated," his sister observed. "So they might be doing it for free."

"Oh, sure, but what I'm really worried about are the side effects, lingering symptoms, that sort of thing. Do we really want to be treated with a cure that they somehow came up with overnight?"

"It's better than nothing," May opined.

"This is Insight we're talking about," Leah reminded her. "Their idea of a cure could be murder."

May raised an eyebrow. "They might be able to get away with a few losses here and there, but no way would they massacre a whole college. As unusual as it is for them, they might really be trying to help here. Also, it's possible the government is forcing them to provide aid. We don't know what the situation is."

"So, are we going to trust them, or not?" Brian asked impatiently. "Noah's going to end up on a bus if we don't move quickly. I don't want to just abandon him like that."

"Then what are we waiting for? Let's go," May said.

"Noah made crossing look easy, but we're still only one startled soldier away from getting captured or shot," Leah warned.

They craned their heads around the vehicle to peer at the nearest uniformed figure looking dutifully out over the assembled students. He was tall enough that even from behind, he seemed likely to be a man.

"He's not paying us any attention, let's move," Brian muttered.

They stepped out of hiding as one and walked briskly towards Noah's line.

Almost at the same time, the soldier began to turn their way.

Leah cursed under her breath. "Turn around and walk towards the soldier, now," she ordered.

"Why?" Brian demanded, but he and May both did as she directed.

Half a second later, the soldier caught sight of what looked to be a couple of students who had broken away from their line. He subtly adjusted his grip on his weapon.

"Halt!" he called, and the three of them instantly obeyed.

"What now?" Brian muttered.

Leah ignored her brother. "We want to know what's going on," she said to the man. Her voice was hesitant at first, but she quickly gained confidence as she continued. "Why do we all have to line up? Where are they sending us?"

For a moment the soldier only stared suspiciously at them, but he finally seemed to realize they were just a few harmless kids. "There's a sickness going around," he allowed shortly. "We need to make sure you're not a carrier."

"Oh, no!" Leah cried, hands moving to her cheeks. Brian somehow managed to refrain from rolling his eyes. "What if we have it?"

"Then Insight will take it out," he answered.

"How will they manage that?" Leah tried to ask, but either the man was fed up with her questions or he didn't know the answer. "Get back in line, you'll find out."

A few nearby students who had clearly been eavesdropping turned away in disappointment.

"Okay. Thank you for your time," Leah said obediently.

The three of them scampered the rest of the way to the lines and slid into place behind Noah.

"Quick thinking," Brian praised.

"Thanks," Leah said, looking relieved.

"Hey, Noah, fancy seeing you here," Brian joked.

Noah didn't seem to hear him, so Brian took him by the shoulders and turned him around. "Hey, man. You doing alright?"

Noah jumped at the sight of them. His eyes moved constantly, darting all around in nervous twitches. "There's, uh, a lot of people here," he muttered.

"Obviously," Brian said, raising his brows. "Will you be okay?"

Noah shrugged. "Most people are infected, to the point that I'm surprised chaos hasn't broken out yet. The uninfected people are just standing around with everyone else. Like her." He pointed at a girl in a nearby line who was wearing a surgical mask. She was looking at something on her phone with earbuds shoved into her ears, seeming wholly unconcerned that she was surrounded by potential zombies. Either she was extremely uninformed, or she had perfect confidence in the security provided by the military presence.

Brian gazed around, realizing almost everyone had a mask. He touched his own face and hoped nobody would single them out for their lack of respiratory protection.

"I keep forgetting that you're like a human diagnostic tester," Leah said to Noah with an amused smirk. "How about that person? They sick?"

Noah reluctantly glanced over. "Yeah."

"How about that one?"

"Infected."

"That guy over there?"

"Infected," Noah said, then looked back in surprise, perking up. "Wait, no. That guy doesn't have it."

"Okay, we get it," Brian interrupted before Leah could point at another random person. "Let's not forget that you're essentially asking if he wants to eat them."

Leah patted Noah on the back. "Aww, don't listen to him. You're doing great."

"Thanks." He smiled half-heartedly, already regretting his decision to place himself in the midst of such a large crowd. Every passing second was a battle to tamp down the urge to wander to one of the uninfected students and just chomp on them. His only saving grace was how rapidly the lines seemed to be moving along; every few seconds everyone would shuffle another few steps forward. Soon enough he would be within a tent and hopefully out of range of any uninfected bystanders.

As he waited patiently, doing what he hoped to be quite the excellent job of pretending to be comfortable and relaxed, a commotion several lines over made both him and everyone nearby look over curiously.

A student in an Oakridge hoodie was pushing people carelessly aside, bulldozing his way through row after row of startled students. His target soon became clear as the girl Noah had pointed out earlier as uninfected.

She didn't seem to realize anything was amiss, although

several people around her certainly did. Someone grabbed her arm and pointed towards the incoming student.

Noah couldn't see anything visibly wrong with the kid, though clearly he had been injured in some way. It could have been anything from a twisted ankle to a brain hemorrhage.

Regardless, he was nearly to the girl before she finally realized she was in danger and stumbled away.

A couple other students tried to hold back the sudden assailant, but they only managed to buy the girl a few seconds before he broke free and lunged for her.

Mid-step, something appeared in his shoulder. A tufted dart with a bright green bush. The student came to an abrupt stop, nearly toppling forward, and clawed at his own eyes. Over the next several seconds he simply collapsed to the ground.

The male soldier with whom Leah had spoken earlier approached the fallen student, dart gun still held at the ready. When a moment passed with no signs of movement, he smoothly holstered the weapon and muttered into a radio clipped to his vest.

Noah couldn't hear his exact words over the sound of everyone shouting excitedly, but it must have been some kind of call for backup, because before long a large cargo vehicle was pulling up alongside him and three soldiers hopped out. Two of them knelt to pull a hood down over the limp student's head before picking him up and carrying him inside the vehicle. The original soldier worked with one of the new arrivals to push back the crowding students and generally exude a threatening aura.

Noah swallowed as their gazes passed over him and tried his very best to look as innocuous as possible. It didn't help that he could tell they were uninfected even from where he stood a dozen meters away.

He needn't have worried; as soon as the tranquilized kid was stashed away in the vehicle, they jumped back inside and it pulled away. The first soldier returned to his previous station and gazed around calmly as if nothing had happened.

The uninfected girl seemed understandably shaken. Despite this, she reclaimed her spot in line and had her nose back in her phone within the minute.

So that's how this whole field hasn't turned into a bloodbath, Noah thought. *The problems are removed as they occur.* He clenched his fists, freshly incentivized to be a good little harmless student.

"So, they know our weakness," Leah mused. "I bet Insight gave them some kind of blinding agent. Damn! Why'd they have to sell us out like that?"

"You're assuming that wasn't just cyanide or something," Brian said.

"Yeah, I am. If they wanted to kill us, why bother with a dart? They would have just used a regular gun."

"Unless that's what they want you to think."

Leah huffed. "The kid was blinded. It's obvious from the way he reacted."

"If we don't do anything dumb, then we won't have to find out either way," May interrupted coolly. "And when I say 'we', I'm talking to you, Noah."

He ducked his head. "I know. I'm doing my best."

She suddenly looked at Brian. "Where are you keeping the pendant? Don't let them take it."

He pulled the collar of his shirt aside to reveal the silver chain glinting coldly on his neck. "Don't worry. I won't give them any reason to steal it from me."

Over the next few minutes they drew closer and closer to their tent. Noah grew nervous in spite of himself as they stood in the shadow of the looming structure, wondering if he had made a mistake to end up here waiting his turn to enter. The entrance was a draping cloth flap that somehow blocked all sight into the tent despite drifting around in the slight breeze. A soldier stood beside it, waving a student in every thirty seconds or so.

It came Noah's turn to enter before he was able to comfortably prepare himself for whatever lay ahead. He pushed his way inside.

46

LOOK INTO HOW TO TIE A KNOT

The tent was illuminated by large plasticky windows sewn into the pitched roof. There were about a dozen health workers garbed in full safety attire and respiratory masks, each with their own small table to sit one-on-one with a student. Noah was immediately aware that all but two workers were uninfected.

Another soldier stationed just behind the entrance pointed Noah towards the far end of the tent, where a worker was disposing of some kind of small plastic tube left over from whomever she had just finished helping. She dropped it into a waste bin and looked up expectantly for the next student. Meeting eyes with Noah, she gestured impatiently for him to hurry over.

"Hello," she said as he nervously took a seat, setting his bundle of clothes under the table.

Noah almost greeted her in kind, but decided against it before he could open his mouth. He hadn't been so close to an uninfected person since last night, at least not without a blindfold. Not trusting himself to be able to close his mouth after a greeting without flesh between his jaws, he opted instead to give her a friendly nod and a smile.

The worker's mask hid her expression as she reached into a box under the table and pulled out a small plastic tube. She fit it snugly into a black device with a green-tinted LCD screen and four red oval buttons, and handed the contraption to Noah.

"Take a deep breath and exhale through the tube," she instructed. "It will test if you are carrying the viral dust infection."

Noah's heart sank. He gazed down at the device helplessly. *Maybe I could just pretend to be able to breathe,* he thought.

But that would be counterproductive. He was here for a cure, and if they didn't know that he was infected, they might very well send him on his way without treatment. It depended on whether they had a kind of immunization that everyone would receive as a preventative measure, or if it was a corrective process that they would only bother to provide to those currently ill.

Deciding he would rather not risk it, Noah set the device down on the table in a slow, deliberate motion and swallowed. He opened his mouth.

"I can't breathe. I already know I'm infected." He couldn't bring himself to meet her gaze, too afraid that it would trigger a lapse in control.

The worker smoothly reclaimed the device. "Ah, you must have been one of the first to fall ill to be displaying such developed symptoms. That's alright, you're not the only one."

Noah risked a hesitant glance up just in time to see her raise her hand. A soldier soon appeared at her station.

"Infected," the health worker said brusquely.

The soldier, a woman wearing a full face mask and so many layers that he genuinely had no idea whether or not she was infected, nodded and jerked her head for Noah to follow her away.

Picking up his personal items from the ground, Noah rose to his feet with one last wistful glance towards the health worker and let the soldier guide him to the back of the tent. He looked across the stations and saw all three of his friends were currently speaking with their health workers, presumably explaining their inability to take the test.

Then the soldier pulled aside the draping cloth covering the tent's exit and led him outside. A different soldier entered the tent at the same time they were leaving. Noah guessed he was tasked with the same duty as the soldier currently leading him away, and was returning to pick up another student in need of an escort.

His thoughts were soon distracted by the dozens of people moving back and forth between the tents and the line of buses idling along the road. Each and every student was accompanied by a soldier, regardless of which bus they were destined for.

Noah glanced back as he was led closer to the road, hoping to catch sight of his friends, but they had yet to appear. The motor of the bus he was approaching suddenly roared to life, making him jump. *Is it about to leave?*

The soldier gestured for him to enter the vehicle. Noah looked back again with increasing anxiety, unwilling to be separated from his friends. His escort noticed him dawdling and narrowed her eyes behind her thick visor. "Get on the bus, kid."

Noah looked around frantically. He had no idea how many seats were left on the bus, but he didn't want to risk that there were only one or two. He noticed a couple students approaching from behind with their own escorts.

Noah surreptitiously stepped on his shoelace and dragged his other foot away, unknotting the laces. "Just give me a sec to tie my shoes."

The soldier stared down at him in exasperation. "Can't you do that on the bus?"

"That would be a safety hazard." Noah picked at his laces like he was struggling to remember how to tie a knot. A kid hesitated behind him, waiting his turn to board, but Noah looked up and gestured graciously towards the bus. "Please, don't mind me. Go right ahead."

The student stepped in with a shrug, followed by the next five arrivals. Noah's friends were still nowhere in sight.

What are they doing, exchanging their full family histories with the workers?

The bus's engine rumbled in a steady hum as more and more students stepped past his crouching form to climb the steps into the vehicle. Noah began to wonder if he was worrying over nothing. Clearly, the bus had plenty more seats to spare.

He was flipping one of the laces mechanically back and forth, stealing impatient glances over his shoulder towards the tent where he knew his friends still remained, when the soldier standing guard beside him suddenly yanked him to his feet. "I don't know what nonsense knot you're trying to tie, but you can finish it on the bus."

She carried him to the door by the scruff of his neck and deposited him on the first step of the vehicle.

"Keep an eye on this one," she told the driver.

The man behind the wheel looked down apologetically at her. "Sorry, ma'am, but the bus is at capacity. You'll have to find another shuttle."

Noah grinned triumphantly as the soldier harrumphed and dragged him off the vehicle. "Look what you've done," she grumbled as the bus pulled away.

"Sorry," he said happily. He finally caught sight of his friends bursting out of their tent and staring around wildly until they noticed him, and he waved to get their attention. The three of them brightened at the sight of him and just about hauled their escorts in his direction.

"What took you all so long?" Noah asked as they fell into place at his side.

"Some girl took a bite out of her health worker," May sighed. "Everyone had to freeze until the soldiers tranqed her and carried her out."

"Oh," Noah said, trying not to feel jealous.

His soldier looked between the four of them and just shook her head with a look of sudden wry understanding.

They followed their guards to the next available bus and climbed aboard with no fuss.

"Look into how to tie a knot, eh?" the soldier called teasingly over her shoulder.

Noah's friends looked at him questioningly, so he pointed at his untied laces and shrugged. "She's really bothered about my shoes for some reason."

There was no shortage of available seats on this bus, and they easily found space for the four of them to sit as a group. As they took their seats Noah nearly tripped on his loose shoelace, to his great embarrassment.

"Careful," Leah warned, smirking.

Noah glanced around sheepishly and bent down, finally getting around to actually tying his shoe. He picked up his laces and tried to loop them around each other, only for a frown to crease his face. He'd forgotten how difficult it was to complete such intricate tasks. He stared down at the laces sitting like two limp white noodles in his numb hands, the prospect of maneuvering them into a knot seeming completely laughable. He settled for shoving the laces beneath the tongue of his shoe. As he patted it into place, pleased with his work, he noticed that he'd picked up a bit of blood on his shoes at some point.

He dabbed at it uncertainly for a moment before deciding it didn't really matter. His shoes were already red, anyway; the blood was hardly visible.

He straightened back into his seat. The bus was filling up quickly. Everyone on board, including the driver, was infected. Noah felt a conflicting mix of disappointment and relief at this realization. At some point he had become able to recognize that it was in his best interest to leave people alone, no matter how delicious they might appear, but that didn't stop him from wishing there was an easy way to satisfy his hunger. He missed the days when he could eat a meal without causing a crisis.

He settled back and gazed listlessly out the window as they pulled away from campus grounds. *Maybe the treatment will include lunch.*

47

SOMETHING AS
STRAIGHTFORWARD AS CASH

The atmosphere on the bus was surprisingly cheerful, considering every single person was ill with an inexplicable sickness. Somebody in the back was playing music on their speaker and there was excited chatter all around.

"Why is everyone so happy?" Noah muttered dourly. There were two soldiers on board, one on each end of the bus, but they didn't seem to put a damper on anyone's mood.

Leah smirked. "Why wouldn't they be? As far as I'm aware, nobody else has been personally threatened by Insight, watched their friend's family murder each other, and spent the night in a mausoleum all in the past twenty-four hours. This is just a free day off from school for most people."

"Nobody's concerned about Insight's involvement in this?"

"Most people don't watch the news. Half these kids might never have heard of the place before, especially if they're not from around the area."

"Even without background knowledge about them," Brian cut in, "You'd have to be crazy not to wonder why a private company would go to all this effort to supposedly help. I wouldn't be on this bus if I could think of literally any other plausible way to find a cure. If anyone could have come up with one, it's the maniacs at Insight. They're the dictionary definition of mad scientists."

"Also, there haven't been any more announcements about the symptoms," May said. "Unless people have seen the worst effects for themselves, and I'm sure plenty have by now, all they'll know about the sickness is that it makes you go numb. And that it makes your heart stop and all that, which is kind of alarming, but it's still not as scary as eating people."

"Why wouldn't they have put out a message?" Brian demanded. "They obviously know about it by now. Keeping it to themselves will only endanger the entire city. If their justification is something as stupid as trying to prevent mass panic, I'll never respect Oakridge again."

Leah raised an eyebrow. "That's probably their reason."

Brian shook his head. "I can't believe I attend this school. What an amateur mistake. This is how the zombie apocalypse starts."

"They must have told the government at some point," Leah countered. "The actual military showed up. That counts for something."

"They're doing a pretty decent job at keeping everything contained," Noah grudgingly acknowledged. "The infection might not have even spread beyond the campus."

"And with Insight helping, this whole thing could be wrapped up nice and neat before the day's out," May said optimistically.

"I'd still like to know why they're even here," Brian grumbled. "Sure, they expressed their interest in us yesterday thanks to a certain scum nugget, but there's a big difference between experimenting on a couple kids and providing emergency medical care to an entire school."

"The government could be paying them," Leah suggested. "Or they're trying to earn some goodwill back from the community."

Brian tried to spit on the floor, but his mouth was so dry that nothing besides the sound came out. "Hah, fat chance. They'd have to cure cancer itself to come close to that. Nobody even knows what this weird sickness is; Insight can parade around all they want crowing they fixed it, but people will just wonder what exactly it was that needed fixing. If they're trying to prove their munificence, they should have waited for everything to get horribly out of hand before they swooped in to save the day."

"So, they're getting paid," Leah repeated.

"I hope."

"Why do you care?"

He gave her a dark look. "It would be comforting to know they're helping for something as straightforward as cash."

"Okay," Leah said, looking bewildered.

Noah looked back out the window to watch the trees blur by. "We're going to Insight Labs, right?"

"I can only assume so," Brian said. "Damn. We went through all that effort to run away, too."

"It's not a complete waste," May said. "There'll be less attention on us this way. We'll just be part of the crowd, getting the same treatment as everyone else."

"The same quick, painless, and extremely effective treatment."

Leah glanced at Brian. "That would be ideal, yeah. We can pretty much rest assured that it'll be painless."

He nodded thoughtfully. "Unless the first step of the treatment is to return our sense of touch. Man, that would suck."

Over the course of their conversation, the trees outside transitioned first into warehouses, shopping centers, and sprawling parking lots, and then into increasingly taller and narrower structures.

Glenmore was not the largest city, though it was the biggest in the area and had grown significantly in the past fifteen years. Insight Labs had been one of several corporations to set up headquarters downtown in that time, adding their monolithic operations center to the city skyline.

Noah caught glimpses of the laboratory's angular shape jutting up in between buildings as they drew nearer. It was like a fat shard of glass, somewhat pyramidal in shape, with a base so wide that it occupied nearly half a city block.

The bus finally turned off the main street onto a one-way covered entrance road that plunged directly into the side of the prism-like building. The walls were entirely composed of mirrored panels, and all of the students peered out the windows at the captivating visual effect. Whoever was playing music in the back turned it off, and silence overtook the bus for an entrancing minute. It felt like they were entering another world.

Then the narrow paved passageway suddenly widened into a larger parking area and the bus screeched to a halt in front of a pair of double doors.

"Everybody off!" the driver called. "Follow the escorts into the building and do as they say!"

"Are you going to bring us back to campus later?" Some random kid asked.

"Nope. Don't know about any return trips," the driver answered. "I hope you brought pajamas."

"What?" the kid muttered, among a few others, exchanging worried looks and trying to figure out if their driver was making a joke.

Before they could ask any further questions, the soldiers aboard the bus stood and began herding everyone off the bus. Noah and his friends stuck close together and followed the pack off the vehicle.

The area was lit well enough that if Noah didn't look up and see the mirrors reflecting a top-down view of the bus and students, he might have believed he was outdoors. Yet even standing here before the entrance, they were really already inside the building. It was all around them, forming a ceiling and walls, and though the space was large enough to accommodate a small parking lot, it was still essentially a very reflective room. There must have been many more such parking areas scattered around beneath the building, because there was certainly not enough space in this single room to accommodate such a large corporation.

Aside from the concrete floor, The doors were the only visible parts of the building that weren't mirrors. They were formed of some kind of heavily frosted glass and had no handles to speak of. Their size and shape were their only characteristics that gave them away as an entrance at all.

They suddenly swung open, both at the same time, to reveal four people dressed in pale blue lab coats and matching respirator masks.

"Follow us," one of them said in a very muffled voice. Noah couldn't tell which of them had spoken.

The students filed slowly into the building, showing a bit more nervousness now than they had on the bus. The two soldiers did not go with them. Noah glanced over his shoulder to see them climbing back aboard the bus without a second glance towards their charges.

I guess whatever security Insight has renders them redundant. Noah watched the bus pull away into the passageway on the far side of the room, delving deeper into the building before presumably exiting somewhere on the opposite side and heading back to Oakridge to pick up another load of students.

He returned his attention to their progression into the belly of Insight. They were being led through a long, featureless hallway, with the walls composed of yet more mirrors. Noah got a good look at himself for the first time since the events of last night. It took a moment for him to realize he was looking at his own reflection.

I hope Insight can fix this, he thought. Everything about him was as pale and sunken as a corpse.

Repulsed, he glanced around surreptitiously, trying to gauge if anyone else was as visibly ill. *Why isn't anyone else this bad?*

He unwillingly looked back at the wall and frowned to himself. If Insight was as fond of mirrors as this entrance seemed to imply, he'd be constantly confronted by his reflection. He wrinkled his nose and turned away, training his gaze firmly on Brian's backpack as his friend walked ahead of him.

Their group finally turned a corner and found themselves

standing before a second set of identical doors. A light
centered above them turned green as they approached, and
the doors automatically swung noiselessly open.

They students were finally met with the sight of something
other than an empty hallway. There were a few workers
hustling up and down this hall, all wearing Insight's signature
blue uniform, but none of them paid their group so much as a
second glance.

They were led through a door immediately on the left.
Instead of a handle, it had another green light that lit up as
they approached. One of the employees pushed the door open.

"Wait here. An attendant will fetch you when it is your
turn for treatment," he informed them in the same muffled
voice as earlier. He waited for the rest of them to file in, then
nodded and retreated after his colleagues from the room,
shutting the door behind him. There was no handle on the
inside, either.

Noah looked around and was somewhat comforted to see
the space was filled with Oakridge students who had already
arrived. There was plenty of seating, though it was incredibly
varied and seemed to be more of an impromptu attempt
to create a sort of traditional waiting room than anything
else. The majority of the chairs were lab stools. There was a
surprisingly normal white door at the back of the room, which
was currently closed. In what must have been an incredible
act of self-restraint, Insight had only made the back wall
mirrored. The other three were painted light blue.

"So, we made it," Leah said. She found an empty stool and
dropped into it, then grinned in surprise as it swiveled her
around in a circle.

The other three friends found nearby seating and dragged
the stools closer together.

"I'm surprised they're already helping us," Brian said. "I
thought for sure there would be at least two hours of waiting
and paperwork."

"Oh, Insight doesn't do paperwork," Leah laughed. "That's
far too incriminating."

"What? Really?"

She grinned and shrugged. "I have no idea."

Brian rolled his eyes and leaned over to a nearby unfamiliar student sitting slouched in one of the few cushioned chairs. He was scrolling on his phone with a glazed look in his eyes.

"Hey, you look like you've been here awhile. About how quickly are people getting treated?"

The guy glanced over and blinked. "Uh, real fast. Somebody gets called back every few minutes. They don't come back, though. No clue where they're getting taken."

"Thanks," Brian said.

He leaned back into their circle with a defeated look in his eyes. "We're definitely getting murdered."

48

DON'T EAT THE SCIENTISTS

"**S**top jumping to conclusions," Leah said, elbowing him. "They're probably already on their way back to Oakridge."

"In body bags," Brian muttered under his breath.

The door at the rear of the room suddenly cracked open and a short blue-coated woman slipped out. She glanced around the room and picked a kid seemingly at random, waving him over to the door. He followed her through and they both disappeared.

"So much for lines," May said, watching the door shut behind them. "We could just as easily be the next picked or the last."

"Something tells me they have no idea how to deal with people," Noah mused after a few minutes. Several more students had been selected and led out of the room in that time.

"Well, Insight's not your typical health center," Leah pointed out. "They're a research lab. They're obviously not focused on improving the client experience."

"Clearly," Brian replied, spinning around and around on his lab stool.

"Hey, I'm not hating these chairs," Leah said. "If anything, it's kind of funny that this is how they decided to deal with all of us. Just shove us in an extra room and make us wait. What are we going to do, file a customer complaint?"

"I wonder if they ever got any use out of those blood

samples Dr. Jansen took," Brian said out of the blue.

May looked at him in surprise. "Did they get sent here? I don't remember where she said she was sending them."

"Well, where else would she pick? She's clearly good buddies with Insight, and what better place to pick for demystifying such a bizarre sickness?"

A few dozen students streamed into the room then, new arrivals from the latest shuttle. They filtered through the space and found seats for themselves.

Noah stared anxiously down at his hands. "I hope the treatment doesn't involve anything that would reveal we're the same people that those blood samples came from. Not sure if it would change anything, but anonymity is definitely the right choice when it comes to this place."

"Hopefully, even if they do realize, we'll be long gone by then," Brian said.

The back door opened and the same woman emerged. She cast her gaze briefly around the room before making eye contact with Noah and beckoning him over.

His eyes flicked to his friends in surprise.

"Well, go on, this is what we came for," Brian said. "They probably won't try to kill you."

"If they try anything suspicious, you can just eat them," Leah said with a grin, then narrowed her eyes. "That's a joke, in case you're wondering. Don't eat the scientists."

Noah swallowed and stood from his seat without responding. He almost forgot his bundle of clothes and personal items, but remembered to grab it at the last second.

"Don't eat them!" Leah yelled again as he walked away, attracting the attention of a few of the nearby students.

Noah turned to smile nervously at her, and then he was through the door and his friends were out of view.

The room he found himself in was about twice the size of a typical doctor's office. There were two male doctors standing near the far wall, where an odd contraption sat whirring quietly, the pitch and volume slowly winding down.

The main body of the apparatus was a thigh-high steel

drum painted a bright blue. There were several tubes with pressure gauges affixed to the top of it, and the entire thing was perched on four small swiveling wheels. An exam table had been positioned next to the machine. There was a second door to his right, as well as a wide counter that stretched nearly wall-to-wall.

"Please take a seat," the woman beside him said. She stepped back beside the door and simply stood there, watching him.

Noah walked hesitantly to the exam table and sat himself on the ledge. He set his clothes down beside him.

"What are you going to do?" he asked.

One of the doctors picked up a plastic oxygen mask which was attached to the end of a tube and began picking at something on its outer shell. "This machine will remove the dust particles from your lungs."

"And that will cure me?"

The doctor gazed at him for a moment before nodding and returning his attention to the mask. "We have found that removing a certain threshold of the particles results in a near-perfect return to normal health within the next twenty-four hours."

Noah raised his eyebrows. "'Near-perfect?'"

"Students who have been injured while they were infected may experience some weight loss, but it's nothing that can't be regained with time."

"Seriously?" Noah complained. "Look at me! What am I supposed to do?"

"I recommend you visit a dietician."

Noah gave the man an appraising look. It was hard to tell under all his layers of protective apparel, but he seemed to have quite a bit of meat on his bones.

"Continuing your current line of thought is ill-advised," the doctor said calmly, somehow reading his mind despite his averted gaze. "We have security measures in place that will prevent any accidents resulting from your poor self-control."

"I have perfect self-control."

"That's good to hear."

The doctor finally seemed satisfied with the mask and stepped closer to Noah. "The process will take about a minute. At the end of that time, we will run a test to ensure you are properly cured. You may feel slightly hungry as the process approaches completion, but the sensation will pass quickly. Let me remind you once again that acting upon your hunger will not end well for you."

Noah glared suspiciously at the oxygen mask, noticing with some dismay that it was attached to the tube by means of a thick wrapping of duct tape. He raised an eyebrow at the doctor, who sighed.

"I am aware that the construction of this device might not inspire confidence, but please bear in mind that we had to come up with a design overnight. We simply did not have sufficient time to fabricate all of the parts we would have liked."

"As long as it works," Noah said uncertainly.

The doctor smiled thinly and placed the mask over Noah's mouth before pulling the elastic bands over his head to secure it in place.

"Don't fight the machine," the man warned. "Keep your mouth open and let it do its job."

Noah nodded mutely. The doctor nodded at his partner, who flicked a switch atop the metal drum. The whirring noise, which had almost died down into nothing, rose suddenly into a headache-inducing whine. The mask pressed itself against his face, pulling the tube which hung between him and the machine almost imperceptibly tighter. Noah couldn't feel it against his face, but he recognized the sound and the visual cues for what they were.

"Did you literally tape an oxygen mask to a vacuum?" he demanded.

The doctors glanced at each other in surprise.

"What? Did you think nobody would be able to tell?" It took some effort to get the words out; the increasing pressure was making it more difficult to speak with every passing second.

"The vacuum is set to run at half power," the second doctor finally said defensively, voice raised to be heard over the piercing sound of the motor. "The suction is not strong enough to harm a human body."

"That's not the point," Noah tried to say, but he couldn't produce an audible sound. *I can't believe this was the solution that a multi-billion dollar company came up with.*

The tube shook slightly, but whether that was because of the dust moving through it or the shaking of the machine's motor was impossible to tell. Noah was quite glad he couldn't feel what it was like for a vacuum to be suctioning at his airways, but it would have been nice to have a visual confirmation that it was being effective. He suddenly realized the mask was transparent and went cross-eyed trying to look at it.

The transparent material had been coated from the inside with an even shade of jet black. The sight promptly inspired an inexplicable spike of panic to shoot through Noah, but he didn't shift or otherwise act on the emotion. *This is what I'm here for,* he reminded himself.

The mask slowly began to its usual unclouded state as the seconds passed. Clumps of dark material pulled away to disappear down the tube, whisked away by the steady pull of the vacuum's power. Before the mask could be considered remotely 'empty', however, the first doctor reached for the machine and hit another switch. The steady whine of the motor began winding down. Both doctors came to stand close beside Noah, and he gazed between them in slight puzzlement. The worsened hunger they had warned him of had yet to set in, although his entire being already ached so terribly to *consume* that it was possible the change had simply occurred beneath his notice.

The dust visible in the mask rapidly dissipated as the vacuum's power waned. Before the machine had gone completely silent, the first doctor pulled the mask away from Noah's face and turned expectantly to his fellow worker. He was handed a large slip of what looked like paper, but was actually what Noah recognized as the filter test-strip material from the small disposable testing contraptions back on campus.

The man slid it over Noah's mouth before letting the mask snap back to hold it in place. Noah realized they were letting the remaining power of the machine 'breathe' for him, suctioning at his lungs and theoretically pulling whatever dust particles remained there into the filter.

After another few seconds the doctor finally took the mask off altogether and pulled the filter away.

"That's it?" Noah asked.

"We need to check the effectiveness of the treatment," the doctor said, setting the mask aside and taking the test strip across the room to the counter. He inserted it into a familiar black device and leaned back patiently for it to produce a verdict. "This is mostly just a formality, but we have had a few cases..."

Noah didn't say anything. He didn't feel any different, but the doctor had said it could take a day for the treatment to kick in, so he didn't let that bother him too much. He just stared hopefully at the device.

There was no visible indication of whether he passed or failed, though the gadget must have conveyed the results somehow. Noah's anxiety mounted as the doctor extracted the test strip, opened the cabinet beneath the counter, and slid the slip carefully into a specific file. He then closed the cabinet and turned back to Noah with a flat expression.

"You still have an unsafe amount of dust particles within your lungs, such that you cannot be considered cured. The treatment process was insufficiently effective."

"Wh-what?" Noah stammered. His heart dropped. "What does that mean?"

"It means you'll be staying overnight as we develop a more potent treatment."

"Just do it again," Noah said quickly. "Run the vacuum at full power."

The doctor shook his head shortly. "We already ran it at the maximum safe power level."

"I don't care about whether it's safe. I'll heal afterwards."

"That's not guaranteed," the second doctor said evenly. "We can keep it as an option if we fail to design a better treatment, but it will not be our first choice."

"And here I thought you guys didn't give a crap about your patients' survival rate," Noah muttered.

All three doctors in the room turned sharply to him. "That is a common misconception," the doctor by the counter said. "Our work is and has always been in the interest of humanity."

Noah huffed and looked away. "Why didn't the treatment work?"

"It's impossible to say with what information we currently possess. There has been no apparent correlation between the few students who have not been effectively treated."

Noah closed his eyes. Frustration welled up within him at how unfair it was that the treatment just inexplicably failed to cure him.

"Fine," he finally snapped. "Where do I go?"

"Follow me."

49

WHAT MAKES YOU THINK I'M FINE

Noah was led into yet another empty mirrored hallway. There were doors spaced evenly down the length of the corridor, all the way to the far end where a larger set of double-doors marked the end of his view.

The doctor walked swiftly down the hall. Lights above each door would turn green for a second as he passed, but he didn't stop at any of them until they were approximately halfway down the passageway.

He paused outside the door and looked at Noah, who was just standing there with his clothes clutched in his arms and a wretched cast to his features. "Wait here with the other uncured students. Somebody will fetch you when we are done treating everyone else, and you will be brought to more suitable accommodations."

With that, he pushed the door open and stepped aside for Noah to enter.

Noah did so slowly, gazing at the doctor with the knowledge that this was probably his last chance in a while for him to take the edge off his awful hunger, but in the end he didn't do anything. He lowered his eyes and trudged inside.

"Good day," the doctor said, and turned back towards the treatment room.

Noah immediately turned to watch him leave, barely taking a moment to observe the new room. As soon as the doctor had moved out of sight, he knelt quickly to the floor and dropped one of the shirts from his clothing bundle on the edge of the doorframe. The door bumped gently against it and remained unlatched by a single inch, and a small smile graced Noah's face.

Noah stood and turned around to face his fellow infected students. Two of them were looking at him with concern, the third was grinning in pleasant surprise, and the fourth was sitting in a shaking wreck on the floor in the corner and didn't seem to be paying any of them any attention.

There were several metal folding chairs leaning against the wall to his left, so he grabbed one and unfolded it before plopping himself down.

The three kids across from him had already set up chairs for themselves. There were two girls and two boys with him in the room, though the second boy was the one on the floor. One of the girls was wearing an enormous winter coat that seemed entirely too hot and bulky for the current season. She was smiling.

"What did you just do with the door?" she asked knowingly.

"None of the doors here have handles, or have you not noticed?" Noah said, playing along. "I'd like to be able to leave if I so choose. I'm just giving myself the option."

She grinned mischievously. "Eh, that method works, I suppose. Personally, I'd go about it in a different manner."

"Yeah? How so?"

She reached into one of the pockets in her coat and pulled out a box of matches, bigger than the small pack Brian carried around, then pointed at a small white disk in the ceiling that had a flashing red light. A fire alarm.

"I dunno if that would work," Noah finally said after he got over his surprise. *Am I the only person who doesn't carry around matches?* "They would probably forget we're even here."

She smirked. "Yeah, I'm counting on it. Once most people have evacuated, I'll initiate stage two." She pulled out an entire hatchet from another pocket. "The doors look all industrial, but they're really just wood. I checked."

Noah shot a glance at the door and his eyes widened. There was a small gash taken out of it to reveal a pale wooden interior.

"Uh, I can't say I expected you guys to have already come up with an escape plan," he muttered. *Okay, I'm not the weird one. She's like Brian with his backpack, except worse. Also, she apparently thinks it's normal to test the material of something by taking a chunk out of it.*

"Just her," the other girl said quickly. "We're not involved in this."

"Aw, don't be like that," she said, slinging the hatchet up to rest casually on her shoulder. "It's just in case."

"How did you even smuggle a hatchet in here? That thing is a weapon," Noah said incredulously.

"They didn't have a security check." She smiled widely.

"They're probably more worried about us trying to eat them than about us pulling an axe on them," he pointed out.

She frowned. "Eating them?"

Everyone else in the room looked at her, including the guy sitting wretchedly in the corner.

She looked around with an uncertain smile. "Am I missing something?"

"Apparently," the guy sitting beside her said. He had shaggy brown hair hanging out from under a white baseball cap. "We're all basically zombies; not sure how you haven't realized that by now. What did you think that kid was doing?" He jabbed a finger at the cadaverous student in the corner, who in turn gave him a dirty look.

She stared around at them like she was waiting for someone to laugh. "Y'all aren't...?"

"No, we're not pulling one over on you, and yes, the sickness does manifest some very zombie-like behaviors," the other girl spoke up. "Not that I've personally experienced any of the more cannibalistic symptoms, but I've seen it happening. You need to be hurt in some way for the effects to kick in, and apparently infected people won't attack other infected people."

"Oh," she said. "Is that why..." She trailed off again.

They all looked at the guy shaking in the corner.

"Yeah," the shaggy-haired kid said. "I was with him when it happened. He sprained his ankle real bad getting off the bus. There must have been some delayed aspect to the injury, because he only started getting really crazy once we had been in the waiting room awhile."

The kid looked up with surprising clarity filtering up from the depths of his sunken eyes. "I tried to go after one of the doctors before they were done treating me, but next thing I knew, I was in this room."

"My man, you should have waited until they were done," Noah rebuked.

The kid shrugged his thin shoulders miserably and buried his head in his hands. "I'm aware."

"I know what it's like," Noah tried to comfort him. "You probably didn't feel like you had an option."

The kid started to nod and say something, but then tremors overtook his body and he no longer seemed in a state capable of continuing the conversation. Noah's gaze lingered on him for a moment, and he felt a faint perverted comfort that somebody was more visibly ill than himself.

He turned away as two sets of footsteps approached from outside the door. Noah glanced quickly at the thin gap through which the hallway was visible, afraid that someone had already discovered his makeshift doorstop, but the footsteps continued down the passageway without slowing.

Thinking he was safe, he stood and crept to the door to peek through the crack. The same doctor who had taken him to the room he currently resided in was now leading another student down the hall. Noah watched them continue all the way to the double doors at the end of the corridor and pass through them when the light turned green. The doors closed automatically behind them. A minute passed before the doctor returned, now unaccompanied.

Noah withdrew from the gap and prayed it was slim enough to pass under the doctor's notice as the sound of his footsteps grew louder. He passed by once again without noticing anything was amiss.

He's not exactly expecting to see a barely ajar door, and the mask he's wearing probably doesn't help matters.

Noah's brow furrowed as he pulled back into the room. He hoped it was nothing, but he couldn't help but wonder why all the Insight employees were still wearing masks when they supposedly had a cure for the infection. He tried not to be too suspicious. *They're perfectly entitled to be cautious, and it would probably be inconvenient to have to constantly suck the dust out. Plus, it could just be normal company practice. I'm sure there's all sorts of other hazardous materials around this place.*

Noah forced his expression back into a neutral position as he sat back in his chair. "It's just the doctor walking by. Nothing to be worried about."

His thoughts went to his friends, still awaiting their treatment, and he realized unhappily that since they were statistically likely to be properly cured, he wouldn't get to see them again until Insight decided to release him. *I can at least send them a text message so they know what happened to me.*

He patted down his pockets for his phone and felt a pang of nervous tension when he came up empty. A moment later he remembered it was still wrapped up in his clothes, so he grabbed the bundle and quickly tugged the device out from the folds of a pair of jeans.

He typed out a message to fill them in on his current situation and hit send. He was unsure what difference it would make, but good communication never hurt anyone.

A few seconds later he received a message in return from Brian. *Don't panic. We'll figure out how to get to you.*

Then a message from Leah: *DON'T EAT ANYONE.*

Noah smirked and sent a dinner plate emoji in reply, then sobered as he realized that Brian was probably going to try something dumb. *Just get yourself cured*, he wrote. *Don't worry about me.*

The lack of an immediate reply only served to make him

more nervous about whatever his friends were planning.

Noah grumbled to himself and leaned back in his chair. He put his phone away and gazed around at the other students. "I never introduced myself. I'm Noah."

"Clarissa," the girl still holding the hatchet said.

"Violet."

"Mark."

They all glanced at the fourth student in the corner, but he didn't seem interested in sharing his name.

"Is he okay?" Clarissa asked.

"He's hungry, I guess," Mark said.

"And?"

"He currently feels like his very life is being drained out of him," Noah flatly informed them. "It's honestly quite impressive that he hasn't passed out yet. If he stays conscious, the next non-infected person to enter this room is probably going to be eaten whole if they're not prepared."

"You look nearly as sick as he does," Clarissa pointed out. "How come you're fine?"

"What makes you think I'm fine?"

"Well, you're holding a conversation, for one."

He smiled. "I guess I'm not as desperate as our friend here." He thought about sharing that he'd already had quite the nice meal last night, but figured there was no need to freak them out. If they weren't hungry, they wouldn't understand.

"Anything interesting happen today?" he asked the room instead. "Or just more of the usual?"

Mark snorted. "Nah, same old, you know."

"I got jumpscared by a corpse in Oakridge's cadaver lab after I coughed on it," Violet announced.

"That must've been exciting," Noah said.

"Yeah. It threw me aside and ran out the door. Not sure where it is now."

"Probably out living its best life," Noah said.

"Yeah."

50

THIS SHOULD'VE BEEN PLAN A

Mark and Clarissa looked between them warily.

"You're saying we can bring back the dead," Clarissa said disbelievingly.

"Well, bring 'em back as zombies, at least," Violet said agreeably. "Not sure how much anyone would want to bring their beloved family member back as a mindless zombie.

"The good news is that a corpse obviously doesn't breathe, so all they can really do is walk around chomping on people and causing chaos. There shouldn't be any danger of them spreading the infection."

"Can they be killed?" Clarissa asked.

Noah dipped his head. "Oh, for sure. I watched my friend get her head chopped off last night, and that was the end of her."

Everyone's mouths fell open.

"She had the *Wager*," he explained. "It basically destroyed her organs and she went crazy trying to heal. Long story short, her dad had to decapitate her. It was pretty terrible."

His explanation didn't appear to lessen anyone's shock. "And I thought my day was insane," Violet muttered to herself.

"At least we know the infected dead can be taken down," Clarissa said hesitantly. She clenched her fingers around the handle of her hatchet and shut her eyes briefly. "I can't believe I'm sitting in a room full of zombies."

"Dormant zombies, more like," Noah said. He eyed the

hatchet warily. "And we're no danger to you. You're just as infected as any of us."

She sighed, releasing a puff of dust and revealing that she had only recently been infected, and shoved the hatchet back into her coat. It disappeared into the massive garment without any visible bulge.

Noah caught the sound of people once more walking down the hall outside, along with an odd repetitive squeaking.

Nobody else in the room seemed interested in the happenings outside, so he shrugged and walked back to the door to peer out curiously.

The two doctors who had treated him were laboriously pushing the large blue metal drum down the hallway. The source of the squeaking was one of its four small wheels wobbling as it moved along. All of the tubes and related apparatus, including the mask, had been balanced atop the metal cylinder in a precarious pile.

"This is, what, the tenth load?" one of the doctors huffed.

"Eleventh."

"Yeah. That's not a small amount of dust. This is a thirty-gallon tank."

They paused at a door about halfway between Noah and the far end of the hall, and waited for the light to turn green before pushing the large canister into the room and out of view. The door closed slowly behind them and the light switched off.

Noah waited patiently for them to return.

The door finally opened several minutes later and the two men reappeared with the metal tank. Noah assumed they had either disposed of its contents within the room or gotten an entirely new empty container, as they were now pushing it with ease.

Noah hoped they would say aloud how they had gotten rid of the dust, but the conversation had moved on to the menu of a cafe that was apparently upstairs. Noah completely tuned them out, his focus locked on the room they had exited. For some reason he found himself desperately wishing he could see what lay within. He had the odd feeling that it was very important somehow.

He stood there, just staring down the corridor at the unlit light above the door and wondering how he could possibly overcome that obstacle, when one of the doctors came walking down the hall once again with another supposedly cured student in tow. He ignored them, but the light above the door went briefly green as the doctor passed.

Noah straightened, eyes narrowing. He wondered how he could use this to get inside. Insight employees must have all been given some kind of card chip or digital key that automatically unlocked the doors. The problem was that he had no idea what form it took or where it was stored on their body.

The doctor came back down the hall and returned to the treatment room, oblivious to Noah watching him.

I don't need to pickpocket them, he thought to himself. *It works by proximity.*

He brightened as an idea came to him, a smile slowly spreading across his face as he mused over it. It was a flawless plan. It even included a backup measure.

He turned to the four students in the room. "I need all of your masks," he announced. "Oakridge gave everyone masks, right? Do you still have yours?"

Violet frowned at him. "Yeah, why?"

He waved aside the question. "Can I have it?"

She narrowed her eyes at him, but acquiesced, slowly pulling a lime-green face mask from her pocket and passing it over to him.

Mark's was hanging on his face by a single ear, and he handed it to Noah with a bemused look. "Why do you need four masks?"

Noah glanced out the door anxiously. The hallway was still empty. "Does it matter?" he asked distractedly.

He shrugged. "I guess not. Will I be getting it back?"

"Sure." Noah looked expectantly at Clarissa.

The girl grinned and pulled a handful of crisp unused

masks from an inner pocket in her coat. "Here, have five."

Noah stared at her, then chuckled. "Alright. Thanks."

He had planned to take the mask from the unfortunate kid in the corner, but with so many extras now he wouldn't have to bother.

He began pulling the masks one-by-one onto his head, much to the confusion of the three students watching him. He layered them into a sort of bonnet that covered the top of his head, left a gap for his eyes to see through, and placed three more to overlap on his nose, mouth, and chin.

Clarissa burst into laughter. "What the hell are you doing?"

"Hiding my identity," he said seriously, but she only laughed harder.

Noah glowered at her. "What? Is it not effective?"

"Well, anyone who sees you is going to wonder why you've bandaged yourself in face masks, but I guess it hides your face well enough. But I have to ask, why bother on top?"

"I'm being thorough."

She snorted. "Okay. If someone tries to identify you using the cameras, though, they'll probably be able to match up your clothes, and you'll find you're not as anonymous as you hoped."

Noah gave her a considering look. "Good point."

He grabbed a shirt and pants from his bundle and pulled them on over his current outfit. The bundle was quickly diminishing, and was less a bundle now so much as a single crumpled undergarment.

"Better?" he asked.

"You just knocked all the masks off," Mark observed.

Noah carefully fixed them back in place. "Okay. How do I look?"

"Like a really crappy medically-themed superhero," Violet said.

"Great, thanks."

Noah picked up his remaining article of clothing, a quite wrinkled pair of underwear, and shoved it in his outer pants pocket. He went to the door and waited for the doctor to make another trip down the hallway with a student.

He didn't have to wait long. Footsteps came briskly towards him, making him tense in anticipation. As soon as they were past his door, he quickly pushed it open, careful not to disturb the shirt doorstop, and slipped out into the hall. He hurried down the passage after the two unaware figures, knowing he had to catch up before they passed the door he wanted to enter or else lose his chance.

He automatically and unconsciously tried to categorize the student as infected or uninfected, only for his instincts to react in confusion. The girl presented a muddled mix of signs that made his senses react strangely, unsure of her status. He wasn't planning on eating her, so he tried not to let it bother him.

He quietly fell into step behind them. He was more worried the student would notice him and raise a fuss than the doctor, who was wearing a full respiratory mask that looked to significantly impede both vision and hearing. Fortunately, both individuals remained oblivious to his presence. He drew yet closer as they approached the door, knowing his opportunity would only last a second.

Then they were right beside it, and the light flicked momentarily on. Noah leapt forward and pressed against it.

He thumped against its unyielding surface. He was too slow. The doctor was already too far ahead, and the light was dim once more.

The student must've noticed the slight noise of him hitting the door, because she turned curiously and jumped at the sight of him standing so close.

Noah held his hands up and tried to use his eyes to express his desire to remain unnoticed by the doctor.

The student stared at him for a second longer and slowly nodded. Noah gave her a grateful nod and backed away towards his room, feeling vaguely frustrated. He would have to try again with the next student escort.

Then the doctor glanced at the girl beside him. "What's

wrong?" He looked briefly backwards down the hall, then did a double-take. He met eyes with the strangely garbed figure standing just behind him and he stepped away in surprise.

Noah froze guiltily, just staring back at him.

"Who are you? What are you doing?" The doctor was more curious than suspicious, although that was quickly changing.

Oh, well. Time for Plan B, Noah thought, and tore away the mask over his mouth, revealing an eager smile. "Don't scream, please," he told the student.

Then, rather than answering the doctor, he stepped forward into the man's personal space and latched onto his throat.

The student, to her credit, didn't scream. She merely stumbled away before she managed to get her feet properly under her and ran to the far end of the hallway. She couldn't go any further, seeing as how every door was locked, but Noah didn't pay her any mind.

This should have been Plan A, Noah thought contentedly, pulling back from the doctor's neck with a small bit of it in his jaws. He couldn't feel it in his mouth, but he could sense the energy it held being bestowed upon him as he swallowed. It was a pleasant sensation.

The man was trying to shout for help, but the mask he wore significantly muffled his voice, and the walls of the building didn't help his prospects. Blood was beginning to stain the collar of his lab coat.

"Looks like your security isn't so airtight, after all," Noah said.

The doctor grit his teeth at the comment and finally managed to shove Noah away. He reached into one of the pockets in his coat and started probing around for something.

Noah didn't know what he was looking for, and he didn't care to find out. He darted once more at the doctor, causing him to flinch, and bit down on his meaty forearm. A lab coat, it turned out, served as terrible armor.

The doctor let out a pained groan. "Stop! Stop! I can get you more people- there's a whole bunch of patients downstairs, I promise- just let me go!"

Noah nonchalantly tore off another piece of his flesh and gave him a dirty look. "I thought you said you cared about your patients."

The guy's eyes darted nervously back and forth. "Well, sure, but desperate times call for desperate-"

"Oh, be quiet," Noah said, and before he could really think about what he was doing, he tore out the man's throat.

51

I HOPE THIS ISN'T GOING TO HAVE
ANY NEGATIVE HEALTH EFFECTS

Noah swallowed whole the large piece of flesh, enjoying the resulting burst of energy, and stood back as the doctor crumpled to the ground. The man's neck was torn wide open, exposing the crushed hole of his pharynx. Blood torrented from the wound.

I did that, Noah thought apathetically.

He flinched suddenly as a dull throb of pain shot through his head out of nowhere. After experiencing absolutely no physical input for over twenty-four hours, the abrupt sensation akin to his brain being squeezed took him by unpleasant surprise. He gritted his teeth and backed away from the body.

"What's happening now?" he muttered to himself.

He knew he needed to get into the room and out of sight before someone wandered into this stretch of hallway, but he was momentarily thrown off by the sudden migraine. He glanced down at his own body, wondering if he had been grievously injured without noticing. There was some blood on his shirt, but he was relatively sure the worst he had suffered was a nasty bruise to his forearm. Even that was already nearly healed, drawing on the energy he had just gained. *The headache isn't a physical injury. I wouldn't be able to feel it if that were the case.*

He took a moment to collect himself. It was a strange and

subtle distinction, but the more he focused on it, the more he became convinced that the pain was mental rather than physical. He glanced back at the mangled body, and horror spiked through him for the briefest of moments before his headache flared uncomfortably and the sentiment abruptly vanished.

His eyes widened, then squeezed shut. A different kind of horror washed over him. *The sickness is messing with my head.*

Not that he hadn't already assumed that was the case, but now the interference was all too obvious. He opened his eyes and focused intently on the body, trying to overcome the invisible force affecting his mind. All he received for his efforts was a dull ache in his skull.

How come it didn't hurt when I was actively eating him? Or Sophie's dad last night, for that matter?

He thought about it and decided that whatever malignant influence was removing his ability to feel disgust at his own actions was probably in constant effect, and only generated pain as a reaction to excess stimuli. Ripping out a man's throat must have qualified as such.

Growing slightly uncomfortable, his gaze focused on the pocket that the doctor had reached for before he died. Half wondering what it was the man had been trying to pull out and half trying to simply distract himself, Noah carefully reached in and withdrew what looked like a very small pistol. It was toylike, with a barrel far too slim for any bullet, and a round vessel sat at the rear of the weapon like a water gun. It had a small switch inset on the top, which Noah flicked without hesitation.

A hypodermic needle slid out from the pinprick hole in the muzzle.

Noah's eyes widened slightly as he realized he was very likely holding a compact and close-range version of the blinding dart guns the soldiers on campus had been equipped with. He flicked the switch back, retracting the needle, and pocketed the weapon. It was nice to have a non-lethal method of attack, although he doubted he would be presented with a situation that would require its use. As terrifying as it was that his mind was being actively affected, the influence was doing its job quite well. He couldn't imagine himself choosing to prick someone with a needle when he could simply take a bite out of them instead.

He glanced down the corridor. It was still empty aside from the student at the far end watching him warily, who he chose to ignore. He figured it was about time to get out of the hallway.

He wondered for a moment if he had been subconsciously lingering out in the open in the hope that another uninfected worker would wander by, and then realized that the thought itself was another form of delay.

Grumbling to himself and wishing his headache would go away, he grabbed the doctor's booted feet and began dragging him down the hall. The blood running from the man's neck streaked the floor like paint from a brush. Noah eyed it unhappily. It pointed a line right to the door he planned to enter.

Let's just get inside before I start worrying about the mess.

Noah might not have been able to directly feel the weight of the doctor's body, but he could certainly perceive the drag it created on his movements, slowing his progress. He finally heaved it in front of the door and stepped back expectantly.

The light on the door flicked green, to his great delight. *Finally,* he thought, pressing it open with his back and dragging the body inside after him. As he passed the threshold, all of the lights in the room turned on at once.

He glanced briefly around the space, taking in several large metallic vats lined up along the side of the room and some tables with odd electrical apparatus scattered upon them. He was quite interested in taking a closer look, but he reasoned he should probably clean up the blood in the hallway before he took the time to properly investigate the space.

"Alright, time for you to help clean the mess you made,"

he told the dead doctor, and got to work pulling his lab coat off of his body. It took some effort, but soon he held the partially bloodstained garment as a balled-up wad of fabric in his hands.

Leaving the doctor's legs partially sticking out into the hallway as a doorstop, he stepped back into the corridor and began wiping the blood off the floor. The lab coat was surprisingly absorbent, although there were a few traces of crimson that had seeped into the cracks in the floor tiles and stubbornly refused to be wiped out.

As he worked, the girl who had been standing at the end of the hallway drifted slowly closer to linger nervously nearby.

"What is it?" Noah snapped, glancing up. He realized he sounded more annoyed than he meant to and gave her an apologetic look. "Sorry, this just isn't coming out."

She was also still wreaking havoc on his senses, and that paired with his fading headache and worry over his state of mind was putting him in a foul mood.

She stared down at the ground with her hands twisted anxiously together. "Why did you attack the doctor like that? By biting him?"

Noah's eyes narrowed at the question, and he was quiet for a moment as he stepped back to inspect his work. He decided it was good enough.

He turned back to the agitated student and would have sighed if he were able. "It was the easiest way to subdue him," he muttered, then shrugged. "And I was hungry."

She stared at him and bit her tongue, clearly wanting to say something. She just stood there silently, though, as the seconds passed.

"Look, if you want to have a conversation, we can do it in there," Noah said impatiently, gesturing down the hall to where the pair of legs stuck out ominously. He swept past her and entered the room, carefully stepping over the body.

To his surprise, she actually followed him, though she cast a horrified look at the doctor as she crossed over him.

As soon as she was over the threshold, Noah pulled the

body further into the room to let the door fully close.

"Alright, what is it?" he asked testily. He had half a mind to just kick her out, but he was afraid she would seek help from one of the other doctors in this wing of the building and end up selling out his position.

She shrunk against the wall. "Ever since this morning, I've felt like- like I wanted to-"

"Eat people?" Noah said flatly. "Yeah, you must've gotten infected, and then injured, and now you're a zombie. Or you were one. Not sure how effective the treatment Insight is handing out is, since it didn't work on me."

He walked over to the row of six identical vats. Each one was slightly taller than him and thick enough that two people standing on either side would have just barely been able to clasp hands. There was a sign warning that the vats were flammable storage, and a large wheel on top to access the contents. There was a smaller wheel on the side.

The student stared at him uncertainly. "A zombie? So that's why you-"

"Yes." He grabbed the large wheel on top of the first vat and gave it an experimental tug.

She blinked. "Huh. I thought I was going crazy."

Noah shook his head. Oakridge's decision to keep quiet about the symptoms of the infection was going to give half their students a personal crisis.

He turned his attention back to the wheel and tightened his fingers around it before heaving it to the left with all his might. It rotated slowly and silently, gradually unscrewing before suddenly coming free in his hands.

Immediately, a dense black cloud expanded from the opening. It blinded him for a moment before he stumbled back out of the worst of it.

He stood a few feet away and stared. The vat was full to the brim of dust. *So this is where they're storing it.* He glanced nervously at the other five massive containers, wondering if they were all full.

The dust was still expanding rapidly from the hole he had

opened, slowly darkening the room.

"I suppose I should close that back up," he muttered to himself, and walked back over to it. He shoved the plug into the opening and screwed it back into place. As he worked, a strange jittery feeling came over him, like he had just downed a week's worth of caffeine.

"I think something's in this dust," he said to the girl standing by the far wall. "You feeling that? Or do you think that's just the normal effect of being in so much dust?"

"I think I just got infected again," she said glumly.

"Oh. Sorry."

She sighed. "Whatever. I can have the doctors suck it back out." She glanced at the body in the corner. "Er, maybe not. I'll find a way to do it myself."

Noah nodded distractedly, staring at his shaking hands. "I hope this isn't going to have any negative health effects. I'm going to check if the other vats are also filled."

She scowled. "Why?"

"I don't know why Insight is storing the dust like this, but I don't think there's a single possible good reason that they haven't already destroyed or otherwise disposed of it. I want to see how badly we're screwed."

52

YOU'RE LITERALLY INSANE

It turned out that only two of the vats were currently being used to store dust. The remaining four were completely empty, though Noah had no idea how many infected students were still waiting to be treated. For all he knew, all of the vats would be filled by the end of the day.

"We've been played," he said portentously.

"Yeah?" The girl was still hovering across the room. She glanced at the door regretfully.

Noah began pacing back and forth in front of the vats, his mind racing. "I'd bet you anything that they only 'treated' us to get their hands on this dust they're so interested in. The fact that it cures the patient is just a convenient side effect. Actually, they probably wish it didn't cure us, so they could keep harvesting from us indefinitely."

He suddenly came to a halt and turned to her, a dark look in his eyes. "I wonder if they didn't cure me and the other kids on purpose. Someone probably realized they would lose their steady source of dust if everyone got cured, so they made sure to set a couple of us aside."

As angry as the thought made him, it was also a source of hope. If the only reason he wasn't cured was because they pulled the plug too early, then it would be an easy thing to remedy.

"Uh," the girl mumbled, unsure of what he was referring to. After a few seconds she hesitantly said, "Well, you don't seem very cured."

"Yeah, that was never in question," he muttered. He stared back at the vats. "What use could they have for so much of this stuff, though? What purpose could it possibly serve?"

His eyes widened. "Oh my gosh. They're gonna make it into a biological weapon and sell it to the government. They're going to end the world."

He looked back at the girl to see what she thought about that, but she just pointed at the tables on the other side of the room. "Or, they're experimenting with using it as a renewable energy source, potentially solving the global energy crisis."

He narrowed his eyes at the tables as he wandered closer. There were spools of copper wire and various electrical paraphernalia scattered upon them. The main item that caught his eye, however, was a brightly shining lightbulb screwed into the handle of a two-pronged metal fork, which in turn was stabbed directly down into the white plastic lid of a glass jar of dust.

"Huh. Would you look at that," Noah said.

"Yeah. It's like a potato battery, except it's a dust battery. Pretty cool."

"Maybe it would be, but this is Insight we're dealing with. Next thing you know, we're gonna be the ones hooked up to a lightbulb."

The student stared at him. "Are you always this paranoid?"

Noah blinked. "My fears are justified. You're the one who's not being cautious enough. I mean, you followed a zombie into a locked and empty room. What kind of idiot does that? Literally right after watching me eat someone, too."

She gazed at him. "You're not still hungry, though, right?"

He shrugged. She had nothing to worry about from him, being too much of an enigma to his senses for him to consider her as good food. Though if he were being truthful with himself, the few bites he had taken out of the doctor hadn't done much for his hunger. He was already looking forward to his next meal and the pleasant burst of energy it would provide.

He wondered briefly if he should be concerned that he was becoming some kind of addict. Even if he was, he decided, it was nothing to be troubled over. He was a zombie, after all; such behavior was perfectly natural. Although he might do well to not announce the fact to his friends when he next saw them.

"Before I opened the vats, did you feel cured?" he asked the girl, forcing his thoughts away from his steady descent into zombiehood. "Also, what's your name? I'm No- uh, no. No. I shall remain unnamed."

"I'm Penelope." She stared at him like he was crazy. "And, well, I guess so. I felt really hungry right after they finished with the vacuum, but now I just feel tired. I can't really say for certain about the other symptoms. I didn't take a moment to really pay attention, to be honest."

"Hmm. Maybe that slapped-together vacuum thing actually worked. That's nice to hear." He stuck a thumb at the door. "You gonna go back for another round of treatment?"

She shook her head. "The doctor and his attendant would want to know where my escort had gone. And when they inevitably find his body in here, it'll seem obvious that I was the one to kill him. Especially when it turns out that I need additional treatment because I seemingly wasn't cured properly. I'd rather just get out of here and find my own vacuum somewhere to do it myself."

"Good point," Noah acknowledged. "Although I wasn't planning on leaving the body out in the open like that. That seems improper. And a downright safety hazard."

"Oh yeah? What are you going to do?"

Noah looked around. "Think he'd fit in one of those vats?"

She gaped at him. "That's horrible!"

"Is it?" He walked over to the body and started dragging it across the room. "Can you just help me get him in?"

She backed away from him. "No."

"Oh, come on! It's in your best interest to delay the discovery of his death. You said it yourself, you were the one last seen with him."

"There might be cameras. They could see it wasn't my fault."

"I didn't see any cameras. And trust me, I was looking."

She didn't respond. Noah went to the sixth vat in the line, figuring it would be the last to be filled with dust, and began unscrewing the top. "I'm going to have some trouble if you make me do this on my own. The guy isn't light. Must've had one too many empanadas at the Insight potluck."

"You're literally insane."

Noah gave her an odd look. "We both know I'm battling a certain illness at the moment. You can't blame me if I don't come across as normal to your sensibilities. Besides, you're probably infected, too. You can't be throwing around these kinds of criticisms."

Her expression said that she very much could. "I haven't eaten anyone. And I'm not currently stuffing a man I killed into a metal vat."

Noah dragged the body over, and after a considerable amount of effort, managed to get the head and shoulders tipped over the rim of the container. From there it was relatively easy to push him the rest of the way in. His skull hit the bottom of the vat with a loud clang. Noah's headache, which was still lingering annoyingly, throbbed in response for some reason, but he did his best to ignore it. He grasped the edge of the vat and pulled himself up a few inches to peer inside, and to his satisfaction, the body was nearly invisible. He dropped back down to the floor, picked up the lid, and sealed the container back up.

He turned back to Penelope. "Alright, I did it. No thanks to you."

"Good. I'd rather not be guilty by association. I feel like I'm committing a crime just by standing in the same room as you."

Noah frowned at her, unsure how to respond to that comment.

"You do realize that all those masks on your face are covered in blood. You look like an actual serial killer."

Noah picked at the masks, nearly pulling one off to look at it himself, before freezing in place and shooting Penelope a suspicious look. "Are you just trying to trick me into revealing my face?" His eyes and mouth were visible, but the rest of his face was still hidden, as far as he was aware.

She stared at him. "No. Are you okay?"

"What kind of question is that?"

"My apologies. The answer is obviously no."

Noah grumbled under his breath. "Alright, we've spent enough time here. I'm leaving before the next delivery of dust shows up."

He walked over to the door and tugged on it, only to find that it was once more locked. A pit formed in his stomach and he looked awkwardly over his shoulder at the vats.

Penelope looked at him blankly for a moment before facepalming. "Did you drop him in the vat before taking his key?"

Noah gulped. "I might actually need your help now. I won't be able to get him out on my own."

She scowled. "I'd rather wait for the next doctor to pay this room a visit. With you right here, it'll be pretty obvious I wasn't the one responsible for the mysterious disappearance of the doctor."

Noah glanced around, beginning to panic. He couldn't let himself be found like this. His gaze panned over the tables of electrical equipment, and he wondered if anything there could be used to somehow short out the lock on the door.

He shook his head. Who was he kidding? He was a bio major, not an electrician. He'd sooner electrocute himself than get any doors open.

A different solution suddenly occurred to him, and he slowly turned to face Penelope.

She must not have liked the look in his eyes, because she flinched and retreated quickly across the room. "I'm sorry, dude, but I'm not going to put myself at risk for a crazy stranger I just met. Surely you can understand."

"Oh, I do," Noah said.

He wondered how much damage it would take for her to go crazy. Crazy enough that it would seem obvious she was the one to have killed the doctor.

He stepped towards her, working his jaw. His instincts warned him she wouldn't be good food, but that was okay; he wasn't trying to satisfy his hunger. He just wasn't sure how else he could effectively damage her. His jaws were the strongest weapon he possessed.

"Wait!" Penelope screeched. She scampered sideways and swiped something off the floor, and Noah nearly sprung at her in response to the sudden movement. Barely restraining himself, he watched as she frantically searched through the pockets of what turned out to be the very bloody lab coat of the doctor. "It could be in here," she said breathlessly.

Noah's eyebrows rose. He had forgotten about the coat, but it would make his life a lot easier if she turned out to be right.

"Here!" she shouted, almost crying in relief as she yanked out a wallet. She glanced at him nervously and slowly edged past him towards the door, holding up the wallet as if to assure him she were just checking that the key lay within. Noah let her cross the room without making a move. As she came within a few feet of the exit, there was an audible click and the light flicked green.

Both of them smiled in relief. "Here," Penelope said, holding the wallet out to Noah before he could say anything. "You can keep it, just let me out of the hall. Alright?"

"Sure," Noah said, surprised at her willingness to give up the key. "Thanks."

She twitched a nervous smile at him before turning and exiting the room. Noah followed with one last look around the space, scanning to make sure there wasn't anything too obviously out of place. There was a bit of blood on the floor by the door, so he scuffed it with his shoe in a quick attempt to make it less visible. Nodding to himself, he stepped out after Penelope.

He went with her to the end of the hallway. As they

approached the double doors the light overhead turned
green and the twin panels automatically swung open. The
next section of hallway looked much the same as every other
he had encountered so far at Insight, though there were a
few people at the far end. Noah noticed a sign indicating a
stairwell somewhere ahead on the left, and pointed it out to
Penelope.

"Yeah, I see it," she said. "I'll ask some people for
directions to get out. Hopefully someone will be kind enough
to lead the way." She looked down the hallway before
reluctantly adding, "You sure you don't want to leave too? You
wouldn't look too suspicious if you took off those masks. And
it looks like you're wearing two layers of shirts; you could take
off the outer bloody one. This could be your last good chance
to escape."

Surprised by her thoughtfulness, Noah nonetheless shook
his head without hesitation. "My friends are still here, and
besides, I want to find out for sure what Insight's planning
with all of this. I don't know how much I'll be able to do about
it, but, well, you never know."

"Okay. Bye, then," she said quickly, stepping through the
door and hurrying away from him as quickly as she could.

53

I'M SURE HE'LL TURN UP

Noah stepped back to let the doors close, eager to get out of view, then turned to begin making his way back towards the room with the other uncured students. He noticed the mask he had discarded earlier laying on the floor, and he quickly picked it up and replaced it back over his mouth. No point leaving it out in the open to invite questions.

The light over each door lit up one by one as he walked down the hall. After the fifth one flashed at him, Noah slowed to a stop and stared consideringly at the door. He put his hand against it, wondering if it would be a good idea to look inside. It would be a waste not to, he thought. There was still no sign of the remaining doctor and his assistant, and it would just take a moment to peek in. He hoped he would find some clue as to what Insight was actually doing with the dust.

He leaned into the door, fully intending to enter the room, only to back off at the last second. He was suddenly paranoid that he would be met with a room full of employees. One or maybe two, he could deal with. But he only had one mouth; any more than that and he would only get himself captured and brought under scrutiny.

He pressed the side of his head carefully against the door, trying to pick up the sound of voices without accidentally pushing it open. He couldn't hear anything, but then again, the walls of this building were clearly quite soundproofed. If a man could get murdered in the hallway without anyone coming out to check what all the noise was about, he doubted he would pick up any noises through the door even if there were a dozen people busy at work inside.

With one final regretful look, he turned away and continued down the hall. Depending on where he stayed the night, perhaps he would have a chance to explore at a later hour.

He had some difficulty picking out his room from all the other identical doors, even knowing it was slightly ajar. The doorways were designed to be set into the wall, which made it difficult to see the subtle gap he knew he had left.

It took him a minute, but he did finally find the correct room. Once he was standing right outside, he could see the barely visible lump of his shirt serving as a doorstop, and he stooped to pick it up before pushing his way inside.

"Hey, guys," he greeted everyone. The same four students were still seated within, and the injured kid seemed to have collected himself somewhat and had taken a seat on Noah's chair while he was away.

A few seconds passed without any response to his return, prompting him to look around quizzically. "What's up?"

"You have blood all over your face," Clarissa said hesitantly, like she didn't want him to panic but kind of thought he should be.

"Oh, yeah. Don't worry, it's not mine," he assured her, ignoring the slightly horrified look he received in return and getting right to work stripping away his outer layer of clothes. He stared at the dirty garments uncertainly, wondering if it would be incriminating to carry them around, but after a moment of thought he just shrugged and bundled everything back together. There was hardly any blood visible.

Once that was done he plucked each of the masks off his face and gave them a cursory glance before holding them out. "You guys want these back?"

"I'm good," Mark said quickly.

Violet just shook her head, seeming horrified at the prospect of even touching the blood-soaked scraps of fabric.

Clarissa sent both students an incredulous look. "Those

are good masks. Hand 'em over."

"Here you go. Good as new."

Clarissa laughed. "Like hell they are. But they'll be fine after a good wash." She tucked them away into her coat. "I'm almost afraid to ask what you got up to out there."

"I ate one of the doctors," he said casually, before realizing that he wasn't in proper company to be disclosing that kind of information. He suppressed a wince and shut his mouth.

Nobody seemed to know how to respond to that announcement, except perhaps the hungry student. He gazed intently at Noah.

"Is- is there any left?" he whispered hopefully.

"Apologies, but he's very dead."

"Oh." He drooped.

"Can I get your name?" Noah asked, feeling a touch of sympathy for him.

"It's Elias Puckett."

"I'm Noah. Pleasure to meet you."

"Yeah. Do you want your chair back? I didn't know when or if you'd return, so I kinda just snagged it for myself."

"You're fine." Noah went to the wall and grabbed another seat for himself. As he was unfolding it beside Elias, the door to the room suddenly opened to reveal none other than Brian, May, and Leah. Behind them were the remaining doctor and his assistant.

"Hi, Noah!" Brian said cheerfully, quick to pick him out from the small crowd. Leah and May waved.

"Guys!" Noah exclaimed in surprise. He narrowed his eyes. "What are you doing here? Why didn't you get cured?"

"It's a bit of a long story," Leah began, but the hollow sound of metal clattering to the floor interrupted her.

Everyone looked over to see Elias standing over his fallen chair. His eyes locked upon the two Insight workers and his hands trembled with barely restrained hunger.

"Buddy, I know they look delicious, but you probably shouldn't," Noah said impassively. "You'll just get knocked out again. You're better off waiting until one of them is alone."

He felt a few pairs of eyes turn to him, but he kept his gaze trained calmly on Elias, waiting. "You know I'm right."

To everyone's surprise, the student slowly nodded and bent to pick his chair back up. He sat back down and glanced around with a slight smile as if nothing had happened.

Noah looked up to see the attendant slowly removing her hand from her pocket, a faintly disbelieving expression on her face as she glanced between Noah and Elias.

The doctor cleared his throat. "Anyways. The three of you will remain here while we finish treating the other students. Our shift ends within the hour, at which point we have been instructed to bring you to Dr. Heinrich."

"Who?" Noah asked.

The doctor sniffed. "He is the head of the temporary unit tasked with investigating the infectious outbreak at Oakridge."

"Oh. So he's the one to blame for dragging you all into our business."

He spluttered. "You ungrateful little-"

"Alright, Phil, let's get back to the office," the assistant said quickly.

The doctor sighed and smoothed back his hair. "Yeah. We'll be back shortly to pick you all up." He turned away, then swiveled right back towards them in the same motion. "Oh! Did my associate happen to stop by this room? I haven't seen him in a minute."

Noah gulped and did his best to maintain a slightly concerned, innocent gaze.

"Ah, I'm sure he'll turn up," the doctor said after it became clear none of them had anything to say. He stepped back, letting the door swing slowly shut behind him, and headed out of view towards the treatment room.

Leah casually stuck an arm out to block the door from fully closing.

Noah laughed. "I did the same thing."

She sent him a glance. "Do you have something I can stick in the door to keep it open?"

His hand went to his pocket and he fingered the keycard hesitantly. He didn't particularly want to deal with the questions it would raise, but after a moment of silence he decided they should be aware he had it, and he pulled it out to brandish it in the air. "No need. I got the key."

"Holy crap," Mark muttered quietly behind him.

Leah's eyes widened excitedly, only to turn to suspicious slits almost immediately. "And where, do tell, did you happen to acquire that?"

54

THIS THING COULD BE USEFUL

Noah cleared his throat. "Around."

She raised her eyebrows. "It wouldn't have anything to do with the mysteriously absent doctor, would it?"

"Why would you think that?"

Brian peered closely at his friend. "Please don't tell me you ate that guy."

"Okay. I won't."

Leah looked around at the other students seated in the room, searching for weakness. Her eyes came to rest on Violet. "Tell me, has Noah been up to questionable activity in the past half hour?"

Noah turned to Violet pleadingly, but the girl ignored him. "Oh, he ate the doctor. One hundred percent. He admitted it himself."

Noah glared at her. "Seriously? I told you that with implied confidentiality!"

She shrugged. "Should've made it explicit."

"Where is the doctor now?" Brian asked.

Noah looked down. "Dead."

His friends stared silently at him. After a few seconds passed, Leah rubbed the bridge of her nose and shut her eyes. "It was bound to happen eventually. Did you at least hide the remains?"

"Yeah." His thoughts went to the vats, and he straightened. "Actually, while I was out, I found something you guys will want to hear about."

"Don't change the subject," Brian scolded.

"Please let him change the subject," Clarissa quickly interrupted. "We don't need to know the exact details of how it went down."

Noah glanced between them and shook his head. "I'm not just changing the subject. Insight is storing all the dust they're vacuuming out of us. They've got these huge vats they're filling up. I think they've figured out how to use it as a sort of energy source."

"Well, that doesn't bode well," Leah said, tilting her head. "Although I'm not surprised the dust can be used as energy. Our bodies obviously aren't currently using oxygen to produce energy; maybe the dust has taken up that function."

"I'm sure the doctors already have it figured all out," Noah muttered. "We can ask them when they next stop by. Speaking of which, how did you convince them to let you all stay?"

"Oh, it was easy," Brian said with a shrug. "We went through this whole plan of bartering with them, but looking back on it, I doubt we even needed to bother. They put up zero fight when we asked to stay."

"What did you trade? Not the pendant, right?"

"Of course not." Brian inclined his head towards May. "We showed the attendant the pictures we took of the tomb, and told her we believe it's related to the source of the dust. She brought us to the doctor- I guess his name is Phil, apparently- and from there we were able to convince him to bring us to you."

"Why didn't you get the treatment while you had the chance? I can tell you're not cured."

"Phil said that we would just get infected again. He still hooked us up to the vacuum and had it run for a minute, which I guess makes sense if the ulterior motive of this whole operation is just collecting dust." He shrugged once more. "Not that I care. If we know where the dust is being stored and you have that keycard, it should be a simple matter to sabotage them."

Noah sent him an amused glance. "Sabotage?"

"Sure." He grinned. "Why not? I've always wanted to give Insight a kick in the pants. Let's sneak over and blow some shit up."

Clarissa looked at Brian in surprise. "Can I have your number?"

Brian blinked at her, then a smile broke across his face. "Of course."

Noah turned away from them to shake his head in mock weariness at Leah and May. "Did you already send them the pictures?"

May nodded. "Phil gave me an email. Apparently the translation work will be outsourced to a friend of Insight. We made the doctor promise to tell us if they successfully translate the images, but who knows if he'll actually follow through on that."

Noah found himself genuinely curious about what they would find, but was hesitant to get his hopes up that it would turn out to be anything interesting. "It better not be the recipe to the dead guy's favorite dinner or something."

Leah shrugged. "It could be anything from that to an instruction guide on how to create the dust from scratch." She paused. "That would actually be pretty terrible if we accidentally gave Insight something like that."

"Let's just hope for the best," Noah said. "They might fail to translate it at all. Or it could end up taking them over a year. It's probably best not to worry about it too much."

"Do you want to sit down?" Mark asked from across the room. "There's a bunch more chairs, if you want."

Leah and May glanced over, and both shook their heads. "It literally makes no difference to me whether I'm standing or sitting," Leah said. "Were you very recently infected? Are you not completely numb yet?"

"Oh, I can't feel anything," Mark muttered. "That's half the problem, though. I'm afraid I'll topple over before I realize my center of gravity is off."

"That hasn't been an issue for us," May said. "And we've

been infected for a while now."

Noah stretched out on his chair. "Speak for yourselves. I'm enjoying my seated position. I'm saving precious mental energy that would otherwise be subconsciously devoted towards balance."

Leah scowled at him. "That's not a thing."

"Sure it is. I'm a bio major; I would know." Noah looked over at Brian, who was grinning at something Clarissa had just said. "Hey, did you ever figure out what the pendant you're carrying around actually does?"

Brian glanced at him. "No. You know as much as I do about the thing. It just sits there and looks pretty."

"Can I see it?" Clarissa asked.

"Uh, sure." Brian carefully lifted the chain up around his neck and handed the entire necklace to her.

Clarissa let it drop heavily into her hand, then flinched in surprise. "It's really hot!"

"You can still feel temperature?" Leah asked, raising her eyebrows. "Did you literally get infected right before stepping on the bus?"

Clarissa shrugged. "No idea. Maybe I inhaled some dust while I was waiting in line on the fields. I guess it's not that hot, I just wasn't expecting it. I can't feel much else at the moment." She peered closer at the pendant, holding it up to let it dangle in front of her eyes. The flat silver square spun slowly on the chain, small waves and imperfections on its surface catching the light. "It does look kind of pretty, for a metal square, I suppose. You said it's supposed to do something?" She clicked it open before Noah or his friends could react.

They all tensed, expecting dust to explode everywhere, but nothing happened at all.

"It's empty," Clarissa said, disappointed. She flicked it closed and held it back to Brian.

Before he could recover from his shock and accept it, she suddenly let out a cough. Dust blew out between them.

"Sorry," she muttered, wiping her mouth.

"Don't worry about it." Brian took the pendant and began to lower it over his head, only to stop and stare at it in surprise.

"What?" Noah asked, leaning over curiously.

"Look at the dust," Brian said quietly.

The small cloud Clarissa had produced was slowly being drawn towards the metal square, funneling towards the bottom of it before disappearing. The room went silent as everyone noticed the strange phenomenon.

Before long, the entire mass of dust that had been darkening the air had been entirely consumed by the pendant. It looked no different, hanging there innocently like it wasn't secretly harboring a biological weapon.

Clarissa looked around. "Is that supposed to happen?"

"No clue," Leah answered. "We've only seen it release dust, not absorb it. Can you open it back up?"

He sent her a nervous glance. "What? You sure?"

She nodded. "I know it'll probably just let everything out, but let's see what happens."

Brian depressed the small locking mechanism, allowing each half of the box to swing open like a book. As expected, the dust it had collected immediately began spewing into the air.

Brian frowned and quickly shut it. For a few seconds, nothing happened, but then it once more began steadily clearing the air, drawing the dark airborne particles inexorably toward itself.

"So, it's a storage container for dust," Leah said. "An ambient air cleaner."

May was staring intently at the pendant. "It must've completely emptied itself back inside the mausoleum. If we had thought to close it, it might have sucked all the dust back into itself. But we just left it open and shut the tomb."

"Hmm," Brian murmured, placing it back around his neck and hiding it once more under his collar. "This thing could be useful."

55

A MARVELOUS CONDITION

"**D**o we even want to visit this Dr. Heinrich?" Noah asked. "The guy is the head of Insight or whatever, so he's definitely a prick. Remember I have a keycard; we can leave anytime."

"I don't mind meeting him," Leah replied. "I kind of like the idea of sabotage, although I'm sure it won't be as simple as Brian seems to hope. We might just have to play along with their scheduled plans until we can get around to throwing a wrench in the works. I'm thinking it would make the most sense to do it tonight after most employees have gone home, maybe mess with those vats you mentioned. Something along those lines. There's just too many people out and about right now. I doubt we'd manage to get out before someone stopped us, even with the keycard."

May nodded in agreement, while Mark and Violet looked away neutrally, clearly wanting nothing to do with their plans. Noah noticed Elias seemed moderately interested, but it was possible he was just wondering if there would be a chance to eat anyone in the midst of whatever chaos they caused.

"Alright," Noah said. "Makes sense to me."

There was very little conversation over the course of the next hour, with the exception of Brian and Clarissa. They soon realized that they both carried quite the collection of random gear and knick knacks, and began rapidly pulling out the contents of their respective storage in a sort of competition. They were quite closely matched in terms of sheer quantity.

Noah tried his best to ignore them, but they kept gasping at whatever the other person pulled out, making it difficult to concentrate on anything else.

"The doctor could be back anytime," Leah eventually reminded them. "It might be best not to have your entire worldly possessions spread across the room."

"Yeah," Brian agreed without sparing her a glance.

"Brian. You don't want them to confiscate your stuff."

Clarissa finally checked her watch and sighed grudgingly. "She's right. We should pack up."

They began the lengthy process of repacking.

"You don't have any batteries, do you?" May asked Clarissa as she carefully placed her possessions one by one in its designated place within her coat.

She looked up. "What kind?"

Understanding May's intention, Brian picked up one of his flashlights and a screwdriver that happened to be lying nearby, and quickly removed the case. He plucked out one of the batteries and held it out. "Got any C's?"

Clarissa shook her head with a sigh, disappointed she didn't have the exact item they needed. "Sorry, I don't carry any of those. If you need another flashlight, though, I've got a couple pen lights right here. Feel free to borrow one until you can get yourself some batteries."

"That would be great, thanks," Brian said, looking relieved. He pocketed one of the small flashlights. "Darkness is kind of our fatal weakness, so it's much appreciated."

She glanced up. "What do you mean?"

Brian hesitated. "Well, if you're not fully numb yet, the condition probably wouldn't affect you, so it's hard to explain."

Violet glanced over. "I lost my sense of touch hours ago. What's the big issue with darkness?"

Brian opened his mouth, then paused. "Close your eyes and cover them with your hands."

She did as instructed.

"Do you know what'll happen to her?" Leah asked the

other three students as they waited for the blindness to take effect.

Mark and Clarissa shook their heads, seeming bemused. Elias, however, dipped his head with a haunted expression. "They blinded me when I tried to attack the doctors in the treatment room. It was probably the single worst thing I've ever experienced in my life."

"Hold up, what?" Violet asked nervously. Before she could further react, she sagged in her seat, nearly sliding to the floor before Brian grabbed her shoulders.

"Open your eyes," he said quickly.

Her hands had dropped away, so her eyesight was immediately returned to her when she blinked her eyes open. "What was that?" she asked shakily, looking around to regain her bearings.

"It just happens," Noah said with a shrug. "Something about not being able to feel makes you go limp in perfect darkness."

"Well, I kind of hate it."

"Oh, for sure. In a lot of ways the sickness is surprisingly subtle. This is probably the only symptom that really sucks."

Several pairs of eyes turned his way. "Does cannibalism not count as a bad symptom?" Leah asked after a moment, eyebrows raised.

Noah gulped as he realized he'd said something wrong. "Of course. Yeah."

Leah exchanged concerned glances with Brian and May, which Noah pretended not to notice.

"What if a blind person got sick?" Violet asked thoughtfully. "Someone without any sight at all."

"They'd probably have a really bad time," Noah answered. "The sickness would be debilitating."

It was at that point that the door finally opened, signaling the return of the doctor and the assistant. Brian quickly swept his remaining possessions into his backpack before anyone could comment on the mess.

"We will now bring you all to see Dr. Heinrich," Phil said

without preamble.

Noah sent Elias a warning glance as they all stood to follow him outside. The starving student just waved his concern aside with a knowing smile.

The kid's learning, Noah thought to himself with pride.

Phil waited until they were all outside, gathered around him, before starting his way down the hallway. As they passed the first door, it lit up green as the doctor and the attendant passed, and then again as Noah walked by a moment later. He looked around anxiously, but neither employee seemed to have noticed.

Noah sidled up close beside the doctor, trying to get close enough that their cards would activate the doors simultaneously and mask the fact that he also had a key. His approach caused Phil to send him a nervous look and his hand strayed to his pocket.

Noah tried to give a reassuring smile, but the doctor flinched and stepped away in response. He ground his teeth, feeling faintly indignant at the zombie prejudice, and settled for trailing a few steps behind. Surely no one would notice if the green lights remained lit for an extra second or two longer than usual.

They went to the end of the hallway and passed through the double doors Noah had let Penelope through earlier. His thoughts went to her for a moment, and he hoped she had managed to find her way out.

"Where do the cured students get sent?" he asked Phil.

The man glanced considringly at him. "Insight is providing transportation back to Oakridge campus."

"Oh, how thoughtful."

The doctor nodded expressionlessly at his response. He led them to the staircase which Noah had noticed the sign for earlier, and they ascended two flights before emerging into a new corridor. Instead of mirrors, one wall was painted a pleasant light blue, while the other was a slanted floor-to-ceiling window presenting a view of the city block below. Noah took note of a camera set discreetly into the ceiling above their heads. It was the first he had seen in the building.

"I didn't realize we were so high up," Leah murmured. "The bus must've taken us up a couple floors."

They turned down another hallway, this one without any windows, before coming to a stop outside a door with a small placard displaying Dr. Heinrich's name. No other information was included. Noah also noticed a distinct lack of any green indicator light over the door; keycards would not be capable of unlocking this room.

A few seconds passed before the door swung open. At first, all Noah could see was the silhouette of a tall man seated behind his desk. Another full wall of windows allowed the harsh midday sunlight to illuminate him from behind. As his eyes adjusted, Noah saw that the office was impressively large, so much so that there was enough space for their group of ten. Dr. Phil and his assistant went to stand on each side of Dr. Heinrich's desk, while the students stood uncertainly just inside the door.

"Please, come in," Heinrich said, his tone warm. He tapped something on his desk and the door shut behind them. "I apologize for the lack of seating, but as I understand it, most of you are not physically capable of feeling discomfort. A marvelous condition, I must say."

56

WILLING VOLUNTEERS

"**W**ell, there are some side effects," Leah said drily. Heinrich laughed. "There certainly are, which I see two of you have already experienced first-hand."

Noah narrowed his eyes as the doctor's gaze drifted to him and Elias. "Are we just here for you to tell us how sick we are? Because we're aware."

Heinrich shook his head with a light smile. "I simply wished to personally greet my new patients. Seeing as we'll be spending some time together in the coming days, I figured it would only be right to get to know you all a little and perhaps satisfy any questions you may be harboring. I would hate for our relationship to start off on anything but a solid foundation of trust."

"Oh man, if I had known that's what we were doing, I would've compiled a list," Brian complained.

"I have a question," Noah announced loudly. "What's happening with all the dust you're taking out of us?"

Out of the corner of his eyes he saw at least two of his fellow students glance questioningly at him, but he just gazed at the doctor, patiently awaiting his response.

Heinrich's smile widened. "I'm glad you asked. We are actively disposing of the vast majority of the 'dust', as you call it, by means of incineration, though a very small amount is being kept strictly for research purposes. Even with what little time we have had so far with it, we have found that it is a highly efficient source of energy, with several very interesting properties that allow it to convert biological material into energy and back. There are, as I'm sure you can imagine, innumerable uses for such a fascinating substance."

So much for trust, Noah thought to himself, flashing a smile of his own at the doctor. "Like what?"

"We believe the dust could be used to- well, not cure the *Wager*, but perhaps ensure a one hundred percent survival rate."

Noah goggled at him. If what had happened to Sophie was anything to go by, mixing the *Wager* with the dust was a very, very bad idea. Perhaps she may have been able to completely heal, given enough victims to feast upon, but that would just have been trading multiple lives for her own. Whatever Heinrich ended up doing with the dust, it would not be saving more lives than it reaped. Whatever so-called 'treatment' he came up with would be used to save those who could afford it, at the expense of whatever unfortunate victims he could get his hands on.

Noah shared a nervous look with his friends. Based on the way they looked bleakly back, they were sharing his thoughts.

Heinrich gazed at the students' expressions and laughed, waving his hand dismissively. "The tests are still in their preliminary stages, though what results we have are very promising. I'll reiterate that we're working with minimal quantities of dust, given that the majority of the substance is being destroyed for safety purposes."

Noah swallowed an angry retort. "It's good to hear that you're being so diligent about destroying the stuff. It would be dangerous to keep such a volatile substance just lying around in a room somewhere, don't you think?"

The doctor's expression became slightly fixed. "I completely agree. As I always say, safety is our highest priority."

Noah briefly wondered if he should just call the man out on his bullshit, but he knew it would be pointless. Heinrich clearly didn't know it, but thanks to Noah's investigative efforts, everyone in the room was well aware that he was lying through his teeth. Pointing it out would only anger the man as well as bring suspicion upon himself. A quick search through his pockets would reveal his newly acquired keycard upon which the dead doctor's name and face was clearly printed, and from there it would only be a matter of time before the body was discovered and Noah was inevitably charged with murder.

Looking like he was already regretting his offer to answer their questions, Heinrich glanced wearily at the rest of them. "If that's all, we can move on to-"

"Why did you bother hooking us up to the vacuum, if not to cure us?" Brian asked, his face a picture of innocent curiosity. His gaze darted to Phil, who stiffened.

Heinrich blinked. Noah could practically see him assembling a convincing reply in real time. "We believe that limiting the quantity of the substance within your lungs can help mitigate the worst of the symptoms and prepare you to more smoothly receive the full treatment when you are ready."

Noah exchanged an impressed look with Brian. That was a pretty damn good response, for having been fabricated on the fly.

"I don't feel any different, though," Brian insisted.

"Oh, the difference is completely internal, and likely won't create any noticeable difference," Heinrich assured him, leaning back in his seat. "If we are not intending to fully cure you, we have to be careful not to remove too much, as that would trigger your hunger response. You are currently operating completely off of the power the dust-like substance provides. It is what fuels your rapid regeneration, though in doing so, it is directly repurposing your own flesh. Fortunately for you, the body mass you lose in this manner is capable of being restored by means of consuming the flesh of others. The material you acquire in this way is entirely converted into 'dust', which is then used to fuel your healing. As your reserves of the substance are diminished, you will find yourself growing hungry, instinctually wishing to replenish your supply. After all, it is not only fueling your healing, but every other biological process supporting your very life. I'm sure you can understand how your body might react poorly if we suddenly removed too much of this substance from your system."

"So you just killed every student you fully removed the dust from," Leah said flatly.

Heinrich smiled. "Far from that. Just as your body seamlessly converted to accept the dust as a source of energy, when a sufficient threshold of the dust is removed, it will simply revert back to its usual state, using the remaining particles to aid in the transition process. It may take as much as a day, and you may feel some amount of weakness in that time, but you will certainly not die."

"Well, that's a relief, I guess," she muttered. "So, what, these guys here just weren't able to reach that supposed threshold?"

"Precisely." The doctor inclined his head. "It may take some time to produce a treatment that is capable of fully curing them. It is a small miracle that none of them succumbed to their hunger, having been brought so close to empty. Thankfully, the vast majority of you have taken well to the treatment, and if all goes well, we should have cured everyone by the day's close."

He switches between truths and lies as easily as taking a dump after Mexican fast food, Noah marveled.

"How come the sickness takes away our sense of touch?" May asked quietly.

"We have found that any bodily processes deemed unnecessary to your survival are simply halted, transforming you into the ideal host. It is quite the efficient use of energy."

May seemed uncomfortable with that answer, but she nodded. "Hmm. I pretty much assumed that was the case."

"Alright," Dr. Heinrich said, clapping his hands together before anyone could raise any more questions. "Part of why I brought you here was to inform you of the accommodations we will be providing for you. The fourth floor has quite a few rooms, most of which are generally occupied by our long-term patients. This is where you will be staying. You will find they feel much the same as regular hotel rooms." He picked a small stack of keycards off his desk and handed it to the assistant at his side, who began distributing them to the students.

"I'm gonna get whiplash if we keep being sent around to different lodgings like this," Brian muttered to Noah.

"Hey, you'll never see me complaining about free stuff," Noah replied. Suddenly feeling anxious, he looked up at the doctor. "Uh, we're not going to have to pay for any of this, are we?"

Heinrich clasped his hands benevolently. "Of course not. Your accommodations are being provided free of charge."

"Are meals included?" Noah asked cheekily.

To his shock, the doctor didn't immediately shoot him down. "Contact an employee if you are feeling desperate. We'll see what we can do for you."

"Wait, you mean-"

Heinrich put his hands up with a laugh. "Apologies, I should have been more clear. We are developing a device that should act as a sort of antidote to your hunger that will, in theory, function by sending a concentrated jet of 'dust' directly into your airways. We are encountering some setbacks in the form of our subjects' bodies failing to fully accept the foreign dust as an acceptable energy source. Initial testing seemed successful, but unfortunately the subjects' hunger was merely delayed and ultimately exacerbated."

"Okay, it's good to know you're working on that, but who exactly are you using as subjects?" Leah asked warily.

Heinrich waved a hand. "They have entrusted us with their confidentiality, but rest assured they are willing volunteers."

"Who the hell would volunteer to become a zombie?" Violet muttered.

"That's what I want to know," Leah agreed, but Heinrich just smiled vaguely at them.

"It was a pleasure to meet all of you. I will be seeing you tomorrow morning for your first scheduled treatment appointment. We will be continuing to use the vacuum until another design has been approved, or until it effectively cleanses you of dust."

Brian raised a hand, and the doctor chuckled and nodded for him to speak.

"What about us?" he asked, gesturing to Leah and May. "Since we volunteered to be here, we were never given the full treatment. We'll probably get cured on the first try, right?"

An uncomfortable expression passed over Heinrich's face. "Hmm, I suppose so. You're free to stay if you wish, though," he added brightly. "You would be contributing to the exploration of an incredible new avenue of study."

"We'll see," Brian said flatly.

Heinrich simply smiled and tapped his desk, opening the door behind them. Phil and the assistant came forward to lead them out of the office, and the students obediently filed after them. As Noah brought up the rear he sent Dr. Heinrich one final glance.

In the moment before he stepped out of view, he caught a glimpse of an eager smile, one that would be better suited on the face of an infected person gazing at a healthy bystander than on a doctor looking upon his patient. Shuddering, Noah hurried away after his friends and tried to shake off the feeling that they were being led into the lion's mouth.

57

THERE'S NO 'GOOD' SIDE WHEN IT COMES TO INSIGHT

A s they retraced their steps to the stairwell, Noah leaned over to Brian and whispered, "Their *Wager* treatment is one hundred percent just going to be them infecting the sick person and throwing bodies at them until they're healed."

"Well, obviously," Brian muttered.

"I hope we're out of here before they start looking around for sacrifices."

Leah leaned over. "You know, we're never gonna be cured, not with them pretending their completely functional vacuum treatment is 'insufficient' or whatever."

Brian gave her a thin smile. "We'll have to take it upon ourselves if we ever want to get out. And I don't know about you, but I'm planning on leaving at the soonest opportunity."

Noah glanced over his shoulder to see Phil glaring daggers at them, too far away to hear them properly but clearly disapproving of their private exchange. Noah pulled a face, letting the aching hunger he felt twist his expression for a fraction of a second, and was gratified to see the man flinch.

They descended one flight of stairs and came out into a corridor that wouldn't have looked out of place in a commercial hotel. The walls were still blue, but the lighting was softer and more tasteful, small rectangular sconces affixed to the walls rather than the harsh ceiling panel lights present throughout the rest of the building. Two broad-leafed potted plants were placed to either side of the stairwell exit. There was even a thin carpet with a gray-and-white spotted pattern covering the floor.

"An Insight employee will pick all of you up tomorrow morning at eight AM for your appointment," Phil said to the group of students after they had come to a halt. "Any questions?"

He was met with silence, so he smiled and turned to follow his assistant back to the stair entrance. As the man turned his back on them, Noah was completely caught off guard by the sudden overwhelming instinct to rush forward and simply tear into his unprotected neck. He staggered forward, helplessly propelled by the force of the compulsion.

The doctor was completely oblivious to his impending death, but Noah's friends immediately caught on to the danger he was in.

"Stop!" Leah shouted, and though Noah did nothing of the sort, Phil paused and looked back with raised eyebrows. The expression morphed into surprise and then horror at the sight of Noah's quickly approaching form.

Noah lurched to a halt as the doctor made eye contact with him, freezing several feet away and gazing forward expressionlessly.

Internally, he was debating whether he would be able to silence the man before he yelled for help and his assistant reappeared from the stairwell. Before he could come to a decision, someone yanked him backwards from behind, and he unwillingly stumbled back a few steps. The doctor was already backing away, within reach of the stairwell now, and Noah unhappily realized that he would not be able to satisfy his hunger at this moment. He simply stood there, not putting up a fight, resigned to the loss.

"Stupid zombie," Phil mumbled, fear coloring his face. He shakily hurried into the stairwell and pulled the door shut behind him. He must have been confident it would keep the students confined to their designated floor, but all it took was a keycard to unlock. If Noah weren't surrounded by his fellow students, it would have been an easy matter of following the unsuspecting man.

"What was that?" Brian hissed angrily. "You're not even injured!"

Noah stared mutely at his friend, struggling to center himself. Despite his numbness, he could somehow feel his stomach complaining that he had let an easy meal get away. His hands were still shaking in anticipation.

"Maybe he got too much dust taken out when he got his treatment," Clarissa offered. Both she and Violet were looking awkwardly at Noah. They had known their infection made them susceptible to rather unseemly behavior, but there was a large difference between being told something and seeing it play out before their eyes.

"That shouldn't matter!" Brian spat out. "Apparently, Noah literally killed and ate a man between then and now! I think my concern is justified!"

"I only ate a little bit of that guy," Noah mumbled. "Just a bit of his arm. And his throat."

Mark shuddered. "My man, you're crazy."

Noah shot a glance at Elias standing quietly to the side, hands jammed in his pockets. "How come you were able to resist?"

The kid shrugged. "You said I should wait until one of them was alone. He wasn't alone."

Noah scratched his neck. Holding himself back would have been utterly impossible; it simply hadn't been an option. "Maybe it's because I've been infected longer," he said to himself.

Brian and Leah looked at each other doubtfully.

"You might want to think about hitting Insight up for one of those devices to keep your hunger under control," Mark suggested.

"You heard the doctor, that would only make it worse in the long run," Brian said, shaking his head. "And as bad as Noah seems now, trust me, it can get worse. It wouldn't end well."

Mark shrugged. "It might be an acceptable stop-gap measure until we actually get cured."

"That depends on how soon they drop the pretense that they can't cure us in the first place," Leah grumbled.

"How about we get out of the main corridor before another person comes along," May proposed before anyone else could add their opinion.

"Good idea," Noah said, relieved. He didn't want to sit around while everyone told him how badly he needed help.

"Wait, before y'all disappear, let's make a group chat," Clarissa suggested. "In case anything happens."

"Oh, yeah! We can use it to coordinate a plan for tonight," Brian said enthusiastically.

"A plan?" May asked warily.

"Sabotage and escape," Brian said with an evil grin. Clarissa smiled with almost exactly the same expression.

"That might not be the smartest idea," Violet piped up. "I mean, they're the ones who can cure us."

"Psht, we could do it ourselves," Brian said. "All it takes is a freaking vacuum. Everyone has a vacuum."

"I don't," Violet said pointedly.

"I'm sure you can borrow someone's." Brian waved her protests aside. "And if you don't want to participate, I don't care. Do what you want to do."

She stared uncertainly at him. "I'll join the chat, but I'm not committing to anything."

Brian and Clarissa both shook their heads. "Can't have you selling us out," Clarissa said.

"Fine. I'm out, then."

"Me too," Mark said after a moment. "I don't want to get on Insight's bad side."

"Suit yourself, but I'm pretty sure there's no 'good' side when it comes to Insight," Brian shrugged. "Everyone else is in?"

Nods all around.

"I'mma turn in," Violet muttered, glancing at her

room card. "Not sure what I'll do for the next ten hours, but anything is better than messing with this screwed-up company." She trudged away towards her room.

"See you guys around," Mark said, stepping away as well. "Please be careful."

Once both deserters had disappeared into their respective doors, the remaining six students turned towards each other with burgeoning excitement.

"So, what's the plan?" Leah asked, eyes shining.

"Well, I definitely want to blow up those vats Noah found," Brian said. "Insight is never going to destroy it, not with how profitable it is. Better to take it off their hands. It's gotta be super flammable, right?"

"Energy sources generally are," Elias agreed.

"It's easy enough to check," Clarissa said, pulling a matchbook from her pocket with frightening speed.

Everyone except Brian stared at her in alarm. "That might not be the safest method-" Elias began, but Clarissa looked him dead in the eyes, hacked up a cloud of dust, and struck a match just outside the hovering blob of darkness.

"You can back up if you want," she said casually, and gave them about half a second to backpedal as fast as they could before she held the flame up into the viscous cloud.

A loud crack and a flash of orange filled the air, and the cloud was gone.

Clarissa was left with a coating of char across her face and outstretched arm. She slowly turned to the other students with wide eyes.

"Okay, that was stupid," Elias said. "You could have burned your face off. And you wouldn't even be dead, you'd be an insane zombie."

Clarissa rubbed her neck. "Yeah, that was kind of impulsive. Sorry."

"At least it answered our question," Leah muttered. "Looks like as long as we can get to those vats we'll have an easy way of destroying the dust. The only problem will be getting there."

"And getting out," Noah added.

"It's great that the plan is coming together, but we should get to our rooms," May interjected. "We've been out here too long. Someone is bound to pass through this hallway sooner or later, and not all of us have the best self-control when it comes to eating strangers."

"Oh, yeah," Clarissa said, glancing at Noah. He just crossed his arms and stared back, unable to deny the accusation.

"We can finish planning over the group chat," May said. "Everyone's in it, right?"

They all nodded. Leah checked her phone and swore. "Geez, my phone is nearly dead."

"Do you need a charger?" Clarissa asked hopefully, already reaching into her coat.

Leah cracked a smile. "Nah, I got my own. I just haven't had a chance to use it."

"Well, let me know if you need another one," Clarissa said pleasantly.

They started to drift apart, peering between their cards and the room numbers along the wall. Before anyone had successfully found their quarters, a door halfway down the corridor clicked open and a woman stepped out.

Both Noah and Elias looked discreetly towards her, waiting to see if anyone else would emerge from the room.

"Don't even think about it!" Leah yelled, rapidly approaching from behind.

"I'm not. She's infected," Noah said flatly. Elias nodded.

"Is she?" Leah asked suspiciously, coming to a halt beside them and peering down the hall at the startled woman.

Noah rolled his eyes. "Can't you tell?"

"No, and I still have no idea how you can."

He just shrugged.

The woman was headed towards them, though her steps were hesitant. "Are you all okay?" she asked as she came within conversational range.

"We're great," Noah said. "Are you here for the same

reason we are?"

She raised her eyebrows. "I doubt it."

The rest of the students drew up behind them, curious about the clearly non-Insight affiliated person.

"Well, you're infected. Aren't you here to be cured?" Noah asked.

"Don't be pushy," Brian muttered beside him.

The woman smiled. "I actually came to Insight specifically to be infected."

She laughed when she was met with six disbelieving faces. "A friend of mine who works here said they'd found some kind of miracle cure. I figured I have nothing to lose, might as well give it a try. So long story short, I showed up this morning and they had me inhale some kind of smoke, and now I'm supposed to wait for a few hours for it to take effect. If the doctors are to be believed, by the time I wake up tomorrow, I'll be cancer-free for the first time in four years."

58

A CURE TO EVERY DISEASE

Silence settled over the group in response to the woman's words.

"I haven't a clue how they'll manage it, and it probably won't be as simple as they've implied," she added with a sigh, "but how could I refuse that kind of offer?"

"You do know that Insight has a certain... reputation," Leah began, trying to figure out how best to broach the subject of the infection's more exotic symptoms.

"I'm well aware," the woman said lightly. "However, they do get results. Something I've not seen much of these past few months. And if worse comes to worst, I'm only losing out on half a year at most. If they can extend that time frame at all, I'll call it a win."

The students glanced at each other.

"Have they warned you about any side effects?" Brian asked hesitantly.

"Oh, they certainly warned me that the treatment is extremely experimental, and I spent about an hour signing release forms, but my friend was adamant that this wasn't an opportunity to miss. As one of their first subjects, I'm getting the treatment for free, but supposedly the cost is going to be pretty much unattainable once it goes on the market."

"The market?" Leah exclaimed, glancing worriedly at her friends.

"Are you seriously surprised Insight is already trying to make a profit off our infection?" Noah asked drily. "Think how much money there is to be made from a sickness that essentially restores your body to peak health. They haven't just found a cure to cancer, they've found a cure to every disease ever. People could regrow missing limbs or recover from paralysis. Insight can pretty much name their price; nobody else can offer the kind of results they'll be able to."

"Only so long as they maintain their monopoly on the dust," Brian commented. "As soon as another company gets their hands on it, the game is up. Unless they make some kind of agreement," he added, brows furrowing.

"Nobody else will get access," Clarissa said solemnly. "Insight's making sure of it. Every single person at Oakridge is being tested for the infection. Last I heard, there were no outside instances of it; Insight is in complete control."

Leah shook her head. "I wouldn't be surprised if the government tries to force them to make it publicly available, or at the very least enforce a price cap."

"I don't think we're concentrating on the real issue here," May broke in. "For every person who is healed, another will have to die."

The woman, swiveling between them as they spoke, finally rounded on May with a startled expression. "What did you say?"

"She's right," Noah said neutrally. "You won't be able to heal from anything serious without eating people."

Her eyes somehow bugged out even further. "What nonsense are you speaking of?" Nobody said anything about-about eating people!"

"Of course they wouldn't," Leah said. "Who would agree to that?"

"How would you even know?" the woman said angrily. Then her gaze slowly shifted to the blood stains spattered about Noah's clothes.

"I don't suppose you were injured earlier," she said, swallowing.

"Oh, I sure was," Noah said, and the woman's visible relief lasted approximately two seconds before he continued bluntly, "Everything healed up after I got a couple bites of my friend's dad. Oh, and a doctor." He squinted contemplatively. "I think there was a raccoon in there too, somewhere. Although I'm not sure how much that really did for me."

Her mouth curled in disgust. "Are you joking?"

"He's not joking," Brian grumbled. "It's not entirely his fault, though. It's what the infection does to you. You're gonna be in the same boat pretty soon, if not worse."

"I don't understand," she said, eyes darting back and forth. "How does healing translate to cannibalism?"

"You should talk to a doctor. They can answer whatever questions you have. If you're having any second thoughts, it's not too late to get the dust sucked out before the healing kicks in."

The woman looked conflicted. "I think I need to have a conversation with my friend. Thank you for sharing this information with me."

Brian nodded. "I know it probably wasn't what you wanted to hear, but better off knowing now than after you've been fed some poor sap, yeah?"

She shuddered and nodded, and with one final glance, hurried past them down the hallway.

Noah turned to watch where she was headed, curious if she had stairwell access. Rather than continue all the way to the stairs, however, she stopped at a vending machine recessed into the wall and pressed a button on the display. She glanced back, saw Noah watching her, and quickly turned back to the machine.

"That poor woman is about to discover she can't eat normal food anymore," May said, peering at her as well. "We probably should've mentioned that symptom."

"Eh, it sounds like she just got infected. She might be able to stomach the food," Leah replied uncertainly. "And if not, well, she'll figure it out real quick."

Noah looked up and down the hall at all the doors, wondering how many other people were here in the hopes of curing themselves of terminal or even simply inconvenient conditions. As incredible as it was that there was even a way at all for them to be healed, the treatment would come with a cost that he doubted most would be willing to pay. The majority of people he interacted with were strongly opposed to the idea of consuming other humans. He shrugged to himself. They'd get over it.

"Let's get to our rooms," Brian suggested. "Before someone who isn't infected decides to take a stroll down this lovely corridor."

"Great idea. I am in desperate need of a nap," Leah muttered.

"Set an alarm for later," Noah said automatically.

"Sure, but I'll need a time for that."

Noah looked at Brian, who shrugged. "Most employees go home around five, right?"

"In a normal workplace, maybe," Leah responded. "We have to assume that not everyone will clock out exactly as expected."

"Midnight, then," Brian said.

"That's really late."

"Correct."

"Fine," she said, throwing up her hands. "I'll see all of you then."

"Noah, if you sleep past the time, I'm banging on your door until you wake up," Brian threatened.

"Aw, it makes me all warm and fuzzy to know you care."

"You are the one with the keycard. We're not getting out of this hallway without you," he said flatly.

Noah rolled his eyes. "Alright. Don't you worry about me, I'll be ready." He stepped down the hall to his room, and a green light exactly the same as those above all of the non-residential doors throughout the building lit up. He waved goodbye to his friends and entered his new quarters.

Noticing the room was cast in darkness, Noah quickly reached out to flick the nearby light switch before the door could shut behind him. He then went around turning on every light he could find in the small bedroom and attached bathroom. There was only a blank wall where a window would usually be located in a typical hotel room, which meant that a power outage would leave him quite helpless until the lights came back to life and restored his mobility. He wondered if he should have asked Brian or Clarissa for a candle or flashlight, but shrugged to himself after only a moment of consideration. He would probably be fine.

Only satisfied once he was burning enough electricity to power a small household, he collapsed onto the small bed and allowed himself to finally unwind. Events were unfolding nearly faster than he could keep track of. *We ran away from school to avoid ending up here, and now we have to run away again. Except this time, it's not as simple as a walk through the woods. We had enough trouble with that; how will we fare navigating the fortress that is Insight?*

He tried not to worry overly much about it. It could be fun to run around and cause some chaos. Ideally, they would build an escape plan into their schedule, and be as far as possible from Insight by the time the next morning rolled around. Although he wasn't sure how far they'd be able to get on foot.

Maybe we can call a taxi or something. He wondered if he would be able to endure a full taxi ride without eating their driver, and his thoughts went to that device Insight was developing to delay their patients' hunger. He knew it wasn't a permanent solution, but it might last him through a short car ride. If all he needed to employ the stop-gap measure was a bit of dust, perhaps he could bag some from the vats before they blew them up.

Though even as he considered that as an option, he could feel his stomach turn in disgruntled protest. He would much rather consume living flesh than subsist himself off someone's dispensed dust.

We'll see what happens. There will surely be a wandering guard or two to solve the issue.

A wave of tiredness passed over him despite the wildly early hour and he realized he was in danger of falling asleep if he didn't move, so he sat upright and pulled out his phone to set an alarm. Upon unlocking the device, he immediately noticed he had quite a few missed calls and texts. He realized he had missed the notifications as they came due to his phone currently being set to vibrate.

Kicking himself for that oversight, he rectified the phone's settings to account for his numbness and then looked closer at who had been trying to contact him.

All five missed calls were from his father. Noah felt a twinge of guilt at that, knowing the man was surely beside himself with worry. There had to have been some form of news coverage on the events currently transpiring at Oakridge campus, and to make matters worse, Noah had never gotten back to him about the results of their school getaway attempt.

Resolving to call his father before he went to sleep, Noah then looked at the texts. They were both in the freshly created group chat and had only just been sent. A text from May read:

Just got translation results back. According to whoever did the actual translating work, it was some sort of cipher. The base language was 'very close to English'.

Noah felt a burst of excitement as he stared at the attachment. This could be the answer to so many questions. He opened the screenshot of a forwarded email, skimmed over a few cautionary words at the beginning indicating that there may be some words that had not been perfectly deciphered, and latched his eyes eagerly upon the short body of translated text.

Here lies a cherished one.

At dusk's last descent, when the rocks of the world have settled and none remain, every clasp across the lands will burst. This one will rise alongside his brethren, wielding an inheritance of rebirth, and bring us all to a second dance.

In patient silence we wait.

59

WE'RE NOT STEALING A VACUUM

Noah closed out of the image to send his own message.

Noah: *Well, shit*

May: *It fits the theme of what we've seen so far, at least*

Noah: *It says there's more pendants and that they're gonna explode. That seems like an escalation to me*

Brian: *Yeah, sounds like they're set up as time bombs or smth. I'm getting real strong apocalypse vibes*

Clarissa: *Insight is definitely gonna try to find them*

Leah: *Insight doesn't know anything about any pendants. We weren't stupid enough to show off the one we found, so for all they know, the 'clasp' could be a metaphor for death or some shit*

Brian: *And even supposing they figure it out, they can't just go around desecrating random tombs. They'd piss off a lot of people and probably wouldn't end up finding anything anyway*

Leah: *Depends on how many pendants are actually out there*

Noah: *Not much we can do to stop them. If they decide they want to launch a world-scale scavenger hunt, that's what they're going to do*

Brian: *It would have been nice for the destruction of the vats to be the end of everything*

May: *Yeah, although I doubt that would have worked. All*

it takes is one infected person for them to rebuild their whole stock, and who knows how many other patients they've got stashed away here. That woman with cancer probably isn't the only one they've offered a cure to.

Noah: *If our goal is to leave Insight with no dust, we could just cure them before we leave. There can't be more than one or two patients, right? You've gotta be pretty desperate to accept a deal with Insight*

Leah: *Maybe. You're saying we stick a vacuum into their face until they're cured? If you're thinking about using the tank from the treatment room, good luck carrying that thing around the building. If it's even still there. Wouldn't be surprised if the doctors store it away somewhere when they're done treating everyone this afternoon*

Noah: *I don't suppose any of you have a portable vacuum currently on your person?*

Brian: *We've already been over this. None of us have a vacuum*

Noah: *How about this- we get out of the building, buy a nice mini vacuum somewhere nearby, then return and cure everyone. Then we blow all the dust up*

Leah: *Where the hell are you going to buy a vacuum? And coming back after we get out is a terrible idea*

Noah: *It's just a thought*

Clarissa: *It's a good idea except for the going off to get a vacuum part. And the coming back part*

Noah: *There might be a vacuum shop next door, how would you know*

Elias: *There aren't any. The whole block is office buildings*

Noah: *Hmmmm*

Noah: *Okay guys, new plan*

Leah: *We're not stealing a vacuum from an office building*

Noah: *Oh come on*

Noah: *If we can overcome Insight's security, we can definitely overcome the comparably pathetic security on a regular old office building*

Brian: *You have an actual skeleton key for this building. How do you propose we get into a neighboring building without a key? We're not exactly seasoned burglars*

Leah: *Also, Insight might deserve to have their property blown up, but the same probably doesn't stand true for their neighbors. I'd rather not commit theft against a random business*

Brian: *For now let's just stick with our current plan and keep our eyes out for any opportunities. Maybe we'll stumble across a vacuum in a custodial closet somewhere*

Noah: *Insight has tiled floors, why would they need a vacuum*

Elias: *Commercial buildings often use vacuums to clean their floors regardless of the material. Although I don't think it'd be the kind of vacuum we'd need*

Clarissa: *You know this whole floor of the building is carpeted, right?*

Noah: *Holy crap you're right*

Noah: *We have to check if there's a maintenance closet on this floor*

Leah: *Don't do it now. Too many people around. You don't want to be caught opening doors you shouldn't be able to*

Noah: *Yeah, yeah. We can check tonight.*

Brian: *Sounds good*

When a minute passed without the appearance of any more messages, Noah wearily set his phone aside and shut his eyes. He welcomed the sense of weightlessness, imagining for a wistful moment that he was back in his own bedroom at home and free of any bizarre infections.

The past two days had been one unexpected event after another, and Noah had always found any deviation from routine to be extremely draining. He was exhausted, and very ready for everything to go back to normal.

He wondered for a moment if another symptom of the infection might be general tiredness, but upon further consideration of his recent sleep schedule, he decided his current fatigue was entirely to be expected. Of course, the sickness probably wasn't helping, especially if his body was involuntarily in something analogous to battery saver mode to somehow make his supply of dust last as long as possible.

Hoping that wasn't the case, and that if it was, it wouldn't get worse, Noah reluctantly opened his eyes and picked his phone back up. He needed to call his dad.

Anxiety coursed through him as he held his phone. For a long moment he made no move to dial. *The last call wasn't even twenty-four hours ago*, he reminded himself. *That's a perfectly reasonable length of time to have passed without checking in.*

Even if the last call may have ended on something of a suspenseful note for him. And then the school got mobbed by the military in response to an outbreak of the very same sickness that I currently possess.

He recognized that he was doing quite the poor job of reassuring himself, so he forcibly halted his spiraling thoughts and jabbed the buttons to dial his dad before he could think of a reason to delay further. He decided right then that no matter what questions he was asked, he would be completely honest. Partly because it had worked out pretty well yesterday, but also because he just didn't have the energy to spin out any lies, let alone maintain them convincingly. And because he would never lie to his father, of course.

"Noah!" His dad picked up within the first ring, his voice heavy with emotion. His tone seemed more relieved than angry.

"Hey, dad."

"Oh, thank goodness. Are you okay? Did you get off campus? Have you seen the news?"

"Uh, I'm doing pretty good, all things considered. I'm not on campus, and I haven't seen the news."

"Where are you now?"

Noah winced. "At Insight."

An unpleasantly long stretch of silence settled over the line before his dad responded, "What? How?"

"The sickness, it's, um, a little worse than we thought."

"What?" he repeated, even more concerned.

"There were a couple late-onset symptoms. Nothing life-threatening, but my friends and I decided our smartest move was to head over to Insight after we heard that the doctors here had come up with a cure. So we got ourselves on a bus to Insight headquarters for treatment."

"Oh," he said uncertainly. "So are you all good now? When will you be back on campus?"

"Er... none of us are actually cured yet. The doctors said the treatment didn't work, but that's only because they're a bunch of lying, horrible excuses for human beings. We figured out pretty quickly that they deliberately refrained from treating us properly. Well, I guess my friends knew from the get-go that they weren't being cured, but the doctors definitely lied to me.

"Anyways. The good news is that the cure is the most laughably easy process imaginable, so now we're just waiting for night to fall to run away and do the treatment ourselves. I have a key that should make navigating our way out of the building pretty easy."

Despite having just been brought up to date on several worrying bits of information, the first question his dad asked in response was, "What's wrong with your voice?"

"What?" Noah was puzzled. None of his friends had mentioned anything about his voice, and he certainly hadn't noticed anything wrong himself.

"You're talking... I dunno how to describe it. Oddly. Like you're trying to get all your words out in a single breath."

"Hmm. I'm not currently breathing, as far as I'm aware. Maybe that's causing whatever seems off to you."

"You're not-!"

"Dad, I'm okay. The infection has a lot of scary-sounding symptoms, but I'm not in any danger. Just trust me on this."

His dad sighed. "Can you understand what this is like for me, Noah? I worry enough for you without hearing about these crazy outbreaks, and military intervention, and shady medical corporations- I did some research on Insight last night, and what I learned was enough to make me wish you were attending school in an entirely different city. That place is bad news. I guess you know that, though."

"Oh, I sure do. When we break out tonight, we're planning on causing some havoc before we go. Hopefully disrupt whatever plans they have to experiment with our sickness."

"Where are you going to go once you're out of the building?"

"We're... not sure yet, actually."

"Hmm. Well, my schedule is open tonight. How would you feel about a getaway ride?"

60

WHERE'S YOUR SENSE OF PRIVACY

Noah stared at his phone in surprise, thoughts whirling. His first instinct was to immediately take him up on his offer, but he forced himself to take a moment to consider what the consequences of his dad's help would be. If he and his friends weren't able to cure themselves before leaving, his father would be in a vehicle with six infected people. None of them were particularly injured at the moment, but anything could happen between now and then. Even as things currently stood, Noah didn't feel certain that he or Elias would be able to resist their instincts for the entire ride.

Worse comes to worst, we can all blindfold each other, Noah thought. *Then we can all be cured once we get our hands on a vacuum somewhere. Assuming we don't find one here, of course.*

With these thoughts in mind, Noah finally responded to his dad.

"I'd need to check with my friends first, but that sounds great," he said gratefully. "It'll save us a whole lot of walking, at least."

"Glad to help. But you have to promise to tell me everything in the car, alright? I don't want to hear any details right now; I'm self-aware enough to know it'll only make me worry more. But once we're safe, I want to hear a step-by-step recounting of every single event since our last call."

"Of course."

"Great. What time should I show up to the party?"

"We're leaving our rooms at midnight, so sometime around then? Maybe stay outside on the street until we're ready to go. I'm not sure Insight would react kindly to a strange car idling outside their front doors for no apparent reason."

"You got it. How many kids am I gonna be transporting?"

"If everything goes according to plan, six people."

"My car is a five-seater, in case you've forgotten."

"I know. But we can make it work, right?"

His dad sighed. "I sure hope so. Anything in particular I should bring? Food? Water?"

"None of that," Noah said automatically, then paused. It was possible he would be cured by the time he saw his dad, and if so, he would probably appreciate the sustenance. "Actually, maybe you should. What would really be nice, though, is a vacuum."

"A vacuum?" Laughter came over the line. "Whatever do you need that for?"

"To cure us," Noah answered vaguely. "Just make sure it's the kind with a nozzle. A portable model, preferably."

"If you actually want me to bring a vacuum, I suppose I can pick one up this afternoon before I head over. You're sure that's what you need?"

"Yes. Trust me, you won't regret having one. Even if we're cured by the time we see you, it can be used to treat anyone else we come across."

"Yeah, alright. Be careful, Noah. What we're doing is risky; don't make it more dangerous than it needs to be. Do what you need to and get out."

"I hear you. See you soon."

"See you."

Noah smiled as he hung up. That call could have gone a lot worse.

He sent a quick message in the group chat to let everyone know they had a ride out of Insight, then double-checked that his alarm was set for a few minutes before midnight and plugged in the phone beside his bed.

He lay back, shut his eyes, and was asleep before any further thoughts could pass through his mind.

***

Despite going to sleep at around 2 PM, Noah soundly slept the day and night away, only waking when the alarm beeped at five minutes to midnight.

He sat up, feeling faintly wistful for some reason, and sat there with a bemused smile for several seconds before figuring the emotion was probably caused by the contents of his dreams. Not that he could remember what had occupied his mind as he slept.

Wistfulness was quickly spiked through by excitement as the plan for the next hour or so came to the forefront of his mind. He glanced at the door, wondering if he should go out in the hallway yet. It was probably safer to wait right up until 12 AM.

He didn't dare close his eyes as he waited, because excitement or not, he certainly would have drifted back to sleep. Instead, he held his phone in his hands and watched the time slowly tick forward, attempting to mentally prepare himself for whatever the night would bring. It would be foolish to assume nothing would go wrong, but the best he could do for the moment was run through the somewhat vague game plan and try to think of possible counters to the most likely complications that may arise. Most of his ideas came down to eating the problem.

He reminded himself that he had a tranquilizing weapon in his pocket, for whatever good it might do. Perhaps if he cured himself and no longer felt up to the task of removing problems by means of consumption, the weapon could take up the slack.

Although, now that he was thinking about it, it would probably just be easier to wait to cure himself until he was off of Insight premises, even if an opportunity for him to be treated arose before then. He recalled Heinrich mentioning something about weakness following treatment, and the last thing he or his friends needed was to be crippled by fatigue before they made it out of the building. His dad would have a vacuum; they could treat each other during the car ride.

At 11:59 PM Noah shook himself from his thoughts and stood from the bed. He quickly tied most of his clothes around his upper arm like a couple of bandanas so he could keep his hands free, then exited the room, leaving all the lights on in a small act of spite.

Noah saw Brian exit his room across the hall simultaneously. The two of them were the last to emerge.

"Great, everyone's here," Leah said briskly. "So, the plan is to check for a custodial closet on this floor, right?"

"Yeah," Noah confirmed. He pulled out the ill-gotten keycard and held it up. "Let's see what this thing can unlock."

He made to do a walk-through of the entire hallway, but before he could take more than a few steps, the nearest door suddenly lit up green.

"That was easy," Brian laughed.

"Uh, wait a moment. That's my room," Elias said nervously. "Why is that keycard able to unlock my room?"

Everyone stared at the card clasped in Noah's hand.

"I don't recall it unlocking any doors earlier," Leah said slowly. "I guess I wasn't really paying attention, though."

"No, you're right. It definitely wasn't working earlier," Clarissa affirmed.

"The card must be set up to only be able to unlock our rooms once night falls," Brian said uneasily. He shuddered. "Why the hell do they need to be able to access our rooms while we're sleeping?"

"Look, we already knew they were shady as shit. This only confirms what we're already well aware of," Noah muttered.

"This is going to make it a lot more difficult to find the supposed maintenance closet," Leah said. "If we knew it was the only door that could be unlocked, it would have been easy to pick it out. But now every single door is gonna light up as we walk by. How are we supposed to find the right one?"

"Maybe it'll look different," May said hopefully. "Or it could be labeled. Let's take a look around before we start despairing."

A full walk-through of the corridor revealed that every door was both visually exactly the same and able to be opened by the keycard.

"Alright, let's start here and work our way down," Noah said once they were gathered at the far end of the hall.

May gave him a dirty look. "You can't just walk into random people's rooms. Where's your sense of privacy?"

"I'm not actually going to enter any of the rooms," he said defensively. "Just crack the door enough to check it's not a custodial closet. Like this."

His friends watched in various states of alarm as he walked to the closest door and silently pushed it several inches open. When it became apparent that it was, indeed, someone's quarters, he calmly shut the door and turned back to his fellow students with a small smile. "See? Easy."

"What if they're awake?" May asked uncomfortably.

"They probably won't notice," Noah said with a shrug.

He went to the next door without anyone moving to stop him, and then the next and the next.

He checked a good two-thirds of the doors in this fashion, encountering no difficulties, until May's warning proved unfortunately accurate.

As he opened the thirteenth door and briefly scanned the room, he was alarmed to see the lights within were all very much on. He quickly closed the door, but in the moment before it shut, an angry shout came from the room.

"You idiot," Brian muttered.

Before Noah hardly knew what was happening, the door was thrown wide open to reveal an infected, middle-aged man standing there with a furious expression twisting his features. He had a pair of narrow reading glasses perched upon the tip of his nose and he held a book with his index finger tucked into the pages, keeping his spot. His eyes narrowed at the sight of the six startled college students arrayed around his door.

Before the man could yell again, Noah pulled the tranquilizing weapon from his pocket, engaged the needle, and lunged forward to stick it into his arm.

The needle easily pierced his skin, but the man simply flinched away, and the needle slid back out with seemingly no effect.

Noah squinted at the weapon for a moment, peeved, before his eyes widened and he darted forward again. The motion somehow caught the man off guard long enough for him to stick the needle into the same arm. Noah depressed the lever, held the weapon in place for as long as he dared, then quickly yanked it out and backpedaled out of range.

Even before Noah removed the needle, the man froze. His hands shot to his eyes.

"Don't worry, I'm pretty sure it's temporary," Noah reassured him. He glanced across the room and considered taking the time to lay the man comfortably on the bed, but quickly thought better of it and instead simply nudged the man (who was currently in the process of slowly collapsing to the floor) so that his body didn't block the door from closing.

"What's happening?!" the guy yelled, panicked.

Noah shut the door without responding and turned to face his friends as he pocketed the needled weapon. Hopefully, it had more than a single dose.

Nobody said anything for a few seconds. Finally Noah smiled weakly and gestured to the right.

"So, next door?"

61

DOESN'T MAKE IT FEEL ANY BETTER

"**N**ot so fast," Leah sputtered. "What just happened? How did you knock him out like that?"

"Hmm? You're asking about this thing?" Noah pulled the syringe gun back out and waved it around. "I picked it up earlier. The doctor I killed was carrying it."

Leah pulled back a little. "Uh, okay. Some kind of tranq gun, then?"

"I think it's the same deal as whatever the soldiers were using yesterday. It injects a blinding agent."

"So that guy you just took out was infected, then."

"Yeah." Noah shoved it back in his pocket and turned away.

In the next several minutes he checked all the remaining doors in the hallway. Each one opened to reveal identical living quarters, about half of which were vacant. The rest of the rooms were mostly occupied by regular, uninfected people, though there were a few who had the dust. Nobody else was awake.

Noah closed the last door with an unhappy grimace.

"What a waste of time," Leah groused.

"I don't understand," Noah muttered. "There should have been at least some sort of maintenance closet, right? They have to clean the rooms somehow! I know this is Insight we're talking about, but if there's one thing they do well, it's clean up after messes."

"I dunno, Noah," Brian said wearily. "We should probably

get moving, though. We've spent too much time here already."

"It was worth checking," Clarissa said consolingly.

With one last disgruntled look around, Noah reluctantly nodded and turned to trudge towards the stairwell access door. Elias and May were already waiting there for him to finish checking the doors, too uncomfortable with the process to stand any closer and associate themselves by proximity.

The access light turned green as Noah approached, and May pushed the door open for them all to file in.

"We need to go down one flight," Noah said, mentally retracing their steps from earlier. "The treatment room and the vat storage room are both on the third floor."

They quickly descended the stairs and paused at the exit while Noah peeked out into the hall.

"It's empty," he said, and stepped out.

"Shouldn't we be covering our faces?" Elias quietly asked. "What if we're being recorded on camera? We could get seriously fined for damages."

"Hidden cameras are a thing, you know."

"Feel free to wear a mask if you want. I'm not gonna stop you."

It's kind of too late at this point," he grumbled, glancing warily around at their imaginary observers. After a moment he pulled a mask from his pocket and equipped it despite his words.

They went through the double doors at the end of the hall into a familiar corridor; this was the section of the building that had evidently been dedicated to researching the dust. The treatment room was at the far end, with their waiting room and the vat room located somewhere between there and where they currently stood.

The building was just as brightly illuminated as it had been during the day, and though that made their lives a little easier at the moment, it also implied the presence of late-night workers. Noah was optimistic that they'd run into a few employees. Shoring up his stores now would do a lot for boosting his confidence that nothing would go wrong when they met up with his father later.

Noah glanced to his right as a door there lit up green, then stopped in his tracks.

"You've gotta be kidding me," he said flatly

"What is it?" Brian asked.

Noah pointed at the *JANITOR* sign affixed to the center of the door and gave his friends a helpless look.

"Huh. Sweet," Leah said.

"Don't just stand there, let's see if it has a vacuum," Clarissa prompted, grinning.

Noah smiled ruefully and pushed into the room. Three bright overhead lights flickered to life as he entered.

The 'closet' was actually somewhat spacious. Metal shelves lined two of the walls, various bottled solvents arranged upon them in colorful rows. The remaining wall was made up of a wooden pegboard from which a mop, broom, and archetypal wet floor sign hung. Sitting below these three items, as if framed, was a vacuum.

It was a canister vacuum, consisting only of a red gumdrop-shaped storage tank and a black coiled hose.

Noah grinned. "Woah! Jackpot!"

"Are we sure that's a vacuum?" Brian asked half jokingly, stepping over to it. The plastic tank was painted with a smiling face to make it appear like the hose formed its protruding nose.

"It's perfect," May said. "I kind of want to name it for some reason."

"Will it be strong enough to work, though?" Clarissa wondered. "The doctors said they were using an industrial-strength vacuum for the treatment. This thing looks like a kid's toy."

"Let's find out. Who wants to go first?" Leah asked brightly, grabbing the power cord and searching the wall for an outlet.

"Wait a moment," Noah quickly interrupted before anyone could volunteer. "Shouldn't we wait until we're out of the building? Heinrich mentioned some side effects following treatment. It's probably safer to get out before we unintentionally take ourselves out of commission."

"Why'd we spend so much time looking for this thing, then?" Leah demanded, gesturing with two arms to the smiling appliance.

"It wasn't that long," Noah protested. "And I thought we were planning on treating the patients upstairs before we left."

"What, all of them? But you'd have to break into their rooms to cure them... Noah! People value their privacy!"

Noah shrugged. "They'll get over it. And only a couple rooms are occupied by infected people. It'll take like three minutes to get them all cured."

"They might not want to be cured," Clarissa said, shooting him a sideways glance.

"Well, then it's a good thing I have a tranq gun."

She paused, then grinned. "That's one way to handle it."

Leah grabbed the handle atop the vacuum and pulled it towards the door. "I got the vacuum. As much as your plan is a massive violation of privacy, it kind of needs to happen. We have to do everything we can while we're still here to ensure that every source of dust Insight possesses is destroyed. They might have stores somewhere we're unaware of, obviously, but there's not much we can do if they've thought that far ahead."

They left the room. The hallway was still clear.

"Alright, if we're going to cure anyone upstairs, we should do it before we blow up the vats," Clarissa said. "Depending on how big the explosion is, it might set off some alarms. And I don't want to be finishing up any business while the building is screaming at us."

"Sounds good to me," Noah agreed.

"Are we really doing this?" May grumbled.

"It's the responsible thing to do," Noah assured her. "Think of it like a public service."

They retraced their steps up to the hotel-like floor.

"Let's start with that guy I already knocked out. Hopefully

he's still out cold."

"He's not actually unconscious," Brian said. "Just blind and helpless."

"Tomato, tomahto," Noah said, marching past him down the hallway. He stopped outside the man's door.

"Are you sure this is the right room?" May asked.

"Yes. I have an excellent memory."

Brian made no effort to hide his incredulous laugh. "No, you don't."

Noah maintained eye contact with his friend as he slowly opened the door, revealing the man splayed across the entryway.

"Who's there?" the man asked fearfully.

"Luck. Nothing more," Brian said resolutely, ignoring the man.

"You just wish you possessed my superior intellect," Noah said as Leah wheeled the vacuum into the room. Clarissa, Elias, and May came in after her, shutting the door behind them.

"Today's your lucky day," Noah told the man, the sight of him prompting a spike of irrational annoyance due to their earlier scuffle. Leah bustled about, plugging in the vacuum and unwinding the hose. There was a flat plastic nozzle attached to the end, which she removed and tossed aside. "You're getting saved from a terrible fate at the hands of Insight."

"What?" he mumbled. "They said they'd fix my heart problems."

Noah glanced around. His friends looked back at him unhelpfully. "Uhh. Well, they probably would have, but you'll just have to trust me when I say it wouldn't be worth it. At least one person would probably have died to heal you. You'll just have to stick out your heart problems for the sake of humanity. Sorry."

"What?" he yelled. As panicked as his voice sounded, he was still incapable of moving an inch. He lay helplessly as Leah gingerly inserted the end of the tube into his mouth.

"Brian, turn on the vacuum. I'll hold the tube in place."

Brian did as instructed. The whine of the motor filled the air, prompting a muffled squeak of terror from the man.

They let the vacuum run for several minutes. They didn't want to cut it off early, of course, but they also didn't want to be sitting around in this guy's room all night. They ended up just standing around awkwardly as the vacuum ran.

"He's not going to suddenly regain mobility, is he?" Leah asked, seeming to only now consider what the results of the treatment could be.

They all shrugged.

"He'll still be blind, at least," Clarissa said, though she stepped forward to stand nearby, ready to react if the man started fighting back.

He never did, and Brian finally announced, "I'm shutting it off."

The vacuum went silent and Leah pulled out the tube.

"Well, the nozzle is clean," she said uncertainly, holding it up. "That's probably a good sign, right?"

"Unless the vacuum was so weak that all of the dust is still in his lungs," Elias pointed out.

"Hmm. Hey, stranger, mind giving us a few coughs so we can confirm the treatment worked?"

"Like hell I will," he said angrily, then coughed, apparently involuntarily. Nothing came out.

"Fiddlesticks," he muttered.

"We appreciate your cooperation," Leah said, rolling her eyes.

The man's hand twitched slightly in response, and she leapt away in alarm. He didn't yet seem capable of further movement, however. "Oh, he's definitely cured," Leah said.

"Alright, great work, gang," Noah said. "Let's pack up and hit the next room."

Brian efficiently wound up the cords and wheeled the vacuum out the door, with everyone else following behind.

Before Noah stepped out of the room, he paused and looked back at the man. "You should feel all back to normal within- uh, what was it, twenty-four hours?" He looked to his friends for confirmation. "Yeah."

"What about my heart disease!?"

"Er, we wish you well on your future medical endeavors. Apologies for the hassle."

"You're so mean," Leah said, shaking her head.

Noah shut the door. "What am I supposed to say? Of course this is gonna be awful for him. This was probably his only hope of fixing whatever was wrong with his heart, and we pranced in and stole it away from right under his nose. He could very well end up dying because of what we've done. What we're doing is trying our best to make sure Insight can't use the dust on a larger scale."

"You don't have to tell me," Leah muttered. "I know why we're doing this. Doesn't make it feel any better, though."

"This is the next door we want," Noah said suddenly. "Everyone ready? This person isn't gonna be pre-incapacitated, so I'll have to stick 'em before we do anything else. Let's go."

They charged in to treat their second target.

62

WE ARE DOING GOOD

Sleeping peacefully in the bed was a young woman. She was still breathing, though the breaths were short and sporadic. Two shoes were placed beside the bed, one of which had a metal pole sticking up from the collar. At the top of the pole was a small black ball socket with a short protruding rod.

Leah pointed at it. "Is that a..."

"A prosthetic, yeah," Clarissa said.

Elias looked down at the woman. "We could just walk out right now and she'll have her leg back by this time tomorrow."

"Yeah, and someone will have been sacrificed to make it happen," Brian said, already working with May to set up the vacuum. He glanced at the nozzle, which was slightly wet with the last man's saliva, and rubbed it on his shirt with a grimace.

Noah walked over with the syringe gun in hand and injected the woman in her exposed shoulder. Numb as she was, she didn't so much as twitch.

Elias glanced at Brian with a small frown. "Not necessarily. If Insight's smart about it, they could use multiple 'sacrifices'. Each of them get a small, non-fatal bite wound, and in exchange this woman regains a limb."

That actually made everyone stop.

"You think they would do that?" Leah asked uncertainly.

"Well, I'm not sure where they would find so many willing people. Maybe the patient's family?"

"It's easier just to lock someone in the room with the patient and let nature take its course," Noah said, a cynical light in his eyes. "I doubt Insight would go to the trouble of saving lives. You think they saw what the dust could do and got all excited that they could change the world for the better? They took one look at us and saw profit."

All the talking was starting to pull the woman from her slumber, and she emitted a soft sleepy murmur.

Noah threw her a glance and continued speaking in a whisper. "If anyone but Insight had found the dust, I might have been more willing to give them the benefit of the doubt. It really, really sucks that Insight got involved with this, because the dust could actually have done a lot of good."

"Well, we'll have a big 'ol tank full of the stuff when we're done here," Brian said quietly, nudging the vacuum with his foot. "We could always hang onto it and see if a more worthy organization could use it."

"That's definitely something worth considering, but let's figure it out later," Clarissa said. "Let's cure this gal."

"Roger that." Brian passed the nozzle to Leah, who set it into the woman's mouth and gave him a thumbs-up. The vacuum roared to life.

Incredibly, the woman seemed to remain unconscious for the entire duration of the treatment. Even when they shut off the vacuum and removed the nozzle, she didn't say anything, though she might well have been roused by the noise and was merely keeping silent.

They packed up the vacuum and hurried out of the room.

"This way," Noah said, leading them confidently to the next door.

Brian watched him with narrowed eyes. "How are you remembering the locations of the rooms?"

Noah shrugged. "How could I forget something so important?"

Brian looked at him suspiciously, but his memory proved once again accurate as the door opened to reveal the woman they had met earlier.

"Oh, it's the cancer lady," Leah said in recognition. "I wonder if she got a chance to talk with the doctors."

Noah walked over with the syringe gun eagerly bared, but Brian stopped him before he could engage the needle.

"I should have said something before you used it on the last woman, but it's kind of a waste to use that thing when they're already asleep. We don't know how many more doses it has, and it's easy enough to just blindfold the person while we treat them. We should save the weapon for emergencies."

Noah put the gun away with a sheepish expression. "Yeah, I guess I haven't been too careful about rationing its usage. It's way too fun to use."

"The needle does theoretically have the advantage of automatically wearing off over time, unlike a blindfold," Brian acknowledged. "We'll have to restore their sight before we leave, or else they'll be stuck here until someone comes to their rescue."

Leah, listening to their conversation, had already laid one of her spare shirts across the woman's eyes. "Is that going to be enough, you think?"

"The room is already pretty dark. It should be fine," May said with a slight nod.

Noah looked around and only now realized that all three rooms they had visited so far had been left illuminated by at least one light. Either the patients had already been warned about their devastating loss of mobility in the dark, or they had figured it out for themselves. Noah guessed it was the former, because otherwise they would have found each of the patients collapsed at the foot of a light switch.

They administered the treatment without any difficulties. Brian turned off the vacuum, Leah pulled out the nozzle, and May took off the blindfold. As soon as she did so, however, she let out a shriek and threw it back into place.

"What?" Elias asked with a concerned glance.

"Her eyes were open," May said, embarrassed.

"Yeah, I'm awake. I haven't been able to sleep all night," the woman said quietly.

"Why didn't you say anything when we walked in?" Leah demanded. "You just let us cure you!"

"I recognized your voices," she admitted. "I've no idea how you got into my room, but I'm glad you did. Thank you for curing me. I talked to the doctors earlier, but they refused to do anything."

May finally reached forward and took off the blindfold for good, revealing calm eyes. "You're welcome," she murmured.

"It sounds like you're treating everyone. Don't dawdle with me; hurry on and finish the job," the woman said. "Do me a favor and destroy the dust when you're done, alright?"

Brian blinked. "You don't think it could be useful? In the hands of someone more responsible?"

She shook her head. "Don't be tempted to save it. The dust is a devil's deal. It's only a matter of time before it causes more damage than it could ever heal."

Brian nodded doubtfully. "Alright."

"Now get moving," she urged. "And be careful."

"Always," Leah said. She grabbed the vacuum and pulled it to the door. "See you around."

The woman didn't respond, just watching from her bed as they exited her room.

"How many more?" Brian asked glumly.

"Just four," Noah said. "Two of which are Mark and Violet."

"At least we're not condemning them to death by treating them," Leah muttered. "Can we go to their rooms next?"

"I've no idea which room is which," Noah shrugged. "It's a fifty-fifty chance."

They went to the next door and entered.

"Oh, excellent," Leah said, seeing Mark out cold on the bed. "Nothing here to make me feel like a rotten human being."

Clarissa stepped forward to secure a satin sleeping mask across his eyes.

"Of course you have one of those," Elias laughed.

"Hmm?" Mark asked sleepily.

"Look, you woke him up," Leah said, shaking her head in disappointment.

"What? What's happening?" Mark's voice suddenly rose as he tried to move and found himself utterly immobile.

"It's just us. Hold still for a moment, we're gonna cure you," Brian said wearily.

"I can't move!"

"Very good."

Leah shoved the nozzle into his mouth, muffling any further words. As soon as it came time to turn off the vacuum and she removed the hose, he let out a shout. "How did you get into my room?"

"Wouldn't you like to know, deserter," Noah said.

"Did you use that stolen keycard?"

"...No."

"If you struggle, Noah will stick a needle in you and you'll be paralyzed all night," Clarissa warned, before tearing off the sleeping mask. Mark stared at her warily and didn't move.

They left the room.

"We're getting good at this," Leah commented. "Only three to go."

"Does the blinding agent really last that long?" Elias asked.

Clarissa shrugged. "Could last a week for all I know."

"This is the next door we want," Noah said.

In they went. Laying in the bed, fast asleep, was a hugely obese man.

"This guy has so much body mass to spare, he could probably regenerate all four limbs from scratch without eating anyone," Leah said, regarding him with an unreadable expression. "I wonder what he's here for."

"He could have the *Wager*... or it could be for weight loss," Elias said thoughtfully. "I wouldn't be surprised if Insight tries to market the dust as a weight loss medicine, in addition to everything else."

"Holy crap," Brian muttered, pausing by the outlet. "They'd make so much money. They might not even have to kill anyone to make it work, either."

Leah walked to the man's bedside with the vacuum nozzle in hand and held it over his mouth, only to pause. "We could do it, you know."

Everyone turned to her. "What?" Brian asked.

"Do what he came here for. You're right that nobody would have to die; the whole point is to use up his own flesh. How long do you think he's been infected? Would it even work?"

Understanding washed over Noah, and he leaned forward with narrowed eyes. "He's not breathing; he must have been infected earlier than the others. It could work."

"I say let's do it," Leah said, setting the nozzle aside. "Assuming he doesn't actually have a terminal illness, it's what he's here for. This is an opportunity for us to do some good."

"We are doing good," Noah muttered.

"You know what I mean. Do something that I can feel good about."

"Hmm. Do you have a knife?" he asked.

Clarissa stepped forward and wordlessly pulled out a small black pocket knife, along with the sleeping mask. Leah took both and quickly pulled the mask around the man's eyes.

Leah glanced around. "Just to check, everyone's okay with this, right?"

May and Elias shrugged.

"Sounds good to me," Brian said. "The guy will probably be overjoyed when he wakes up."

"Alright." Leah turned, flicked out the blade, and drove it through the blankets into the man's heart.

Elias let out a snort of surprise, but Leah didn't stop there, plunging the knife repeatedly into his chest.

Finally she paused. "Let's see if that's enough."

For a long moment nothing happened. Then the man let out a long groan and began to deflate like a punctured balloon. Leah watched carefully, administering another stab each time the deflation slowed.

"Don't do too much," Noah warned.

"I'm being careful."

By the time Leah stepped back with a satisfied nod, the sheets were a mess of ragged holes. There was some blood, but it wasn't covering the entire bed like it might've been if the man wasn't infected.

"Do you think he's even hungry after healing all of that?" Clarissa asked.

"Who knows. He's still asleep, so he's probably fine." Leah snapped the blade shut and handed it back to her. "Nice knife. Thanks for letting me use it."

"You're welcome," she said, pleased.

The man looked like an entirely different person; what was visible of his upper body above the sheets had gained definition as the layers of fat were consumed to fuel his healing. He had probably lost half his body weight in the past five minutes.

"We did good," Leah said proudly, picking up the nozzle. "Brian, turn on the vacuum."

Over the next few moments the man was cured without him any the wiser, and Leah gave him one last appraising look as they left the room. "I hope he appreciates what we've done."

Clarissa dipped her head. "Yeah. Who knows what his situation was. Hopefully he's not also dying of a fatal illness."

Noah took them to the second-to-last room, which turned out to be Violet's quarters. She woke up halfway through the treatment, but rather than fight back, she seemed appreciative. She watched them pack up with a pensive expression, and when they made to leave, she called for them to stop.

"Can I come with you?"

Noah shook his head without hesitation. "No. My dad's car is already short on seats. Besides, you made your choice. You can go home tomorrow. Insight won't have any need for you if you don't have the dust, and you're better off having nothing to do with us. Insight isn't going to be too fond of us after tonight."

Violet reluctantly lay back in bed. "Yeah, yeah. I'll see you back on campus."

They filed out into the hallway.

"Where's the last room?" Brian asked Noah, wandering slowly beside him down the corridor.

"No idea." Noah grinned.

"What?" his friend demanded, staring at him.

Noah laughed and came to a stop beside a door. "This is the one."

Brian shot him a dirty look as they entered the final room, though his annoyance was soon forgotten, superseded by the state of the room.

"Holy crap," Leah muttered, fanning a hand in front of her face. "What happened here?"

Dust hung heavily in the air, obscuring their sight of the room's occupant. Several lamps were turned on, but they shone through the dark clouds like distant suns and only managed to create a faint muffled glow.

"Imagine if it's Dr. Jansen," Brian whispered.

"No way would they do her dirty like that," Leah scoffed.

"This is actually dangerous," Noah muttered as he peered around. "I can hardly see anything."

Brian suddenly straightened. "Hold on just a moment. I might be able to do something about that." He fumbled at his shirt collar for a moment before extracting the pendant and holding it aloft. "Let's see how good the suction on this thing is."

The air darkened about the silver square as if it were exuding a malicious aura rather than cleansing the air, and a foul vortex soon formed above it. As more and more particles were caught in the pull, the air steadily cleared, until at last the final wisp of dust disappeared into the pendant.

"Sweet," Brian murmured. He let it drop back around his neck.

They all looked at the person laying in bed, the one responsible for contaminating the entire room.

A tiny shriveled slip of an old woman was curled beneath the blankets, her skeletal form hardly displacing them at all. Her breath sounded like a broken radiator, gurgling and rattling in irregular bursts, each sound making Noah instinctively wince. Even as they watched, she let out a feeble cough, and more dust appeared around her wrinkled face. The faint clouds hovered there for only a moment before drawing inexorably to the pendant left uncovered on Brian's chest.

"I'm almost afraid to touch her," Leah murmured.

"We have to," Noah said coldly. He took the vacuum's cord and plugged it in himself, then held the tube nozzle out to her. "Come on."

Leah gave him a worried look and slowly took hold of the hose. "Clarissa, blind her."

Noah hit the switch once everything was in place. The blindfold seemed wholly unnecessary; the old woman didn't so much as twitch at the sound of the vacuum's whining motor.

"Noah..." May said, her voice strained. "The effects of the treatment, the weakness... she's not going to survive this. She's already too feeble."

She might survive, he didn't say. "You're probably right. She likely won't."

May looked around at everyone, but nobody would meet her gaze. The only sound was the vacuum's motor.

"I know it's horrible," Brian said quietly.

"I'm going outside," she muttered.

They watched her shuffle out of the room and carefully shut the door behind her.

No one said anything until Noah finally shut off the vacuum several minutes later. The silence was deafening.

"Let's get out of here," Leah muttered.

They wrapped up the vacuum's tubes and cords and processed out of the room.

Noah was the first back into the hallway. He looked around for May, not seeing her immediately beside the door, and found her halfway down the hall towards the staircase.

As soon as he caught sight of her, he realized she wasn't alone. A woman garbed in the signature blue uniform of Insight stood in front of her, backed up against the far wall. In her hands, pointed at May, was a pistol.

Before anyone could do anything, she fired.

63

I'D RATHER NOT BE A ZOMBIE, THANKS

May stumbled back at the impact. When she didn't go down, the woman fired again, but she only took one more step back. She dazedly touched the holes in her chest.

"What the hell, May?!" Leah yelled, sprinting down the hallway towards her. "We leave you alone for five minutes and you get yourself shot!?"

"Stand back!" the guard commanded, adjusting her aim towards Leah. She ignored the threat of the weapon, only stopping once she stood beside her injured friend.

"Oh, excellent," Noah murmured. The four of them still hovering around the door began cautiously making their way down the hall as well. The vacuum was left forgotten by the door.

"I will fire," the guard warned.

"Jeez, trigger-happy, much? What if I just wanted to grab a snack?" Leah said, pointing at the vending machine innocently.

"You'll have to wait until morning. Curfew was two hours ago."

"Curfew?" Brian laughed. He turned to Noah. "Nobody told us about a curfew. I would remember being informed about a lethally-enforced curfew."

"Whoever brought you to your rooms should have ensured

you were aware of the rule," the guard said neutrally.

Elias glanced at Noah knowingly. "It must've slipped the doctor's mind."

Noah stared at the guard, standing with the pistol braced in her hands, her eyes cold. "Do you know what we are?" he asked curiously. *Not that I'm complaining, but shouldn't she have a syringe gun rather than a pistol? Did she skip the daily briefing? And if she's completely clueless, which seems to be the case, what kind of sicko do you have to be to fire at an unarmed kid?*

She deserves what's coming for her. As does the rest of Insight.

"Yes. You are disobeying company policy." The woman narrowed her eyes when none of them made any move to clear out of the hallway. She shifted the gun to a single hand, keeping it trained on them as if they had given her any reason to suspect they would present a danger to her, then grabbed a radio on her hip and held it to her lips. "I've got a couple of kids making trouble on four."

Noah almost laughed out loud. Nobody had eaten anyone yet and she was already calling in reinforcements. *This is fantastic,* he thought, unable to suppress a grin. *There'll be plenty for everyone.*

Clarissa leaned towards Leah and May. "How's she doing?"

There was no response from May, but Leah laughed mirthlessly. "She just got shot twice in the chest. What do you think?"

May's eyes were fixed unblinkingly on the guard, though she still made no move towards her. She simply stood there, growing more gaunt with every passing second. Noah was impressed with how long she was fighting her instincts, but he knew it would inevitably be a lost cause. Two bullets were lodged somewhere in her chest; the damage they caused was surely extensive.

"Go get 'em, captain," Noah encouraged. "You can have this one, but I want the next."

"Speak for yourself," Elias said with a mad grin, just about bouncing in place with poorly restrained excitement. He had already taken off the mask he had equipped earlier and shoved it in his pocket in preparation for his anticipated meal.

"Holy crap, shut up, both of you," Brian growled. He pulled off the pendant. "May, I know it's tough, but just try to hold on for a moment. Let's see if getting some dust into you can make you feel any better."

"Oh, good thinking," Clarissa said.

May's eyes snapped suddenly to Brian and she gave him a look of immense disgust. "That's only for emergencies. This isn't an emergency."

"Oh?" Brian said, squinting uncertainly. "You're okay? You don't seem, uh-"

"There's a person right there," May interrupted with a wide gesture forward. "You can keep your dust."

The security guard, watching them from a short distance down the hall, seemed to reach the limit of her patience. Revealing an astounding disregard for life, she lifted her weapon once more and fired.

Noah didn't see if anyone had been hit. The sound was like a starting pistol for May, and she bolted forward without hesitation. Elias shrugged apologetically at Noah before giving into his own hunger and racing after her.

"Wait!" Leah yelled, reaching out impotently.

Noah patted her on the shoulder. "This is for the best. The guard isn't going to leave us alone until we're back in our quarters, and I don't ever plan on returning to that room. They're hungry. Let them take care of her."

Leah turned to her brother for support, only for her eyes to widen in horror. "Brian! Seriously?"

"Did- did I get hit?" he asked incredulously, then murmured to himself, "Is that what that was?"

He brought his hand to his neck to brush against the dark red mark, glancing around fearfully, until his neck finally began to mend itself. It was as if a switch suddenly flipped within him; his eyes went hazy for a moment, and then, as if by magnetic pull, shifted to the guard. "Sorry. I'll be right back."

He hurried after Elias and May, shoving the pendant in his pocket as he went. Leah slumped and watched him go with a resigned grimace.

When May had gone after the guard, she had only been able to fire off four ineffectual shots before the girl's jaws fastened themselves onto her shoulder. In the next moment Elias had arrived and immediately set to chewing on her arm, narrowly avoiding three more shots before the gun fell from the woman's hand.

The guard now seemed an equal mix of bewildered and horrified. She scrambled to push them aside and extricate herself, but then Brian came flying out of nowhere, and upon impact she simply collapsed, the collision force too great to stand against. She was wearing some sort of blue body armor, but it only covered her vital organs, and ultimately did little more than to prolong her suffering. Her body was hidden from view, but the sounds carried far too well.

"That's just plain disgusting," Clarissa mumbled, turning away with a gag.

Noah glanced at her. "If it's bothering you, a small wound would take care of your discomfort."

She scowled. "I don't *want* to be comfortable. I'd rather not be a zombie, thanks."

"Hmm." Noah couldn't disagree more. The woman's uninfected presence called out to him like a siren's song, but he held himself back with the knowledge that she wouldn't last much longer. Besides, if her brief message on the radio was indeed a plea for backup, he would soon have more people than he could possibly eat.

Noah was aware of the exact moment she passed. The pressing urge withdrew into a more tolerable prick at the back of his consciousness, and he nudged Clarissa and Leah. "It's over."

"How can you...?" Leah trailed off. "Okay. Thanks."

Their three friends slowly pulled back from the body,

revealing an unappetizing mess.

"That was fantastic," May said, beaming. Brian and Elias appeared equally satisfied.

"Isn't it?" Noah enthused, any lingering regret squashed at the sight of their joy. Pride and fellowship welled up within him.

"We need to move," Leah said. "I'm so glad you all had fun, but there could be more workers showing up at any moment."

"Maybe we should wait," Noah protested weakly, but despite his best efforts, he couldn't come up with a convincing reason to stay.

Leah glared at him. "We're here to blow up some dust and get out. Nothing more."

Noah glanced around. "I'm just saying, if an opportunity were to arise... the world would be a better place with a few less of these people, right?"

Leah didn't favor him with a response, merely sweeping past him towards the stairs.

"Come on, Noah," Clarissa sighed.

"Oh, wait!" he brightened. "The vacuum! We should probably take care of that now, right?"

Leah slowly turned around. "What?"

"Er, we can't just leave it here, full of dust as it is," he began. "And I don't really feel like carrying it around, so wouldn't now be a good time to destroy its contents?"

Brian came trudging forward with the pendant in hand. "Or we could use this; it won't take much longer, and we can decide later what we want to do with the dust. Take off the vacuum's lid and I'll hold the pendant close."

"What about what that woman said?" Leah asked.

Brian dipped his head. "We'll probably end up destroying it, yeah. But it's a decision better made when we're not in a time crunch."

The group retraced their steps to the abandoned vacuum.

"Alright, let's see," Noah murmured, bending down to look at the release mechanism. "This looks highly complex. It could very well take all night to get this open."

"Oh, shove off," Leah snapped, pushing him aside and flicking the twin spring latches on each side of the container. The lid lifted easily off. Beneath was a disk-shaped filter, which also came out without any trouble.

"Oh..." Noah said sadly.

Leah paused to give him a dark look. "What's wrong with you? Do you not want to get out of here?"

Noah swallowed, realizing that watching his friends eat had perhaps roused his appetite a bit more than he had realized. "Of course. I'm- I'm being dumb. Sorry."

She shook her head and looked back at the vacuum's contents. "There's a bag here that I doubt I'll be able to open properly. Clarissa, you still got that knife?"

"What do you think?" she said with a smirk, passing it over.

Leah took it and smoothly ripped it into the fabric vacuum bag, sending dust streaming up into the air. "Brian! Your turn!"

"I'm right here," he said, leaning over her shoulder to dangle the metal square above the torn dust bag. "Give it a minute."

They all watched as the dust spread seemingly without end, expanding to fill their section of the corridor.

"You don't mean an actual minute, do you?" Elias muttered.

Despite their fears, the pendant was doing its job, albeit at a slower pace than the rate of release from the vacuum. A familiar vortex formed around them, dark tendrils waving wildly about as the suction force of the pendant overcame the dust's natural proclivity to spread far and wide. Even the far-drifting particles could not escape the pull, finally being drawn inward like fish on a line.

The pendant's power slowly picked up, gradually overcoming the amount pouring from the vacuum and eventually tearing the dust straight from the bag directly into itself. The fabric began to tear beneath the force.

All at once, the air was still once more. Brian lifted the pendant to drop back around his neck.

"That thing doesn't have a storage capacity, does it?" Elias asked warily.

Brian shrugged. "How would I know? There's already so much more dust in it than seems plausible, so I don't think it's worth worrying about. As long as it doesn't break, we should probably be fine. And it's literally a metal square; I think we're safe."

Noah gazed at the disassembled vacuum for a second before opening the door beside them and shoving it inside. "There. We're all set to head downstairs."

"What about the body?" May asked. "Aren't we going to clean that up, too?"

"Nah, there's too much blood," Noah said as they walked towards where it lay beside the stairwell entrance "It would take forever. And Leah's absolutely right that we have to leave. My dad's waiting for us outside." *And if anyone were coming, they'd already have arrived by now.*

Brian paused by the remains. "Anything worth taking from the body, you think?"

"Maybe the radio," Clarissa suggested. "I'd leave the gun, though. We don't need it, and it'll only bring us trouble."

Brian poked at it for a moment before turning away with a faintly nauseated expression. "Actually, I think I'll just leave everything as it is."

"You do realize you made that mess," Leah pointed out.

"Yeah, but it's dead now," Brian muttered. "Come on, I'm sick of this floor. Let's go blow some vats up."

64

INVESTIGATION

"Alright," Leah said, turning to May as they climbed the stairs. "What I want to know is how you managed to piss off that lady so bad in the span of five minutes that she felt the need to shoot you."

May chuckled darkly. "You heard her going on about the curfew. She came out of the stairwell just in time to see me leave the room, and she gave me a warning to get back inside. Obviously that wasn't my room and I don't have Noah's magic keycard, so I couldn't very well do that. So she came right over and kind of got in my face, and said I have three seconds to get back inside. And when she got to zero I'm pretty sure she tased me."

"Pretty sure?"

"Look, I've never been hit by a taser before. I'm sure if I wasn't infected it would've been a lot worse, but it only made me fall over for a few seconds, and as soon as I was able, I just picked myself back up and pulled the wires out. I think we were both a little confused at what was happening.

"She didn't pull the gun until she realized the taser was ineffective. She pointed the gun at me and backed up, and that's when you all finally decided to come out. I wonder what she thought when we all came out of the same room, if she was even paying attention."

"So she really was just crazy," Clarissa said, shaking her head. "Must be part of the Insight hiring process. A checkbox, 'Are you comfortable shooting at a kid'?"

"Seriously," Brian muttered. "Everyone here is insane."

"Looks like nobody gave that guard's radio message a second thought," Noah commented. "No alarms going off, no people anywhere."

"They probably assumed she could handle a 'couple of kids making trouble,'" Brian grinned. "After all, she's apparently at liberty to shoot everyone and everything. What hope do we have against that?"

"But that's the thing," Noah said, furrowing his brows. "All she did was shoot. She didn't even try to blind us. It's like she had no idea about the dust at all."

"Insight's a big place," Elias replied. "They're probably working on all sorts of crazy stuff. I wouldn't be surprised if she was never told about their most recent project."

"That seems like somewhat of a security oversight," Noah muttered.

"I would say so, yes."

By now they had arrived back in the hallway with the treatment room. There were still no employees to be seen.

Noah glanced around. "For some unfathomable reason, all the doors look exactly the same, so it might take a bit of trial and error to find the vat room. I can't remember exactly which one it was."

"That's fine," Brian said. "We should probably check the other rooms anyway. For all we know, there could be a dozen more vats stuffed to the brim with dust hidden away somewhere."

"I'm almost afraid of what we'll find," Clarissa said wearily. "They're probably committing war crimes in here."

"That's Insight for you," Brian murmured. "Pushing the limits of science with complete disregard for laws, morals, or sanctity of life in general."

"Says the guy who literally ripped someone apart, what was it, ten minutes ago?" Clarissa glanced sideways at him.

"I'm sick," he replied easily. "There's no comparison."

They went to the very first door and paused there. "What if we find Insight workers inside?" Leah asked.

Everyone except Clarissa gave her an odd look.

"Do you really have to ask?" Noah muttered.

Leah frowned. "Do you possibly think you could avoid killing everyone? A lot of the people here might not be as evil as the company they're working for."

"I sincerely doubt that."

"Just try not to go for any vital bits, alright? Incapacitation is fine."

"I'll try," Noah mumbled. His friends nodded their halfhearted assent.

"You can have this," Noah said after a moment, pulling out the syringe gun and holding it out to her. "I know I won't need it, and you'll be practically defenseless until you pick up an injury."

She grimaced but accepted the offering. "Thanks."

"What about me?" Clarissa pouted.

Brian stared at her. "Is your hatchet just for show?"

"'Is it for show?'" She laughed. "You just watch, buddy."

"There probably won't be anyone inside," Leah said, giving Clarissa a slightly worried look.

"Let's find out." Noah pushed the door open and led the way into the room.

It was about the same size as the vat room, though most of the available floor space was taken up with filing cabinets and several large freezers. A long table at standing height extended down the center of the room, written notes strewn across it. There were no workers present.

"Check the cabinets and freezers for anything that looks like it could be a receptacle for the dust," Brian ordered. "If they're unlocked, that is." He went to the closest one and gave it a tentative tug. He smiled when it slid out easily.

To no one's surprise, the filing cabinets held files. They didn't have time to go through the endless papers, but a brief page-through of one of the drawers revealed old funding requests and project plans dating from six years ago. They soon moved on to the freezers.

Noah half feared they would be filled with the bodies

of Insight's past victims, but the contents were perfectly mundane, consisting of countless capped vials, labeled and lined up in wire racks. The transparent material allowed him to see that they contained some kind of liquid varying in color from transparent to dark pink. Noah grabbed one to peer at the label, but it was an indecipherable mix of letters and numbers, so he shrugged and put it back.

The next freezer was full of cardboard boxes, which upon further investigation contained sealed packets of congealed amber sludge. None of them could identify what it was, but it wasn't dust, so they left those be and moved on to the final freezer.

It was locked shut.

"Well, that's inconvenient," Brian said. "And not a little suspicious."

Elias stepped over to the first two freezers and inspected the closing mechanism, opening and shutting the doors. They were both currently set to be unlocked, but the unengaged plastic bolt was clearly visible when the doors were open.

"These things aren't built to be vaults, they're built to be freezers," Elias observed. "The lock looks pretty fragile. We might be able to break it, with enough force."

Brian acknowledged him with a nod and braced himself against the frame of the locked freezer, straining on the handle with all his strength. The door remained firmly shut. Noah joined him a second later, barely fitting his hands beside his friend's on the small handle, but even their combined might was insufficient to snap the plastic bolt within the door.

"Er, I might have misjudged the strength of the lock," Elias admitted.

"Clarissa," Brian huffed, stepping back. "You think your axe could make a dent in this?"

"Come on, you know it's a hatchet," she corrected. "And no. It is designed to chop wood, not metal. At best, the blade would dull, and at worst it would completely break off, hit one of you, and make you go crazier than you already are."

"Wouldn't want that to happen," Brian muttered.

"I don't suppose the key is laying around nearby," May said.

Noah glanced at the table. There wasn't a key immediately visible, but he leaned over anyway to get a better look at the various papers which someone had failed to gather up at the conclusion of some past meeting.

He quickly realized the subject of the notes was the dust. Observations, experiments, and data were recorded in neat lines, almost more than seemed possible from a single day of research.

"Look at this," he said, gesturing vaguely to the table in its entirety. "They've been busy."

He picked up a paper at random and scanned down its contents, then laughed. "They've made a whole acronym for it already. DUST: Dispersing Unicellular Survival Toxin." He wondered if 'Survival' referred to the dust, or the person who had it.

"Sounds about right," Brian remarked, peering at his own sheet of notes. "Listen to this- after a subject has been injured, the hunger 'persists even beyond the event of total physical recovery. Given the opportunity to consume additional flesh following regeneration, test subjects will do so every time. Once exposed to the compulsion, a subject will not return to their normal mental state until they are cured.'" He turned to Noah. "But we already know that, don't we?"

"Sure. Does it say why?"

Brian narrowed his eyes at the paper. "No, although down here it mentions that there is no known maximum capacity for dust storage within a subject's lungs."

"That makes sense," Elias reflected. "That tiny pendant is holding enough dust right now to fill a gymnasium. The dust can pack itself impossibly tightly."

"So I'll never feel sated," Noah murmured.

Leah glanced over with a frown. "That's what you get out of all of this? Sure you will, as soon as you're cured."

Brian flipped the page over. "It says 'see further notes,' but there's nothing else here."

"This might be it," May said, holding up another sheet of paper. "Or it's related, at least. Remember the device Heinrich mentioned that's supposed to assuage a subject's hunger? Well, apparently the scientists discovered some side effects while they were trying to figure out how to make it have more than a temporary effect. 'When a subject achieves a certain concentration of dust within their body, they begin to display elevated physical faculties, with an approximate twenty-five to thirty percent increase in categories including strength and speed. This effect can be achieved through either consumption of flesh or a large dose of dust directly into the lungs, and scales proportionally to the amount ingested. While in this state, a subject's supply of dust will be rapidly deplete until they have returned to their usual capabilities.'"

65

SHH, I'M GETTING SUPERPOWERS

Noah thought back to the odd hyper feeling he'd momentarily observed back in the vat room when he'd opened the container and gotten a faceful of pressurized dust. "I think I already experienced a little of that," he said slowly.

"Through which method?" Leah asked suspiciously. "Eating people, or dust?"

"Dust. When I opened one of the vats."

"I'm surprised you haven't gotten it the other way," Clarissa commented.

"Hey, I've been showing commendable self-restraint," Noah protested. "There were like twenty uninfected patients upstairs in those rooms, you know."

"Great job, Noah. We're all proud of you," Leah muttered. "What I want to know is how the doctors managed to figure any of this stuff out. Exactly how much 'consumption of flesh' is required, and who's being eaten? None of the patients upstairs had that half-starved look you get after you've regenerated from an injury."

"Oh man, *I* was injured," Brian realized, gazing around with a horrified expression. "Do I look like Noah now?"

Elias sighed. "The building is literally made of mirrors. Did you not check your reflection? We're all in the same boat."

"Guys," Leah ground out. "Listen. I think there are more patients somewhere. All of these notes had to come from somewhere."

"We get it," Brian said. "They're probably somewhere in this hallway, right? We'll find them and get them cured, just like all the others. We've come too far to just leave infected people laying around."

"The sunk cost fallacy, except with human life," May murmured melodramatically.

"We should've brought the vacuum with us," Leah said, ignoring her. "We'll have to make yet another trip upstairs to get it."

"Er, we might need to find another vacuum. The bag ripped, remember?"

"We're spending an awful lot of time running around not blowing up vats," Clarissa observed. "The more time we spend here, the higher the chance we'll be discovered."

"We already were discovered, and I think that went pretty well," Elias said.

"Yeah, and she was an ignorant idiot who had no idea how to handle us. Who's to say the next guard we stumble across won't be more informed, and better equipped? The sickness makes us all terribly vulnerable. If they so much as turn off the lights, we're screwed."

"Keep one of your flashlights on," Noah suggested. "So we won't be in total darkness if that happens."

Clarissa paused. "That's smart; I should've thought of that." She took out a penlight, turned it on, and clipped it to one of her coat pockets so that it shone towards the floor by her feet. "Okay. We need to get moving."

"I know, I know," Brian said, pulling the pendant off his neck. "But I might have an idea of how to get that freezer over there open. You think there's enough dust in this thing to activate super zombie mode?"

Noah snorted, his lip unconsciously curling. "You actually want to do that?" Even knowing the potential benefits, releasing so much dust into his lungs did not appeal to him in the slightest, and a deep-seated revulsion rose up in him at the thought.

"Yeah, it'll suck," Brian acknowledged. "But there's gotta

be something important locked up in that wannabe vault. If this pendant can grant me the strength to open the door, I'm willing to put up with a little discomfort to make it happen."

"How noble," Clarissa said, looking between them in visible confusion.

Noticing her expression, Leah said, "I don't know either. More dust shenanigans, I'm guessing. Something about the pendant makes them weirdly opposed to using it to boost their, uh, dust supply."

Elias shook his head. "I don't think it's specifically related to the pendant. It's the idea of using an external source of dust at all. If I had to guess, the dust doesn't like the fact that we're using it up for no good reason. It wants us to eat people and make more of it, not expend it unnecessarily."

"So it has a mind of its own?" Clarissa asked skeptically.

"More of an evolved affectual instinct, I would say. Or maybe it does. I don't know."

"Well, I have the dust too. Shouldn't I feel the same as them?"

Leah glanced at her. "At this point I think it's pretty obvious that it stays in a sort of dormant state until you get injured. It doesn't seem to really start messing with your head until that point."

"Yeah. You're not a real zombie yet, poser," Noah shot out, grinning at Clarissa.

"Shh, I'm getting superpowers," Brian interrupted gleefully. He pressed the pendant to his lips and compressed the opening mechanism on each side. He looked somewhat silly, trying to fit his mouth around the rectangular piece of metal, but to his credit, hardly any dust escaped around the corners of his lips.

"What if I wanted to try?" May complained. "Your saliva is going to be all over it."

Brian gave her a dirty look, but didn't bother attempting to respond around the pendant.

"Can you feel anything happening?" Noah asked after a few moments had passed.

Brian waggled his eyebrows.

"I don't know what that means."

There was no response, though the blood vessels in Brian's body grew darker and more prominent as the seconds ticked by. A slight shaking became noticeable throughout his entire form.

He finally pulled the pendant away from his mouth and folded it closed before too much of the dark particles could leak out into the air. "It means shut up and let me finish," he said in a strangely blurry voice, as if his voice was coming through a fan. Dust poured out of his nostrils, and when he opened his mouth to speak, it cascaded from his lips as well. The dark wisps were dragged after him as he swept across the room towards the locked freezer.

Noah noticed his friend's gait was strangely stuttery, like an old hand-cranked film playing out before his eyes. Each step consisted of a hundred small jerky movements. Noah could hardly imagine how much dust was permeating Brian's body.

Brian reached the freezer and reached forward for the handle, grabbed it, and pulled it open like it had never been locked to begin with. A loud snap echoed through the room.

"Twenty-five to thirty percent increase in strength?" Leah muttered. "Something tells me they were being a tad conservative with that estimate."

Or they weren't using so much dust in their experiments, Noah thought.

"I did it," Brian said in that same odd voice, turning back to them.

"Yes, we can see that," Clarissa said drily.

"I think I might just explode now," Brian said, looking down at his vibrating hands. The dust was no longer wafting from his mouth, though he clearly had some excess energy.

"Can you suck the dust back out with the pendant?" Elias wondered. "Like you would with a vacuum?"

Brian looked at the necklace doubtfully. "This thing doesn't really start suctioning until it's actually in the presence of a decent amount of dust. It won't just draw it out from my lungs like that."

"The note said that this strengthened state doesn't last long," May recalled. "I'm not sure what else you can do besides wait it out."

"Yeah. It's fine, it doesn't exactly hurt," Brian muttered. "C'mon, take a look at what they were keeping in here."

They all gathered around the freezer as a mist drifted out from within and danced around their feet. At first glance, the box seemed completely empty. There were no items on any of its wire racks, with the exception of the bottommost shelf. There they found four familiar stoppered vials. Leah stepped forward to take them out.

"Is that...?" Noah trailed off.

Leah nodded. "Our blood samples. Has our names right on them."

"When did they get your blood?" Clarissa demanded. "And why would they lock it up?"

Noah shot a questioning look at his friends who had been by his side from the beginning. Leah and May nodded shortly, and Brian seemed ambivalent. *Alright then.*

"We were some of the earliest people to get infected," Noah bluntly informed Clarissa and Elias. "The first four, actually."

A moment of silence passed.

"You were *what*?" Clarissa spluttered. "How?"

Noah leaned back against a nearby freezer. "It started with that pendant Brian's carrying, which we found in a mausoleum nearby campus. We opened it up, the dust came out, and we got sick. And then things escalated before we realized what was wrong."

"Why didn't you vacuum it out? How did the whole school end up with it?" Elias asked, his brows furrowing as he tried to wrap his head around the fact that he was standing in a room with the four people responsible for the current crisis.

"We had no idea what was happening," Noah grumbled. "We didn't know if a cure even existed at the time. And we did get ourselves quarantined, but it was too late. I'm sincerely sorry for everything that's happened as a result."

Clarissa briefly shut her eyes. "Okay. So how did they end up with your blood?"

"We provided the samples back on campus," Brian said. His voice had nearly returned to normal, though dark lines still traced beneath his skin, and he shuddered with what energy he yet retained. "Who knows if they even got any use out of them. I just don't understand why they would be locked up."

They looked back to the four vials clutched in Leah's hands.

"Is it just me, or are they darker than they should be?" Noah suddenly asked suspiciously.

They all leaned a little closer. The contents were certainly red, but the color was perhaps just a shade darker than typical.

"Yeah, that doesn't look normal," Clarissa agreed.

"Did they mix something in, or is our blood just naturally darkened by the infection, you think?" Brian asked.

"I don't know," Leah said finally. "I'm not leaving these behind, though."

"I can carry them," Clarissa offered.

Leah passed them over and the girl pocketed them.

"Alright, we opened the freezer, let's go," Elias said. "Hopefully we can move a little quicker through the rest of the rooms."

Clarissa began gathering up all of the papers on the table and shoving them into her coat. When she was finished, they left the room. The hall was empty.

They moved as one to the next door, which turned green, allowing them inside.

66

YOU ARE NOT EATING THIS GUY

The next several rooms consisted of unoccupied labs, furnished with tables, stools, and whiteboards. It took quite a bit of time to thoroughly search through the many cabinets and drawers in each room, which contained all manner of science paraphernalia, though their efforts were eventually rewarded.

In the fourth room Elias happened across a collection of metal containers shaped like wine bottles. Each vessel sported a knob where the cork would be on a regular bottle, which when sufficiently loosened would begin to release dust. They opened each of these containers and relocated the dust into the pendant.

One of the bottles, however, was hooked up to a delicate array of narrow glass tubes. Dust had flooded from it to fill the entire contraption.

They were stumped on how to deal with this until Clarissa stepped forward, raised her hatchet, and swung it clear through the delicate apparatus. An awful screeching sound of shattering glass filled the room and dust flew everywhere. Brian used the pendant to clean the air, and they left the broken pieces of glass scattered across the desk and floor.

They continued on, generally ransacking each room for any sign of the dust and gradually making their way closer to the vat room, until they came across something different. They found a room that was not vacant.

The first thing Noah noticed about the space were the

lights; they were dimmed well past half power, casting the room in shadow. It was not so dark that he was unable to see, however, and his attention soon fastened onto the twin glass cubicles located on the far side of the room. Within each compartment was an examination table, and laying on each table was a person. One of the people had a hood around their head, while the other's head was free, though they seemed to be sleeping. Both individuals were bound in place by wide fabric bands akin to car seatbelts, and the cubicles were locked by a sliding bolt from the outside. The entire enclosed space around the hooded person was shrouded in dust.

"What's happening here?" Brian asked quietly, gazing around with a frown. His voice had returned to normal and the dark lines under his skin had disappeared, but he was the worse for wear. He had become increasingly gaunt as the extraordinary effects of the dust wore off, and his current state was truly macabre. He must've been mind-numbingly hungry, but he bore it without complaint.

They crossed the room to the enclosures, their established routine of combing through every nook and cranny momentarily forgotten.

As they grew closer it became apparent that though both individuals had the distinctive malnourished appearance of an infected person who had healed from a wound, only one of them was currently infected, and was in fact in a far worse state than the other. The person wearing the hood was so dreadfully emaciated that she was hardly more than a skeleton. Her exposed arms were covered with bite wounds.

Clarissa barely spared the hooded woman a glance before she pressed her nose against the glass of the uninfected man's enclosure. "Hey, that's the guy who owns the Corner Market. David, right? What the hell is he doing here?"

Noah was struck by a sensation akin to being punched in the gut as his gaze locked onto the man's face. *Is that really him?* Like most Oakridge students, he had seen David's mammoth form bustling around his store countless times, his presence as much a part of the building as its yellowed windows and cracked floor tiles. The man in front of him, however, could have been the store owner's older, feebler brother. He had lost most of his prodigious muscle and looked to have aged ten years in the past two days.

"Insight must have been curing Oakridge staff in addition to all of us students, even if I haven't seen any of 'em around," Brian mused thoughtfully. "Maybe they were tested and treated the night before we arrived? Anyway, the Corner Market is so close to campus that I guess somebody went over to test the people there, too. I don't know how else David could have ended up here."

"Some dumb infected kid must've gone to the store and spread the dust to him," Elias said.

Brian glanced furtively at Noah, who gave a glum shrug. Yeah, he had pretty much known from the beginning that had infected David. The man's current situation was entirely his fault, but if he were being honest, he found he was actually somewhat relieved that the guy had been brought to Insight. It meant he wasn't in danger of spreading the dust to his unsuspecting patrons, or picking up an injury somehow and suddenly eating one of them. Sure, something strange was obviously going on in this room, but he was cured now, and had been for quite some time. That's what mattered.

"That doesn't explain what he's doing locked up in a glass cage," Leah said. "And why him in particular? If Insight cured all the staff and faculty at Insight, they could've stuck any one of them in here if they needed some kind of test subject."

"Maybe they thought it'd be easier to get away with trapping a random store owner rather than a professor or someone backed up by a whole institution," Elias suggested. "Or maybe it was completely random and they don't care."

"Why don't you ask him?" May said to Leah, gesturing to the door.

Noah stepped closer. "We should do that."

Leah glanced back and forth, clearly unwilling. "I'm okay. He's probably fine."

Noah squinted at the infected woman in the other

enclosure, momentarily distracted. "Hey, this person is infected, but someone clearly tried their best to eat her anyway. What kind of idiot tries to eat another infected person?"

"She probably wasn't infected at the time," Elias sighed. "See her wounds? They look old, like they've had some time to heal. She must've gotten halfway through the process of healing them before running out of energy."

Noah glanced back at the store owner, separated from the infected woman by a sheet of glass. He wasn't injured at all. In fact, if one could ignore his stick-thin limbs and sunken face, he was more or less in perfect condition.

"There's a vacuum here," Clarissa's voice came from behind him. Noah spun around to see her picking up a portable hand-held vacuum from a table pushed against the wall. "It's empty," she added, peering into the transparent dust compartment. She turned it on, testing its battery, and it whirred for a moment before she shut it back off.

"Excellent, we can use it to cure this lady, and then get out of here," Leah said. "You want to do it or should I?"

"You're not even a little curious to know why they're locked up?" Brian prodded, turning to his sister.

"Nah."

Brian went to the glass door of David's cubicle and slid the latch open. "Well, I think we should take a closer look," he said, just a touch too eagerly.

Leah's eyes widened. "Don't you dare," she snapped, leaning over to snatch him away from the door. "Do we need to cure you first?"

"No," Brian muttered quickly. "I really was just curious. I figured the infected woman probably wouldn't feel much like talking, based on the looks of her."

Leah shot the skeletal woman a look, then turned grudgingly back to her brother. "I suppose I can spare a minute to see if he knows what the hell is going on in here. But not while you're anywhere close. Clarissa, keep an eye on him."

"Oh, I can do that." She grinned.

Noah couldn't help but edge forward as Leah opened the door. She paused and leveled a glare at him. "Get back, all of you," she growled.

Noah glanced around and realized May and Elias had casually drawn up beside him, equally interested to 'speak' to David. Sure, the guy was a staple of Oakridge campus life, universally known- even loved- by approximately every single student, but Noah was hungry. They all were.

"I just wanted-"

"I know *exactly* what you want. You are not eating this guy," Leah said firmly. "I'm going to wake him up now, and I don't want to hear so much as a word out of you. Stay behind the glass. In fact, if you want to be useful, take the vacuum and cure the other person." She pushed the syringe gun back into his hands before he could refuse.

Noah stared evenly at her. Nearly his entire conscious mind valued his own hunger over Leah's request. Yet somehow, that tiny sliver of himself that still cared was digging in its feet, putting up a fierce struggle to make its voice known. In the end, though he hardly understood why, he simply stood and watched as she entered the glass cage alone.

May and Elias tried to walk forward past him, but he grabbed their forearms and held them back. If he didn't get to go in, neither did they.

"I don't mind curing the skeleton," Brian offered, taking the vacuum in hand. "Can I borrow the syringe gun, Noah? I'll have to pull her hood up to get the vacuum into her mouth, so it'd probably be safest just to-"

"Of course," Noah agreed. He handed it to his friend. "Again, not sure how many doses are left in there, so be careful."

Brian grabbed the weapon and shook it experimentally by his ear, then shrugged with a goofy expression. "I'll be fine. It's not like I'm in danger of getting eaten."

"Don't make any assumptions," Clarissa said. "We don't

know what Insight did to these people."

"Okay, good point," Brian said, sobering. He unlatched the enclosure and let himself inside, leaving the glass door open behind him. Dust wafted out through the gap.

"Are you, ah, are you awake?" Brian asked quietly, clearly hoping the answer was no. He received no response, but he brought the syringe gun to the person's shackled arm anyway and slid the needle through the skin. The poor woman barely had enough flesh on her bones for Brian to be able to pierce her arm at all, and what little she did have was marred by half-healed bite wounds.

Noah reflected that proper medical practice probably should've had them replacing the needle between each person they punctured, but there wasn't much they could do about it at this point. Hopefully nobody would die to any unfortunate infections.

Brian tore the hood off and raised the vacuum, only to freeze as the thick haze of dust trapped beneath cleared away.

"Penelope?" he asked.

Noah's head swiveled, recognizing the name. The person laying on the examination table looked a far cry from the girl he had met earlier, though the facial structure was about the same.

Brian noticed his reaction. "You know her, too?"

"Not really, I just ran into her yesterday in the halls," Noah replied, joining his friend in the cramped glass enclosure. "I thought she got out, but clearly she wasn't so lucky. How do you know her?"

"We're in the same writing seminar. I really only know her name, to be honest."

Noah glanced over to see if Leah happened to recognize the girl as well, but she had managed to awaken David and was busy interrogating the confused man.

"Penelope!" Brian shouted in the girl's face, apparently deciding she should be awake as well.

"She's not going to be in her right mind, and in any case, you've just blinded her," Noah reminded his friend. "I'm not sure why you'd want her to wake her."

Brian slumped. "Oh, yeah." He powered up the vacuum, but rather than move it to Penelope's lips, he just stood there motionlessly for a few seconds before turning it back off.

"What? What is it?" May asked, stepping into the cage.

Brian swallowed uncomfortably. "Is she even alive?"

Noah stared down at the girl. She looked downright cadaverous. In normal circumstances, it wouldn't have been a question of whether any life lingered in her body.

"She's gotta be," May said finally. "This space is full of dust. She's still breathing, or at least she was recently."

"That's right," Brian said, relieved. "She's probably fine."

"She might not be once we cure her, though," May said. "Depending on how debilitating the supposed post-treatment weakness is."

Brian threw his hands up despite the fact that he was currently holding both a vacuum cleaner and a needled weapon. "Well, what do you want me to do?"

"I don't know. She might be okay," May said hesitantly.

"She'll probably just need a nice big meal or two. The kind regular people have," Noah said, though he frowned worriedly even as he spoke.

Brian stared unhappily at them for several long moments, then reluctantly brought the small vacuum to life. "Let's hope so. She seemed like a decent person."

He pressed the nozzle into Penelope's mouth. The vacuum's storage canister was transparent, allowing them to watch as dust rushed into the small space and swirled around, gradually tinting it darker and darker until it was an even shade of jet-black. She remained unconscious through the entire process.

Eventually he shut it off and pulled the nozzle free. He hesitated then, his gaze panning across the fabric bindings locking her down to the table. He glanced over his shoulder at May and Noah. "I've got a knife," he informed them. "It would be easy enough to cut through these straps."

"Go for it," Noah encouraged. "It's the least we could do."

When May nodded in agreement, Brian dropped his backpack to the ground to retrieve a silver pocket knife from within its pockets. He flicked it open and brought its serrated edge against Penelope's bindings before pausing to glance back, a faint frown tracing across his gaunt face. "Noah, you mind doing the actual cutting? My arm feels about like a cooked noodle right now. I haven't quite recovered from using the pendant yet."

"Of course," Noah readily agreed, accepting the knife and sawing easily through the bindings. They fell limply to the floor one by one. When Penelope was wholly unfettered, he snapped the blade shut and returned it to his friend. The tool quickly disappeared back into the backpack.

Before the three of them left the room, Brian fished the pendant out from his shirt collar, then detached the vacuum's dust compartment to allow its contents to be swallowed up into the necklace. The dust in the glass cage was drawn in as well, and when they rejoined Elias back outside in the wider room, so too were the few enterprising wisps that had escaped out the door.

Noah drew the door shut, leaving the latch unlocked. The hood was left behind on the ground beside the table. There was no guarantee that Penelope would be able to escape the building upon waking up- after all, she'd clearly failed on that count once already- but what else could they do?

Brian paused outside the enclosure. "Good luck," he whispered. He returned the syringe gun to Noah and shoved the vacuum into his backpack, defying several laws of physics to make it fit.

They wandered to the second enclosure. Elias nodded casually at them before turning back to stare through the glass with undisguised hunger. Clarissa had joined Leah at some point to cut David free of his own restraints with her own knife, though the man wasn't making any moves to get up.

"Almost done there?" Brian asked. "We're all finished administering the treatment, if you need any help."

All three people turned to peer out through the pane of

glass. "We'll be out soon," Leah said. "You stay right there."

True to her word, she exited the enclosure with Clarissa less than a minute later. She closed the unlatched door behind her with David still inside. "The things Insight put these people through," she muttered.

"He told you what happened?" Noah asked.

"Oh, he sure did, or at least what he could remember of it. Apparently the military closed off Oakridge Street yesterday afternoon before checking if anyone in the stores were infected. Out of the entire street, he believes he is the only one to have been carrying the dust. His symptoms had not yet progressed to the point that he was coughing the stuff out, so he'd had no idea that he was ill at all until the results of the test said otherwise. They brought him straight here in an Insight vehicle alongside several Oakridge professors from campus who had also tested positive for the dust. Upon arrival, however, he was separated from the group and brought directly to this room. The doctors didn't even pretend to try to cure him. They just locked him down to that table. They... they damaged him, and then they brought in an animal. A live pig."

"A pig?" Brian exclaimed. "Where'd they get it from?"

Leah shook her head. "Just listen. He ate it, obviously, and it let him regain lucidity for a little while. The doctors said it didn't noticeably facilitate his healing, even though it seemed to temporarily help with his hunger. But they didn't stop there; they barely finished cleaning up from that before they moved on to their next test. They hurt him again, until he was out of his own mind with hunger, and they left him like that for several hours. Then they brought in a girl. He says her name was Penelope. She was uninfected.

"The doctors separated them before he could completely consume the girl. She's in that enclosure now," Leah said, pointing to Penelope without recognition. "They then took all the dust from him and gave it to her."

"What? What's the point?" Clarissa demanded.

"I can hazard a guess," Elias said. "It seems that they used him to answer a few of their questions. They wanted to know if animals could be used to heal a person, and if two infected people could heal each other infinitely. The answer to both questions, clearly, is no."

"That poor man. He's going to need therapy," Brian said matter-of-factly, gazing through the glass at him. The usually cheerful store owner was laying flat on the table despite the bindings having been cut away, eyes staring hollowly up at the ceiling. There were tears running down each side of his face, pooling in the crinkles of the plastic cushion beneath his head, though his expression remained empty.

Clarissa stared at the four students standing before her, their cheeks sunken and their limbs reduced to hardly more than frail sticks, blood not their own freckling their faces and drenching their clothing. "Hmm. Something tells me you all will."

67

THAT'S A GRENADE

They left both Penelope and David behind in the room, the door to which was currently propped open by fabric straps, repurposed from their previous role in life as bindings.

Even if Penelope had awoken before they left, she would not have been in any state to run around with them. David, on the other hand... he declined to leave with them. Whether that was because he knew he would probably be eaten before making it to the next room or because he was simply incapable of such action while recovering from his recent trauma, Noah couldn't say for sure. The man had barely acknowledged their departure.

"Even if they don't get out on their own, Insight would let them go when they realize neither of them are infected anymore. Right?" May wondered, dragging her hand along the wall as they walked.

Nobody bothered to answer her. How could they know?

Noah pushed open the next door to reveal the vat room. The six massive metal cylinders were exactly where he had last seen them, lined up ominously along the wall. He stared at the sixth vat. Unless some poor employee had made an unpleasant discovery, the body of the doctor he had killed remained hidden within.

"Well, this is it," Noah said. "Where Insight is keeping enough dust to turn the whole city into zombies."

"Let's finish checking the other rooms before we destroy

the dust here," Brian said. "If the pressure of these vats
are being monitored, alarms will go off as soon as we start
messing with them."

"I opened one of them earlier and nothing happened,"
Noah said.

"Sure, but we're going to completely destroy the contents,
not just peek inside. We should look through the rest of the
rooms before we leave. Better to do it now while we're still
operating under the radar."

"I don't know if your reasoning is sound," Noah muttered,
but he untied a shirt from his arm and dropped it outside the
entrance to the room, marking it. "Fine. We'll come back."

"We could split up," Elias offered.

"You have a keycard?"

"Ah, right. Forget it."

"That security guard upstairs certainly had one," Clarissa
said thoughtfully. "We should've grabbed it."

"We still could," Brian suggested.

She shook her head. "We're nearly done here anyway.
Let's not push our luck by crossing floors yet again."

So they continued on down the hall. There were only six
remaining doors, including the treatment room at the far end
of the corridor. The first two rooms held nothing of interest,
though they took several minutes to comb through each of
them. The third was their private waiting room from the
previous morning. The chairs had been folded and returned
to the wall. The fourth was a vacant operating room, judging
by the central table surrounded by equipment and computer
monitors. On a cart beside the main table was another one
of the wine-bottle shaped metal containers, but when they
loosened the cap, they found it was empty. There were no
drawers or cabinets, so they soon moved on to the fifth door.

As they entered there came a startled yelp from inside.
Noah's focus immediately snapped to the source of the noise,
zeroing in on a relatively young masked employee hunched
over a standing desk, a few somewhat alarming items laid out
on the tabletop before her. *Is that a grenade?*

The woman's head tilted up to reveal wide, nervous eyes. "I was just trying to finish-" she began, then cut off as she realized who she was speaking to. Her eyes narrowed into slits. "Who are you people? How did you get in here?"

"Get her," Leah said coldly. There was no question of who her words were meant for.

Noah hardly needed her permission. An uninfected person stood before him; he had hardly paused between entering the room and continuing forward towards her.

He was aware of his friends' presence at his side. Rather than try to outpace them, he instinctively fell into step with the three of them, recognizing that the woman before them could likely be armed. Together they would present a greater threat.

There were half a dozen vacant workstations lining the wall between them and their quarry. Before they could cross more than half the distance, she withdrew a familiar syringe gun from her pocket and leveled it at them as if it was a long-range weapon. Her expression was almost neutral, though her eyes were just a little too wide, and Noah knew she was afraid.

"You're infected," she said, as if they weren't already well aware. "You don't really want to do this."

Noah almost laughed. Clearly, despite whatever research she might have been involved with, she had no idea how the infection worked. He could say with full honesty that he wanted nothing more in that moment than to devour her until nothing remained.

They continued forward as if oblivious to the words she spoke and the weapon she wielded. The distance between them shrunk until Noah could see the nervous tremors running through her body. Her eyes darted to her desk. She reached for the grenade, but almost immediately gave a small shake of her head and withdrew her hand.

Then her eyes lit up with an ember of hope, and with a short gasp she snatched a small device from the edge of the desk and hooked it behind her ear. It wasn't a radio like the security guard had used, but rather an earpiece that seemed to serve a similar purpose. She pressed it with her free hand and began muttering quickly. "I'm in 3-C-20. Six intruders just entered the room, and they have the dust. Er, that means they're zombies. I need immediate help."

"Can you guys maybe walk faster than an arthritic sloth?" Leah demanded behind them. "There is no reason she should've had time to call for help."

Noah paid her worry no heed. Whatever backup came to the employee's aid would be too late. They were nearly upon her.

The woman's face was squinched in concentration as she listened to whoever was on the other end of her earpiece. She must not have liked what she heard, because her face suddenly paled visibly. "No, wait! I'm still in here! How long-?"

Brian broke from the formation first, throwing himself at the employee. He tried to maneuver around the needle, but it speared him squarely in the chest. Rather than use his last moments of mobility to attempt a bite at her, he flashed a satisfied smile before clasping the weapon to himself and drooping to the floor. The weapon was carried down with him.

The woman frantically dropped down, urgently rolling him off of the weapon to recover it before she could be overwhelmed.

It was too late. Noah descended upon her, buried his face in her back, and chomped down over and over. Energy flooded through him, and he only now realized how close he'd been to empty. He could all but physically feel it as dust spread comfortably through his limbs, restoring his strength.

He was dimly aware of May and Elias to his either side, but they were courteous enough to keep to themselves.

All too soon, the life faded from the employee, and Noah stumbled back at the sudden disgust that rose up in him in response to the lifeless corpse. He blinked the blood out of his eyes and looked around, remembering where he was. His sight was drawn back to the body despite himself, and he winced as a painful jolting throb ran through his skull. He clenched his teeth and backed away.

"Is it done?" a voice came from behind him.

He spun around to see Leah and Clarissa standing by the door. Leah was gagging uncontrollably despite having turned away.

"We're done, yes," Elias said. "Brian, are you...?"

"I think I might need a little help," he said from where he lay in an undignified crumpled position on the floor. "I'm blind and I can't move."

"What were you thinking?" Clarissa said, exasperated. "You could've at least tried to avoid the needle."

"I did." A slight frown somehow formed on his features despite his immobilization. "Did you take her out?"

"Yes, Brian," Noah muttered. "You were very brave and noble. Thanks to your selfless sacrifice, we were able to overcome our foe."

The frown disappeared. "Oh, it was nothing. Thank you for acknowledging my greatness."

"Did he say selfless sacrifice? I think he meant to say exceptionally moronic behavior," Clarissa said sternly. "We're going to have to drag you around now until the blindness wears off, and since you took three years to walk across the room, she had time to call security. We're going to be neck-deep in Insight workers if we don't get moving."

"What are you waiting for, then?" Brian demanded. "I don't hear anyone dragging me."

"I'll get him," Noah said before Clarissa could explode. He felt full to bursting with energy, and it was with almost no effort at all that he grabbed his friend's sneakers and began hauling him towards the door. Even if he hadn't just enjoyed a meal, the numbness throughout his body would have made it feel like an easy task. Elias graciously came around to support Brian's shoulders. They left his truly massive backpack where it was, strapped to his body.

"Wait," May said, glancing around the room. "We still need to check for dust."

"We don't have time for that," Clarissa said. "We'll just have to hope there isn't any."

"There's a fridge over here. It'll only take a second."

"Forget the fridge," Leah said suddenly. "Do you see what the employee was working on? If I'm not mistaken, that's a *grenade*."

Noah dropped Brian's feet to step closer to the desk. "That's not all. There's a vial of dark blood here as well. Just like how the vials with our blood looked."

"We can take everything with us, but we need to leave," Clarissa said impatiently. "Come on."

Noah didn't feel entirely comfortable pocketing a grenade, but he did so anyway, then tucked the vial of blood into the opposite pocket. Worse came to worst, he was pretty sure there was a squad of Insight workers currently making their way to his location. An explosive device might come in handy.

"Guys..." May trailed off nervously. Despite Leah's words she had gone to the fridge and thrown it open. "This thing is stocked with racks and racks of vials, and they're all full of blood."

"Are they dark?" Noah asked, glancing over his shoulder.

May slowly shook her head. "No."

"Great. We need to go," Leah said insistently.

"Why are they here?"

"I don't know, May! There are plenty of perfectly normal reasons why a medical laboratory might keep a supply of blood!"

Noah went back to Brian and helped Elias carry him to the front of the room. May reluctantly closed the fridge and joined them after a moment.

Leah tugged at the door and nearly face-planted into it when it remained firmly shut.

"Noah! Get over here," she snapped. "Unlock the door."

"I'm right here," he replied, a strange tone in his voice. "It should be opening."

Leah tugged once more, but even when she braced against the wall and threw her weight against it, the door didn't so much as budge. She slowly stepped back and stared around at her companions. "We've been trapped."

68

I GUESS WE'RE JUST NOT
EATING ENOUGH PEOPLE

"The door must've locked right after the employee contacted security," Clarissa mused.

"You don't seem very concerned," Leah said.

Noah smiled mischievously. "I bet she's thinking the same thing I am."

Clarissa grinned. "Yeah?"

He pointed towards the corpse at the back of the room. "We can take her earpiece and impersonate her voice to convince security that it was all a false alarm."

His enthusiastic words were met only by silence, and he slowly deflated. "What is it?"

Clarissa could only gape at him. "That's... quite possibly the worst plan I've ever heard in all my years of life on this planet. A child wouldn't fall for that."

"Oh yeah? Enlighten us on your superior thoughts, then," Noah said peevishly.

"I should've thought they were obvious," she smirked, reaching into her coat and procuring her hatchet. She took a stance in front of the door with it poised over her shoulder. "We'll be out of this room in no time."

"You're right. I should've known," Noah conceded. "I still think my idea would make a good backup plan, though."

"Noah, I hate to break it to you, but your plan is stupid," Brian said.

"I'm carrying you around," Noah muttered. "The least you could do is take my side."

Clarissa glanced at them. "A good friend isn't afraid to hit you with the ugly truth."

"Are you going to break the door down or what?" Leah said impatiently.

Clarissa shuffled her feet slightly. "As much as I've fantasized about it, I've never actually demolished a door before."

"Use the pendant," Brian suggested. "Elias, can you grab it?"

Elias took it off Brian's head and held it out to Clarissa.

"I don't think there's a lot of dust left inside, but it should be enough to at least speed up the process," Brian said, still staring sightlessly up at the ceiling.

Clarissa reached for it, then hesitated. "Will it end up having the same effect on me as if I were injured? I don't want to use it if it'll make me end up like you guys."

"Probably," Noah said lightly.

"You do it, then. I'm not touching that thing."

"You sure? I'd hate to steal a lifelong dream right out from under your nose."

Clarissa waved her hand. "There are plenty of doors in this world. I'll destroy another one."

Noah reluctantly accepted the pendant from Elias. "This is going to suck, isn't it."

If anything, the revulsion he had felt earlier towards allowing the dust to flood into his lungs had only multiplied now that he had been recently sated.

"Not so much initially, but you'll feel like crap afterwards," Brian said. "As in, weaker than a soggy piece of bread. And hungry."

Noah struggled to strengthen his resolve. "Well, I guess one of us has to do it." Fighting past every instinct in his infected body screaming at him to stop, he pressed the metal square to his lips and released the clasp.

It wasn't as bad as he'd feared. In fact, as energy exploded into him, he realized it was something like a watered-down version of the rejuvenating sensation he enjoyed while consuming flesh.

However, there was simply so much dust within the pendant that it very quickly surpassed any burst of energy he'd previously received. There was so much- almost too much.

Noah didn't pull the pendant away until it had emptied itself into his lungs. With a shuddering jerk, he brought it away from his mouth and snapped it shut. He tried to give it back to Elias, but it fell from his grasp before the boy could take it. May bent down to pick it up instead.

"The hatchet," Noah gasped, dust pouring from his nose and mouth. He hardly recognized his own voice, but he couldn't keep it steady.

Clarissa quickly handed it over to him before backing up, retreating with the others to the rear of the room. Noah watched them come to a halt a respectable distance from the corpse, then turned his attention to the hatchet in his hands.

Noah had never held a hatchet before in his life, let alone attempt to break down a door with one. There was probably a proper way to go about it, to maximize the effort to result ratio.

Rather than overthink it, he struck out with abandon, letting the blade shoot forward as if released from a slingshot. It bit through the door with an awful creaking scream of snapping wood.

Noah pulled the hatchet back to himself and gave the door an appraising look. It had given way with almost no resistance. If his stance had been unstable, he could easily have overextended and lost his balance. He wondered if Insight had skimped on the material.

"What are you waiting for? Keep going," Leah urged from behind him.

Noah glanced back at her with an odd light in his eyes, then let the hatchet drop to the floor. His friends watched in surprise as he proceeded to turn and press his fingers through the door as if it were made of soft clay. There was some resistance at first, but he narrowed his eyes and increased the pressure, and his hands punched through without much difficulty. The sound this action produced was horrendous.

Noah then pulled the entire fine piece of carpentry clean off the wall and looked falteringly around, clutching it between his hands, before settling on placing it carefully to the ground beside the newly opened doorway.

"It's done," he announced, as if they hadn't watched the entire process.

"And so are my eardrums," Brian complained. "Seriously, what did you do to that poor door?"

"It doesn't matter. We can leave," Clarissa said, coming forward to pick up her hatchet from the ground and tuck it safely back into her coat.

"Your worry about there not being much dust left was entirely unfounded," Noah informed Brian in that same strange voice. "Although there's none left now."

"I must have left more inside than I thought," Brian said. "The amount we got from Penelope was pretty pathetic, so I don't see how else the pendant would be very full."

"You know it's coming out your nostrils, right?" Elias asked.

Noah waved a hand in front of his face. "Yeah, the same thing happened to Brian. It's kind of annoying."

Elias stared at the smoke. "I bet that's how it spreads- by reaching or exceeding capacity. It doesn't make sense otherwise; how could it infect people from inside someone's lungs? Once a person stops breathing, they wouldn't be able to infect anyone else."

"Unless they consume so much- or cheat and use a secondhand source like Brian and I did- that it overflows," Noah said thoughtfully, finishing Elias' thought for him. "I haven't seen it happen naturally yet, though. I guess we're just not eating enough people."

Leah sent him a wary look. "You're doing fine."

They left the room. May took over the duty of helping

Elias carry Brian, because Noah was afraid he would
accidentally crush his friend's ankles. Neither of them would
realize it had happened until it was too late.

The hallway outside was anticlimactically empty and
quiet. Looking down the barren corridor, Noah could
almost convince himself that Insight wasn't going to bother
responding to the dead employee's plea for help. Perhaps they
had decided the best course of action was to simply cut their
losses and leave everyone locked up until they felt like dealing
with the problem.

Then again, the building was huge. Perhaps there was
currently a response team racing towards them, and they
hadn't arrived yet because they were two miles worth of
hallways away.

"Alright," Leah said, striding forward. "I know it's a risk,
but we can still destroy the dust in the vats. All it takes is
a match to incinerate the stuff; it won't take long and we
can rest assured we won't be leaving any behind. I think we
should do it."

"You don't have to convince me," May said.

The others nodded.

"We're doing this," Brian said firmly.

"Oh, shut up. You just have to sit there and let yourself be
carried around," Noah said, grinning.

"I'm in as much danger as any of you," he protested.
"More, probably."

They crossed the hall to the vat room. As they crossed
through the doorway, Noah felt the power from the dust ever
so slowly beginning to recede. He grimaced. Based on Brian's
precedent, he wouldn't end up completely incapacitated, but
the sensation was akin to being injured. He felt every scrap
of energy that left him like the departure of a good friend;
the tighter he clung to the dissipating strength, the worse the
emptiness was when it disappeared. Though he still possessed
greatly elevated strength to his usual standard, it wouldn't be
long before that energy abandoned him.

He picked up the shirt he had used to mark the door and

tied it with the others around his arm. Security would be coming to investigate the location to which they had been summoned; with any luck, they wouldn't think to check any of the other rooms until Noah and his friends were long gone. The final moments of their escape would likely turn into a chase.

"Quickly, now," Clarissa said. "Someone start opening the vats. I'll get the matches ready."

Noah went to the first vat. He still had more energy left than he knew what to do with, so he stuck a single finger into the wheel and spun it open in less than a second, his arm whirring round and round. He grabbed the cylindrical hunk of metal before gravity could send it to the floor and gently lowered it down, then stepped back. Dust began to billow up from the mouth of the vat.

"Jeez, speedster, give me a moment," she muttered, fumbling with a match. She couldn't seem to get it to light.

"We could just use the pendant," Elias suggested. May was standing close enough that the dust was already beginning to swirl towards the necklace draped around her shoulders.

"No," Clarissa snapped. "We're not here to steal the dust, we're here to destroy it." She glared down at the tiny slip of cardboard that was her match. "I don't know why I'm having so much trouble with this."

"You're numb," Leah said simply.

"I'm aware, but I still don't understand why it would be this difficult." She spoke slowly, her concentration on her hands rather than her words. After another moment the match finally let out a soft *whoomph* as it caught fire. Almost in the same instant, a deafening crack boomed and a flash of orange light filled the room as the dust in the air immediately combusted.

Everyone froze, startled.

"We're lucky the explosion is harmless," Elias finally murmured.

"Open the next one," Clarissa demanded, throwing aside the suddenly dead match and tugging another from the matchbook.

Noah tried to open the second vat in the same manner as the first, but with his strength draining out of him, he couldn't make the wheel turn with anything less than both hands. As he stepped away, the lid slipped from his grasp to fall heavily to the ground. The heavy metal plug barely missed his toes.

Clarissa had the next match ready, and she tossed it into the vat before dust could begin to pour out in great clouds. There was a flash of sound and light from the hole, and then it darkened, leaving the container empty.

"I can't do any more," Noah said shortly.

May came forward to open the next vat. As she worked to unscrew the lid, they began to hear shouts from the hallway. Even with the significant noise-cancelling properties of Insight's walls, the racket of a large group of people stomping around and barking orders at each other just outside the door was impossible to miss. The guards had arrived. By the sound of it they had noticed that the door, which was supposed to be locked and closed, had been torn off its hinges. They didn't seem pleased about it.

The students glanced nervously at each other. Noah had no idea how they'd get past security, but they'd have to find a way. They didn't have any other option.

May kept working through the noise, and now she slid the third lid free, revealing dust boiling up from within. Only the first two vats had been filled when Noah had visited the room yesterday; Insight had clearly been busy. Clarissa threw in the match and they moved on to the fourth vat.

They were producing quite the loud bang with each explosion they set off, but there was nothing they could do about the noise. Hopefully all the clamor outside would mask their activity.

As May began working to remove the fifth lid, Noah pulled out his phone and sent his dad a message: *We'll be out soon. Sorry for the delay.* He started to put the phone away, but then he received a response:

OK. Which entrance?

We're on the third floor. Does that help?
Yes. On my way.

Noah hesitated before sending one more text: *If we're not there in twenty minutes, get out of here.*

He pocketed the phone, uninterested in whatever reply would inevitably come. By now the fifth vat was open, though Clarissa was having trouble igniting the match again. The air was still clear due to May standing so close that the particles were immediately pulled into the pendant before they could escape into the wider room.

"Got it," Clarissa whispered, and held the flame to the opening of the vat. *Boom.*

"Not much point in whispering when you turn around and set off an explosion," Leah commented.

"Shh," Clarissa whispered.

Leah rolled her eyes and shut up.

May stepped to the sixth and final vat. Noah gave the container a nervous look. A corpse was hidden within. His friends knew he'd killed the doctor, but they didn't know where he'd left the body. *There's no reason to be furtive about it. I should just tell them.*

He opened his mouth, but before he could speak, the indistinct sounds of commotion outside in the hall suddenly got a lot less muffled.

He whirled around to see the door open, a startled guard staring in at them.

69

THE BEING THAT WAS
ONCE DR. CARL

The six students froze. Even May paused for a moment to glance over her shoulder at the man before redoubling her efforts to open the final vat.

The guard looked sideways down the hall, then back at them, all the while slowly backing up.

"Just close the door," Leah encouraged him. "Pretend we're not here. Honestly, you'll probably just get eaten if you stay."

His eyes bulged and it was clear he didn't intend to take her suggestion. "I found the zombies," he called over his shoulder. "All six of 'em, right here."

"What's happening?" Brian demanded. He was laying on the ground against the back wall.

"Exactly what it sounds like," Clarissa said. She was fumbling with her matchbook, trying without success to light a match. She cursed. "I need to get better matches. These things burn out too fast."

The guard in the doorway stepped back to allow his comrades entrance to the room. There were about a dozen of them in total, though only half were appreciably prepared, equipped with gas masks and syringe guns.

The sight of these weapons was the only thing that kept Noah rooted in place. Not a single guard was infected, and every second that ticked by drained him of a little more energy, replacing it with a persistent and growing hunger.

As the security force was entering the room May finished unscrewing the top of the sixth vat, and dust came streaming out like steam from an uncovered pot of some terribly burned stew.

Most of it wafted towards the pendant, but a fair quantity escaped past her and spread rapidly through the room. A few of the guards stared at the dark plumes and began muttering to each other.

Dammit, half of them are going to end up infected, Noah realized unhappily.

A voice came from within the ranks like a bucket of ice water, dousing the murmurs. "Shut up."

Noah glanced at his friends. "Is that...?"

"Move aside," the voice spoke again.

The guards divided down the middle, stepping away to reveal Heinrich standing at their center. He wore a bulky respirator mask that concealed his lower face and shielded his eyes behind a plastic visor. Clutched in his hands was an entirely blue, cordless chainsaw with the Insight logo plastered across its chassis.

The doctor cleared his throat. "Well, this is disappointing."

"Do you actually live in this building?" Leah demanded. "What are you doing here?"

"I could ask you the same," Heinrich said calmly. "You have damaged Insight property."

"Is that what you call it when your employees get murdered?" Leah asked acidly.

Heinrich frowned. "I am referring to the door you ruined, as well as your tampering with the containment vats." He suddenly noticed what Clarissa held in her hands, and his eyes bulged. "Drop the matchbook."

When Clarissa ignored him, he gestured to the guards around him. Half a dozen pistols were suddenly pointed at the girl.

Clarissa went still, a startled expression crossing her face. She slowly looked up at Heinrich. "You- you think bullets will keep me down?"

"Enough damage kills anything." The doctor smiled thinly. "The dust can only heal so much. And if bullets aren't enough, I brought a chainsaw."

"What happened to the doctor's oath?" Noah muttered.

Heinrich tilted his head, amused. "I'm not that kind of doctor."

Clarissa waved the matchbook around. "What's got you so worked up about a single match, anyway?"

"Don't feign ignorance. We are both aware of why you are here."

"I'm not sure why you're just standing here talking to us, then. Every moment you wait, more of your precious dust leaks away."

"It can be recollected," Heinrich said, though a look of doubt flickered across his face. He must have finally noticed that the dark haze hovering about the room was gradually clearing, drifting in lazy wafting clouds towards the pendant exposed on May's neck.

"What is that?" Heinrich muttered, peering intently forward. "What do you have there?"

"She's got nothing," Leah snapped, stepping in front of her friend. "Mind your own business."

May looked down at the pendant in surprise, clutching at it. She tucked it beneath her shirt collar, halting its invisible, unexplainable pull, but its purpose had already been made apparent to everyone in the room. There was no dust left in the air, and it wasn't because Clarissa had managed to ignite a match.

Heinrich turned his agitated gaze to the guard at his left. "Blind the girl and bring me her necklace."

Before the selected man could step forward, a dull metallic knock suddenly sounded from the rear of the room. Everyone paused.

"What now?" Heinrich demanded, narrowing his eyes.

The students were silent.

"Look behind that vat," the doctor ordered, pushing

another two guards forward. "I believe we may have a seventh wayward child on our hands."

The three members of Insight's security force approached the sixth vat, May momentarily forgotten. The students took a few steps away, giving the guards plenty of space.

Noah's eyes widened in unexpected understanding; he suddenly knew exactly what had caused the sound. He watched the unfortunate guards stride obliviously towards the metal monoliths. Dust no longer streamed from any of them, and they stood empty and still.

Before any of the three guards could get close enough to peer around the vat, a second muffled bang came from it and a hand suddenly appeared, reaching up to grip the lip of the container from within. Following the hand came a head covered with a dense map of dark twisting lines. It rose up into view with agonizing slowness, revealing a face twisted with unnatural hunger.

"What is *that*?" Leah cried, stumbling away in alarm.

I really should've thought the hiding spot for that doctor through, Noah thought, feeling faintly embarrassed for his oversight.

"Carl?" One of the guards standing before the vat tilted his head in recognition.

The second one, displaying far superior situational awareness, grabbed her fellow and pulled him away.

"Well, wouldn't you know it," Heinrich said thoughtfully. "So this is where the man ended up. And here I thought he was skipping shifts."

Looking up, he called out to the guards, "Blind the creature. It is not Carl, and it is not human. It is a corpse being puppeted by the primitive mind-construct of the dust."

Noah stared at the doctor. *How does he know that?*

The being that was once Dr. Carl pulled itself from the vat and tumbled out to land in a discombobulated heap on the floor. Dust seeped into the air from its nostrils like ink pouring into water. Noah was intrigued to see that all of the wounds he had inflicted on the man before his death had been healed; if not for the dark web that ran beneath every inch of his skin, his neck would have been unblemished. He looked almost like a normal human, or perhaps one who had arbitrarily decided to scribble over themselves with a black marker. The expression was the only indication that something was truly wrong.

The creature landed awkwardly, and so the three guards approached it with ill-considered confidence, needled weapons bristling at the ready. And then the creature moved.

They had no chance to react. In the span of a second, the closest guard had been eviscerated and thrown against the wall. The creature now stood in the man's place with a piece of his stomach clutched in its hands. It chewed rapidly on its prize, like a rabbit with a carrot, and gazed unblinkingly at the remaining guards.

Noah was suddenly very, very glad he and his friends were infected.

"Ah, of course," Heinrich said. "It has been steeping in dust for about twelve hours. It will have elevated physical abilities, though it should soon begin to lose its strength. If it stops eating, that is." As he spoke he edged backwards to stand behind the formation of guards.

"Shoot it," he commanded. Six pistols fired, and the creature fell backwards. One of the two remaining guards standing nearby seized the moment to dart bravely forward, syringe gun bared, but the creature reacted before it could be impaled. The woman suddenly found her hand trapped in an iron grip. She could only watch as the tranquilizing gun was plucked away from her and crushed into broken metal. The creature uncurled its fist, letting the pieces clatter to the ground, and then simply leaned forward to bury its teeth into the woman's shoulder.

The other guard tried to take advantage of the creature's distraction, approaching it from behind. Before he could get into striking range, the creature spun around, wielding the body of the first guard like a club and striking the second man with enough force to send him flying across the room.

He hit one of the vats with a hollow clang and collapsed in an unmoving heap to the ground.

"What's happening?" Brian asked again.

"Zombie," Noah answered. "Er, it's the guy I ate yesterday. I probably could have hidden him in a better spot, now that I'm thinking about it."

"No, this is excellent. Has he eaten Heinrich yet? Can we leave?"

"No," Heinrich snapped, his voice carrying from across the room.

"Aw, shucks," Brian muttered unhappily.

The zombie turned its attention to the remaining guards.

"This is our chance," Clarissa murmured. She stepped over to Brian and scooped him off the ground in a fireman's carry.

"Wait, now?" Leah said in surprise. "There's still like ten remaining people over there!"

"Trust me," she insisted. "This is our best shot."

And so all six of them fell into step behind the creature, using it like a shield as it crept jerkily towards Heinrich and his security force. The only weapon the guards possessed that could truly take any of them out of commission were the syringe guns, and since these were close-range tools, the guards would have to approach the creature if they wanted to have a chance to attack. Quite understandably, they did not seem eager to do so.

"Blind the kids!" Heinrich shouted. "Blind all of them now!"

"How about you try, Doc," one of the guards muttered. Nobody moved.

The zombie suddenly darted forward. The entire formation of guards broke apart like a school of fish dividing around a shark, and Heinrich dove to the floor alongside everyone else.

One poor guard, just a little too slow to move, found himself the target of the creature's attention. Though it was perhaps slightly slower now than when it had first emerged from the vat, it still easily outpaced the man's pathetic attempts to escape, and the guard was disemboweled within moments.

"Don't let it eat you!" Heinrich snapped. "It won't get weaker if it keeps eating!"

"I don't think they're getting eaten on purpose," Leah said as she swept by. The way to the door was now clear; none of the guards were willing to stand and make themselves a target to the creature. The students hurried towards the exit.

The creature stood amidst the flattened forms of the guards, absorbed in its meal. Noah suddenly noticed a man, laying almost motionlessly by the creature's feet, slowly beginning to reach for the creature's ankle. A syringe gun was primed in his hand.

Noah slowed to a halt despite himself. "Move!" he yelled, startling his friends, but the creature didn't- couldn't- acknowledge him. The needle pierced the creature's lower leg, right through the cuff of its blue scrub pants. For a few seconds it didn't react, chewing unheedingly on whatever piece of the last guard it had managed to snag, and then it simply dropped to the ground.

"No!" Leah groaned, seeing it fall. "What an idiot!"

They were nearly to the door, but it was still too far away. The guards were already picking themselves off the ground. Five syringe guns remained between them; perhaps if they made a sudden dash towards the exit, one of them would make it out, but Noah knew they weren't going to take that chance. They halted before they could come into range of the guards blocking the door.

"Very good," Heinrich said slowly. Noah heard an odd whirring sound, and it took him a moment to realize it was the electric chainsaw coming to life. The doctor raised it towards the ceiling with a crazed glint in his eyes. "You don't deserve the dust you carry," he began.

"Deserve it?" Leah muttered. "What, like it's a prize?"

"Oh, but it is," he nodded, waving the chainsaw back and forth as he spoke. "It will change the course of history.

Sickness, injury, almost any affliction that ails mankind, it will all become a thing of the past. The *Wager*- I've cured the *Wager*," he cackled.

"Yeah, in the most perverted way imaginable," Leah muttered. "People are going to be eating each other over mundane wounds. You can't possibly think the dust is going to prevent more suffering than it causes."

"An unfortunate, yet unavoidable consequence," Heinrich had to yell to be heard over the chainsaw's motor. "But I'll find it awfully hard to care, I think."

Okay, I knew this guy was the mad scientist to end all mad scientists, but perhaps he's beginning to lean into that role a bit too hard, Noah mused.

The guards around them were standing awkwardly, syringe guns poised and ready, yet unsure if they should interrupt while the doctor was still talking.

"Oh, just stick them already," Heinrich said, waving them forward impatiently. "It'll make my job easier."

Noah wanted to backpedal as the guards closed in, but there was nowhere to go. What could he do to ten of them? His thoughts went to the pendant. There should be a fair amount of dust in the thing now, made up of whatever leakage it had managed to snag from the vats. There wouldn't be much, but perhaps it would be enough to overwhelm their foes and escape.

He nearly told May to use it, but then another idea struck him. The guards weren't the only ones armed with a weapon. Perhaps if he waved it around threateningly enough he could make them hesitate, if only long enough for the six of them to make their exit. Or worst-case, he could always blow everything up. He and his friends would probably survive.

He reached into his pocket and pulled out the grenade.

70

HE DOESN'T GET TO HIDE

Both the guards and Noah's own friends paused warily, staring at the bomb, but Heinrich only laughed. "That won't do anything. You got that from 3-C-20, correct? The detonator has been removed."

Noah stared at it. *Seriously? Is he bluffing?*

"Well, I put it back," he declared.

"I don't think you did," Heinrich replied, smiling. "You know what we were going to use them for? They were going to be dust bombs. But the dust- in its natural state, at least- combusts too quickly for it to be an effective weapon when paired with explosives, and the effect of exposure is too delayed for most practical field use." Heinrich paused for a moment, seeming to be lost in thought for several seconds before he recollected himself and continued speaking. "Before we solved both issues, we found that a non-explosive auto-release timer worked somewhat better. The dust spreads well enough on its own, though it unfortunately loses its potency when dispersed too thinly."

Solved both issues? What does that mean? Noah stared suspiciously at the doctor.

"You're going to sell *dust bombs*?" May spluttered, horrified.

"No, of course not. It was considered, but ultimately, we decided there was more profit to be made in the field of medicine rather than weaponry. Selling the dust in that fashion would be the same as handing our competitors the keys to our success. We have far better control over who can access it this way." Heinrich suddenly looked around at the guards surrounding them. "What are you waiting for?"

"Er, you seemed to be interested in conversing-"

"They don't have to be able to see to carry a conversation," Heinrich snapped.

"Of course, sir."

Seeing they were out of time, Noah didn't hesitate. He tugged the pin free of the safety mechanism, just for fun, and hurled the grenade as hard as he could at Heinrich's face.

However, he currently possessed a fraction of his usual strength, and rather than impact Heinrich's face as intended, the projectile drooped and hit the man in a somewhat lower region. In the moments before a guard dove between them, too late to shield Heinrich, Noah saw the doctor silently double over.

"That was beautiful," Clarissa breathed.

A woman standing beside Heinrich tracked where the grenade landed and kicked it away in the direction of the doorway. Her aim was poor, but the device rebounded off someone's boot and came to rest exactly in the center of the doorframe.

The initial guard, seeing he had failed to protect Heinrich, turned his attention to Noah and lunged forward needle-first. Noah couldn't dodge in time.

Clarissa dove in between them with Brian held before her like a body shield. The needle sunk into his neck with quite a bit of force behind it.

The guard gaped in surprise and tried to tug the weapon free, but before he could recover it, a deafening boom shook the room.

Several people began shouting. Noah looked around in shock, his vision slightly blurry for some reason, and saw dust pouring in huge dark clouds from the door. Those closest to the grenade had been thrown to the ground.

"I think your bomb was live," Brian informed him. "Also, why does my neck feel warm?"

"Don't worry about it," Clarissa said, after checking to make sure he hadn't actually been hit by shrapnel in addition to the syringe gun hanging from below his left ear.

Elias saw Brian's predicament and tore the weapon free, then turned and emptied it into the nearest guard. The unwitting man was staring at the door and failed to notice that he'd been impaled until his vision was gone. His hands shot to his eyes and he stumbled sideways into another guard.

"I think this is our cue to leave," Elias said. "Did any of you get hit?"

Noah glanced down, but he didn't seem to be bleeding. His vision was beginning to clear as well. "I think I'm good."

"What did you *do*?" Heinrich howled. Noah was disappointed to see he too seemed to have avoided taking any shrapnel, perhaps in part due to his crouched position. "Do you have any idea what was in that grenade?"

"Ignore him," Leah said. "Come on."

They picked their way in the general direction of the door. Dust was rapidly filling the space, creating such poor visibility that Noah could barely make out anything or anyone out of arm's reach.

May could have taken the pendant out from behind her collar to clear the room, but the chaos was to their benefit. They would just have to accept that some dust would be left behind, because the alternative was letting themselves be captured. It was unfortunate, considering all the work they had done up to this point, but it was necessary. As it was, they were just a few nameless shadows moving around in the gloom, and they made their way forward unchallenged.

A scream suddenly cut through the air. It cut off with a gurgle less than a second later. Noah spun around, wondering if one of his friends had taken an opportunistic bite out of a passing guard, but the five of them stood close around him, eyes forward and intent on escape.

What was that? He ducked away as the dark form of a guard suddenly loomed before him, but the person was suddenly bowled over by another figure, and both shadows disappeared back into the haze. There was another scream.

There are more zombies in here, he realized, but he couldn't understand where they were coming from. "The dust may have infected the guards, or at least those of them that are unmasked, but it shouldn't cause them any symptoms for at least a few hours yet. Right? What's happening?"

His friends didn't have any answers, but Heinrich did.

"What you're seeing isn't just dust, as much as it may appear so," the doctor's voice came despondently from the darkness. "Do you know why an infected individual only begins to display symptoms after nearly half a day has passed?"

Noah frowned. What did that have to do with anything?

"We didn't either," Heinrich said as if they had responded. "Not until we looked at some blood samples we had come into possession of a day prior. These provided several crucial pieces of information by allowing us to watch the dust develop through several evolutions within the blood in real-time."

Elias glanced at Noah and spoke under his breath. "You don't suppose that blood would happen to be the samples you had taken on campus, would you?"

Noah ran his hands over his face. "They probably are."

Heinrich continued speaking like he was a teacher lecturing his students. "The dust is a parasite, and it needs time to adapt itself to its host. However, the blood samples revealed that it can continue adapting to human blood *outside* of a human body. We realized it was progressing through its standard stages of development from within the vials. This pre-acclimation means that when inhaled in either a mist or gaseous form, the blood of an infected person will create symptoms of an identical stage of progression to rapidly develop in a previously uninfected subject."

Noah had turned most of his attention towards getting to the door, which seemed to have simply disappeared. He feared he and his friends had gotten turned around at some point, as they had yet to find so much as a wall. The room was big, but it wasn't that big.

Despite being distracted, enough of Heinrich's words registered for him to know he didn't like where the monologue was headed. Or where it began, if he were being honest.

"This 'bloody dust', as I call it, does not immediately combust as does its regular counterpart, which makes it an ideal substance to be paired with a standard grenade. Shrapnel injures the target, and then they immediately become infected by the fast-acting dust and turn on their fellows. It's honestly such a lost opportunity that we cannot market the dust as both a medicine and a weapon."

"Where is that man?" Clarissa muttered, adjusting how Brian was positioned over her shoulder so that she could grab her penlight and shine it around. The beam of light hit the clouds in front of her like a wall, failing to penetrate whatsoever. "I think he needs another kick in the balls."

"Now, what I can't understand," Heinrich resumed flatly, "is how the grenade you stole from down the hall ended up with its detonator reinstalled. I watched it be removed with my own eyes just a few hours ago when the decision was made to discontinue further development of the dust as a biological weapon."

"What *I* can't understand is why the hell you'd mess with something that's probably capable of turning half the continent into a zombie movie," Leah shot back. "Did you seriously think the stuff wasn't dangerous enough to begin with? I can't believe the only reason you decided against it at all was because it *wouldn't make as much money* as other alternatives. How scummy can you get?"

Noah was beginning to feel quite lost within the room, and so he stopped and identified May from the five silhouettes behind him. "Do you think you could get the pendant out? We're never going to find the exit at this rate, and if it gets any darker in here, we could find ourselves as incapacitated as Brian."

"Plus, you know, it probably wouldn't be good for the dust to get out into the rest of the building, if it's not too late," Leah added.

"I already have the pendant out," May said. "It's not working like it should. It's trying to draw in the dust, and it kind of is, but the suction is really weak."

Noah groaned. "Because it's not just dust, it's aerosolized blood with dust mixed in?"

"I would guess so, yes."

"Screw you, Heinrich," he muttered.

At least the grenade seemed to have stopped spewing dust. The air began clearing as the clouds dispersed out into the hall outside. The pendant helped as well, though the effect was greatly reduced from its usual potency. It was gradually strengthening, as it was wont to do, but as of yet its power was still just about negligible.

Noah's range of vision incrementally increased until he could finally take in the state of the room. Most of the guards were on the floor, either because they were wounded, dead, or trying their best to look dead so as to avoid the four unmasked guards who had clearly been zombified by the grenade. Even from where Noah stood, disappointingly far from the door despite his efforts to escape, he could tell which people were faking at a glance. Only six people, not including Heinrich, had entered the room with gas masks, and four of them had already been killed. Noah watched as one of the infected guards suddenly descended on a seemingly dead man, who began screaming as he lost a piece of his back to the zombie's jaws.

He tore his gaze away in search of Heinrich, but the man seemed to have disappeared.

"Over there," Leah said, pointing at the vats. Heinrich had hidden himself behind them, and now as the dust began to clear, he was trying and failing miserably to get himself up into the open top of the fifth container.

"He's trying to hide," Noah muttered angrily. "He doesn't get to hide." He nearly went after the man himself, but the guy still had a chainsaw, so he went with another option.

"Hey, you four!" he shouted at the guards. They looked over at him with conflicting expressions, urgent hunger warring with horror, though the hunger was clearly prevailing. *Their infection isn't developed enough to censor as much of their thoughts as it should be,* he realized.

He tilted his chin at Heinrich once he had their attention. "You might wanna grab him before he seals himself up," he suggested helpfully.

They looked over at the doctor.

"He has a chainsaw," one of them said.

"You outnumber him," Noah responded. "Besides, you don't want to eat that lady." He gestured at the last surviving uninfected guard. "She's one of you, just a fellow guard doing her job."

"Pauline," another guard said, nodding.

"Yeah! See, you're good buddies. Heinrich, on the other hand..." Noah paused thoughtfully. "He's probably a terrible boss. Nobody would blame you for taking a couple bites out of the guy."

The four guards looked at the doctor consideringly.

"One move and you're fired," Heinrich warned, stepping away from the vat. "And then decapitated." He revved the chainsaw and raised it threateningly, his expression twisting. The teeth turned into a silver blur and it emitted a high-pitched motorized whine.

The guards looked at each other. One of them nodded, and as one they stepped forward. Heinrich flinched.

"I don't know how you do it," Leah muttered, watching the guards creep towards the doctor.

Noah looked at her. "What?"

"Make them listen to you like that."

"There's no secret," he laughed. "They're just normal people. Er, as normal as you can be and still decide to work for Insight. The dust doesn't erase who you fundamentally are, it just tacks on a few quirks. There's no reason they wouldn't heed a valid suggestion."

"...Sure," she said skeptically. "You think they can really take Heinrich down?"

"Of course. It's four against one, and they're trained

security guards."

"They don't have a chainsaw."

"It'll be fine," Noah said unconvincingly. "Just watch."

71

DO YOU KNOW MY NAME

Heinrich grew increasingly pale as the guards approached. He looked between them desperately, seeking for any sign of hesitation he could exploit.

"Why come after me first?" he asked, apparently trying to replicate Noah's feat of convincing them to switch targets. "Why not go after the other person? She doesn't have a chainsaw!" He waved the bladed tool around as if to remind them of its existence.

The guards didn't seem to consider his words for even a second, though they eyed the weapon warily. Their faces were masks of hunger, and Heinrich was food. No argument could turn them away from him now.

On some unspoken cue all four darted forward. Each of them had picked up some wounds from the grenade, but the dust they inhaled had been enough to remedy the most debilitating effects of their injuries, and they moved with startling speed.

Heinrich slashed forward, catching one of them on the teeth of the chainsaw, but the other three reached him without issue. Each of them tore a small piece away from his left side. Not lethal wounds, but certainly painful ones.

The man struck by the chainsaw, however, was not so lucky. The blades bit into his neck, and the damage he was accruing was too great to be overcome by the healing power of the dust. If he could steal a bite out of Heinrich, he would be able to recover, but the doctor was clearly aware of this.

He pressed the injured guard away with the edge of the blade even as the other three tore at him from his other side. Blood was beginning to drench Heinrich's shirt and his face was rapidly losing color beneath his respirator.

Without warning Heinrich whirled away from the man, swinging the chainsaw like a club to dislodge the three other guards from where they hung onto his side with their jaws buried in his flesh like leeches. One of the guards took the brunt of the attack and fell back with a cry, while the other two were forced to step away, managing to evade the blow.

Heinrich crouched slightly as he faced them, his whole body shaking, his breaths shallow and quick. He raised the chainsaw again, barely managing to bring it to chest height. He was holding it with one arm; he had sacrificed the functionality of his left to buy himself time to take down the first guard.

Noah was surprised Heinrich was still upright at all; he was losing blood at a tremendous rate, mostly from a wound one of the guards had managed to inflict on his neck.

The two guards left standing stalked forward. Heinrich stumbled away, nearly tripping over the body of a woman who had been fatally injured by the initial blast of the grenade.

"Fine," Heinrich growled. "I'm not playing this stupid game." He grabbed his respirator and tore it away, revealing a face plastered with sweat.

Before he could inhale, one of the guards was on him, hands around his neck. Heinrich's eyes bulged and he fell backwards to the floor, though he still somehow maintained his grasp on the chainsaw. Tremors wracked his entire body as he fought to bring it up against the back of the infected man.

Then the second guard reached him. She grabbed the discarded mask from the floor and brought it back into place over his mouth.

Heinrich's hand went to his face, finally letting the chainsaw drop to the ground. He barely had the energy to grip its handle, let alone wield it as the weapon he intended it to be. His only hope now was to become infected. The spinning saw chain hit the floor and jerked away across the room where it idled quietly.

"Let me go, I command it," Heinrich wheezed. His fingers dug at the edge of the mask, weakly fighting to create even the smallest gap that would allow dust to flood in.

"No," the guard said. "You're done."

"Why?" Heinrich asked, seeming genuinely confused. He stared desperately at her, then switched his gaze to the other guard, but neither of their faces betrayed any sympathy. "If you're not going to eat me, you might as well let me go."

The male guard rose to his feet and stared down at the man with disgust. He nodded at the other guard, who lifted a hand to clear the blood off her face.

"Do you know my name?" she asked.

Heinrich squinted at her through bloodshot eyes. "Is this really the time?"

"I've worked for you for twelve years. I see you every day."

The doctor sighed. "Jane?"

"Sumati," she said with a flat look.

He coughed. "That's what I meant to say."

Sumati just looked at him.

"What's the point of this? Why aren't you doing anything?"

"I just killed my best friend."

"...My condolences."

"And then you tried to kill me with a chainsaw."

"You were going to eat me!" Heinrich rasped. "You did eat me! You can't blame me for defending myself. I'm bleeding out because you ate half my neck."

"It was hardly half. More like a sixteenth, at most. I can assure you that you wouldn't be missing *any* of your neck if I hadn't been infected by a weapon you designed. Nor would my friend have died."

"I don't understand how that detonated," Heinrich mumbled. "It was decommissioned."

"You should never have made such a thing in the first

place."

Noah wanted to yell at the guards to get on with it and finish the man off already, but they seemed to be having a moment, so he just stayed silent and watched. Heinrich clearly wasn't long for this world, anyway.

His attention was momentarily diverted as Clarissa began meandering her way across the room to where the chainsaw had fallen. She picked it up, gave it an appraising look-over, then shut off its idling motor and stuck it into her coat. She did all of this with Brian still draped over her shoulder with his rear in the air.

When Noah looked back at Heinrich only a moment later, the man's eyes had closed and he no longer seemed to be breathing. He was unconscious and fast approaching death. The guard named Sumati was still talking to him.

"When I attacked you earlier, my actions were driven by hunger. Now, my actions are driven by spite. You could have survived this day."

Heinrich died as she went silent.

Noah wanted to clap, but he thought it would probably be inappropriate, so he settled for giving the two guards his best smile. "Well done."

Sumati looked past him at Clarissa. "You took the chainsaw. May I borrow it for a moment?"

Clarissa hesitantly drew it out and stepped forward to pass it over. "What are you going to-"

The guard flicked the chainsaw on and pressed the trigger to its limit, then leaned down and separated Heinrich's head from his body.

When she was done, she turned the tool off, wiped both sides of the guard bar off on Heinrich's shirt, and handed it back to Clarissa handle-first.

Clarissa accepted it with a startled expression.

"Now he cannot rise again," the guard said. She looked around at all the other bodies scattered around the room and tilted her head. "Actually, can I have the chainsaw back?"

"How about you just keep it," Clarissa suggested, handing

it over. "We're about to leave; you can deal with the bodies once we're gone."

"Don't forget that there's one person still alive and uninfected in here," Elias said, glancing across the room to where she quietly lay. "Please don't cut her head off."

That's right, Noah realized. He stared over at the woman. She was still playing dead, clearly unaware that it was entirely pointless.

Leah elbowed him. He nearly fell over, and when he recollected himself, he gave her an affronted look. "What?"

She just shook her head.

"Would you like to be cured?" May asked Sumati. "We can do that for you before we go."

The male guard looked over. "Me as well, please."

Noah helped May cure the two guards, as well as three others who had been infected and soon thereafter immobilized by their uninfected comrades. Or in the case of one of the guards who had attacked Heinrich, wounded nearly to the point of death. The man had taken a nasty gash to his side and had almost managed to fully heal it before he ran out of energy and was reduced to little more than a skeleton. He was alive, however, which was more than could be said for most others in the room. Included among the dead was the guard who had led the attack against Heinrich.

When the vacuum's dust bin was full he brought it to the pendant and opened it up, forgetting that the guards had been infected by altered dust.

To his surprise, however, the pendant had no trouble suctioning the particles out of the air.

"Not that I'm complaining," he said as he watched the dust disappear, "but how is this working?"

Elias looked over at the dust flowing between him and May and immediately understood what was puzzling him. "Interesting. The dust is behaving as if it's in its unaltered, neutral state, despite having been inhaled in its 'attuned' form. Do you suppose something about it being exhaled or otherwise pulled directly from a person's lungs somehow resets it to its unattuned state? Assuming that attunement to human blood renders it incapable of infecting other life forms, converting back to normal would give it the greatest chance of infecting another being upon being expelled from someone's lungs."

Leah glanced at him. "You're pretty smart, aren't you."

Elias blushed faintly. "Thank you."

"With all this talk of attunement and whatnot," Brian said from his position over Clarissa's shoulder, "should I be worried about random animals getting infected? Or what about people's pets? If the dust has to attune to a person, it stands to reason it would be able to attune to just about any respiring creature."

"Probably," Elias said.

"I ate a raccoon a couple days ago," Noah said. "I already mentioned that, right? Anyway, it tasted pretty awful, so with any luck the same will be true the other way around, and whatever animals that hypothetically get zombified will only act like zombies to others of their own species."

Clarissa clapped her hands. "Alright, I think we've veered sufficiently off-topic. Can we go now?"

"There's still some dust in the air," Leah said.

"It's getting better, though," May observed. "The pendant gets stronger the longer it's surrounded by dust, and we've been in the room long enough that it's actually beginning to do a somewhat decent job at clearing the air."

Noah peered at the pendant and saw she was right, though there was a somewhat unpleasant side effect of it absorbing the altered dust, in the form of blood beading at the bottom of the metal square. Red droplets formed one after another at the center of the small siphon of dust being continually pulled into the pendant. Each one was immediately wicked into May's shirt.

"It's filtering out the blood," Noah said. "It must only be able to store unattuned dust."

"Fortunately, your shirt is already covered in blood, so you won't even notice the extra stains," Leah said drily.

They waited around for another minute, letting the air clear.

"Alright, enough's enough," Clarissa said. "It's not going to get any better than this. And for all we know, the dust has already gotten into the vents and spread to half the building."

"Don't say stuff like that," Leah muttered.

The six of them made their way to the exit, and with a final wave at Sumati and the other unnamed guard, left the room.

They headed towards the end of the hall, past the gaping hole in the wall where Noah had destroyed the door. The keycard unlocked the treatment room and the six of them filed inside. The vacuum had been disassembled and pushed into a corner.

They went through that room into the main waiting area, where the dimmed lights and empty chairs made for a somewhat eerie scene, and then out into another hallway. A right-hand turn took them through a pair of double doors out into the long entrance hall. The exit lay at the end of the corridor.

Noah smiled. *Almost there, dad.*

72

INFECTED FOREVER

A single set of doors was all that remained between them and escape. As they approached, a large, bright orange blob became vaguely visible though the frosted glass.

"That's my dad's car," Noah said. "Let's go."

Leah grabbed the collar of his shirt and yanked him back. "Forgetting something, are we?"

Noah gazed at her blankly.

She narrowed her eyes. "It's time to be cured. No more delays."

Noah smiled hesitantly. "Ah, right. Of course."

"Brian should get the treatment first," May said.

Nobody had any quarrel with that suggestion, so in short order Brian was laid across the ground and cured. They were quite well-practiced with the process by this point.

"It doesn't feel particularly pleasant," Brian commented after the vacuum had turned off. "On a metaphysical level, I mean. I still can't feel anything."

"Unless the blindness wears out anytime soon, you'll probably be immobile for another few hours at the very least," Elias said. "It depends how soon you regain feeling in your limbs."

Brian didn't seem very pleased about that estimate, but there was nothing any of them could do.

"I can go next," May volunteered. Her eyes tracked the vacuum as Clarissa brought it to her mouth, and she sat perfectly still until it was over.

"It wasn't that bad," she declared without elaborating.

Elias went after her, and then it was Noah's turn.

A nervous energy gathered in the pit of his stomach as he watched Clarissa empty the vacuum in preparation. "What did you think, Elias? How bad is it?"

"It's kind of like you're dying," he said after a moment of thought. "Like you're having all of your vital organs sucked out."

Noah blinked. "May, you said it wasn't that bad, right? Right?"

Clarissa approached him with the vacuum. Her expression was neutral, but somehow the way she held the device seemed very threatening.

"Are you wiping the nozzle off between each person?" Noah asked before she could turn the vacuum on. "Because if not, that's just gross."

Clarissa raised an eyebrow and wiped it quickly on her shirt. "Yeah," she said unconvincingly.

"You can do a better job than that."

"Noah! Just let her cure you," Leah said, exasperated. "You'll be fine."

He gave a short, somewhat unwilling nod and tried his best to convince himself there was nothing to be nervous about. Clarissa pressed the vacuum against his lips and turned it on.

The motor whined, held a pitch for about two seconds... and died.

Noah gazed at it in surprise, hardly believing his luck. He knew he shouldn't feel relieved, but he couldn't stop the emotion from rolling through him.

Clarissa brought the nozzle away from his mouth and gave it an irritated shake, then jammed her thumb repeatedly into the power button, but it was well and truly dead. "I do believe our vacuum just ran out of battery."

"Didn't you say your dad was bringing one?" Elias asked Noah. "I can step out and grab it."

He shook his head. "My dad doesn't know you; why would

he hand it over? I should be the one to get it."

Leah peered at him wearily. "You're not going outside until you're cured."

He threw her a hurt look. "I wouldn't eat him. He's my dad."

"Maybe so, but there's also a fair chance he won't recognize you. It's better if I'm the one to talk to him. Or Clarissa, I suppose. The rest of you are covered in blood and gaunt like death itself."

Noah paused. The dust tried to make him uncaring of the people around him, either to push its own objectives or to protect his sanity. Despite its best efforts, however, he still cared for his dad. Maybe that would change with enough time, but he had no intention of letting himself get to that point. He handed her the keycard.

She smiled. "Thank you. Now back up. I'm not opening the door until you're at the other end of the hall."

"Oh, come on. Have some faith." Despite his complaints, he smiled good-naturedly and retreated down the corridor. When she deemed him a safe distance away Leah slipped through the door and out of sight.

A minute later she reappeared with a handheld vacuum very similar to the device they already possessed, although this one was slightly smaller, and painted red rather than blue.

Noah returned to his companions. Leah turned the vacuum off and on, testing the battery as he approached. "Your dad seems nice," she said. "He's excited to see you."

Noah came to a stop directly in front of her and smiled. "It'll be good to see him."

Leah held the nozzle of the vacuum to his mouth and turned it on.

Noah closed his eyes as he waited to feel the treatment taking effect. There was no tactile feedback at its touch, though as the seconds passed, he felt an almost imperceptible, intangible tug, as if it were pulling at his very soul. The sensation was accompanied by a pang of deep loss. If he didn't do anything, he would lose something of vital importance, never to see it again. He pushed down the sentiment, knowing it was artificial, but the sense of desperation suddenly strengthened, and in an instant it had smothered him.

He suddenly realized he was making an awful mistake. The dust had been nothing but beneficial. It granted him capabilities straight out of a comic book; who in their right mind would turn down such incredible boons? He failed to think of a reason he shouldn't remain infected. Remain infected forever.

He tried to tell Leah to stop, but the vacuum over his mouth whisked the words away before he could get them out.

Panic seared through him, but the emotion suddenly turned to anger as he realized what Leah was doing. She was stealing his dust for herself.

He wound his fist back and punched her in the face.

His body was a feeble, weakened wreck, but the blow took her by complete surprise, and she stumbled back. The vacuum fell to the floor

"What the hell, Noah?" Clarissa shouted.

Noah ignored her. His attention was on the vacuum on the floor, on its darkened dustbin. He needed to reclaim its contents.

He reached for it, but Clarissa tackled him from the side and he tumbled to the ground several feet away.

"What is wrong with you?" Leah demanded.

"We should have blinded him before treating him," Clarissa muttered. "Do any of you have a syringe gun?"

"Noah has the only one," Elias said.

"Of course he does," Clarissa sighed, though she was already pulling a blindfold out of her pocket. She picked the vacuum up from the floor. "C'mere, Noah. Let me put this on you and then we can finish up the treatment."

"Give that to me," he said, looking at the vacuum.

She gave him a flat look. "Come and take it."

He stepped towards her cautiously before suddenly darting forward to grasp the device. He tried to yank it out of her grip, but she was as immovable as a marble statue.

She let him tug ineffectually on the vacuum for another moment before slowly shaking her head. "You're so weak." She pulled the blindfold over his head with pitying eyes.

Noah heard the vacuum turn on. The sound filled him with such dread that he nearly passed out.

The vacuum droned on, unheeding, and the awful feeling gradually lessened until he felt almost normal again. Unconsciousness beckoned, though now it was due to simple, overwhelming fatigue.

The vacuum wound down into silence. The blindfold was pulled off his head and Clarissa's hopeful face filled his vision.

"How are you feeling?" she asked.

A combination of exhaustion and shame made Noah reluctant to meet her gaze, but it was awfully difficult not to with her eyes hovering several inches from his own. "Like I could sleep through to next year. But better. Thank you."

"You're welcome." She maintained his gaze for another moment, nodded to herself, then turned away to cure Leah.

Noah slumped down against the mirrored wall and closed his eyes. He heard the sound of a match catching fire and the sharp crack of dust as it combusted, but he didn't care enough to look. Never in his life had he ever felt so completely drained.

I'm cured. It was a strange thought. He cracked his eyes open to peer down at his hands, but they remained as skeletal as he had grown accustomed to over the past few days. It would take time for him to recover to his pre-infected state. The dust had used him up and spat him out.

The treatment may not have remedied his outward physical state, but it had certainly done something for his psyche. For the past two days hunger had sat in his mind like a heavy stone at the center of a trampoline, sending all of his other thoughts rolling inevitably towards it.

Now that stone had been lifted away. He felt like he could finally think in his own head again.

He dipped in and out of consciousness as Clarissa and

Leah quietly cured each other. He was pretty sure his brain had already shut down and gone to sleep despite the fact that his eyes were still open. May and Elias seemed to be in a similar state, and Brian... Well, he was probably already dreaming.

Several peaceful minutes passed before Clarissa slammed the doors open, startling everyone from their stupor. "We did it! We're cured! Let's go!"

"Shh," Brian groaned. "Some of us are sleeping."

She ducked down to scoop him back over her shoulder. "I'll be as loud as I want to be, thank you very much."

Noah pulled himself to his feet and gazed out the open door. His dad's car was parked exactly where the bus had stopped yesterday to let the students off. The window was rolled down.

Noah stepped out of the building and slowly brought his eyes up, almost afraid of what he would see. He was suddenly horribly aware of his appearance, and shame made him duck his head as if he could hide what had become of him.

"You made it," a familiar voice said, cracking in raw relief. "Took you long enough, eh?"

Noah's heart jumped. He stumbled forward and leaned against the side of the orange car to see his dad sitting inside, hands on the wheel, looking at him with poorly concealed worry.

Noah smiled weakly at him. "Thanks for picking us up."

"Of course. You- you're not hurt, are you?" he asked hesitantly.

"No. I'm okay." Noah winced and looked down at his hands again before he could stop himself. Feeling suddenly uncomfortable, he leaned away from the car and turned back toward his friends.

"What are you waiting for? Get in," he prompted.

They stepped out from under the doorway.

Clarissa gave the car an appraising look. "Nice whip."

"Is it?" Brian asked. "I want shotgun."

73

SOME PRETTY CRAZY STUFF
HAS HAPPENED

"Where are we all going to sit?" Elias wondered. He peered into the open door. "Including Noah's dad, there are seven of us, and only five seats."

"We can make it work," Noah said, walking around to the back of the vehicle. He waved Clarissa over. "Brian said he wants shotgun, though. Let me help Clarissa get him situated and then we can figure out who's sitting where."

He popped the trunk and stepped back. Clarissa dropped Brian in.

"You're all set," she said.

"Thank you," Brian said, immensely pleased.

She closed the door and walked with Noah back to the front of the car.

"Six people and five seats," Noah quietly corrected Elias, grinning.

Noah ended up taking shotgun while the four remaining students squeezed into the back seat. They were all just about sitting on each other, but they got the doors closed. It helped that two of them were essentially skeletons.

"Everyone's all set?" Noah's dad threw a glance back at them. He chuckled at how tightly packed they were, then started the car and pulled away from the entrance.

The walls reflected the car back at them as they drove along. Despite his exhaustion, Noah stared ahead unblinkingly, nervous that they'd round a corner and find the way blocked off.

"This stinking building," his dad muttered. "It's like driving in a house of mirrors."

"How'd you find the right entrance?" Noah asked.

"I counted the floors," he answered, smiling self-consciously. "I figured each branch in the road was another level. 'Course, that's not the most accurate way to keep track, so I was awfully glad when that friend of yours appeared. I was about ready to find another entrance."

The car angled down as they hit a ramp and began descending.

"I guess their fancy built-in parking garage only has three floors," Noah mumbled to himself.

Down they went, curving slowly to the left, until the floor evened out. Directly ahead was the exit.

There were no gates or people to stop them, and they pulled out of the building unimpeded. Noah leaned out the window to stare back at its looming shape as they left it behind.

"It feels like we were in there for ages," he said. "Do you think we really destroyed all of their dust? If we left even a little bit laying around somewhere..."

"Well, Heinrich's dead," Elias murmured sleepily. "And he seemed to be the head of the snake."

Clarissa nodded as she gazed out the window. "We'll have to keep an eye on the news. Not that Insight's generally keen on public communication, but you never know."

The building slowly fell out of view behind them. There were a few other people out and about despite the hour, though as they drew further from the heart of the city, the roads soon became empty.

"Do you mind if I close the window? The air is a little chilly," the dad said.

"Go ahead," Noah sighed. Cold night air was one of his favorite things, but it seemed he hadn't quite recovered enough to feel it yet. "Where are we going?"

"If I didn't have five other kids in my car, I'd take us to my hotel room. I don't think the staff would take kindly to all of you, though, so I figured we could just find a parking lot somewhere and stay put until morning."

"Sounds good." Noah closed his eyes. "Thank you for doing this for us. Some pretty crazy stuff has happened these past few days, but I'll have to tell you everything tomorrow. I don't think I'd be able to get through all of it right now before I pass out."

His dad peered sideways at him over his glasses. "Yeah, I can see that."

The only sound for the next several minutes was the quiet hum of the motor. A gas station with an attached cafe eventually appeared on the side of the road, and they turned into the empty parking lot. The store was closed, as it was currently approaching 2 AM, though the lights over the pumps were still on.

Noah's dad backed into a parking spot next to the building and pulled the key out of the ignition. He sat quietly in his seat for a few moments before almost reluctantly turning to look at Noah. The boy's head had already dropped to his chest.

He would never admit it, but when Noah had stepped out from the building, there had been a moment that he failed to realize he was looking at his own kid. He knew Noah like the back of his own hand, but the sickness had changed him so much. Even now, he had to suppress the feeling that a stranger sat beside him.

I should've done more, he thought unhappily, though the thought was borne more of vague helplessness than any specific regret. After Noah had mentioned Insight two days ago, he had spent the night going down the rabbit hole of old press releases covering all the horrifying things the company had gotten away with over the past fifteen years.

The next morning, he had decided to drive himself to Oakridge to see if his son had successfully escaped. He got no further than the very edge of campus grounds before he found himself confronted by a military blockade. A soldier informed him that there was a viral contagion on campus that needed to be contained, which was both extremely worrying and frustratingly vague, so he went back to his hotel and spent several hours alternating between checking his phone for any word from Noah and scouring local news outlets for updates on what was actually happening at Oakridge. There was simply no media coverage to be found. When he finally received a call from Noah, he nearly cried from relief, and shortly after the call ended, he finally crashed.

He woke up several hours later with barely enough time to go out and buy the vacuum he had promised to bring, considering he also had to charge it up to a usable state. By the time he had shown up to Insight, he'd felt on the verge of a nervous breakdown, afraid of what could have happened since their phone call.

He sighed and glanced over his shoulder. All four kids were passed out, their heads resting on each other's shoulders. He was pretty sure there was a boy in his trunk as well, but he hadn't heard any complaints from the back, so the kid was probably fine.

He sat back in his seat and closed his own eyes. It took quite a while, but he finally drifted off into his own restless sleep.

***

Noah awoke to an annoying repetitive banging.

"What is that *racket*?" he complained, opening his eyes. Sunlight streamed through the windshield, warming his lap.

His dad was out cold, slumped against the window with his glasses askew. Noah turned to peer into the back seat. His friends were in the process of waking up. May tried to stretch and accidentally punched Elias instead. Neither of them were awake enough to notice.

The banging was beginning to grate on Noah's nerves, so he unlocked the car with his dad's keys and got out to look around. There were other people in the parking lot now that morning had broken, walking in and out of the convenience store and using the gas pumps. He glanced to the side and made eye contact with a young man frozen halfway through the motion of stepping out of his own car. His gaze conveyed a mix of fear and surprise.

Noah froze as well, struck with a bolt of self-consciousness. He still had blood soaked down the front of his outfit, but he didn't have any spare clothes he could change into that weren't also covered in blood.

Before he could say anything, the guy slowly withdrew back into his car and shut the door. The vehicle squealed as it turned out of the parking lot and flew away down the road.

Noah didn't move for another few seconds. *I need new clothes,* he thought dispiritedly. *And even that will only solve half the problem.* Trying not to let the interaction bother him, he stomped around the back of the car. He stared around in confusion when the origin of the noise seemed to shift around to behind him. An embarrassingly long stretch of time passed before he realized what was going on. *Oh, snap! Brian!*

He reached down to pop the trunk, but it suddenly swung open on its own, nearly knocking him upside the chin.

Brian looked up at him with slightly wild eyes.

"Oh, hey," Noah said awkwardly. "I was just coming around to let you out."

"You... you put me in the *trunk*!" he said, flabbergasted.

Noah scratched the back of his neck. "We were short on seats."

Brian stared at him in disbelief as he slowly clambered out of the enclosed space.

"How'd you manage to open it from inside?" Noah wondered.

His friend pointed wordlessly to a T-shaped emergency release handle dangling from the open door.

"Ah."

"Unbelievable," Brian muttered. The rest of their companions were beginning to emerge from the vehicle, roused by their conversation, and he turned his glare on them.

"Were you in on it? Clarissa! You must've been!"

"Hey, hey," Noah said quickly. "I'm sorry we stuck you in there, but it was the only way everyone would be able to fit into the car. Somebody had to do it."

"And I was the clueless blind guy," he sighed. "I should've known."

"That's not what we..." Noah began, but he trailed off at Brian's flat look. "Yeah, alright. It won't happen again."

Brian rolled his eyes. "Good to know."

Noah's dad finally opened his door and stepped out. "Oh, excellent, you're all awake. I was thinking we could grab breakfast here at this place, if you guys don't mind."

He received six eager smiles in response.

"Breakfast sounds amazing," Leah said. "Also, I should've said this last night, but thank you for giving us a ride out of Insight. And the vacuum, too. I think I speak for all of us when I say your help has been hugely appreciated."

The man smiled. "You're very welcome."

74

IT'S WHAT I DID

Noah hesitated outside the store entrance, prompting his dad to glance at him. "What is it?"

"Are we really going to go into the store like this?" he asked, tugging at his shirt.

He had noticed that his dad had yet to directly question why any of them were covered in blood. The man's only immediate concern had been for his health, and when it became clear that he wasn't in immediate danger, he hadn't pressed for more information.

May suddenly seemed to realize she was in an equally gruesome state. She blanched. "Maybe we should stay in the car."

"I have a couple extra shirts," Brian offered.

Elias looked at him doubtfully. "They'd be huge on all of us now."

"It'd be better than nothing, right?"

"I don't think it will be an issue," Clarissa said. "People can assume whatever they want. You might get some funny looks, but I bet you right now, nobody will actually say anything."

Noah considered mentioning the exchange he'd had with the random guy in the parking lot. He didn't say anything, however, and they walked into the convenience store as they were. The cashier's jaw dropped open as they walked by, but he remained silent.

Noah's dad waved vaguely towards the aisles. "Grab

whatever you want. If you don't have any cash, I'll cover it for you. I'm going to use the bathroom now."

"That's very generous, thank you, sir," Elias said.

Noah gave his friends a slightly nervous look after his dad had walked away. "I don't know about you guys, but I haven't used a bathroom in three days."

"Oh, man, that's right," Brian muttered, eyes widening.

"I'm kind of terrified at what's going to come out when nature finally calls."

"There might not be anything to worry about," Elias said. "The dust stayed in our lungs, right? It may never have touched our normal digestive systems."

"Speaking of which," Leah interjected impatiently, "I'm starving. I'm going to get some soup." She marched away with May following close behind.

Clarissa grabbed Brian's hand and pulled him away down another aisle, leaving Noah standing alone with Elias.

"I think I want a sandwich," Noah said thoughtfully. "Possibly multiple sandwiches."

They meandered between rows of shelves. Neither of them had ever been to this particular convenience store before, so spent several minutes just peering around at what it had to offer. Elias came across a small tub of peanut butter, which he tucked under his arm with a grin, and shortly afterward he also grabbed a single banana.

Noah was very pleased to find a case of plastic-wrapped sandwiches in a refrigerator at the back corner of the store. He grabbed a turkey-and-ham, and then instead of immediately closing the door, he simply stood there for a moment as the cold air washed over him.

Elias shivered and shut the door for him. "Are you not able to feel yet?"

"Oh, I can," Noah said. "You know, generally speaking, the experience of feeling is pretty uncomfortable."

"Are you saying you *preferred* being completely insensate?" Elias asked, raising an eyebrow.

Noah laughed and shook his head. "Being uncomfortable

is awesome, are you kidding?"

The look Elias gave him made it clear he thought he was bonkers, but he just shook his head and turned away without saying anything.

Neither of them had money, so they found Noah's dad before checking out and bringing their food to the small attached cafe. Leah and May had already arrived and had claimed a long, bar-esque table with enough seats for their group of seven. Placed before each of them was a plastic spoon and an unopened can of minestrone soup.

"Where's Brian when you need him?" Leah complained. "I don't have my can opener on me."

Noah stared at her. "How are you planning on cooking your soup?"

"I'm not. It comes pre-cooked."

Noah looked at the can. "I'm pretty sure those are cooking instructions on the side."

She peered down with narrowed eyes. "Mere suggestions for those weak of mind and body."

Brian and Clarissa soon arrived. Brian had a can of pasta, while Clarissa was bearing a loaf of unsliced bread and nothing else.

Noah gave her a slightly incredulous look, but nobody else seemed concerned, so he kept quiet. Maybe it was normal to eat straight bread for breakfast.

Brian slung his backpack to the floor and sat down across from his sister. He pulled out a purple can opener and passed it over to her without a word, then got out *another* one, which was yellow, and opened his own can of pasta. Noah didn't bother asking if he would cook the food before eating.

At that point Noah's dad finally joined them and took a seat next to his son. He had bought an apple and an energy drink.

Noah nodded at him and began unwrapping his sandwich. The last time he had eaten proper food had been... he slowly frowned. Not counting the pre-made meal he had barely touched at the housing units back on campus, the last thing he had eaten had been the sandwich Brian made for their visit to the cemetery.

No, that's not the last thing I've eaten. A sense of *wrongness* suddenly flooded through him, and he gagged. The noise attracted the attention of his companions.

"Noah?" his dad asked.

Noah looked at him. For a horrible moment he felt his hunger lean towards the man, or perhaps he *expected* to feel his hunger do so, and he froze, horrified. The feeling passed before he could act on it, but it left his mind disoriented and guilt-ridden. His dad was gazing at him with a slightly confused, worried expression, unsure what was wrong, but eager to help.

Everything he had done in the past several days hit him in that single moment. He curled over, nearly planting his face in the sandwich, and sobbed.

He felt a hand patting his back. "It's okay," his dad said quietly. "You're not at Insight anymore."

Noah couldn't bear to look at him. "It's not what they did, dad. It's what *I* did."

The man didn't respond. He probably had no idea what to say.

"It's not your fault," he heard Clarissa murmur. "You can't blame yourself for what you did there. Plus, they kind of deserved it. Don't beat yourself up."

Over a minute passed before he finally raised his head. He wiped his eyes quickly and looked around. To his surprise, his friends looked about as miserable as he felt. Elias was staring at his own hands, shaking, while May sat listlessly with tears streaming down her face. Brian stared down at his food with a frown, though that could just have been because he had bought himself canned pasta. Clarissa and Leah were looking around at them all with wretched expressions.

His dad was sitting very still, eyes darting back and forth. He seemed hesitant to speak, but he finally asked in a quiet voice, "What happened?"

"How much do you know about the infection?" Clarissa

asked after it became clear nobody else wanted to answer.

"Noah told me some of the symptoms a few days ago. Numbness, decreased heart rate and breathing... he said he wasn't in any danger, even though that seemed impossible."

She sighed and opened her mouth, but Noah interrupted her in a flat voice.

"The sickness makes you into a zombie. It makes you eat people, like a monster."

Several seconds passed. His dad blinked. "Oh. *Oh*. So all of you..."

"Not her or I," Clarissa said, nodding at Leah. "The rest of them, though... yes."

"I see," he murmured.

"I was hungry the whole time," May suddenly burst out. "From the moment Dr. Jansen cut me. It never got better."

Noah stared at her, momentarily shocked out of his self-misery. "Really? The wounds didn't look that bad."

She glared at him. "I'm glad you thought so."

He held his hands up. "I don't mean to offend you. If your words are true, you've shown incredible self-restraint. I don't know how you did it."

She shut her eyes. "It was so hard. And it didn't matter, in the end. I failed."

"Yeah, but not until you got shot," he said, genuinely impressed. "And it does matter. Think of all the people you *didn't* eat, up 'till that point."

She smiled weakly. "Yeah. Thanks."

"Kid." Noah turned to see his dad looking right at him. "It sounds like you went through some horrible stuff. I wish you had talked to me about what was happening, but there's nothing I can do about it now. What I *can* do is tell you this: you're not a zombie, and you're not a monster. You're a victim. And if you don't believe that right now, that's okay, but sooner or later you're gonna realize I was right."

Noah stared at him for several seconds, then leaned forward and hugged him. "I hope so," he whispered.

A long moment passed before they separated. "Now, eat

your sandwich," the man said sternly. "That thing wasn't free."

Noah obediently took a bite. It tasted so good that he nearly started crying again, but he had to pause to take a drink of water before he could swallow. He hadn't realized how dry his throat was. He only intended to take a sip, but before he knew it, he was setting down the empty bottle. He then proceeded to devour his entire sandwich in about five bites.

His friends tore into their own food with equal gusto, and Noah's dad had barely picked up his apple before the rest of them were finished eating.

"What happens now?" Leah asked.

"We go back to school," Elias said. "What else?"

"You think it's safe?"

"Well, it's not as if I've seen any zombies roaming the streets, and nobody seems to be panicking. This could have been the beginning of a disaster, but by some miracle, the crisis was caught before it could spiral out of control. Classes have probably already resumed."

"So, that's it, then." Brian sighed. "Everything goes back to normal."

Noah shot a look at his friend. "I hope so."

When Noah's dad finished eating they cleared the table and exited the cafe. Brian took one look at the car and shook his head. "I'm not going back in the trunk."

"Understandable," Noah said. "You go ahead and sit in the front. I'll squeeze in with everyone else."

Brian grinned. "Good luck with that."

Everyone did finally manage to fit into the car, though Noah doubted there was a square foot of cumulative spare space left in the back seat by the time everyone was situated. It was certainly an unsafe arrangement.

They drove back to school.

***

"Is this really the best place to put this thing?"

Brian gave Noah a sharp look as he pulled the door to the mausoleum open. The door was just as stubborn as usual. "Can you think of a better spot?"

"I'm still not convinced we shouldn't just destroy it," May murmured. She sneezed. "Sorry, allergies. What if someone finds it?"

Leah shook her head. "It won't be discovered. The only people who will ever know where it is will be us four."

Brian tugged the lever to open the tomb and they all stared down at the motionless corpse.

"Put it as far back as you can reach," he said.

May gave him a long, worried look, but in the end she did as they had agreed. Brian closed the tomb.

They didn't linger, although Noah gave the dark room one last uneasy look as he stood by the door.

"Just in case," he whispered, and slipped outside after his friends.

www.ingramcontent.com/pod-product-compliance
Lightning Source LLC
Chambersburg PA
CBHW010512100726
47903CB00009B/2718